U0536686

Supported by Science Foundation of Beijing Language and Culture University
(the Fundamental Research Funds for the Central Universities) [17YBG28]

王秋生 著

英国动物诗歌研究
A STUDY OF BRITISH ANIMAL POEMS

中国书籍出版社
China Book Press

图书在版编目（CIP）数据

英国动物诗歌研究 / 王秋生著. -- 北京：中国书籍出版社，2020.5
　　ISBN 978-7-5068-7630-8

　　Ⅰ.①英… Ⅱ.①王… Ⅲ.①诗歌研究—英国 Ⅳ.①I561.072

中国版本图书馆CIP数据核字(2019)第282234号

英国动物诗歌研究

王秋生　著

责任编辑	朱　琳
责任印制	孙马飞　马　芝
封面设计	东方美迪
出版发行	中国书籍出版社
地　　址	北京市丰台区三路居路 97 号（邮编：100073）
电　　话	（010）52257143（总编室）　（010）52257140（发行部）
电子邮箱	eo@chinabp.com.cn
经　　销	全国新华书店
印　　刷	北京九州迅驰传媒文化有限公司
开　　本	710毫米×1000毫米　1/16
字　　数	299千字
印　　张	22
版　　次	2020 年 5 月第 1 版　2020 年 5 月第 1 次印刷
书　　号	ISBN 978-7-5068-7630-8
定　　价	59.00元

版权所有　翻印必究

Acknowledgements

I would like to show my heart-felt and sincere thanks to all those who have helped me in the writing process of the book, without whom the completion of the book would be impossible.

First and foremost, I would like to thank the publishers of my previous essays on the study of British animal poems which contribute to some extent to the content of this book, including *English Language Learning*, *Journal of Literature and Art Studies*, *the Northeast Asia International Symposium on Linguistics, Literature and Teaching*, and *the Northeast Asia International Symposium on Language, Literature and Translation*.

Next, my thanks go to my dear friend David Sulz, a librarian at the University of Alberta in Canada, who has helped me in finding some valuable research materials and answering my related questions timely and patiently.

Last but not least, I am grateful to editor Zhu Lin from China Book Press, who spares no effort in the proofreading and editing of this book, which guarantees its high-quality printing.

Contents

Introduction / 1

Chapter One   High Praise of Animals / 28

    I. Beauty and Loveliness / 28

    II. Happiness and Carefreeness / 38

    III. Loyalty and Dutifulness / 54

Chapter Two   Great Concern for Animals / 70

    I. Showing Concern, Love or Sympathy to Animals / 70

    II. Harmony Or Good Relationship Between Man and Animals / 85

    III. Irony or Criticism of People's Lack of Concern for Animals / 99

    IV. Remorse for Wrongdoings / 119

    V. Elegies or Epitaphs to Dead Animals / 126

Chapter Three   Animals' Functions in People's Mental Life / 139

    I. Animals as Stimulus to Good Mood / 139

    II. Animals as Source of Wisdom / 147

    III. Animals as Evoker of Empathy / 164

Chapter Four   Criticism Against the Cruelty to Animals / 171

    I. Pain of Animals with Bondage / 171

    II. Distress of Performing or Racing Animals / 184

    III. Suffering of Hunted Animals / 194

    IV. Abuse of Other Animals / 223

    V. Theme of Nemesis / 249

Chapter Five   Advocacy of Animal Freedom and Rights / 261

    I. Proposal for the Protection and Welfare of Animals / 261

    II. Protest Against Experiment on Animals and Vivisection / 268

    III. Promotion of Vegetarianism / 276

    IV. Proposition of Anti-Anthropocentrism / 292

Conclusion / 310

References / 313

Index / 339

Introduction

In concept, animal poetry is "that kind of poetry which attempts to portray the animal, bird, or insect objectively, and sympathetically" (Sells xiii). The reason why I choose animal poetry as the research object of my current study is that, on the one hand, I am personally an ardent animal lover and am always intrigued by poems dedicated to animals; on the other hand, animal poetry as a poetic genre is becoming more and more significant in the reading circle and academic field. My interest in animal poetry was particularly developed in 2010 when I published in the journal *English Language Learning* the translation and critical analysis of an animal poem by Thomas Hardy, entitled "The Blinded Bird", and the interest was deepened when I further published during the years 2015 and 2016 two more conference papers related to the study of Hardy's animal poems. As to the reason for the public interest in animal poetry, just as Vanessa Robinson puts it, in the twentieth century, literary animal figures have become more prominent in revealing — and at times informing — our understanding of non-human beings (28). The significance of the academic study of animal poetry is proposed by Susan McHugh in the following way: "By furthering the investigation into new and old means of representing animals, literary animal studies can contribute to a broader understanding of porous species forms and can help model knowledges and responsibilities attendant to life in the twenty-first century" (491-92).

My current study of the British animal poetry will be done in the light of animal ethics or animal rights, that is, "views supportive of the protection of animals against human misuse" (Beauchamp 1), or "a term used in academia to describe human-animal relationships and how animals ought to be treated" (Wikipedia Editors). Accordingly, the literature review of my study will be dealt with in this regard.

The time during which animal poetry first flourished is the Romantic period. According to Laurence W. Mazzeno and Ronald D. Morrison, most of the major figures in Romantic literature directly addressed animal issues in one way or another, and most did so through one dominant genre: poetry (7). For the sake of convenient discussion, the British animal poetry will be roughly grouped into the pre-Romantic period, the Romantic period, and the post-Romantic period.

As for the study on animal poems in the pre-Romantic period, there is not much. One of the earliest essays is the study of two animal poets in the medieval period, that is, Florence H. Ridley's "The Treatment of Animals in the Poetry of Henryson and Dunbar" (1990). Ridley argues that animals play a major role in the poetry of the fifteenth century Scottish poets William Dunbar and Robert Henryson. Most of Dunbar's poetry is inner directed, consistently conveying a sense of self-concern, one striking aspect of his poetry being its tendency to turn men into animals to serve the poet's own ends. In contrast, Henryson's poetry is outer directed, and conveys a strong sense of concern for others, to serve whom he humanizes animals, turning them into all manners of men, to entertain but most often to demonstrate lessons against greed, vanity, hypocrisy, and to protest against the injustice both of the social and even the divine order of his world (364).

Another study about animal poems or bird poems to be exact in the medieval period is Michael J. Warren's monograph *Birds in Medieval English Poetry: Metaphors, Realities, Transformations* (2018). By attending to the ways in which birds were observed and experienced, this book aims at offering new perspectives on how and why birds are meaningful in five major poems, namely,

"The Seafarer" (by anonymous author), *Exeter Book Riddles* (by anonymous author), *The Owl and the Nightingale* (by anonymous author), *The Parliament of Fowls* (by Geoffrey Chaucer) and *Confessio Amantis* (by John Gower). Warren argues that birds are relevant to the medieval mind because their unique properties align them with important religious and secular themes.

One of the most prominent critics of animal poetry is David Perkins who has published a monograph and several related essays, one of which is "Human Mouseness: Burns and Compassion for Animals" (2000). The essay is devoted to the study of the eighteenth-century Scottish poet Robert Burns. Perkins argues that no poet writes of animals with more sympathy than Burns does. By a detailed study of Burns' poem "To A Mouse", Perkins shows us the role the poetry of Burns plays in the transformation of human and animal relationship, and he concludes that in the career of Burns' poem, compassion for the mouse becomes pity for the poor, then pity for all existence (13).

A large majority of the studies focus on animal poems in the Romantic period. One of the earliest essays with relatively comprehensive study on Romantic animal poetry is Frank Doggett's "Romanticism's Singing Bird" (1974). By analyzing the Romantic poets' famous bird poems such as Coleridge's "The Nightingale: A Conversation Poem", Wordsworth's "To the Cuckoo", Shelley's "To a Skylark", and Keats' "Ode to a Nightingale", as well as the Victorian poets Arnold, Swinburne, Bridges and Hardy's bird poems, the essay reviews the development of the singing bird poetry and examine its importance in the English poetry of the nineteenth century, and argues that the Romantic poets saw in the image of the singing bird an instance of creativity in the natural world (551).

One of the latest comprehensive essays on Romantic animal poetry is Johansen Quijano's "Morality, Ethics, and Animal Rights in Romantic Poetry and Victorian Thought" (2013). This essay takes a critical look at the poetry of

British Romantic poets like Blake, Wordsworth, Coleridge, Shelley and Keats, and proposes that with the shift in attitudes towards animals during the Romantic period people stopped seeing animals as things towards which no moral or ethical duty was owed and began to consider them as divine gifts having a spirit of their own (126).

Another latest essay is Isabel Karremann's "Human/Animal Relations in Romantic Poetry: The Creaturely Poetics of Christopher Smart and John Clare" (2015), which examines the relationship between man and animals by studying the poems of two less well-known Romantic poets. Karremann argues that from a biocentric and biosemiotic perspective that acknowledges non-human modes and experiences of existence as meaningful, the poems of Smart and Clare serve as a stepping stone toward the creaturely poetics that regards non-human creatures as "significant others" (94).

In addition to the essays, there are also some monographs which provide comprehensive studies on the Romantic animal poetry, the earliest one of which is Christine Kenyon-Jones's monograph *Kindred Brutes: Animals in Romantic-period Writing* (2001). The book consists of six chapters, namely, "Animals Dead and Alive: Pets, Politics and Poetry in the Romantic Period", "Children's Animals: Locke, Rousseau, Coleridge and the Instruction/Imagination Debate", "Political Animals: Bull-fighting, Bull-baiting and Childe Harold I", "Animals as Food: Shelley, Byron and the Ideology of Eating", "Animals and Nature: Beasts, Birds and Wordsworth's Ecological Credentials", and "Evolutionary Animals: Science and Imagination Between the Darwins". The study covers all the major Romantic poets including Blake, Wordsworth, Coleridge, Southey, Byron, Shelley, and Keats, from perspectives related to children's books, parliamentary debates, vegetarian theses, encyclopedias and early theories about evolution. Most important of all is that the study shows how in the Romantic period animals were seen as subjects in their own right, rather than simply human beings' tools or subordinates and they also have the ability to feel and perhaps to think like human beings.

Another monograph is David Perkins's *Romanticism and Animal Rights: 1790–1830* (2003). This book shows how extensively English Romantic literature takes up issues of what we now call animal rights or ecological concerns. The book is divided into eight chapters, namely, "In the beginning of animal rights", "Grounds of argument", "Keeping pets: William Cowper and his hares", "Barbarian pleasures: against hunting", "Savage amusements of the poor: John Clare's badger sonnets", "Work animals, slaves, servants: Coleridge's young ass", "The slaughterhouse and the kitchen: Charles Lamb's 'Dissertation upon Roast Pig'", and "Caged birds and wild". These chapters deal with problems like keeping pets, hunting and baiting of animals, working or laboring animals, eating animals as food, and the various harms inflicted on wild birds, which might influence people's feelings or arouse their protest. Apart from the poets like Cowper, Clare and Coleridge, who are mentioned in the chapter titles, other popular Romantic poets including Burns, Blake, Wordsworth, Byron, Shelley and Keats are studied as well.

The latest monograph is Chase Pielak's *Memorializing Animals during the Romantic Period* (2016). The book is composed of six chapters, namely, "Beasts at the Table: Charles and Mary Lamb and Roast Animals", "Living Together: John Clare's Creature Community", "Mourning in Eden's Churchyard: Clare's Animal Bodies", "Dead(ly) Beasts: Samuel Taylor Coleridge and the Wandering Cemetery", "Eccentric Beasts: Byron's Animal Taboo and Transgression", and "Landed Beasts: William Wordsworth, the White Doe, and the Cuckoo". Pielak deals with animal encounters from the communal life, the dinner table, to the countryside, and finally to the cemetery. He argues that Romantic writers intend to expose anxiousness over what it means to be human, what happens at death, the consequences of living together, and the significance of being remembered.

He shows us that these animal representations are not only inherently important but also foreshadow the ways we continue to need images of dead and deadly Romantic beasts.

In addition to the studies of Romantic animal poetry as a whole, there are also some essays devoted to the study of individual Romantic poets, and the one studied most is not one of the so-called six major Romantic poets, but Clare, a less renowned one. There are several related essays on Clare. The first one is Perkins' "Sweet Helpston! John Clare on Badger Baiting" (1999). After reading some poems of compassion for animals written by Clare, Perkins says that he is struck that even though Clare sympathizes with the badgers, he does not idealize or sentimentalize them. He argues that in the "Badger" sonnets, Clare views the baited animals with a somewhat affectionate realism and the baiting villagers with a somewhat humorous distance, and his strongest desire is to keep both at an emotional distance (406).

The second essay is Sehjae Chun's "'An Undiscovered Song': John Clare's 'Birds Poems'" (2005). Chun aims to approach Clare's "Bird Poems" from an environmentally oriented perspective. Chun argues that it is not as a sentimental writer of nature but as an expert naturalist and environmentalist poet that Clare succeeds in poetizing birds with a naturalist's eye, through demonstrating the mutually constituent relationship between ornithology and poetry (47). Chun concludes that Clare's engagement with birds actually becomes the basis for an environmental ethic of dwelling and a sustainable reading of non-humans (62).

The third one is Stephanie Kuduk Weiner's "Listening with John Clare" (2009). By analyzing some of Clare's poems of singing birds, Weiner argues that the sounds of Clare's poetic language embody the vitality and sensuous appeal of the natural world which he tries to capture in his poetic work. Clare's techniques for placing his readers within his auditory vantage point, his use of onomatopoeia and sound effects enable his readers to listen with him to the birds' singing, fully to hear both the music of nature and the music of language (390).

Finally, let's take a look at the study of the animal poems in the post-Romantic period, which for the convenience of discussion will be divided into the Victorian period and the modern period.

Among the Victorian poets who paid heed to animals, Thomas Hardy undoubtedly deserves most attention and is also a dominant figure among all British animal poets. There are many studies devoted to Hardy. One of the earliest essays is George Witter Sherman's "Thomas Hardy and the Lower Animals" (1946), which also turns out to be one of the earliest studies on British animal poetry as a whole. In this essay, though Sherman employs more examples from Hardy's novels (such as *Tess of the d'Urbervilles*, *Far from the Madding Crowd*, *The Return of the Native* and *The Mayor of Casterbridge*) in his argument, he also uses several animal poems, such as "The Caged Thrush Freed and Home Again", "The Puzzled Game-Birds" and "The Blinded Bird", as well as Hardy's long verse drama *The Dynasts,* so as to show his compassion and sympathy for all of nature's defenseless creatures and the treachery and hypocrisy of man in their relationship with animals (307, 309).

The next essay about Hardy is J. O. Bailey's "Evolutionary Meliorism in the Poetry of Thomas Hardy" (1963). Bailey argues that evolutionary meliorism is the third and final stage of the development of Hardy's thought, with bleak pessimism and meditation about the Unconscious Will being the first and second one. In his view, Hardy thinks man's inhumanity to man and the lower animals is an ill practice that can be remedied through the evolutionary development of compassion as a universal human trait, and despite the fact that Hardy deplores violence in his poetry, he believes that the impulse to cruelty is dying out in the world (586).

One more essay about Hardy, which is one of the latest publications, is

Christine Roth's "The Zoocentric Ecology of Hardy's Poetic Consciousness" (2017). Roth argues that in both the form and the content of Hardy's novels and poems, he consistently challenges the prevailing anthropocentrism of Victorian culture, and his target is the series of zoological links and institutional disjunctions that characterize "the animal" (79). She also argues that Hardy's animal poems go so far as to anticipate modern discussions about speciesism and offer paradigmatic scenarios of Derrida's theorization of the "non-criminal putting to death" of animals (80).

Up to now, regretfully, there are still no monographs holistically devoted to the study of Hardy's animal poems, though there is a monograph devoted to the study of the animals in his novels by Anna West, entitled *Thomas Hardy and Animals* (2017).

The early twentieth century poet D. H. Lawrence published a collection of poetry entitled *Birds, Beast and Flowers* (1923) and is thus also regarded as an important animal poet. One of the essays about Lawrence's animal poems is Del Ivan Janik's "D. H. Lawrence and Environmental Consciousness" (1983). By analyzing Lawrence's novels, essays and some poems in his poetry collection *Birds, Beasts and Flowers*, such as "Fish" and "Snake", Janik tries to show that Lawrence has a deep respect for the land, the plants, and the animals which Westerners used to consider as mere instruments of progress toward human goals, and that Lawrence is a pioneering figure in the development of a new environmental consciousness in literature (371).

M. J. Lockwood, in the third chapter of his monograph *A Study of the Poems of D. H. Lawrence: Thinking in Poetry* (1987), argues that Lawrence's poetry collection *Birds, Beasts and Flowers*, among other things, is an effort to win right recognition again for creatures human beings have disowned or denied in whole or in part, or which we have loved too indiscriminately (118).

In Roberts W. French's essay "Lawrence and American Poetry" (1987), he argues that Lawrence has reached the second level of the three levels of consciousness put forward by the American writer Robert Bly, that is, the individual moves out from his own ego into the non-human world of plants and animals. In French's view, *Birds, Beasts and Flowers* is the collection of poems in which Lawrence is most open to the non-human world (123). He also argues that Lawrence's respect for the natural world is constant, as is shown in poems like "Snake" and "Man and Bat", in which Lawrence recognizes animals' claims to a place within the scheme of things since they are equally created beings just as he is, and hence he cannot assume superiority over them (125).

Another essay on Lawrence is one of the latest publications, that is, Jamie Johnson's "The Animal in D. H. Lawrence: A Struggle Against Anthropocentrism" (2016). By studying the poems of human-animal engagements such as "The Fox", "Reflections on the Death of a Porcupine", "Snake" and "Man and Bat", Johnson argues that the poems on the one hand show that nonhuman animals act as sources of inspiration for human beings, and on the other hand show human beings' disturbing violence towards animals, and such opposing attitudes or so-called contradictions actually reflect Lawrence's progress struggle against anthropocentrism. He also argues that human beings' unmistakable ontological connection to animals creates an ongoing tension in our illusory separation, and Lawrence's texts expose this tension in a dialectical manner (145).

One more important animal poet in the twentieth century is Philip Larkin. One essay about Larkin's animal poems is Roger Craik's "Animals and Birds in Philip Larkin's Poetry" (2002). By analyzing poems like "Pigeons", "Midwinter Waking", and "Wires", Craik looks at the role of birds and other animals as the main characters in Larkin's poems, discusses the career background of Larkin, the genre of his literary works, and the concept of human suffering.

Another essay about Larkin is James Booth's "Larkin as Animal Poet"

(2006). Booth makes a comparison between the animal poems of Larkin and Hughes, shows the major differences between them and points out that Larkin is an animal poet who deals with the life of ordinary animals around us in our daily life from the ecological perspective. In Booth's view, Larkin's animal poems show the concept of the harmonious co-existence between man and animals.

One more essay about Larkin is A. Banerjee's "Larkin Reconsidered" (2008), at the end of which he argues that there is an appeal for kindness toward animals in Larkin's poetry by analyzing one of his animal poems "The Mower", in which the accidental killing of a hedgehog fills him with deep remorse (441).

Ted Hughes is generally considered as the most important animal poet in the twentieth century, who published many poetry collections about animals. There are many essays devoted to the study of Hughes' animal poems. Herbert Lomas' essay "The Poetry of Ted Hughes" (1987) argues that though Hughes' poetry centers on animals, they are heavily anthropomorphized, are in fact excruciatingly lifelike mask, and he visualizes animals as human beings peeping out of beaks and snouts. Thus, Hughes has sought himself in the animal kingdom and presented humanity to the readers in the form of a bestiary (413, 425). He proposes that some of Hughes' animal poems are immortal and are likely to be read as long as English poetry is read (426).

Tuba Gonel and John Dayton's essay "Animal Images as Metaphors in Ted Hughes' Poetry" (2012) aims at analyzing some of Hughes' poems in which he employs animal figures to represent his association of human beings with nature, so as to convey the message that human beings, despite our civilized appearance, are as primitive and violent as other creatures in nature.

In Laura Webb's essay "Mythology, Mortality and Memorialization: Animal and Human Endurance in Hughes' Poetry" (2013), she thinks that the strategies of memorialization in Hughes' poetry are threefold. First, poetry is a means of endurance, of conjuring and commemorating the absent subject, shown first of all in the poem "The Thought-Fox" and later on in the poetry collection *Moortown Diary*. Second, as symbols of survival, animals in Hughes' poetry are often used as metaphors for an endurance that transcends animality and extends towards the human. Finally, beginning in the late 1970s and early 1980s, animals come to be memorialized in their own right, as is proved in many poems in poetry collections such as *Moortown Diary*, *River* and *Wolfwatching* (45).

Ashik Istiak's essay "Human Animals in Ted Hughes' Poetry: A Thorough Study of the Animal Poems of Ted Hughes" (2016) first presents the description of the violent and sometimes exotic animals in many of Hughes' animal poems and then tries to explore the hermeneutics of them. It aims to prove that the vicious animals in Hughes' poems are more humans than animals. Literary theories like deconstruction and psychoanalysis are employed to find out how the cruelty, the vendetta and the ferociousness of the animals in Hughes' poems go beyond their animal identities.

In Michael Malay's up-to-date monograph *The Figure of the Animal in Modern and Contemporary Poetry* (2018), Chapter 3 "Rhythmic Contact: Ted Hughes and Animal Life" is devoted to the study of Hughes' animal poems. The study examines some of Hughes' poems from different stages of his writing career, with a special emphasis on poetry collections like *The Hawk in the Rain*, *Crow* and *River*. This chapter is divided into several parts, namely "The Hawk in the Rain", "Violent Transformation", "Becoming-Animal", "The Machine in the Garden", "The Animal Body", "The Misfortune of Being Physical", and "The River's Wheel". For example, "The Animal Body" concludes that Crow's "super-ugly language" is a primal reminder of our own animality, as well as a testament to the power of trauma to disable language and incapacitate thought (134). In "The Misfortune of Being Physical", the author draws a conclusion that the poetry collection *Crow* invites the readers to see nonhuman animals differently, not from the lofty vantage point of humanism, but from the perspective of ecological continuity (141). In "The River's Wheel", the section ends with the study of Hughes' poems on the salmon, such as "An August Salmon", "October Salmon" and "Salmon Eggs", which is closely related to Hughes' distinctive concerns: energy, vitality, renewal, and rebirth (145).

Last but not the least, there is a newly-published comprehensive study of British animal literature, that is, Mario Ortiz-Robles' *Literature and Animal Studies* (2016). This book is divided into six chapters, namely, "What is it like to be a trope", "Equids (might and right)", "Canids (companionship, cunning, domestication)", "Songbirds (poetry and environment)", "Felids (enigma and fur)", and "Animal revolutions (allegory and politics)". In terms of British poems, the book touches upon animals including the ass, jaguar, lamb, tiger, rat, and especially the nightingale, written by British poets such as Shakespeare, Milton, Charlotte Smith, Blake, Wordsworth, Coleridge, Clare, Keats, Browning, Mrs. Browning, T. S. Eliot, Ted Hughes, and Muldoon. As the introductory remark on the half-title page goes, "Ortiz Robles examines the various tropes literature has historically employed to give meaning to our fraught relations with other animals" and "The book makes us see animals and our relation to them with fresh eyes and, in doing so, prompts us to review the role of literature in a culture that considers it an endangered art form".

From the above literature review, we can find that most overseas criticism on animal poems are devoted to Romantic poets, the Victorian poet Hardy and modern poets like Lawrence, Larkin and Hughes. However, there are still many more poets who have written animal poems, but they are not paid enough attention to or neglected.

Comparatively speaking, the study of animal poetry in China started much later than that of the study overseas, as the earliest study is in 1985 and most of the researches are actually done in the twenty-first century. In China, there are not so many scholars who are devoted to the study of British animal poetry and hence there are not so many related publications. Statistics from CNKI show that there are only over 60 essays, 7 MA theses, 3 Ph.D dissertations, and 1 monograph about or concerning British animal poetry, but they almost unanimously focus on the works of Thomas Hardy, D. H. Lawrence, Philip Larkin and Ted Hughes, with only a few exceptions, and what's more, there is a severe lack of related monographs.

The one and only study solely devoted to the animal poems in the pre-Romantic period is Hu Jialuan's "Peaceful Kingdom: British Garden Poetry and Animal Symbols in the Renaissance Period" (2006), which argues that British garden poetry in the Renaissance Period uses animal images as emblems of choice between good and evil, as representations of human passions, or as metaphors of political organization and social order, thus giving the fullest expression to their earnest wish for universal harmony between man and animals (32). In this essay, Hu touches upon the poems of over ten British poets, including famous poets like William Shakespeare, Henry Howard, Edmund Spencer, Thomas Nashe, John Donne, John Milton, Andrew Marvell, as well as Margaret Cavendish, Thomas Tryon, and Thomas Traherne, who are not so well-known.

There are two essays as regards the study of animal poetry in the Romantic period, which is relatively insufficient compared with the abundant study abroad. In 2006, Chen Hong published an essay entitled "To Set the Wild Free: Changing Images of Animals in English Poetry of the Pre-Romantic and Romantic Periods" in *Interdisciplinary Studies in Literature & Environment*, which is one of the couple of related essays published in a foreign journal. Chen's essay examines the changes in the images of animals in English poetry of the Pre-Romantic and Romantic periods and suggests that the Romantic period in literature and art is a crucial turning point in terms of human-animal relationship.

The latest essay is Xie Chao's "The Representation of the Human-Animal

Relationship in the British Romantic Poetry" (2018), and it is the second essay after Chen Hong's essay that deals with the animal poetry of British Romantic poets as a whole. From the perspective of eco-criticism, this essay explores the human animal relationship represented in the British Romantic poetry against the social and cultural background, focusing on the poets' sympathies for animals, the connection between sufferings of animals and those of humans, and the poets' appeal for a harmonious relationship between human beings and animals (41).

One of the major focuses of the study of British animal poems in China is on Thomas Hardy's works. About 20% of the essays and theses are devoted to Hardy's animal poems, but the majority of the study focuses on one of his most anthologized individual poem "The Darkling Thrush".

The earliest study of Hardy's animal poems begins just from the analysis of "The Darkling Thrush", that is Xiao Yi's "Meditation at the End of the Century: Comment on Hardy's 'Darkling Thrush'" (2000), in which Xiao argues that Hardy shows his hope for a more promising future through the image of an optimistic thrush (53). There are eight more essays devoted to the study of "Darkling Thrush" published between the years 2003–2015, and most of them restate the theme of optimism and tenacity in depressing situations, some with the assistance of the analysis of Hardy's writing techniques.

In 2011, Fang Ying and Fang Ling published the essay "Hardy's Ecological Ethics". A part of the essay is devoted to Hardy's advocacy of the subjectivity of animals, in that animals' rights should be respected and animals' feelings should be recognized (25), but most of the examples are from Hardy's novels and only two animal poems are taken into consideration; one is "Snow in the Suburbs", the other is "The Bird Catcher's Boy".

In 2015, Jiang Huiling's essay "An Analysis of the Eco-ethics Reflected in Thomas Hardy's Animal Poems" came out. Jiang's view is that in Hardy's animal poems, he gives animals subjectivity, is filled with sympathy towards animals, and criticizes sharply against human beings' ill-treatment of animals. She argues that as a man of ecological consciousness and humanistic ideas, what Hardy looks forward to is the harmony between man and animals.

In the same year, I myself published a conference paper "Animal Ethics in Thomas Hardy's Bird Poems" in *Proceedings of the 2015 Northeast Asia International Symposium on Linguistics, Literature and Teaching*. My view in this paper is that by writing poems showing his concern and love for birds, poems revealing the lack of concern and love as well as its bad consequence, and poems criticizing the inequality between man and birds as well as man's cruelty to birds, Hardy proves himself to be an ardent supporter of animal rights, a fighter against brutality to animals and a poet with animal ethics (105).

In 2016, I published another conference paper "Thomas Hardy's Animal Poems Seen in the Light of Animal Ethics", in *Proceeding of the Fifth Northeast Asia International Symposium on Language, Literature and Translation*. In this paper, I continue to prove Hardy as a lover of animals, an ardent supporter of animal rights, a fighter against cruelty to animals and a poet with animal ethics by using his animal poems other than bird poems, including poems about dogs, cats, horses, cattle, and sheep, so as to show again his concern, care, love and respect for animals, poems revealing the lack of the above-mentioned virtues, and poems criticizing man's brutality to animals (302).

Another focus of the study of British animal poems is on D. H. Lawrence's works. About 20% of the publications are devoted to Lawrence whose collection of poetry *Birds, Beasts and Flowers* are concerned with creatures, reptiles, tortoises, birds, and animals.

The earliest one is Pan Lingjian's "D. H. Lawrence's *Birds, Beasts and Flowers*: An Invocation for Human Return and Universal Harmony" (2002). Through the construction of a systematic, symbolic, metaphorical world, the poet explores human existence in three dimensions, namely, "Man and Nature", "Man and Civilization" and "Man and Self", and proceeds to invoke human return and universal harmony. He argues that the personification of the essence of nature and the grandeur and profundity of the poet's ideological system have paved the way for this collection of poems to a share of immortality in the twentieth century poetry (102).

The next essay is Chen Hong's "Romantic Morality in D. H. Lawrence's Animal Poems" (2006). Chen argues in this essay that Lawrence's animal poems express his moral attitude regarding nature, which is basically anti-anthropocentric or biocentric, and which is closely connected to the anti-rationalist Romantic tradition. Through the reading of three of Lawrence's animal poems, i.e. "Snake", "Fish", and "Tortoise Shout", the essay presents Lawrence's deep exploration into nature, especially the internal nature of human beings. It draws attention to a crucial and yet often neglected point in Lawrence's moral view, that is, his acute sense of balance between one's social-consciousness and blood-consciousness, or between our humanity and animality (47).

Also in 2006, Miao Fuguang finished his Ph.D dissertation "An Eco-Critical Reading of D. H. Lawrence" (published in 2007 by Shanghai University Press), and the fourth section of Chapter Three of this dissertation is "Lawrence's Eco-Ethical View on Animals". His argument is that Lawrence is an extreme bio-centrist who shows his love and respect to animals and possesses the eco-ethical view of treating animals equally. Pitifully, there is only one example, that is, "Snake", which is a shortcoming in terms of argumentation.

In 2007, Liu Yingqian and Liu Xuming published the essay "Exploring into Man's Future in Nature: Reading Lawrence's *Birds, Beasts and Flowers*", the first section of which, entitled "Revelation of Nature", analyzes the poem "Mountain Lion" and criticizes man's cruel killing of the lion.

Introduction

In 2010, Zhang Liping published the essay "Lawrence's Ecological Consciousnesses Seen Through *Birds, Beasts and Flowers*". She argues that some of the poems in this collection, such as "The Jaguar" and "Snake", criticize anthropocentrism which promotes conquering nature and controlling nature, and Lawrence pays attention not only to the balance between man and nature, but also man and man, and man's body and soul.

In 2011, Zhou Weigui's essay "World of Innocence and World of Experience: A Study of the Existentialist Theme in D. H. Lawrence's Animal Poems" came out. In Zhou's view, Lawrence's animal poems create a series of animal images who follow natural instinct and are not bothered by self-consciousness. The world of innocence demonstrated by animals' way of existence forms a sharp contrast with man's world of experience. Due to the world of experience created by human beings' self-consciousness and cultural tradition, human beings cannot experience the charm of the world of innocence and obtain the independence enjoyed by animals.

In 2012, Zhang Jing's "On D. H. Lawrence's Animal Philosophy" was published. In her view, Lawrence loves nature passionately and puts almost all kinds of animals into his works. Meanwhile, he criticizes the western industrial civilization severely, trying hard to find the true value of life and the rebirth of mankind. This essay focuses on Lawrence's ideas on the non-human animals and explores his particular animal philosophy (156), that is, the unity between man and nature, the disadvantage of the gradual disappearance of man's animal instinct (such as being free from self-consciousness), and the necessity of man's respect and gratitude towards nature.

The next two essays came out in 2016; one is Yu Juan's "On the Wiring of Animals in D. H. Lawrence's Poems", the other is Jiang Huiling's "'View of Equality of All Creatures' Reflected in D. H. Lawrence's Animal Poems". Yu's standpoint is that with poems on "inferior animals", Lawrence promotes the equality between animals, with the rhetorical device of personification and the description of animals' sexual behaviour, he shows the similarity and link between man and animals, which is a refute against the binary opposition between man and animals, forward-looking and enlightening to the ecological consciousness of modern men. Jiang proposes that Lawrence shows respect and love to animals, criticism against anthropocentrism, and longing for the harmonious co-existence between man and animals, and states that Lawrence's "view of equality of all creatures" will influence later poets and shed light on the cross-disciplinary study of literature and ecology. Regretfully, the essay is only a one-page essay without sufficient examples. The ideas in both these two essays are not novel but kind of restatement of previous essays.

In 2018, Ding Liming published the essay "On Aesthetics and Anthropocentrism in D. H. Lawrence's Poem 'Snake'". Based upon Jacques Derrida's concept of animal ethics, Ding argues that the philosophical thoughts of animal "other" shared by Lawrence and Derrida overturned the philosophical tradition of western anthropocentrism since ancient Greece and reshaped the image of animal sovereignty (122).

In addition to the preference for Hardy and Lawrence, one more focus is on Philip Larkin and about 10% of the study on British animal poetry are devoted to him.

The earliest studies on Larkin are two conference papers, i.e. Chen Xi's "Living Things, Ecology and Environment: The Eco-ethics in Philip Larkin's Poetry" and Lv Aijing's "The Lost Eden: Looking at Larkinian Views", published in *Proceedings of International Conference on Literature and Environment* (2008). By analyzing animal poems like "At Grass", "First Sight" and "Take One Home for the Kiddies", Chen's paper argues that the nature depicted in Larkin's poems is against the nature of Romanticism and Anthropocentrism and analyzes Larkin's eco-egalitarian and his concern about the environmental degradation brought by modern industrialization (442). Lv's paper proposes that natural scenery, free animals and beautiful girls are the making of Larkin's dreamy Eden which is lost. Only the second part of her paper is devoted to the study of Larkin's animal poems, in which she discusses the animals in great distress, such as the ape in "Ape Experiment Room", the rabbit in "Myxomatosis", the horses in "At Grass" and the cattle in "Wires".

Lv published another essay in the following year, "Beauty of the Small: Non-heroism in Larkin's Animal Poetry" (2009). In her opinion, Larkin's animal images, such as rabbit, calf and little swallow, are unlike the strong and huge animals with power and they are the most common animal references which embody the common men in the human world, i.e. the non-heroes, a group of responsible citizens responsibly employed and they are a realist's and mature man's heroes (110).

In 2010, Lv published one more essay "Seeking for the English Garden: Ecological Thinking in Philip Larkin's Poetry". She thinks that the ill-treatment of animals and the rape of the sanctuaries of nature make Larkin extremely sad. To Larkin, natural scenery, playful animals and simple life are the making of the English garden, and man should respect animals, preserve the beauty of nature and poetically dwell on the Earth garden (16). However, both the major argument and the examples used in this essay are very much similar to her own paper in 2008.

In 2011, Chen Xi finished her Ph.D dissertation "The Flaneur's Ethics: A Study of Philip Larkin's Poetry". In the second section ("Larkin's Eco-Ethics") of Chapter IV ("Eco-Ethics and Urban Civilization") of her dissertation, she discusses Larkin's animal poems and the ecological equality that Larkin advocates. She thinks that Larkin's animal poems promote the ecological morality of caring for animals, loving living things, and protecting nature, and criticizes anthropocentrism imposed by man upon animals. From the main argument and the examples employed, this is practically a restatement of her paper in 2008.

In the same year, Wang Yufeng and Chen Zhijin published the essay "A Preliminary Exploration of the Ecological Thoughts in Philip Larkin's Poetry". In the abstract, the authors state "this paper employs a brand-new perspective of the newly-developed ecocriticism to study some of Philip Larkin's poems" (72), which shows that they fail to do enough literature review, because the eco-critical reading of Larkin's poems is far from being "brand-new" in the year 2011. The essay analyzes the ecological thoughts in Larkin's poetry, pointing out that Larkin is a poet with ecological consciousness (72), which is not an innovative argument either.

In 2016, Shao Xiaxin's essay "An Analysis of Ethical Thought in Philip Larkin's Poems" came out. The essay analyzes the religious ethic, moral ethic and ecological ethic of Larkin's poems, and in the ecological ethic part, the author analyzes several of Larkin's animal poems and shows his eco-ethical view that living things should be equal, which does not break away from the argument of Chen Xi's essay in 2008.

All in all, Chen Xi and Lv Aijing have made the most contribution to the study of Larkin's animal poems.

Most domestic essays and theses (about 40%) were devoted to Ted Hughes who is often referred to as "a poet of animals" with his various volumes of animal poetry such as *The Hawk in the Rain* (1957), *Lupercal* (1960), *Crow: From the Life and the Songs of the Crow* (1970) and *Wolfwatching* (1989). Hence, it is almost impossible for critics to comment on Hughes' poetry without making use of or touching upon his animal poems.

In a broad sense, the earliest essay devoted to Hughes' animal poetry is Zhang Zhongzai's "Ted Hughes: British Poet Laureate" (1985), which is also the earliest study on British animal poetry. The essay is a general introduction to Hughes and his poetry, and in which Zhang analyzes Hughes' animal poems such as "Thought-Fox", "Hawk Roosting", "A Childish Prank", "Examination at the Womb-Door" and "Crow's Last Stand" and argues that Hughes' poems show violence and portray bloody scenes of animal killing, and some of them even make the readers feel sick and disgusting, however, there are also poems showing light, warmth and hope, such as "The Horses" and "Crow and Mama".

The next essay on Hughes did not come out until over ten years later, which is Yao Zhiyong and Wu Wenquan's "Ted Hughes and His 'Animal World'" (1997). By analyzing poems in early poetry collections like *The Hawk in the Rain, Lupercal, Wodwo*, and *Crow*, the two authors think that the violent and cruel animals in Hughes' early poetry changed into the docile and lovely domesticated animals in the later poems in poetry collections like *Moortown* and *River*.

Coming next is Lin Yupeng's "Emotion Behind Wildness and Power: Review on Ted Hughes' Poetry" (1999). Lin thinks that Hughes puts his emotions into the writing of the animal poems, and his emotions enter into the body of the animals, emerging with them. Hughes seems to become the animals, and run and howl like them.

Li Chengjian is one of the major contributors to the study of Hughes' animal poetry who published five essays within three years from 2000 to 2002. However, only the essay "The Return of the Romantic Spirit under Postmodernist Vision: A Revaluation of the Significance of Ted Hughes' Poetry" (2002) is to some extent related to my current study. In this essay, by analyzing animal poems like "Thought-Fox", "A Childish Prank", "Disaster", and "The Crow's Last Stand", Li thinks that the intimate relationship with nature and high praise of heroism indicate the return of the romantic spirit in Hughes' poetry. However, Hughes' poetry is far from being a simple repetition of history and the structure of his poetry with a plurality of possible meanings and his textual deconstruction and reconstruction have imbued his works with postmodernist features (169).

There are two essays published in 2006. One is Zhang Lin and Zheng Xiaoqing's "Hawk, Man and Nature: On the Writing of 'Animal Poems' by Ted Hughes from 'Hawk Roosting'", the other is Chen Hong's "Who is Violent? Man or Animals? — Further Discussion on Ted Hughes' Animal Poems". Zhang and Zheng's essay proposes that as a poet full of conscience and consciousness of suffering, Hughes can penetrate into the latent crisis in the development of modern industrial civilization and worries about the development and the future of human beings. Therefore, Hughes gives a deep thought of the embarrassing relationship between man and nature, ascribes it directly to anthropocentrism, and aims at warning people to try to build up a harmonious man-and-nature relationship (46). Chen's essay argues that Hughes' poetry, especially his early animal poems, are not aimed at advocating violence as many readers or critics consider them to be. His animal poems do not only show his deep insight into humanity and animality, but also his strong eco-environmental consciousness. In Hughes' mind's eye, animals are not to blame for their instinct to survive, and it is not that animals are cruel and violent, but the dehumanized human beings are.

In 2007, there are also two essays published. One is Liu Haoduo's "The Lonely Brave Man: A Review on Ted Hughes the Poet of Animal Fables", the other is Li Yudi's "The Relationship between Man and Animal in Ted Hughes' Poems". Liu's essay points out that Hughes vents out his complaint and worry about the human society through portraying some animals in nature. Hughes often uses animals to reflect the world, and his animal poems are like animal fables, such as the poems "Howl" and "Hawk Roosting". Li's essay is the first one published in a foreign journal called *Canadian Social Science*. It discusses the significance of Hughes' animal poems, and finds out the relationship between man and animals. It analyses man-animal relationship in Hughes' poems from three aspects, i.e. man expecting to acquire animal power, animals reflecting man and man's enlightenment from animals (95).

There is only one essay in 2008, that is, Hu Jiewen and Wang Liming's "Modern Animal Fables of Ted Hughes", which proposes that through his unique animal fables, Hughes shows his ecological concerns about nature, calls for human beings' ecological consciousness and guides us along a green ecological road (127). The view in this essay is not so innovative, or so to speak, it is a reconsideration of Zhang Lin and Zheng Xiaoqing's view.

There is also a Ph.D dissertation in 2008. Liu Guoqing's Ph.D dissertation "Closing Rifts: The Study of Ted Hughes' Ecological Thought in His Poems" analyzes the formation of Hughes' ecological outlook, the consciousness of ecological crisis in his poetry, the ecological appeal in his poetry and his pursuit of ecological harmony, in the analytic process of which many animal poems are employed, especially poems from *The Hawk in the Rain*, *Crow* and *Gaudete*.

In 2012, Chen Baiyu published "The Construction of Ted Hughes to the Relationship between Human and Nature: Ecological Interpretation of Poetry Collection *Crow*". The essay uses Arne Naess' theory of deep ecology to analyze the inquiry of Hughes into the relationship between man and nature in the poetry collection *Crow*, as well as his self realization of deep ecology. In Hughes' mind, only by abandoning the overbearing anthropocentric attitude, and making deep ecology internalized, can man establish a firm identity with all other creatures, which means the reunification of human spiritual world and the outside world, and it is the only way to solve the environmental crisis the western society is confronted with (58).

In 2014, Hu Peng's "Multidimensional Complex in Ecological Civilization: Re-understanding of Ted Hughes' Animal Poems" was published. The author thinks that in the era full of ecological crisis, Hughes practices his poetic quest of the re-establishment of the harmony between man and nature. The essay discusses the multidimensional complex of "animal complex", "ecological complex", "violence complex" and "anti-traditional creation complex" in Hughes' animal poems (86).

In 2016, there were two related essays. The first one is Zhao Yue's "An Analysis of Ted Hughes' Animal Metaphors in *Lupercal*", and the second one is Zheng Siming's "Man's Violence towards Nature — The Ecological Consciousness in Ted Hughes' Poetry". Zhao's essay explores Hughes' metaphors on man, nature and humanity, shows Hughes' sharp insight into the unbalanced relationship among man, nature and human nature, and clarifies his intention to warn the human beings of their centralism and to build a balanced man-and-nature relationship (99). This essay, like Hu and Wang's essay, is again a reconsideration of Zhang Lin and Zheng Xiaoqing's view. Zheng's essay discusses man's violence towards animals, man's violence towards nature and the revenge of nature on man, so as to arouse people's ecological consciousness.

There is only one publication about the study of post-50s modern animal poetry, that is, He Ning's essay "On Contemporary British Animal Poetry" (2017), which is the only one that deals with contemporary post-50s poets who are still alive today, namely John Burnside (1955–), Alice Oswald (1966–) and Kathleen Jamie (1962–). He's viewpoint is that the above-mentioned three poets are the most prominent poets who reflect on the relationship between human world and animal world, understand the significance of animal world's connection with nature, and explore a harmonious relationship between human beings and animals. They abandon the tradition of using animal images to describe the human society, regard the animal world as an equal of the human world in their poetic works, and promote a non-anthropocentric representation of animal in contemporary British poetry (78-80).

So far, the most comprehensive study concerning British animal poetry is one of the major animal poetry critics Chen Hong's *Bestiality, Animality, and Humanity* (2005), being one of the earliest studies on British animal poetry. This book is divided into three chapters, namely, "To Set the Wild Free", "To Brave the Wild" and "To Have the Snake Crowned Again". It provides a retrospect of the history of the Romantic tradition of regarding bestiality in nature and animality in humanity as a positive force, pays attention to the background of its creation and development, including British poetry's concern about animals, especially wild animals, from the later part of the eighteenth century and second half of the twentieth century, as well as various changes in non-literary aspects such as culture and social reality. The major argument of the study is that British poets like Lawrence and Hughes hold a critical attitude towards the traditional view on the relationship among bestiality, animality and humanity held by ancient Greeks, especially Christianity.

Apart from the study on individual poets and certain literary periods, there are several essays of comparative study as well.

In 2016, Jiang Huiling published "Animals in Distress: A Comparative Study of Hardy's and Larkin's Eco-ethics Reflected in Their Animal Poems", in which she argues that Hardy writes more about birds in the countryside while Larkin writes more about domesticated animals like oxen, horses and sheep; Hardy's criticism is more conservative while Larkin's criticism is more thorough and downright; Hardy is more subjective while Larkin is more objective (32).

As a major contributor to the study of British animal poems, Jiang published two more essays in 2017, in collaboration with other authors. One is by Jiang and Su Xiaoli, entitled "Treating Animals Kindly and Pursuing Harmonious Beauty: Ecological Ideas in the Animal Poems of Larkin and Hughes". The argument of the essay is that the two poets are similar in that they both show the eco-ethics of giving concern to animals, sharing a common fate with animals and pursuing harmonious beauty. The other is by Jiang and Cui Xiyun, entitled "From Non-Hero to Hero: Looking into the Change of the Social Mentality of the Post-war British People Reflected in the Animal Poems of

Larkin and Hughes". The contention of this essay is that despite the similarities between the two poets in their writing of animal poems, they are different in a couple of ways, for example, Larkin is better at describing the small animals and domesticated animals while Hughes is more well versed in depicting wild animals like foxes, tigers and hawks; what's more, Larkin's non-hero view is distinct from Hughes' view of "supremacy over all".

The latest comparative study was published in 2018, that is, Chen Guicai and Yuan Yichuan's "Intertextuality and Modernity in the Animal Writing of British Romantic Poetry: A Case Study of Ted Hughes' 'Hawk' and D. H. Lawrence's 'Eagle'", which deals with the textual and cultural dialogues between Hughes' "hawk" texts such as "The Hawk in the Rain" and "Hawk Roosting" and Lawrence's "eagle" texts such as "Eagle in New Mexico" and "The American Eagle", and argues that through the dialogues there exists intertextuality in terms of romanticism, anthropocentrism and colonialism between Hughes' "hawk" texts and Lawrence's "eagle" texts (32).

As can be seen, relatively speaking, the studies of British animal poetry home and abroad both mainly focus on those well-known poets, the number of whom is limited. However, as a matter of fact, there are many more poets who have made contribution to the development of British animal poetry. My study is going to bring into discussion as many as 82 poets, with the analysis of nearly 230 poems in total, aiming at providing the readers with a panorama or a comprehensive study of the British animal poetry. Apart from poems, I will also include some verse-plays by Shakespeare and Hardy.

The study is composed of five chapters. Chapter One is "High Praise of Animals", in which the animals are complimented in three aspects, i.e. their beauty and loveliness, their happiness and carefreeness, as well as their loyalty and dutifulness. Chapter Two is "Great Concern for Animals". First, it studies how the poets show their concern, love or sympathy to animals. Then it deals with the harmony or good relationship between man and animals shown in these poems. Third, it deals with how the poets ironize or criticize some people's lack of concern, love or sympathy to animals. Fourth, it discusses some people's remorse for their wrongdoings in the treatment of animals. Finally, it touches upon some elegies or epitaphs written to dead animals as a way of showing love to them. Chapter Three is "Animals' Functions in Poets' Mental Life", in which we can see that animals can function as stimulus to good mood, source of wisdom, and evoker of empathy among poets or human beings in general. Chapter Four is "Criticism Against the Cruelty to Animals". The first four sections of this chapter show human beings' brutality to or abuse of various kinds of animals, such as caged animals or animals with bondage, performing or racing animals, hunted animals, and butchered animals. The last section of this chapter deals with the theme of nemesis, that is, supernatural revenge on human beings' ill treatment of animals. The last chapter is "Advocacy of Animal Freedom and Rights", which is the most animal-rights-oriented part of the whole book. Section one is about the proposal for the protection and welfare of animals. Section two is devoted to the protest against experiment on animals and vivisection. Section three deals with the promotion of vegetarianism. The last section is with regard to the proposition of anti-anthropocentrism, which is one of the root causes of human beings' unfair or cruel treatment of animals.

However, some people's praise and love cannot cover other people's abuse and cruelty, and criticism is not for the sake of criticism. The study aims at providing some remedy for the endangered or corrupted human-animal relationship, and achieving human and animal harmony.

Chapter One   High Praise of Animals

To praise, commend or eulogize is one of the major functions of poetry and a large number of the British animal poems are devoted to the praise of the animals' good qualities or virtues, in terms of their beauty and loveliness, their happiness and carefreeness, as well as their loyalty and dutifulness. Animals are so praiseworthy that Edward Searl even edited a collection of writings commending animals, that is, *In Praise of Animals: A Treasury of Poems, Quotations and Readings* (2007), in which he calls on his readers to join him "in celebrating our animal brothers and sisters who accompany us on the great adventure we share" (vii). Following his footstep, this chapter will focus on the praise of animals in the three above-mentioned perspectives. To make it clear, the arrangement of the examples employed in this chapter will not be that of a rigid or absolute chronological order, but in the type of animals, namely, pet animals, domesticated animals, common wild animals, and less common wild animals. Within the analysis of a certain type of animal poems, the discussion will be based on their chronological order.

I. Beauty and Loveliness

Some animal poems are written in order to show the beauty and loveliness of the animals in people's household or in nature. Among animal poems, there are a number of pet poems, and the most favorite pets for poets are cats and dogs. Let's first look into two poems about dogs.

Chapter One High Praise of Animals

William Cowper (1731–1800), who is considered as a precursor to Romantic ideas, has written a lot about nature, with animals included. David Perkins thinks highly of Cowper, and in his view, if literature has practical influence on man, no writer in the eighteenth century had more effect than Cowper in transforming attitudes to animals and stimulating reform (*Romanticism and Animal Rights* 44). In Cowper's "The Dog and the Water Lily. No Fable" (1788), he praises his dog with the name of "Beau" who accompanies him to a walk on the side of the river Ouse as "prettiest of his race, / And high in pedigree" (lines 5-6), so much so that he even thinks that it is "Two nymphs adorn'd with every grace" who find the dog for him (7). The naughty and lovely dog runs in a carefree and playful way, and sometimes it runs out of sight in "flags and reeds" (9), sometimes it runs after the swallow on the meadow, which shows the loveliness of the dog. As a Romantic poet, Cowper does not only care about nature, he is "much concerned also with animals and their treatment" (Newey 41).

The second poem is "To Flush, My Dog" (1844) by the Victorian poetess Elizabeth Barrett Browning (1806–1861, henceforth referred to as Mrs. Browning). In the first stanza of the poem, she calls her dog "Loving friend" and "Gentle fellow-creature" (line 1, 6). The colour of the dog is dark brown; his silken ears are "Like a lady's ringlets brown" (7), his breast is "silver-suited" and his sleek curls "Flash all over into gold / With a burnished fullness" (10, 17-18). The color of the dog's bland and kindling eyes is that of hazel. From Mrs. Browning's portrayal, we can envisage the beauty of the dog. What is more impressive is her description of the dog's leaping. The dog leaps "like a charger" (24), and when he is leaping, its "broad tail waves a light" (25), his "slender feet are bright" and his ears "flicker strangely" (26, 29). Mrs. Browning loves the dog so much that, according to Deirdre David, she even went "on a rare cab trip to Shoreditch in search of Flush, dog-napped from Wimpole Street" (124). Mrs.

Browning's praise of the dog continues with another poem entitled "Flush or Faunus", in which she "associates Flush with the masculine sexual energy of the classical deity Faunus or Pan, the part man, part beast god of fields and forests, crops, flocks, wildlife, and fertility" (Stone and Taylor 187).

Next are two poems about pet cats. The first one is "For I Will Consider My Cat Jeoffry" (1762) by Christopher Smart (1722–1771) from his long poem "Jubilate Agno". According to Katharine M. Rogers, in the eighteenth century, "Tenderness toward all pets became more widespread, and, in addition, cats began to be regularly included among animal friends" (88). Biographically, Smart was once kept in a mental asylum for several years, and Jeoffrey was his only companion during that period of time. As a result, Smart wrote this moving celebration of his animal friend.

At the beginning of the poem, Smart says that the cat is "the servant of the Living God" (line 2), who worships God in his own special way by "wreathing his body seven times round with elegant quickness" (4).

The cat is such a friendly one that when he comes across a female cat in the neighborhood, he "will kiss her in kindness" (20). He is so kind that he even plays with the mouse and sometimes gives one of his preys a chance to survive. All this contributes to his loveliness.

The cat also has another good virtue, that is, gratefulness, because "when God tells him he's a good Cat", "he purrs in thankfulness" (32), so much so that "he is an instrument for the children to learn benevolence upon" (33). Coming next is a long list of the cat's good qualities or virtues, in a way of paralleled lines as follows:

> For he is the cleanest in the use of his forepaws of any quadruped.
> For the dexterity of his defence is an instance of the love of God to him exceedingly.
> For he is the quickest to his mark of any creature.

Chapter One High Praise of Animals

For he is tenacious of his point.

[...]

For there is nothing sweeter than his peace when at rest.

For there is nothing brisker than his life when in motion.

[...]

For his tongue is exceeding pure so that it has in purity what it wants in music.

For he is docile and can learn certain things.

For he can set up with gravity which is patience upon approbation.

For he can fetch and carry, which is patience in employment.

For he can jump over a stick which is patience upon proof positive.

For he can spraggle upon waggle at the word of command.

For he can jump from an eminence into his master's bosom.

For he can catch the cork and toss it again.

[...]

For he killed the Ichneumon-rat very pernicious by land.

For his ears are so acute that they sting again.

For from this proceeds the passing quickness of his attention.

[...]

For, tho he cannot fly, he is an excellent clamberer.

For his motions upon the face of the earth are more than any other quadruped. (38-41, 44-45, 49-56, 63-65, 70-71)

In the above long-listed praises, Smart makes use of several superlative forms of positive adjectives, namely, "the cleanest", "the quickest", "nothing sweeter" (the sweetest), "nothing brisker" (the briskest), and "motions...more than any other quadruped" (having the most motions), to show the incomparability and matchlessness of the cat in various ways. In addition, the cat is also described as being dexterous, tenacious, pure (tongue), docile, patient, obedient, playful, dutiful, acute (ears), quick (in attention) and excellent (clamberer). All of the words Smart uses are commendatory words of the cat's beauty and loveliness, which will impress the readers and they may also give their love to this "celebrated" cat (Wild 111). No wonder Jeoffrey is called the "most famous cat in the whole history of English literature"[1] by Neil Curry, one of Smart's biographers.

Another poem about the pet cat is "The Kitten and the Falling Leaves" (1804) by William Wordsworth (1770–1850). As a Romantic poet, Wordsworth does not only write about the people in the rural area, but also sings "the praises of the lesser members of the animal and plant kingdoms" (Barker 210). The kitten is so cute and lovely that we can see her "Sporting with the leaves that fall" (line 4). Wordsworth draws our attention to the movements of the kitten as to "how she starts, / Crouches, stretches, paws, and darts!" with "intenseness of desire / In her upward eye of fire!" (17-18, 22-23). She catches one falling leaf and then lets it go, and then she plays with several falling leaves "Like an Indian conjurer" (29). Wordsworth says that even if there were thousands of audience applauding for her, she would not care about it, because she is

> Over happy to be proud,
>
> Over wealthy in the treasure
>
> Of her own exceeding pleasure! (37-39)

He goes on praising the cat's movements with many commendatory words like "Lithest, gaudiest Harlequin! / Prettiest Tumbler ever seen! / Light of heart and light of limb" (71-73). The cat is the showiest amusing character and the prettiest acrobat with nimbleness and agility, and it makes Wordsworth's daughter Dora laugh, "Sharing in the ecstasy" (119); it also has some influence

---

[1] 10 Classic Poems about Cats Everyone Should Read. https://interestingliterature.com/2016/01/12/10-classic-poems-about-cats-everyone-should-read/

Chapter One High Praise of Animals

on Wordsworth himself, since he says "Find my wisdom in my bliss; / Keep the sprightly soul awake" (121-22). As a result, when he meets with some troubles or sorrowful things in life, he will not be in low spirits or in a bad mood, but have "a jocund thought" (125). He ends the poem with "Spite of care, and spite of grief, / To gambol with Life's falling Leaf " (126-27). The last line is symbolic, which means that we should be like a cat with jollity and liveliness when we are in adversity. The praise of the lovely cat playing with the falling leaves actually shows Wordsworth's "love of nature in all its forms" (85)[①].

The lamb can be both regarded as a pet and a domesticated animal. "The Lamb" (1789) by William Blake (1757–1827) is one of the most anthologized English poems. In the poem, Blake first praises the clothing of the lamb as "Softest clothing, woolly, bright" (line 6), and then praises its tender voice which makes "all the vales rejoice" (8). Even though the lamb is a reference to Jesus Christ and the poem is usually interpreted as a praise of God, the creator of the lamb, it is first of all a praise of the lamb itself, whose brightness, delight and tenderness impress the readers.

Apart from pets, the bird is another favorite character for animal poets. Wordsworth's "Water-Fowl Observed Frequently over the Lakes of Rydal and Grasmere" is taken from his long poem *The Recluse* (1813), Part One, Book One, "Home at Grasmere", and is sometimes considered as an individual poem. Wordsworth thinks the motion of the bird is so graceful that it "might scarcely seem / Inferior to angelical" (lines 2-3), which is a very high praise. While the birds are flying, in height, they may fly as high as the mountain tops with their "ambitious wing" (5); in width, they may fly a larger circle than the lake beneath. What's more, their flight is so jubilant, unperplexed and indefatigable that "They tempt the sun to sport amid their plumes; / They tempt the water, or

---

① *American Quarterly Review*. Vol. XX. Philadelphia: Adam Waldie, 1836.

the gleaming ice, / To show them a fair image" (20-22). The word "fair" denotes beauty and prettiness. In Kenneth R. Johnston's view, "The point about the birds is that they exercise their freedom within bounds" (14). Only in freedom can the birds demonstrate fully their beauty. The ending of the poem goes like "then up again aloft, / Up with a sally and a flash of speed, / As if they scorned both resting-place and rest" (25-27), which creates an image of a bird of pride who looks down upon earthly things. The very ending line of the poem may have influenced Shelley's "thou scorner of the ground" in his poem "To A Skylark" (1820).

W. H. Auden (1907–1973) has ever written a poem entitled "Short Ode to the Cuckoo" (1971). In terms of virtue, the cuckoo is not a bird worthy of being praised and does not deserve an ode. By instinct, the cuckoo is a brood parasite who does not make a nest of its own, but lays eggs in the nests of other birds, such as reed warblers, meadow pipits or dunnocks, and let other birds hatch the eggs and raise the newborn birds for them. That's why Geoffrey Chaucer says "the cuckoo all unkind"[1], and that's also why "our most hardened crooks are sincerely shocked by / your nesting habits" (lines 7-8). What's more, the cuckoo is not a great singer because "Compared with arias by the great performers / such as the merle, your two-note act is kid-stuff" (5-6). However, why does Auden still persist in writing an ode to the cuckoo? There is a peripeteia in the following stanza:

> Science, Aesthetics, Ethics, may huff and puff but they
> cannot extinguish your magic: you marvel
> the commuter as you wondered the savage. (9-11)

Here Science, Aesthetics and Ethics stand for science, ration or sense,

---

[1] From Chaucer's *The Parliament of Fowls*. Translated by A. S. Kline in 2007. https://www.poetryintranslation.com/PITBR/English/Fowls.htm

while the cuckoo stands for arts, passion or sensibility, which can be regarded as beauty in different forms. Even though we all need the former, the latter is also indispensable, and sometimes, the latter is even more important than the former, because it can create magic, marvel and wonder in life.

> Hence, in my diary,
> where I normally enter nothing but social
> engagements and, lately, the death of friends, I
> scribble year after year when I first hear you,
> of a holy moment. (12-16)

Auden explains at the end of the poem why he annually puts the cuckoo in his diary where he usually records only important events such as social engagements or the death of friends. The reason why Auden pays so much attention to the cuckoo is that when the migrant cuckoo returns home, it signals that warm spring has come back. To Auden, as well as other people, it is "a holy moment" and a season of hope. As Rainer Emig puts it, "The poem declares the cuckoo humanly relevant exactly in human terms" (221).

After talking about birds, let's move on to the fish. In the household of Harold Monro (1879-1932), there is a small "zoo", which is made up of several dogs, a cat and a goldfish. As far as his wife Alida is concerned, "she needed them all as a bond with Harold. She treated them almost as though they were his and her children" (Hibberd 220). At the beginning of Monro's poem "Goldfish", he calls the goldfish "angels of that watery world" (line 1), who

> move themselves on golden fins,
> Or fill their paradise with fire
> By darting suddenly from end to end. (3-5)

In the evening, when the room is in the gloom, "their movements growing larger " (12); in the morning, when the sun shines into the room, they glide to meet the sunlight, and "their gulping lips / Suck the light in" (17-18). According to the poet, the function of the goldfish or what the goldfish can do to the atmosphere of the room is that "they give the house some gleam of faint delight" (23). Therefore, it is the goldfish who brings liveliness, vigor and pleasure to the house, and in turn cheers up the people living in it.

The next poem is about the whales. Whales look like fish, but scientifically speaking, they are not fish as many people think, and they are actually mammals living under water. In "Little Whale Song" (1989) by Ted Hughes (1930–1998), he thinks that the whales have "global brains", which are "perfectly tuned receivers and perceivers" (line 8). The personified whales think of themselves as follows:

> We are beautiful. We stir
> Our self-colour in the pot of colours
> Which is the world. At each
> Tail-stroke we deepen
> Our being into the world's lit substance,
>
> And our joy into the world's
> Spinning bliss, and our peace
> Into the world's floating, plumed peace. (12-19)

From the remark of the whales, we can see that they are proud of themselves, taking pride in their beauty and their contribution to the world. They play an important role in the world in that they are an indispensable part of the world's colours, lit substance, bliss and peace. Hughes goes on praising the whales by saying that they have

> The loftiest, spermiest
> Passions, the most exquisite pleasures,
> The noblest characters, the most god-like
> Oceanic presence and poise — (29-32)

Chapter One High Praise of Animals

Hughes makes use of five superlative forms of adjectives to describe the passions, pleasures, characters, presence and poise of the whales, which means they are unparalleled both spiritually and physically. And the word "god-like" denotes the poet's admiration and reverence for the whale's elegant manners. As Yvonne Reddick puts it, this poem "articulates a deep respect for whales, cataloguing their remarkable attributes and the reasons why their survival is important" (276).

Finally, there is a poem about an animal which does not appear frequently in animal poems, because it is too region-specific, that is, the Australian kangaroo. In "Kangaroo" (1923) by D. H. Lawrence (1885–1930), we can see that the mother kangaroo is very delicate and has a "beautiful slender face" and "sensitive, long, pure-bred face" (line 3, 7), who is more beautiful than a rabbit or hare. Her eyes are "so dark / So big and quiet and remote" and "wonder liquid" (8-9, 42). The portrait goes on with her "little loose hands", "drooping Victorian shoulders", "great weight", "vast pale belly", "long thin ear", "big haunches" and "great muscular python-stretch of her tail" (11-12, 14, 17-18). Her movements are described as "she wistfully, sensitively sniffs the air, and then turns, / goes off in slow sad leaps" (20-21), and "Stops again, half turns, inquisitive to look back" (24), from which we can see that she is sensitive, cautious and full of longing. As J.C. Squire argues, Lawrence "seems to have penetrated to the essence" of animals, "attempting to wrest from them, as though no one had ever looked at them before, their essential characteristics" (334). The reason for the mother kangaroo's cautiousness is that there is a baby kangaroo in her pouch. The cute and lovely baby kangaroo peaks out from its mother's pouch, feels dismayed by the outside world, and withdraws "to snuggle down in the warmth" (29), from which we can see that the mother kangaroo's pouch is a harbour of coziness and safety for the baby kangaroo. In Kenneth Inniss' view, the mother kangaroo is not only a natural "wonder", but also serves as an emblem of motherhood incarnate, allied with the rabbit, the lamb and other figures of peace and increase (81).

The description of the beauty and loveliness of the animals reflects the poets' love of them. We, as readers, cannot help being deeply impressed by these beautiful and lovely animals portrayed in the poems, and cannot help thinking that human beings are blessed with so many beautiful and lovely creatures in nature, beautifying and decorating the world we live in. Accordingly, what we are supposed to do is to observe, appreciate and marvel at their beauty instead of taking advantage of it or bringing destruction to it.

II. Happiness and Carefreeness

Apart from the poems devoted to the depiction of the beauty and loveliness of the animals, there are also some poems unfolding before our eyes their happiness and carefreeness, especially those animals in nature.

Cowper's long poem *The Task: A Poem, in Six Books* (1785) is a meditation on the blessings of nature as well as other things, and "strongly urged compassion for animals" (Perkins, *Romanticism and Animal Rights* 45). In Book VI "The Winter Walk At Noon", there is a vivid description of the life of animals, which is sometimes singled out as an individual poem with the title of "Animals Enjoying Life". At the very beginning of the poem, Cowper says that someone who is not pleased with seeing the animals enjoying their life has a heart that is "hard in nature", "void / Of sympathy" and "dead alike / To love and friendship" (line 1, 2-3, 3-4). Then he shares with us his pleasure of seeing the animals enjoying their life.

>The bounding fawn, that darts across the glade
>When none pursues, through mere delight of heart,
>And spirits buoyant with excess of glee;

Chapter One High Praise of Animals

> The horse as wanton and almost as fleet,
>
> That skims the spacious meadow at full speed,
>
> Then stops and snorts, and, throwing high his heels,
>
> Starts to the voluntary race again;
>
> The very kine that gambol at high noon,
>
> The total herd receiving first from one
>
> That leads the dance a summons to be gay,
>
> Though wild their strange vagaries and uncouth
>
> Their efforts, yet resolved with one consent
>
> To give such act and utterance as they may
>
> To ecstacy too big to be suppress'd; — (7-20)

From the above lines, we can see that the happiness of the fawn (a deer less than one year old) is shown by its bounding and darting movements, and the synonymous words of happiness Cowper uses is "delight" and "glee". The horse's happiness is shown in its lively movements of skimming, snorting, and throwing high his heels. The happiness of the kine (ancient word for "cow") is indirectly shown by the word "gambol", which means to jump or run about in a lively way, and directly shown by the word "gay" and the description "ecstasy too big to be suppress'd", since "gay" signifies "cheerfulness", and "ecstasy" denotes "very great happiness".

According to Cowper, apart from the happiness of the above mentioned animals, there are still "a thousand images of bliss" which cruel men who damage nature cannot defeat (21), and benevolent people who love nature will be imparted with "far superior happiness" and "comfort of a reasonable joy" (26, 27). No wonder Vincent Newey proposes that this poem "is rich in self-stabilising endeavour and personal therapeutic gain" (44).

The nightingale is a favorite bird in British bird poems or oscine poetry, and according to Mario Ortiz-Robles, "In the European lyric tradition, no songbird is more prominent than the nightingale" (88). In "The Nightingale: A Conversation Poem" (1798) by Samuel Taylor Coleridge (1772–1834), he invites us to listen to the nightingale's singing, "And hark! the Nightingale begins its song" (line 12), for the reason that it is the "'Most musical, most melancholy' bird!" (13), which is a quotation from John Milton's poem "Il Penseroso" (line 62). But soon he negates himself by saying that this is "idle thought" (14), or he "rebukes himself for his inattentive response" (Blades 61), because it dawns upon him that "in nature there is nothing melancholy" (15).

> Nature's sweet voices, always full of love
> And joyance! 'Tis the merry Nightingale
> That crowds, and hurries, and precipitates
> With fast thick warble his delicious notes,
> As he were fearful that an April night
> Would be too short for him to utter forth
> His love-chant, and disburthen his full soul
> Of all its music! (41-48)

We can see that it is the nightingale that contributes to the sweet voices of nature and makes nature full of love and joy, because he is merry and his notes are delicious. His daytime singing is fast and thick because he is afraid that the April night is not long enough for him to sing fully. Then, Coleridge continues to tell us that there are a lot of nightingales and it is the first time that he has seen so many nightingales at one place.

> They answer and provoke each other's song,
> With skirmish and capricious passagings,
> And murmurs musical and swift jug jug,
> And one low piping sound more sweet than all –
> Stirring the air with such a harmony,
> That should you close your eyes, you might almost

Chapter One High Praise of Animals

Forget it was not day! (55-64)

We can see that the nightingales regard singing as a team work and are singing in a cooperative or collaborative manner, by answering and provoking each other's songs, which leads to a harmonious chorus, as if a sudden wind "had swept at once / A hundred airy harps!" (81-82).

At the end of the poem, Coleridge brings his son Hartley into the poem and talks about the influence of the nightingales' singing on the child.

his childhood shall grow up

Familiar with these songs, that with the night

He may associate joy. — Once more, farewell,

Sweet Nightingale! (107-10)

The child may make a connection between the dark night and joy only because of the affect of the nightingales, who are sweet singers. So the poem begins with the nightingales' joy and ends with their joy as well, from which we know that they are birds of happiness and have positive influence upon human beings, adults and children alike. As is argued by Blades, "The nightingale itself has a mollifying influence because it is specifically associated with happiness and harmony" (66).

As the "Northamptonshire Peasant" poet of the Romantic school, John Clare (1793-1864) is an ardent lover of nature. In one of the letters to his son Charles in 1848, he puts it very frankly: "Birds bees trees flowers all talked to me incessantly louder than the busy hum of men" (*By Himself* 277). In Clare's "The Nightingale's Nest" (1832), we can see that the poet cares about the bird so much that he shuts the gate softly for fear that "The noise might drive her from her home of love" (line 4). In the line "For here I've heard her many a merry year" (5), the rhetorical device transferred epithet is employed since it is not the year that is merry but the bird and the poet who hears her singing are merry. The bird sings all day long, all year long, "As though she lived on song" (7). Then

Clare reminisces his observation of the birds when he was a small boy.

> Her wings would tremble in her ecstasy,
>
> And feathers stand on end, as 'twere with joy,
>
> And mouth wide open to release her heart
>
> Of its out-sobbing songs. The happiest part
>
> Of summer's fame she shared, for so to me
>
> Did happy fancies shapen her employ. (22-27)

In the above selection, Clare uses several words or phrases with the meaning of happiness to show the happy life of the bird, namely, "ecstasy", "joy", "happiest part" and "happy fancies". Clare goes on with his recollection:

> ... our presence doth retard
>
> Her joys, and doubt turns every rapture chill.
>
> Sing on, sweet bird! may no worse hap befall
>
> Thy visions, than the fear that now deceives.
>
> We will not plunder music of its dower,
>
> Nor turn this spot of happiness to thrall. (77-82)

Even though Clare did not bring any harm to the bird as a child, just as Storey says "Clare is an admirer, not an intruder" (123), Clare still felt sorry for the bird since he and his partners' close observation did affect her joy. Therefore, he gives a blessing and makes a promise to the bird as recompense, by wishing that there would be no accidental happenings to the bird and assuring that they would not bring damage or destruction to the happy nest of the bird. Neither would they rob the bird of its home, nor would they steal the bird of its eggs, since Clare ends the poem with the following two lines "So here we'll leave them, still unknown to wrong /As the old woodland's legacy of song" (104-05). As Storey proposes, "Clare decides not to continue with his search, contenting himself with a glimpse of the nest. The place is too sacred to harm" (125).

Another nightingale poem is "To A Nightingale" by George Meredith

(1828–1909), which sings praise of the function of the nightingale in gloomy weathers.

> Rich July has many a sky
> With splendour dim, that thou mightst hymn,
> And make rejoice with thy wondrous voice,
> And the thrill of thy wild pervading tone! (lines 5-8)

The temperature in July in Britain is 10 to 18 degrees centigrade on average, which is a little bit cold, especially during the night, when the light is not bright. But the thrilling and permeating singing of the nightingale brings rejoice to the atmosphere.

The skylark is another favorite bird in British bird poems, and two of its earliest appearances are in "The Knight's Tale" of *The Canterbury Tales* (1387) by Geoffrey Chaucer (1343–1400) as "bisy larke, messager of day / Saluëth in hir song the morwe gray" and "Sonnet 29" by William Shakespeare (1564–1616) as "the lark at break of day arising / From sullen earth, sings hymns at heaven's gate".

The skylark is also a favorite subject for British Romantic poets, among whom the Scottish poet James Hogg (1770–1835) is not so well-known. But since Meiko O'Halloran has emphasized Hogg's significance in the contexts of Scottish Romanticism, as well as his place in British Romanticism and the history of British literature more broadly (257), it is advisable to analyze his poems in the light of Romanticism. At the beginning of his poem "The Skylark", Hogg describes the bird as "Blithesome" (line 2), which is identical to Shelley's addressing the skylark as "blithe Spirit", and Hogg calls it "Emblem of happiness" (4), whose dwelling place is blessed, so that the poet would like to live together with it. Why is the bird's singing wild and loud? The answer to the question is that "Love gives it energy, love gave it birth" (9). Hence the skylark is not only a bird of happiness but also one of love. Hogg also calls the skylark

"Musical cherub" (18), a lovely angel, who can be seen singing everywhere, such as over the fell (i.e. hill), fountain, moor, mountain, morning rays, clouds, and rainbow. In the last stanza, Hogg repeats the last three lines of the first stanza "Emblem of happiness, / Blest is thy dwelling-place — / O to abide in the desert with thee!" (4-6), through which he emphasizes the happiness of the skylark and his hope to share its happiness. As James V. Baker argues, this poem shows the poet's envy of the lark for its apparent freedom, for the wildness of its life in the "wilderness", and the desire of the poet to be identified with the lark (71).

"To a Skylark" (sometimes entitled "Ode to a Skylark" or "Ode to the Skylark", 1822) by the well-known Romantic poet Percy Bysshe Shelley (1792–1822) is one of the most anthologized animal poems or bird poems in English literature. In the very first line of the poem, Shelley addresses the skylark as "blithe Spirit" (line 1), through which the carefree, happy and lighthearted nature of the bird is directly shown. The bird pours its full heart "in profuse strains of unpremeditated art" (4), so its singing is impromptu and spontaneous. It is singing while it is flying very high in the sky, "like an unbodied joy" (15). And even though the bird is too high to be seen, Shelley can still hear its "shrill delight" (20), which is keen as arrows. The bird's singing is so powerful that is surpasses "All that ever was / Joyous, and clear, and fresh" in nature (59-60). Shelley uses an indirect superlative form of praise by saying "I have never heard / Praise of love or wine /That panted forth a flood of rapture so divine" (63-65), which means the skylark gives out the most divine flood of rapture, so that compared with its singing, "chorus hymeneal" of the choir or "triumphal chaunt" of the army is just "an empty vaunt" (66, 67, 69). Hence we can see that the happiness of the skylark is emphasized through the repetition of many synonymous words like "blithe", "joy", "delight" and "rapture". In Leigh Hunt's view, "In sweetness" this poem is "inferior only to Coleridge, — in rapturous passion to no man" (qtd. in Bloom, *Classic Critical Views* 46). What is the result

Chapter One High Praise of Animals

of being so happy? Shelley tells us that

> With thy clear keen joyance
>
> Languor cannot be:
>
> Shadow of annoyance
>
> Never came near thee:
>
> Thou lovest, but ne'er knew love's sad satiety. (76-80)

Therefore, the skylark's happiness dispels, drives away or gets rid of laziness, angry feelings and love's sad satiety. Then what is the origin of or the reason for the bird's happiness?

> What objects are the fountains
>
> Of thy happy strain?
>
> What fields, or waves, or mountains?
>
> What shapes of sky or plain?
>
> What love of thine own kind? what ignorance of pain? (71-75)

The answer is summarized into one phrase, that is, the bird is the "scorner of the ground" (100). The bird looks down upon the worldly or earthly things of which human beings are in hot pursuit. Shelley analyzes the reasons why human beings are not happy as the nightingale is.

> We look before and after,
>
> And pine for what is not:
>
> Our sincerest laughter
>
> With some pain is fraught;
>
> Our sweetest songs are those that tell of saddest thought. (86-90)

From the above stanza, we can see that we human beings are always in search of something, either material or non-material, and when we fail to make it, we usually feed sad for the failure, even though as a matter of fact we are not entitled to or qualified for such things. Even if we laugh, our laughter is filled or tinted with sadness. And when we sing, our songs express the most grievous thought, though sounding very sweet. In other words, we are bound by chasing personal fame and gains and we cannot enjoy pure happiness as the skylarks do. In this way, the skylark's happiness forms a sharp contrast with human beings' sadness. "Shelley's lark symbolizes the ideal poet, the poet Shelley himself wanted to be" (Baker 72).

Shelley ends the poem very much like the way he ends "Ode to the West Wind" (1819), in which he wants to be the lyre of the west wind, and he hopes the west wind to drive his dead thoughts over the universe and scatter his words among mankind. In this poem, Shelley wants the skylark to teach him "half the gladness" (101), and as a result, "the world should listen" to what he expresses in his poems which contain "harmonious madness" (103). In Perkins' view, the nightingale is idealized to the point that it transcends mortal limitations and is no longer a subject for compassion (*Romanticism and Animal Rights* 181), but one for admiration instead in my mind's eye.

Just as Shelley earnestly requests the skylark to teach him "half the gladness", in "To a Skylark" (1805), Wordsworth implores the skylark to fly together with him into the bird's "banqueting-place in the sky" (line 15):

> Up with me! up with me into the clouds!
> For thy song, Lark, is strong;
> Up with me, up with me into the clouds!
> Singing, singing,
> With clouds and sky about thee ringing,
> Lift me, guide me till I find
> That spot which seems so to thy mind! (1-7)

There are two reasons why Wordsworth makes such an appeal to the skylark. The first one is personal reason, that is, "I have walked through wildernesses dreary / And to-day my heart is weary" (8-9), showing his boredom of the earthly life. The second one is related to the skylark, who is a bird of joy, as "There is madness about thee, and joy divine / In that song of thine" (12-13). In addition, the skylark is a "Happy, happy Liver", "Joyous as morning / Thou art laughing and scorning" (22, 16-17). Even though the poet's life journey is "rugged and uneven" (26), yet hearing the skylark's cheering and heartening singing, "As full of gladness and as free of heaven" (19), he will not complain about his fate, but instead "will plod on, / And hope for higher raptures" (20-21). So the gladness and raptures of the bird has positive influence on Wordsworth.

Wordsworth's homonymous poem "To a Skylark" (1825) hails the skylark as "Ethereal minstrel! pilgrim of the sky!" (line 1). "Dost thou despise the earth where cares abound?" is a rhetorical question which needs no answer at all (2), but to emphasize the fact that the carefree skylarks look down upon human beings who are indulged in worldly pursuits and who are troubled by worry and anxiety. Wordsworth's skylark which despises the earth is much similar to Shelley's "scorner of the ground". Wordsworth talks to the skylark:

> Leave to the nightingale her shady wood;
>
> A privacy of glorious light is thine;
>
> Whence thou dost pour upon the world a flood
>
> Of harmony, with instinct more divine;
>
> Type of the wise who soar, but never roam;
>
> True to the kindred points of Heaven and Home! (7-12)

In sharp contrast to the nightingale which favors shady wood, the skylark is fond of glorious light, symbolizing good mood. The singing of the skylark is harmonious and divine. The skylarks fly very high into the sky, but never without aim or direction, and they regard heaven as their home. In Baker's view, "Wordsworth has loaded the bird with a moral meaning" (75).

"A Green Cornfield" (1875, sometime entitled "The Skylark") by the Victorian poetess Christina Rossetti (1830–1894) is taken from her *Sing-Song: A Nursery Rhyme Book* in which there are some animal poems, such as "Bread and

Milk for Breakfast" in which a caring kid gives "a crumb for robin redbreast / On the cold days of the year" (lines 3-4). "A Green Cornfield" is influenced by Shelley, because she quotes the line "And singing still dost soar, and soaring ever singest" from his "To a Skylark" in front of her own poem. As Christina's biographer Jan Marsh records, "She claimed to read 'only what hit her fancy'... Shelley's *Skylark* was an early favourite" (39).

The setting of the poem is very pleasant and agreeable, with green grass, blue sky and sunny weather. The skylark is flying as well as singing over the corn field. Because it is flying very high, it seems like a small speck. The singing of the skylark high in the sky is "in gay accord" with the dancing of the butterflies below (5), from which we can see that both of them are happy. The two lines "And still the singing skylark soared, / And silent sank and soared to sing" are much similar to her quote from Shelley (7-8). The poem ends:

  And as I paused to hear his song

  While swift the sunny moments slid,

  Perhaps his mate sat listening long,

  And listened longer than I did. (13-16)

Time passes quickly as Christina is listening to the happy singing of the skylark. It is a pity that she can only enjoy the beauty of nature temporarily.

The Victorian poet Frederick Tennyson (1807–1898) is the elder brother of the well-known poet Alfred Tennyson. In his "The Skylark"[1], Frederick calls the bird as a "blithe Lark" who fills the air "with jubilant sweet songs of mirth" (line 1, 4). All the words like "blithe", "jubilant" and "mirth" denote happiness.

  What matter if the days be dark and frore,

  That sunbeam tells of other days to be,

  And singing in the light that floods him o'er

---

[1] https://www.poemhunter.com/poem/the-skylark-5/

Chapter One High Praise of Animals

In joy he overtakes Futurity; (9-12)

If we can be as optimistic as the skylark, to us it does not matter if luck does not favor us today, because tomorrow is another day and it might be prospective. The sanguine bird always sings in joy and gives us the hope that the future is bright.

> Singing thou scalest Heaven upon thy wings,
>
> Thou liftest a glad heart into the skies;
>
> He maketh his own sunrise, while he sings,
>
> And turns the dusty Earth to Paradise;
>
> I see thee sail along
>
> Far up the sunny streams,
>
> Unseen, I hear his song,
>
> I see his dreams. (57-64)

The last stanza talks about the influence of the skylark's happiness on human beings. By singing like the bird, one can change a dirty, dull and unpleasant place into a beautiful, perfect and holy place. The poet can not identify the person who is influenced positively by the bird, but he can perceive the influence.

Meredith's poem "The Lark Ascending" (1881) is a long couplet poem which describes in detail the flying and singing of the skylark. It is a paean to the skylark, in which happiness is a key note as well. For example, the skylark has a "happy bill" (line 25), his voice is "Renew'd in endless notes of glee" and "he is joy, awake, aglow" (29, 32). The skylark is supposed to

> ... know the pleasure sprinkled bright
>
> By simple singing of delight,
>
> Shrill, irreflective, unrestrain'd,
>
> Rapt, ringing, on the jet sustain'd (35-38)

So we can see that not only is the skylark himself cheerful and joyous, but his delightful singing also brings pleasure to his multitudinous listeners, human beings in particular.

> The song seraphically free
>
> Of taint of personality,
>
> So pure that it salutes the suns
>
> The voice of one for millions,
>
> In whom the millions rejoice
>
> For giving their one spirit voice. (93-98)

The skylark's happiness is so contagious that millions of people rejoice in his angelic, free, and pure singing. He seems to be the mouthpiece of human beings who are actually lacking in happiness due to their unrestrained egoism, to express their happiness on their behalf. As James Moffatt puts it, "Meredith combines the joy and the link with earth in a higher synthesis" (501).

Vexed by "the anxiety of influence" (to quote Harold Bloom's phrase) of Shelley's "To a Skylark", later poets feel reluctant to write about the skylark, but according to an unsigned review on June 25th, 1883, in the journal *St. James's Gazette*, "Mr. Meredith's 'The Lark Ascending' must be read with admiration, even after Shelley's famous ode" (*Critical Heritage* 244). And in another unsigned review in September, 1887, in *Westminster Review*, the critic remarks that "'The Lark Ascending' challenges an incomparable model; it is the highest possible praise to say of it that it may be enjoyed even after Shelley" (*Critical Heritage* 300). The two reviews show Meredith's contemporary critics' approval of the poem.

The last bird poem I'd like to analyze in this section is Auden's short poem "Bird-Language" (1967), which I will quote in full length:

> Trying to understand the words
>
> Uttered on all sides by birds,
>
> I recognize in what I hear

Chapter One   High Praise of Animals

Noises that betoken fear.

Though some of them, I'm certain, must

Stand for rage, bravado, lust.

All other notes that birds employ

Sound like synonyms for joy.

Assuming himself as someone with supernatural ability to understand the birds' language, Auden finds that part of the birds' language is conveying dread, anger, pretended confidence, or desire, but the large majority of their language is expressing joy, which is the dominant or universal feeling among the birds. To quote Anthony Hecht, while he is making a comment on another poem by Auden entitled "The Fall of Rome", the birds "are therefore a permanent reminder of how alienated we are from that pastoral union with the natural world that comprises our idea of Eden" (330-31).

After the discussion of bird poems, let's move on to poems concerning other animals. "On the Death of Echo, A Favourite Beagle" by the Romantic poet David Hartley Coleridge (1796–1849), the eldest son of Samuel Taylor Coleridge, is the lament of a hunting dog, in which Hartley recollects the happy moments when the dog was alive.

With drooping ears, keen nose, and nimble feet.

In the glad Chase she raised her merry voice

And made her name-sake of the woods rejoice (lines 4-6)

From the above recollection we can see that the dog enjoys fun in the chasing of the preys as she is barking merrily while running after them. In the woods, the dog has become a synonym of the word "rejoice" and her happiness makes the woods full of joy.

Lawrence's "Little Fish" (1929) is a very short five-line poem. The whole poem goes as follows:

The tiny fish enjoy themselves

> in the sea.
>
> Quick little splinters of life,
>
> their little lives are fun to them
>
> in the sea.

Though the poem is tiny just as the tiny fish is, the happiness of the fish is shown very clearly, as we can see that the fish enjoy themselves and their lives are fun. Just within several short lines, two words denoting happiness are used to show the happy life of the fish even though they are petty in comparison with the enormous sea and they are apt to fall victim to bigger fish. The joy of the fish is also echoed in Lawrence's short novel *St Mawr* (1925), which goes:

> This is sheer joy — and men have lost it, or never accomplished it. The cleverest sports men in the world are owls beside these fish. And the togetherness of love is nothing to the spinning unison of dolphins playing under-sea. It would be wonderful to know joy as these fish know it. The life of the deep waters is ahead of us, it contains sheer togetherness and sheer joy. (221-22)

Thereby the happiness of the fish in Lawrence's poem and that in his novel are identical. According to Glenn Hughes, Lawrence has become one with the animals he observes, as he "sucks blood with a mosquito, darts with a fish, swoops with a bat, wriggles over the desert floor with a snake, shuffles through the tropics with an elephant, hops with a kangaroo, and makes love with goats and tortoises" (122).

Clare's sonnet "A Spring Morning" (1828) depicts a harmonious picture of different kinds of animals, together with other things in nature. The poem goes:

> Spring cometh in with all her hues and smells
>
> In freshness breathing over hills and dells
>
> O'er woods where May her gorgeous drapery flings
>
> And meads washed fragrant with their laughing springs

Chapter One High Praise of Animals

> Fresh as new-opened flowers untouched and free
> From the bold rifling of the amorous bee
> The happy time of singing birds is come
> And love's lone pilgrimage now finds a home
> Among the mossy oaks now coos the dove
> And the hoarse crow finds softer notes for love
> The foxes play around their dens and bark
> In joy's excess mid woodland shadows dark
> And flowers join lips below and leaves above
> And every sound that meets the ear is love.

In Clare's poem, an Eden-like picture is thus portrayed, where there is no snatching, no baiting and no hunting to disturb the animals' peaceful life. In Clare's vivid description, we can see that the amorous and affectionate bees are stealing honey from the flowers; the singing birds are enjoying their happy time; the dove is cooing in the oak tree; the crow is using more refined expressions to voice its love; and the foxes are playing in excessive joy. Not only the animals are happy, but also the personified springs which are laughing as they wash the meadows. All in all, "every sound that meets the ear is love" and is filled with happiness. As Stephanie Kuduk Weiner puts it, "Indications of the emotions that motivate birds to sing and insects to hum, similarly, point toward the meaning of their sounds and the pleasures of listening" (378).

"The Donkey" (1900) by Gilbert Keith Chesterton (1874–1936, often referred to as G.K.) depicts to us a very optimistic donkey. The congenital condition of the donkey is not good. First of all, at the time when he was born, there appeared some strange phenomena, one of which is a weird celestial phenomenon of ill omen, that is "Some moment when the moon was blood" (line 3). Secondly, the donkey has very ugly appearance:

> With monstrous head and sickening cry

And ears like errant wings,

The devil's walking parody

On all four-footed things. (5-8)

Given such innate disadvantages, the donkey knows clearly what kind of life attitude he is supposed to have. "Starve, scourge, deride me: I am dumb, / I keep my secret still" (11-12). He has to swallow humiliation and bear a heavy load silently. He addresses those who do not understand his forbearance and endurance as "Fools!" (13). He firmly believes in the English proverb, "every dog has his day", and is fully confident that "I also had my hour / One far fierce hour and sweet" (13-14). He could hear "a shout about my ears" (15), which is people's cheer and acclamation for his success. The last line "And palms before my feet" is symbolic (16), because the palm is usually a symbol of victory in the western culture. The donkey is portrayed as one with sanguine character, which is praiseworthy.

From the examples analyzed above, we can see that the animals in nature (including the domesticated hunting dog chasing preys in nature) are very happy and carefree, because they enjoy much more freedom than animals in bondage (such as animals in cages or in the zoo) or serving as pets in households.

III. Loyalty and Dutifulness

Loyalty and dutifulness are considered as one of the most praiseworthy qualities in animals, to which a number of animal poems are devoted and most of them are about dogs.

The Neo-classical poet Alexander Pope (1688–1744) portrays the devoted dog of Ulysses in his poem "Argus" (1709). As is known, Ulysses is a hero in the Trojan War and is away from his home for over ten years. Not only his faithful wife Penelope is waiting for his return, but also his old loyal dog.

Chapter One High Praise of Animals

> The faithful Dog alone his rightful master knew!
> Unfed, unhous'd, neglected, on the clay,
> Like an old servant now cashier'd, he lay;
> Touch'd with resentment of ungrateful man,
> And longing to behold his ancient lord again.
> Him when he saw he rose, and crawl'd to meet,
> ('T was all he could) and fawn'd and kiss'd his feet,
> Seiz'd with dumb joy; then falling by his side,
> Own'd his returning lord, look'd up, and died! (lines 10-18)

This is really a very moving story. In order to see his owner for the last time, the dog Argus lingers on with his last breath of life in a miserable living condition. When he sees his owner coming back, he summons up his last ounce of strength, fawning and kissing him, so as to show his yearning and affection towards his owner. After the ultimate intimacy is expressed, the dog breathes his last and dies. As Joshua Scodel puts it, the relationship between Ulysses and his dog "combines the master-servant relationship with the intimacy of friendship" and the dog is Ulysses's "truest servant, devoted onto death" (377).

In the previously-mentioned poem "The Dog and the Water Lily. No Fable" by Cowper, his dog "Beau" accompanies him to a walk on the side of the river Ouse. During the ramble, Cowper wants on an impulse to reach for one of the beautiful water lilies in the river with his cane, but in vain. The considerate dog notices that and comprehends Cowper's "unsuccessful pains" (line 21), just as Samuel Drew proposes, the poem "gives an amiable instance of the reasoning of the lower animals" (137). As a result, the dog quickly plunges into the water, swims offshore towards the lily, crops it, swims back to the shore and drops it at Cowper's feet, which he considers as a "treasure" (36), not only because the lily is pretty but also because it shows the dutiful dog's love expressed to him in this thoughtful behavior. By adding "No Fable" in the title, Cowper means that this is not an untrue tale but an account of real happening, which denotes that such intriguing stories between man and animal do occur in real life.

"Beth Gêlert, or The Grave of A Greyhound"① (1800) by William Robert Spencer (1769–1834) is devoted to a dog named Gêlert owned by Prince Llewellyn in a traditional Welsh story in the thirteenth century. Spencer praises the dog as follows:

"O, where doth faithful Gêlert roam,

The flower of all his race,

So true, so brave, — a lamb at home,

A lion in the chase?"

'T was only at Llewellyn's board

The faithful Gêlert fed;

He watched, he served, he cheered his lord,

And sentineled his bed. (lines 9-16)

Spencer has a high opinion of the dog and considers him as "the flower of all his race" and a "peerless hound" (17). A series of positive adjectives are used to modify the dog, namely, "true", "brave" and "faithful". The dog has adorable double characters; at home he is mild and obedient like a lamb, while chasing the preys he is brave and fast like a lion. His dutifulness is not only shown in his chasing the preys in hunting but also in his serving as a soldier on guard at home.

Wordsworth's "Fidelity" (1805) tells the readers the story of a faithful dog who does not leave his owner who has been dead for three months and waits for somebody to come to find his body.

In order to draw the attention of the shepherd, the dog is barking with

---

① https://www.poemhunter.com/poem/beth-gelert-or-the-grave-of-a-greyhound/

Chapter One　High Praise of Animals

something "unusual in its cry" (line 12). Since the look of the dog is "not of mountain breed" (9), the shepherd wonders why the dog appears in a rocky place with a precipice and a tarn, so he thinks there might be something behind this. Curiously, he follows the dog quickly, only to find "a human skeleton on the ground" (38), which is the corpse of the dog's owner, a traveller who has fallen off the precipice and died by accident.

> Yes, proof was plain that, since the day
> When this ill-fated Traveller died,
> The Dog had watched about the spot,
> Or by his master's side:
> How nourished here through such long time
> He knows, who gave that love sublime;
> And gave that strength of feeling, great
> Above all human estimate! (57-64)

Since the place where the traveller's body lies is far away from the "public road or dwelling, / Pathway, or cultivated land / From trace of human foot or hand" (22-24), we can imagine how many times the dog has tried in order to let people discover his owner and how many times he has run to and fro inexhaustibly between the place of the accident and the public road or residence, before he finally succeeds in arousing the attention of the shepherd. According to the Wordsworthian biography written by Juliet Barker, "The discovery caused a brief sensation, not least because of the loyalty of the dog in maintaining her lonely vigil beside the corpse for three long months" (243). The shepherd also wonders what kind of food the dog lives on and how he manages to survive for such a long time, since this is a "savage place" (56), which even keeps the winter snow although it is already summer time. "The more kindly disposed of the Lakers decided it ate grass" (Barker 243). So the shepherd thinks this really is a wonder and "This wonder merits well" (52). The love, affection, and fidelity of the dog towards his owner is beyond our imagination and estimation.

The Romantic poet George Gordon Byron (1788–1824) is a well-known animal lover. According to Robert Schnakenberg, Byron owns a domestic menagerie, which includes "horses, geese, monkeys, a badger, a fox, a parrot, an eagle, a crow, a heron, a falcon, a crocodile, five peacocks, two guinea hens, and an Egyptian crane" (20). Byron's Italian lover Teresa Guiccioli tells us an anecdote of Byron and two geese: "during the journey from Pisa to Genoa, on Michaelmas eve, he saw the two white geese in their cage in the wagon that followed his carriage, and felt so sorry for them that he gave orders they should be spared. After his arrival at Genoa they became such pets that he caressed them constantly" (293).

Byron's "Epitaph to a Dog" (1808, also referred to as "Inscription On The Monument Of A Newfoundland Dog") is devoted to the mourning of his five-year dog Boatswain who died of rabies. The epitaph at the tomb of the dog goes:

>Near this spot
>
>Are deposited the Remains
>
>Of one
>
>Who possessed Beauty
>
>Without Vanity,
>
>Strength without Insolence,
>
>Courage without Ferocity,
>
>And all the Virtues of Man
>
>Without his Vices.

From the epitaph we can see that Byron sings high praise of the dog's beauty, strength and courage, concluding that the dog has all the good qualities of man but without man's evilness. The epitaph is "as condemnatory of man as laudatory of the dog" (Preece, *Sensibility to Animals* 196).

The related poem "Epitaph to a Dog" commends the faithfulness of the dog as follows:

> But the poor dog, in life the firmest friend,
> The first to welcome, foremost to defend,
> Whose honest heart is still his master's own,
> Who labors, fights, lives, breathes for him alone (lines 7-10)

In Martin Garrett's view, the poem "contrasts canine loyalty with human untrustworthiness" (22). The dog is first of all praised by Byron's use of a superlative adjective "firmest" and we can see that firmness and honesty are the good qualities of the dog. When the owner comes back home from outside, the dog will always be the first one to welcome him back; when the owner is in trouble or in danger, the dog will always be the first one to rescue him or protect him. The dog has an honest heart and does everything for the benefit of his owner. That the dog does everything for his owner alone shows its steadfastness in its allegiance to man. In Schnakenberg's view, "Byron immortalized Boatswain in verse" (21).

Mrs. Browning's "To Flush, My Dog" has already been used previously as an example to show the dog's prettiness and loveliness. However, what is most praiseworthy is the dog's dutifulness, who "watched beside a bed / Day and night unweary" (lines 38-39). Mrs. Browning makes a comparison between her faithful dog and other dogs. Other dogs "Tracked the hares and followed through / Sunny moor or meadow" (50-51), while her dog "crept and crept / Next a languid cheek that slept" (52-53); other dogs "Bounded at the whistle clear, / Up the woodside hieing" (56-57), while her dog "watched in reach / Of a faintly uttered speech / Or a louder sighing" (58-60). Therefore, she would like to "Render praise and favor" (81) to the dog, say benediction to him forever and give back more love to him. As Fabienne Moine contends, the dog is Mrs. Browning's "faithful companion" and "has since become a staple of literary history" (151).

A Study of British Animal Poems

In the poem "Ah, Are You Digging on My Grave?" (1913) by Thomas Hardy (1840–1928), as a sub-theme, he sings praise of dogs' virtue of loyalty by saying "What feeling do we ever find / To equal among human kind / A dog's fidelity!" (lines 28-30) Despite the generally-accepted interpretation of the ironic ending of the poem which shows that the dog's visit to the mistress's tomb is just by accident, as far as the major theme of the poem — no love or hate outlasts death — is concerned, the dog's failure to commemorate its mistress does not negate the fact that he was once "one true heart " to her when she was alive (27).

The twentieth century poet Robert Graves (1895–1985) is a poet who is in favor of "very much wider use in poetry than in daily speech of animal, bird, cloud and flower imagery" (68), and so he has also contributed to the animal poetry by writing "Epitaph on a Favorite Dog", which goes:

> True to his master, generous and brave;
> His friend, companion; not his slave:
> Fond without fawning; kind to those
> His master lov'd; but to his foes
> A foe undaunted; whom no bribe
> Could warp, to join the faithless tribe
> Of curs, who prosperous friends caress,
> And basely shun them in distress.
> Whoe'er thou art, 'till thou canst find
> As true a friend amongst mankind,
> Grudge not the tribute of a tear,
> To the poor dog that slumbers here.

Even though the dog's characters like generosity and bravery are also mentioned, what is emphasized is his faithfulness. The relationship between the poet and his dog is that of friends and companions, instead of master and slave. The word "true" is used twice to emphasize the faithfulness of the dog, which is reemphasized in his refusal to become a member of the faithless gang of unfriendly and aggressive dogs. The faithfulness of the dog is also shown in his drawing a clear demarcation between whom to love and whom to hate, to be specific, to love his owner and hate their mutual enemies.

After focusing on the dutifulness and loyalty of dogs, let's move on to some other animals. Wordsworth's "Peter Bell. A Tale" (1798) is a long ballad about the hero Peter Bell who changes from "the wildest of his clan" to "a good and honest man" (3.397; 3.400). He wickedly steals the ass away from a man who is drowned by accident, but later miraculously the "enduring", "trusty" and "faithful" ass travels a long way and takes him back to the dead man's house. Peter is conscience-bitten and asks himself:

> When shall I be as good as thou?
>
> Oh! would, poor beast, that I had now
>
> A heart but half as good as thine!" (363-65)

As Janyce Marson puts it, Peter Bell "transforms after witnessing the touching and devoted response of an ass that remained faithful to its deceased owner" (321). Apart from exerting moral influence on an immoral person, the ass is such an important figure in the household of the dead man, and that is why when the son of the dead man who is looking for his missing father sees the ass coming back, he shows his passionate love to the ass in the following way:

> In loving words he talks to him,
>
> He kisses, kisses face and limb, —
>
> He kisses him a thousand times!" (377-80)

With the man's sudden death, his wife becomes a widow with seven young children. And hence the return of the ass is crucially significant to the family.

> And many years did this poor Ass,
>
> Whom once it was my luck to see
>
> Cropping the shrubs of Leming-Lane,

A Study of British Animal Poems

> Help by his labour to maintain
> The Widow and her family. (391-95)

From the above stanza we know that it is the ass who eats coarse food but works very hard to support the poor family without a husband and a father. But for the dutiful ass, it might be hard for the family to survive.

"How They Brought the Good News from Ghent to Aix" (1845) by the Victorian poet Robert Browning (1812–1889) talks about how three cavalrymen bring the good news From Ghent to Aix, namely, the narrator, Joris and Dirck, and their horses galloped with "Good speed" (line 3). However, when they arrive at Hasselt, Dirck's horse Roos "shuddered and sank" with "quick wheeze / Of her chest" and "stretched neck and staggering knees, / And sunk tail, and horrible heave of the flank" (36, 33, 34-35). So only the narrator and Joris are left. When they arrive at Dalhem, Joris's horse is so exhausted that it "Rolled neck and croup over, lay dead as a stone" (44). As a result, only the narrator and his horse Roland are left, which in his view is a horse "without peer" (52). And finally they successfully reach Aix. The narrator recalls the moment of the triumph as follows:

> And all I remember is — friends flocking round
> As I sat with his head 'twixt my knees on the ground;
> And no voice but was praising this Roland of mine,
> As I poured down his throat our last measure of wine,
> Which (the burgesses voted by common consent)
> Was no more than his due who brought good news from Ghent. (55-60)

Upon the narrator's arrival, his friends come to congratulate him and celebrate the success of the mission of sending good news from Ghent. People are praising the horse for its stamina and perseverance. So in addition to Stefan Hawlin's hailing the poem as "an interest in extreme virtue, aggressive heroism and chivalry" (76), it is also a praise of the horse's dutifulness, without which man's heroism and chivalry could not have been achieved. The poem is so vividly-written and touching that, according to the literary life written by Richard S. Kennedy and Donald S. Hair, it "became one of Browning's most popular dramatic narratives, read and recited by schoolchildren throughout the English-speaking world for the next century and a half" (104).

"The Cow" (1885) by Robert Louis Stevenson (1850–1894) is a rather simple poem both verbally and thematically, which is like a nursery rhyme.

> The friendly cow all red and white,
> I love with all my heart:
> She gives me cream with all her might,
> To eat with apple-tart.
>
> She wanders lowing here and there,
> And yet she cannot stray,
> All in the pleasant open air,
> The pleasant light of day;
>
> And blown by all the winds that pass
> And wet with all the showers,
> She walks among the meadow grass
> And eats the meadow flowers.

First of all, Stevenson shows the relationship between him and the cow, that is, the cow is friendly to him and he loves the cow wholeheartedly. The reason for his love towards the cow is that she spares no effort to provide him with milk, even though there is some exaggeration in the strength the cow uses in producing milk since "whatever might is expended in the process is that of the hands and arms of the milker" (Hollander 253). What's more, the living environment of the cow is not so good since she is blown by the wind and sprinkled by the rain.

And what she eats are just apple-tart and meadow flowers. The simple poem just shows us a simple and universal truth — the cow eats coarse grass but produces nutritious milk, which shows that the cow is a dedicatory and dutiful animal.

Not only the pets and domesticated animals are praiseworthy, some beneficial insects are also commended by poets. A case in point is "The Mower to the Glowworms" (1651) by the Metaphysical poet Andrew Marvell (1621–1678), in which we can see how the glowworm is a helpful insect who makes full use of his own advantage or forte to provide light to people at night and guide people who have lost their way in darkness. Firstly, it is the glowworm who serves as "living Lamps" (line 1), enabling the nightingale to study and meditate "all the Summer-night" (3). According to Michael Craze, the nightingale here may stand for the "scholar-poet such as Marvell himself" (155). Secondly, it is the glowworm "whose officious flame / To wandering mowers shows the way" (9-10). In Sir E.K. Chambers's view, "[Marvell's] complete absorption in nature, the unreserved abandonment of self to the skyey influences, is the really true and sanative wisdom" (269). Even though the concluding stanza brings about Juliana, the mower's lover, whose brilliance seems to overshadow the glowworm's "courteous Lights" (13), the latter's illuminating role cannot be neglected with regard to other people in need.

Another example is Cowper's "The Silkworm" (1799–1800). First and foremost, the silkworm is not an insatiable and greedy eater, once he grows big enough, he will begin to fast and not eat any more and will start his work.

> He spins and weaves, and weaves and spins;
> Till circle upon circle, wound
> Careless around him and around,
> Conceals him with a veil, though slight,
> Impervious to the keenest sight.
> Thus self-enclosed, as in a cask,

Chapter One   High Praise of Animals

> At length he finishes his task (lines 14-20)

So we can see that the silkworm works industriously and tirelessly until he accomplishes his task of making the cocoon. And then he will transform into a chrysalis and then into a moth. After the moth whose life lasts only several days lay some eggs, it will die. This is the brief and transient life of a silkworm which lasts no more than two months, but as Cowper says "Though shorter-lived than most he be, / Were useful in their kind as he" (30-31). The silkworm is a useful and dutiful insect, whose life is meaningful and valuable in spite of its ephemeral lifespan. In Lodwick Charles Hartley's view, Cowper portrays many useful animals in his poems, including "the silkworm whose usefulness excels that of many human beings" (230).

To conclude this chapter, I would like to bring in Auden's "Address to the Beasts" (1973), which is an overall praise of the animals without special focus and thus cannot be easily categorized into any of the three sections above. Actually it is more than praise, since in Emig's view, there is also certain envy, of course innocent envy, "envy of all natural creatures' groundedness in their environment and harmony with creation" (223). Before giving praise to the animals, Auden first shows us the attitude of the animals towards the arrogant and self-conceited human beings.

> though very few of you
> find us worth looking at,
> unless we come too close.
>
> To you all scents are sacred
> except our smell and those
> we manufacture. (lines 10-15)

First of all, the animals as a whole do not think human beings are worth paying attention to. Secondly, they don't think the scents of human beings are worthy of reverence. Such negligence on the animals' side may result from the threat or harm that human beings have brought or are bringing to the animals. Therefore, human beings have to do something to improve the corrupted relationship. One of the ways is to give due respect to the animals, taking into consideration their good qualities or advantages, just as Kelly Sultzbach proposes, "the speaker's attitude is one of respect and admiration for the non-human other" (182). In terms of conduct,

> How promptly and ably
>
> you execute Nature's policies
>
> and are never
>
> lured into misconduct
>
> except by some unlucky
>
> chance imprinting. (16-21)

As Om Prakash Singla argues, "Auden feels that birds and beasts are superior to man in many ways" (198). The first one of their good qualities is that they usually stay far away from misconducts, and even if they sometimes transgress, it is due to accident or unfortunate occurrence. This forms a sharp contrast to human beings, who are much more easily "lured into misconduct". In regard to the relationship with others,

> Endowed from birth with good manners
>
> you wag no snobbish elbows,
>
> don't leer,
>
> don't look down your nostrils
>
> nor poke them into another
>
> creature's business. (22-27)

And unlike human beings who are inherently sinful according to

Chapter One High Praise of Animals

Christianity, animals are born with good manners. They are not snobbish, they do not look up to the superior while looking down upon the inferior, they do not look or smile at others in an evil or unpleasant way, and they do not bully others or interfere into others' business. With regard to the dwelling place,

> Your own habitations
>
> are cozy and private, not
>
> pretentious temples. (28-30)

Different from human beings who are fond of building grand, pompous, and sumptuously decorated houses or buildings, animals pay much more attention to the comfort and privacy of their residence. As for the purpose of hunting,

> Of course, you have to take lives
>
> to keep your own, but never
>
> kill for applause.
>
> Compared with even your greediest
>
> how Non-U
>
> our hunting gentry seem. (31-36)

Like human beings, animals, especially carnivorous ones, also kill other animals for food in order to survive, which is a way of keeping the balance of nature as well. However, the animals never kill other animals for their own entertainment or for hand-clapping from the audience. In comparison, the hunting men of noble birth or from the higher social class are far more greedy or rapacious. As far as literacy or culture is concerned,

> Exempt from taxation,
>
> you have never felt the need
>
> to become literate,
>
> but your oral cultures

> have inspired our poets to pen
> dulcet verses,
>
> and, though unconscious of God,
> your Sung Eucharists are
> more hallowed than ours. (37-45)

Even though the animals are illiterate, their cryings are inspirations to poets' writing of poems, particularly nature poets or animal poets. And even though the animals are irreligious, their "eating ceremony" is holier than that of human beings'. As regards art and philosophy,

> If you cannot engender
> a genius like Mozart,
> neither can you
>
> plague the earth
> with brilliant sillies like Hegel
> or clever nasties like Hobbes. (49-54)

In the animal world, it is a pity that they cannot totally understand and appreciate tuneful music, however, they are also not bothered or baffled by stupid and undesirable philosophies, which are seemingly magnificent and intelligent.

> Distinct now,
> in the end we shall join you
> (how soon all corpses look alike),
>
> but you exhibit no signs
> of knowing that you are sentenced.
> Now that could be why

Chapter One High Praise of Animals

> we upstarts are often
>
> jealous of your innocence
>
> but never envious? (61-69)

Even though animals die earlier than human beings in general, sooner or later, human beings will join animals in the underground. What's more important, animals are ignorant of life and death, and therefore are not at all disturbed or bothered by aging and impending death. And that is the reason why arrogant and presumptuous human beings are jealous of animals' ignorance, innocence as well as their simple life.

So on the whole, animals have many good qualities and life attitudes, in which human beings are lacking and from which human beings are supposed to learn from. Human beings should relinquish their haughty airs, pay due respect to animals and be friends with animals. Only in this way, can a sound and harmonious human-animal relationship be established. Otherwise, "Humans destroy animals in the same way that they destroy what they call their environment, and are also likely to destroy themselves" (Emig 223-24).

Chapter Two   Great Concern for Animals

Apart from singing high praise of the animals' beauty and loveliness, happiness and carefreeness, as well as loyalty and dutifulness, the poets also show great concern to animals, which is much more important in establishing the harmonious human-animal relationship, since the animals may not be conscious of the praise but they are aware of the love and concern shown to them. This chapter will be devoted to the analysis of various poets' concern for animals and will be divided into four parts, including showing concern, love or sympathy to animals; harmonious relationship between man and animals; irony or criticism of people's lack of concern for animals; remorse for wrongdoings towards animals, and some elegies or epitaphs dedicated to dead animals.

I. Showing Concern, Love or Sympathy to Animals

The German philosopher Arthur Schopenhauer (1788–1860) proposes that whoever is filled with compassion, all his actions will bear the stamp of justice and loving-kindness (213-14). Accordingly, there are some poems which directly and straight-forwardly show the poets' concern, love or sympathy to animals without beating about the bush. As a rule, let's first discuss the pet poems. In Book III "The Garden" of Cowper's *The Task*, there is a part often taken as an individual poem, sometimes entitled "My Pet Hare", sometimes entitled "The Garden", which goes:

  Well — one at least is safe. One shelter'd hare

Chapter Two Great Concern for Animals

has never heard the sanguinary yell

of cruel man, exulting in her woes.

Innocent partner of my peaceful home,

Whom ten long years' experience of my care

Has made at last familiar; she has lost

Much of her vigilant instinctive dread,

Not needdful here, beneath a roof like mine.

Yes — thou may'st eat they bread, and lick the hand

That feeds thee; thou may'st frolic on the floor

At evening, and at night retire secure

To thy straw couch, and slumber unalarm'd;

For I have gain'd the confidence, have peldg'd

All that is human in me to protect

Thine unsuspecting gratitude and love.

If I survive thee I will dig thy grave;

And, when I place thee in it, sighing, say,

I knew at least one hare that had a friend. (lines 334-51)

The phrase "at least" in the first line indicates that safety is one of the most basic requirements for the living or survival of an animal. And so Maslow's hierarchy of needs applied to man to some extent can also be extended to animals, here in this case the security needs. The word "sheltered" signifies protection, synonymous to the "peaceful home", which prevents the lamb from the bloody yell of slaughters, who take pleasure in its misery. In return for the undoubted gratefulness and love of the lamb, the narrator offers it protection and care. So in the narrator's house, the lamb enjoys a comfortable and carefree life, in which it eats, plays and rests in a happy, secure and unalarmed way. From the last line of the quoted part, we can see that the narrator and the lamb have become very good and intimate friends.

At the beginning of Wordsworth's ovine poem "The Pet-Lamb. A Pastoral" (1800), he shows us how a little girl is feeding a lamb,

> With one knee on the grass did the little Maiden kneel,
> While to that mountain-lamb she gave its evening meal.
>
> The lamb, while from her hand he thus his supper took,
> Seemed to feast with head and ears; and his tail with pleasure shook.
> "Drink, pretty creature, drink," she said in such a tone
> That I almost received her heart into my own. (lines 7-12)

In order to let the lamb eat in a comfortable way, the little girl kneels down. She talks to the lamb in a loving and gentle voice, and the lamb shakes his tail happily. This scene arouses Wordsworth's empathy with the girl, and so he watches them "with delight" and thinks "they were a lovely pair" (14). What the little girl feeds the lamb with are "Fresh water from the brook" and "warm milk it is and new" (42, 44).

The little girl recalls how the lamb comes into her household. When her father first saw the lamb at a faraway place, it is "owned by none" (35), so to speak, an "orphan". What her father did is "He took thee in his arms, and in pity brought thee home" (37). So it is the heart-felt sympathy towards the lonely lamb that makes the girl's father take it home.

After the recollection, the girl makes some predictions of the future life of the lamb, such as "My playmate thou shalt be; and when the wind is cold / Our hearth shall be thy bed, our house shall be thy fold" (47-48). In other words, the little girl is making promises to the lamb, which may remind us of the shepherd in Christopher Marlowe's "The Passionate Shepherd to His Love" who promises his love many things, including "I will make thee beds of roses / And a thousand fragrant posies". Likewise, the girl's love to the lamb is also very passionate. When the future weather is bad in the cold winter, the girl will let the lamb stay indoors and sleep by the warm fireplace. She is not simply showing love and concern to the lamb, but kind of spoiling or pampering him, since sheep usually stay in the fold, nevertheless, the image of the girl as an animal lover is crystal clear.

After feeding the lamb, the girl will go back to her household. Before leaving, she assures the lamb by saying:

> Here thou need'st not dread the raven in the sky;
>
> Night and day thou art safe, — our cottage is hard by
>
> Why bleat so after me? Why pull so at thy chain?
>
> Sleep — and at break of day I will come to thee again! (57-60).

As is shown that the lamb feels reluctant to let the girl leave, from which we can see that there exists a harmonious and friendly relationship between the girl and the lamb.

Shelley's "Verses On A Cat" (1800) shows his concern to a cat who is in distress in the following way:

> A cat in distress,
>
> Nothing more, nor less;
>
> Good folks, I must faithfully tell ye,
>
> As I am a sinner,
>
> It waits for some dinner
>
> To stuff out its own little belly. (1.1-6)

Shelley says that he must tell the truth, as a sinner is supposed to make a confession and atone for his sin. The truth is that the cat is in difficulty and needs help. Specifically speaking, it is suffering from hunger or starvation. He is kind of calling on the good folks to care about the cat or cats. Or maybe "good folks" is the use of verbal irony implying that people who fail to show enough concern and care to animals are not kind enough.

In comparison with people's various pursuits, such as society, variety, tranquil life, delicious food or a good wife, the cat's requirement is very basic and rudimentary, equivalent to the physiological needs in Maslow's hierarchy of needs.

> But this poor little cat
> Only wanted a rat,
> To stuff out its own little maw. (5.1-3)

The word "maw" means "stomach". So at the end of the poem, Shelley is repeating the same idea, that is, the cat is lacking in food, and thus needs people's care. What is worthy of being mentioned is that Shelley was only eight years old when he wrote this poem, which shows that his rudimentary concern for the welfare of animals germinated when he was still a little child. Though the diction of the poem is simple, the ethical thought expressed viscerally never dwindles down.

The renowned biologist Charles Darwin once said in his *Descent of Man* (1871), "Sympathy beyond the confines of man, that is, humanity to the lower animals, seems to be one of the latest moral acquisitions" (101). Darwin's idea has a profound influence on contemporary poets, one of whom is Hardy.

Hardy is one of the poets who shows the greatest love and concern to animals. He has written over twenty animal poems and his position as one of the most important animal poetry writers in Britain is unwavering. Hardy's basic concept concerning animal ethics is shown in his letter written to a lady of New York in answer to an inquiry she has made, "The discovery of the law of evolution, which revealed that all organic creatures are of one family, shifted the centre of altruism from humanity to the whole conscious world collectively" (qtd. in F. Hardy 346). As far as the meaning of the word "altruism" is concerned, human beings should also show unselfish concern for animals' happiness and welfare. In Hardy's tragic novels and poetry, his empathy with animal life infuses the texts (Kean 127).

Chapter Two Great Concern for Animals

Among the over twenty animal poems mentioned above, several of them are about pets. Hardy is a passionate cat-lover. In his old age, at least eight cats were living at his residence Max Gate and in the afternoon, saucers of milk were placed on the lawn for visiting cats. In April 1901, one of his favorite cats was run over on the nearby railway line, Hardy exclaimed woefully, "The violent death of dumb creatures always makes me revile the contingencies of a world in which animals are in the best of cases pitiable for their limitations" (Millgate 380).

In the poem "Snow in the Suburbs" (1878–1881), after describing the heavy snow and the comic movement of a sparrow in the tree to avoid the falling snow-lump, Hardy brings into sight a black cat:

The steps are a blanched slope,

Up which, with feeble hope,

A black cat comes, wide-eyed and thin;

And we take him in. (lines 17-20)

The stray cat is rather thin, suffering from coldness and hunger, and he comes to Hardy's house "with feeble hope", presumably because he has been rejected or dispelled by other households, possibly due to its symbol of evil omens. As luck would have it, the Hardys generously and considerately take him in, which shows Hardy as a man of benevolence and compassion in the treatment of animals. The poem ends with a moving and effective coda, and Hardy's characteristically unemphatic conclusion reminds us with its matter-of-fact compassion (T. Johnson 112).

The last poet to be discussed showing love to pets is Stevie Smith (1902–1971). Stevie is originally named Florence Margaret Smith, and as a twentieth-century female poet and novelist, she is overshadowed by other contemporary well-known writers. Nevertheless, she has contributed a lot to the writing of animal poems, one of which is "My Cat Major" (1957). The whole poem goes as follows:

> Major is a fine cat
>
> What is he at?
>
> He hunts birds in the hydrangea
>
> And in the tree
>
> Major was ever a ranger
>
> He ranges where no one can see.
>
> Sometimes he goes up to the attic
>
> With a hooped back
>
> His paws hit the iron rungs
>
> Of the ladder in a quick kick
>
> How can this be done?
>
> It is a knack.
>
> Oh Major is a fine cat
>
> He walks cleverly
>
> And what is he at, my fine cat?
>
> No one can see.

  The love of the poetess for the cat lies in three aspects. First, she hails the cat as "a fine cat" and repeats this address three times. The word "fine" connotes satisfaction and acceptance, and hence signifies the love of the poetess towards the cat. Second, the cat is named "Major", which shows the position of the cat in the household is not subordinate. Third, the cat enjoys total freedom in the household in that he can go anywhere he wants, such as the hydrangea, the tree, and the attic. He can either be the hunter of birds, or the ranger taking care of the household, or he just walks in the courtyard randomly without any special purpose. The last line "No one can see" emphasizes the unpredictability and unrestraint of the cat's movement. Only the true lover of animals will give his or her pet total freedom, rather than bondage or captivity.

In addition to pet animals, a number of animal poems are devoted to birds. Thomas Erskine (1750–1823), Lord Chancellor of the UK between 1806 and 1807, known for his contribution to British law, is the pioneer of legislation against cruelty to horses. His love and care extend to other living things as well, such as birds. In his sonnet "The Liberated Robins" (1798) which is published in *Animal World*, the journal of the RSPCA (Royal Society for the Prevention of Cruelty to Animals), he says to the robins which are set free: "Now harmless songsters, ye are free! / Yet stay awhile and sing to me" (lines 1-2), which shows his sense of reluctance to part from the birds. Even though they are set free, Erskine's home is always their shelter, where there is "no dark snare" (6), "No artful note of tame decoy" (7), but "blossomed shrubs" and "sweetest berries" instead (9, 10). Especially in the cold and bleak winter when there is a scarcity of food in nature, his "friendly hand shall furnish more" (12). Accordingly, I cannot agree with Feuerstein who thinks "As the human governor, Erskine grants the birds protection and freedom, yet they become his property in the last line" (32). As far as I am concerned, the phrase "my robins" in the last line does not necessarily mean his possession of the birds, but rather to show his intimacy with them. If he really wants to possess the birds, he would not set them free. The sequel poem "The Robins' Reply to Their Benefactor (Lord Erskine) at Hampstead" (1870), written by Erskine's daughter Mrs. Holland, is also published in *Animal World*, in which the robins express their gratitude to Erskine.

The next poem is Clare's "The Nightingale's Nest" (1832), at the beginning of which he tells us:

> Up this green woodland-ride let's softly rove,
> And list the nightingale — she dwells just here.

> Hush! let the wood-gate softly clap, for fear
>
> The noise might drive her from her home of love (lines 1-4)

Clare advises people to walk or wander softly, and close the wood-gate softly. The reason is that he is afraid of disturbing the nightingale and driving her away from its nest.

He recollects that when he was a boy, in order to observe the nightingale feeding the baby birds and singing songs without disturbing her, he crept "on hands and knees through matted thorn" and "nestled down" (13, 18). He then goes on suggesting again moving quietly and not disturbing the nightingale.

> Hark! there she is as usual — let's be hush —
>
> [...]
>
> ... Part aside
>
> These hazel branches in a gentle way,
>
> And stoop right cautious 'neath the rustling boughs (42, 44-46)

Clare remembers that once, despite his and his friends' carefulness, the sensitive nightingale still stops singing for fear of betraying her home and flies to a high tree. So the young Clare says, "Sing on, sweet bird! may no worse hap befall / Thy visions, than the fear that now deceives" (67-68). He is blessing the nightingale and telling her that her fear is unnecessary since they will do no harm to her. And he guarantees her that "We will not plunder music of its dower, / Nor turn this spot of happiness to thrall" (69-70). In Chun's view, "Clare is extremely cautious of his possible threat to the privacy of birds and tries not to disturb them" (53).

At the end of the poem, we find that when the nightingale is frightened to leave her nest, Clare and his friends look into her nest which is not at a high place and not well decorated, and they see

> Snug lie her curious eggs in number five,
>
> Of deadened green, or rather olive brown ;

Chapter Two Great Concern for Animals

And the old prickly thorn-bush guards them well.

So here we'll leave them, still unknown to wrong,

As the old woodland's legacy of song. (89-93)

Unlike other naughty boys, who rob the birds of their eggs on purpose, Clare and his friends leave the eggs where they are, which shows their concern and love to the birds.

The hedge-sparrow is a kind of tame and gentle birds which deserve people's love and care. In Clare's "Hedge-Sparrow" (1848), we can see what a charitable female bird-lover usually does to the bird in winter seasons, "And the bird-loving dame can do no less / Then throw it out a crumble on cold days" (lines 3-4). The lady's kind and benevolent deed forms a sharp contrast with the "skulking cat with mischief" who "Catches their [hedge-sparrows'] young before they leave the nest" (13, 14).

Given the love and concern that human beings give to birds in the two poems analyzed above, it is difficult for me to agree with L. J. Swingle's argument that "Clare's 'love' is less a matter of sympathy and good-will for the creatures he writes about than of a pure, almost scientific curiosity simply about seeing them" (280).

In Hardy's "Birds at Winter Nightfall" (1899), we can clearly perceive his concern and love for birds. The whole poem goes as follows:

Around the house the flakes fly faster,

And all the berries now are gone

From holly and cotoneaster

Around the house. The flakes fly! — faster

Shutting indoors that crumb-outcaster

We used to see upon the lawn

Around the house. The flakes fly faster,

And all the berries now are gone!

The setting of the poem is a winter day; the weather is cold and it is snowing heavily. As a result, there are no berries available for the birds. To make things worse, Hardy, an old man of nearly sixty years old, who used to feed the birds with crumbs, is prevented from going out by the heavy snow and what he can do is only to feel worried and concerned for the hungry birds. According to J. O. Bailey, Hardy and his wife even used this poem as a Christmas card in 1919 — Perhaps as "propaganda" for kindness to birds (*Handbook and Commentary* 163). The care for starving birds is related to an incident that Hardy experienced as a child. As is recorded in *Life*, he witnessed his father idly throwing a stone at a fieldfare, ending in the killing of the bird though not meaning to do so. Young Hardy picked up the bird, finding it "as light as a feather, all skin and bone, practically starved" (F. Hardy 444). The tragic incident has a strong influence on the young Hardy and "the memory had always haunted him" (F. Hardy 444).

"Nesting-Ground" (1975) is a short prose poem written by the twentieth-century poet Seamus Heaney (1939–2013), in which he narrates,

> The sandmartins' nests were loopholes of darkness in the riverbank. He could imagine his arm going in to the armpit, sleeved and straitened, but because he once felt the cold prick of a dead robin's claw and the surprising density of its tiny beak he only gazed.
>
> He heard cheeping far in but because the men had once shown him a rat's nest in the butt of a stack where chaff and powdered cornstalks adhered to the moist pink necks and backs he only listened.
>
> As he stood sentry, gazing, waiting, he thought of putting his ear to one of the abandoned holes and listening for the silence under the ground.

We can see that the protagonist in the poem only imagines his sleeved and strained arm reaching into the sandmartins' deep nests at the riverbank, and he only gazes at the "loopholes of darkness", and only intends to listen to the underground silence, instead of taking actions to snatch the eggs or baby birds from the nests. What's more, the word "sentry" shows that the protagonist is like a soldier whose job is to guard the nest, protecting it from potential danger. Instead of being a cruel snatcher, the protagonist is only a silent observer. Instead of being a thief or robber, the protagonist functions as a protector. As Randy Malamud argues, "Heaney describes in 'Nesting-Ground' how he has come to the aesthetic of distanced, detached watching, and it is an aesthetic that may facilitate a valuable relationship with animals" (172).

Finally, let's talk about poets' love and care for other creatures. Wordsworth's "To a Butterfly" (1802) deals with a child's care for a common insect.

> Oh! pleasant, pleasant were the days,
>
> The time, when, in our childish plays,
>
> My sister Emmeline and I
>
> Together chased the butterfly!
>
> A very hunter did I rush
>
> Upon the prey: — with leaps and springs
>
> I followed on from brake to bush;
>
> But she, God love her, feared to brush
>
> The dust from off its wings. (lines 10-18)

At the very beginning of the stanza, instead of regarding the poem as one showing care to insects, we might as well treat it as its opposite, since Wordsworth describes to us a scene of kids chasing the butterfly and finally catching it, which is not a friendly behavior. Kids are kids after all, and they are not to blame so much for their childish and playful character, since running after some living creatures is what most of us did while we were kids. Nevertheless, if Wordsworth and his younger sister Dorothy go on to torture and even kill the butterfly, they should still be censured despite their identity as kids. As luck would have it, we see Dorothy is reluctant to brush the dust from the wings of the butterfly for fear that she may damage its wings and hurt it. This shows that Dorothy is a girl possessing love and care for living creatures and that is why Wordsworth prays "God love her".

Christina's "Hurt No Living Thing" (1872) is also taken from her *Sing-Song*. The poem is a very direct appeal for the kindness to living things, insects in particular:

> Hurt no living thing:
> Ladybird, nor butterfly,
> Nor moth with dusty wing,
> Nor cricket chirping cheerily,
> Nor grasshopper so light of leap,
> Nor dancing gnat, nor beetle fat,
> Nor harmless worms that creep.

Christina calls on kids not to hurt the insects, no matter they are the beautiful ladybird and butterfly, or the dusty moth and the fat beetle; no matter they can tunefully sing like the cricket and gracefully dance like the gnat, or just leap like the grasshopper and creep like the worms. Every insect is supposed to be kept out of harm's way. Even though Christina's kindness goes not only to the beneficial insects but also to the injurious ones, which is not necessary at all, it does not prevent us from regarding her as a poet with tender love towards the living things.

"Seal Lullaby" (1902) by Rudyard Kipling (1865–1936) is one of the few poems that are dedicated to the love of the seal, which I will quote in full length:

> Oh! hush thee, my baby, the night is behind us,
> And black are the waters that sparkled so green.
> The moon, o'er the combers, looks downward to find us
> At rest in the hollows that rustle between.

Chapter Two Great Concern for Animals

Where billow meets billow, there soft be thy pillow;

Ah, weary wee flipperling, curl at thy ease!

The storm shall not wake thee, nor shark overtake thee,

Asleep in the arms of the slow-swinging seas.

"[L]ullaby" is a soft gentle song sung to help a child to go to sleep, which shows the love of the parents or other elders for the child. The lullaby in this poem is not used to lull a child to sleep but a seal. Best wishes are given to the baby seal's sleep, such as the soft waves would serve as the pillow, there would be no storms to disturb its sleeping and there would be no sharks attacking and endangering it. The pacifying lullaby shows the love and concern of the poet towards the seal.

"The Sea Horse" by Ruthven Todd (1914–1978) deals with a sea horse which comes to the shore by mistake and is caught by the narrator of the poem, in reality the poet himself.

... Its tail,

Prehensile, curled strongly round my finger,

A rigid band, harsh for one so very small,

As if its horror of the air had forced an anger

Against my hand... (lines 6-10)

By instinct, the sea horse curled strongly round the poet's finger just like its habitual holding on to the tentacle of corals or the leaf of seaweed. But compared with the soft tentacle or leaf, a human finger is rigid and harsh. The sea horse living underwater in the sea is not accustomed to or even afraid of the open air on the land. Hence it clutches the poet's finger firmly and angrily as if he is afraid of being swept away by rapid currents in the sea. Todd goes on describing the sea horse.

...and flexible armor

Was not crisp and brittle as in the dry

> One before me on my table as I write here; (12-14)

Todd contrasts the armor of the living sea horse and that of the dry dead one. Even if the armor of the sea horse is not very strong compared with other stronger sea animals, it can protect itself to some degree. But once it is dead and dry, its armor will be easily broken. People catch sea horses for its medical or nourishing use, especially for improvement of men's sexual function. No wonder the poet says "This strange and amulet fish attracts / As no other" (16-17). So Todd is in a dilemma, that is, whether to let the sea horse go or turn it into another dry one.

> In my imagination still cannot destroy
>
> My appreciation of this so unfamiliar stranger,
>
> Which, for a long moment, I held, let lie
>
> Convulsive in my palm, then watched it linger
>
> In reorientation before it twirled away (21-25)

After some mental struggle, Todd decides to set the sea horse free. The "long moment" shows his hesitation or procrastination, but finally his concern for the life of the sea horse conquers his desire to keep it, and thus the sea horse survives and regains freedom. It goes back to the familiar sea, "Where once more on its own errantry it could go / Compelled by will or hunger, wish or need" (28-29).

The last poem in this section is Heaney's poem "The Badgers" (1979). At the end of the poem, Heaney appeals:

> How perilous is it to choose
>
> not to love the life we're shown?
>
> His sturdy dirty body
>
> and interloping grovel.
>
> The intelligence in his bone.
>
> The unquestionable houseboy's shoulders
>
> that could have been my own. (lines 32-38)

Heaney's poem serves as a kind of warning to people, emphasizing the significance of loving animals by questioning at the very beginning of the stanza "How perilous is it to choose / not to love the life we're shown?" The badger does not only have the negative side of dirty body and interloping grovel, but also the positive side of high intelligence, which makes it worthy of being loved by human beings.

II. Harmony Or Good Relationship Between Man and Animals

Since people on the whole tend to show love, care and concern to animals, the human-animal relationship turns out to be harmonious by and large. Some animal poems are devoted to show the harmony or good relationship between man and animals. I tend to divide this section into two parts; one is about the harmony between man and animals in the mass, the other is that between man and an individual animal.

One of the earliest poems that show the harmony between man and animals in general is the well-known nature poem "Spring" (1600) by the Renaissance-period poet Thomas Nashe (1567–1601). The poem is actually taken from Nashe's play *Summer's Last Will and Testament*, and it portrays a pleasant picture of spring, the first stanza of which shows us that flowers bloom luxuriantly and girls dance happily. In the following stanza, we see

> The palm and may make country houses gay,
>
> Lambs frisk and play, the shepherds pipe all day,
>
> And we hear aye birds tune this merry lay,
>
> Cuckoo, jug-jug, pu-we, to-witta-woo! (lines 5-8)

In the above lines, a harmonious picture is drawn in which plants like palm and may, animals like playful lambs and singing birds, and human beings like the piping shepherds all peacefully co-exist in nature, and together they are enjoying the warmth and beauty of spring.

In Book VI "The Winter Walk At Noon" of Cowper's poem *The Task*, a harmonious picture of man and animal relationship is portrayed as follows:

> These shades are all my own. The tim'rous hare,
> Grown so familiar with her frequent guest,
> Scarce shuns me; and the stock dove unalarm'd
> Sits cooing in the pine-tree, nor suspends
> His long love-ditty for my near approach.
> Drawn from his refuge in some lonely elm,
> That age or injury has hollow'd deep,
> Where, on his bed of wool and matted leaves,
> He has outslept the winter, ventures forth
> To frisk awhile, and bask in the warm sun,
> The squirrel, flippant, pert, and full of play:
> He sees me, and at once, swift as a bird,
> Ascends the neighb'ring beech; there whisks his brush,
> And perks his ears, and stamps, and cries aloud
> With all the prettiness of feign'd alarm,
> And anger insignificantly fierce. (lines 305-20)

From the above selection, we can see that a scene of harmony is depicted and an intimate relationship between man and animals is established. The first animal portrayed is the hare. As is known to us, the hare is labeled with "timidity", which is vividly shown in the English idiom "as timid as a hare". However, the hare in this poem is very familiar with the poet and does not shun him or keep far away from him. Coming next is the stockdove. The stockdove is not alarmed when the poet gets near and does not stop singing his love song. Finally comes the squirrel. He is the only animal that runs away from the poet, climbs up the tree and cries aloud while seeing the poet's approach. But the poet thinks that the squirrel's alarm is pretended and his anger is mild. In other words, the squirrel's fear is not genuine and his running away is due to his playfulness. All in all, there exists a friendly relationship between man and various kinds of animals. As far as Cowper is concerned, "the woes of animals in the wild come from human beings" (Perkins, *Romanticism and Animal Rights* 137), so if human beings do not inflict woes upon animals, their relationship can be one of harmony.

In Shelley's long poem *Revolt of Islam* (1817), the main character Laone appeals to the enfranchised nations:

> My brethren, we are free! The fruits are glowing
>
> Beneath the stars, and the night-winds are flowing
>
> O'er the ripe corn; the Birds and Beasts are dreaming.
>
> Never again may blood of bird or beast
>
> Stain with its venomous stream a human feast,
>
> To the pure skies in accusation steaming;
>
> Avenging poisons shall have ceased
>
> To feed disease, and fear, and madness;
>
> The dwellers of the earth and air
>
> Shall throng around our steps in gladness,
>
> Seeking their food or refuge there.
>
> Our toil from thought all glorious forms shall cull,
>
> To make this earth, our home, more beautiful;
>
> And Science, and her sister Poesy,
>
> Shall clothe in light the fields and cities of the free! (5.51.5)

In "the fields and cities of the free", all human beings and animals become free and equal members of the society. Human beings will not butcher animals and their feasts will not be stained by the blood of the birds and beasts. Instead, the animals will gather around human beings happily, relying on them as food-supplier and shelter-provider. According to Shelley, the harmonious co-existence between man and animals on the earth will make our mutual home more beautiful.

Comparatively speaking, many more poems are devoted to the harmony between man and an individual animal. Let's start from poems about pet animals. Anna Seward (1742–1809) is an English poet who was acclaimed as the "Swan of Lichfield" and "the immortal Muse of Britain". Seward's "An Old Cat's Dying Soliloquy"[①] (1792) is not a well-known poem but it is a touching and poignant one, in which the personified cat recollects her previous beauty and grace while young, envisages her forthcoming death, reveals the kindness of her owner and expresses the pity that her owner will not be together with her in the afterlife. The kind treatment of the cat from the "more loved master" (line 44) and their harmonious relationship are shown as follows:

  'Ne'er shall thy now expiring puss forget
  To thy kind care her long-enduring debt,
  Nor shall the joys that painless realms decree
  Efface the comforts once bestowed by thee;
  To countless mice thy chicken-bones preferred,
  Thy toast to golden fish and wingless bird;
  O'er marum borders and valerian bed
  Thy Selima shall bend her moping head,
  Sigh that no more she climbs, with grateful glee,
  Thy downy sofa and thy cradling knee; (33-42)

The cat with the name of Selima promises that she will never forget her owner's kind care, deeming it as a debt she owes to him, which she is not able to pay off during her short life. Even though heaven is a painless place which

---

① http://www.mustlovecats.net/an-old-cats-dying-soliloquy.html

endows the cat with abundant joy, she will never forget the comforts given by her owner. In terms of food, compared with what are supposed to be a cat's favorite food, such as mice, fish and birds, the cat prefers the chicken-bones and toast her owner offers her. She often lies comfortably on her owner's soft sofa or his knees which may serve as a cosy cradle. "From a distance, the reader watches sympathetically and is taught to think by this exemplary cat that they too desire to commodify a similar relationship with an adoring animal" (Milne 172).

Christina's "The Dog Lies in His Kennel" (1872) is also taken from her *Sing-Song,* and it is a very simple nursery poem with only eight lines.

> The dog lies in his kennel,
> And Puss purrs on the rug,
> And baby perches on my knee
> For me to love and hug.
> Pat the dog and stroke the cat,
> Each in its degree;
> And cuddle and kiss my baby,
> And baby kiss me.

Though the poem is short, it reveals to us the peaceful co-existence of the dog, the cat, the narrator of the poem (probably a mother), and the narrator's baby. As is known, "pat" means to touch somebody or something for several times gently, especially as a sign of affection, and "stroke" means to move one's hand slowly and gently over somebody or something. So both words denote tenderness and affection, and show the love of the narrator towards the animals. She is not only kind and affectionate to her baby but also to the animals. As Lona Mosk Packer puts it, "each little creature receiving its due in affection according to its need and nature" (266).

In Monro's "Dog"[①] (1918–1919), at the very beginning of the poem he calls the dog "little friend" (line 1). The dog is "walk-ecstatic" (14), that is, he shows great enthusiasm for walking. Every day, he asks for "that expected walk" by way of sniffing (2), and he is so eager for the walk that he almost talks though he cannot. When his owners are making preparation for going out, we can see him "scamper the stairs" (8). The word "scamper" means to move quickly with small, light steps, from which we can sense his happiness. The moment he goes out, his "head is already low" (15), which means he is sniffing the flowers though according to the narrator he cannot smell the fragrance. The dog is so lively and vigorous that the narrator says to him "your limbs can draw / Life from the earth through the touch of your padded paw" (17-18). The dog who walks in the front sometimes looks back at his owners "Who follow slowly the track of your [the dog's] lovely play" (20). And his owners say:

> Thus, for your walk, we took ourselves, and went
>
> Out by the hedge and the tree to the open ground.
>
> You ran, in delightful strata of wafted scent,
>
> Over the hill without seeing the view; (23-26)

From this remark we can see that it is for the purpose of walking the dog that his owners go out every day in the evening, and the dog takes great delight in the walking. Upon coming home from the evening walk,

> ... and further joy will be surely there:
>
> Supper waiting full of the taste of bone.
>
> You throw up your nose again, and sniff, and stare
>
> For the rapture known
>
> Of the quick wild gorge of food and the still lie-down
>
> While your people talk above you in the light

[①] https://www.poemhunter.com/poem/dog-15/

Chapter Two Great Concern for Animals

Of candles, and your dreams will merge and drown

Into the bed-delicious hours of night. (29-36)

Thanks to the care of his owners, the dog's joy does not come to an end by walking, and his further joy will be the taste of the bone, a dog's most favorite food, which he will gorge on. After eating supper, he lies down quietly, fall asleep and go into the dreamland to the accompaniment of his owners' chitchat at night. The phrase "bed-delicious hours of night" makes use of the rhetorical device of synaesthesia, since "delicious" is related to the sense of taste, while "bed" is concerned with visual sense and tactile sense. And this shows that the dog's sleep is sound and his dream is sweet, which is the result of his happy walk and tasty supper provided by his considerate owners.

Hardy's "A Popular Personage at Home" (1924) is about the pet dog "Wessex" in his household, to be specific, a terrier. The poem is narrated in the first person point of view, in which the personified dog tells us his story instead of the poet. Just as the title shows, the dog wins great popularity in Hardy's home, and from the use of the word "personage", we can judge that it has already been regarded as a person and a family member. If we take into consideration the fact that the Hardys have no child of their own, the dog may be deemed as a child for the Hardys. The dog says:

With a leap and a heart elate I go

At the end of an hour's expectancy

To take a walk of a mile or so

With the folk I let live here with me. (lines 5-8)

From the above lines, we can see that like the "walk-ecstatic" (14) dog in Monro's poem who asks for the expected walk, the dog in Hardy's poem is also full of expectancy for the walk with his owners and when the time for the walk comes, he is filled with high spirits and jumps merrily. That the dog regards the Hardys as "the folk I let live here with me" is witty and funny, since it seems as if he is the owner of the household. The reason for such a bold idea on the dog's side is that he is somewhat pampered and he "regularly trespassed conventional animal-human boundaries himself (and apparently was encouraged to do [by the Hardys])" (Roth 91).

Like Monro's dog who sniffs the roses, Hardy's dog "sniff, and find out rarest smells" (10). Again like Monro's dog who looks back at his owners, Hardy's dog "Gazing back for my mistress till / She reaches where I have run already" (15-16). The mistress here in this poem is Hardy's second wife Florence, to whom the dog serves as a companion for 13 years. At the end of the poem, the dog envisages his own mortality while the eternal natural scenery will "stay the same a thousand years" (20). Upon Wessex's death, Hardy sets up a headstone for him, on which it is inscribed:

THE

FAMOUS DOG

WESSEX

August 1913–27 Dec. 1926

Faithful. Unflinching.

(F. Hardy 435)

This shows that the dog Wessex is very loyal as a pet at Hardy's home and it wins a high position in Hardy's heart. To a certain extent, the dog who has a harmonious relationship with his owners also gains literary immortality in Hardy's poetic work.

In "Puppy Dog"[①] by George Bernard Shaw (1856–1950), at the beginning of the poem, he says that he is "mesmerized" (line 2), that is, enchanted by the dog's beautiful deep brown eyes. He will clean him or brush him, provide him with a doghouse, and teach him some special tricks or skills. The dog will listen

---

① https://www.poemhunter.com/poem/puppy-dog/

Chapter Two   Great Concern for Animals

to his talk, sleep near his bed and is indiscriminate about the food his owner gives him. Every day, they will go for long walks as companions. Thus a picture of the harmonious co-existence of man and animal is depicted. At the end of the poem, Shaw says:

> We were together for many a long year.
>
> To me he was someone very dear.
>
> If you get the chance to look into a Puppy's eyes,
>
> I just know that you are in for a surprise.
>
> It might be that you too will have found a true friend,
>
> Some one to help you your time to spend. (19-24)

Shaw is not only emphasizing that he and the dog are long-term dear intimate friends, but also suggesting that the readers should keep a dog as a pet on the ground that the dog is human being's true friend and it helps us to spend our time in a leisurely and pleasant way.

Auden's "Cats and Dog" (1939) is taken from the opera *Paul Bunyan* (1939–1941), the libretto written by Auden for the operetta by the British musician Benjamin Britten (1913–1976). The titular figure Paul Bunyan is a giant lumberjack in American folklore. In the following selected part, the dog and the cats are talking about their relationship with the man:

> DOG   The single creature leads a partial life,
>
>   Man by his mind, and by his nose the hound;
>
>   He needs the deep emotions I can give,
>
>   I scent in him a vaster hunting ground.
>
> CATS Like calls to like, to share is to relieve
>
>   And sympathy the root bears love the flower;
>
>   He feel in us, and we in him perceive
>
>   A common passion for the lonely hour.
>
> CATS We move in our apartness and our pride

>   About the decent dwellings he has made:
>
> DOG   In all his walks I follow at his side,
>   His faithful servant and his loving shade.

From what the dog says, we can see that the man and the dog rely on each other, the man for the dog's deep emotions and the dog for the man's food supply as well as the shelter. The faithful dog follows the man like a shadow and accompanies him to wherever he goes. From what the cats say, we find that the man shows sympathy and love to the cats, and the cats requite the man and accompany him in his solitude. As is shown, the love between the man and the pet animals are reciprocal, and their relationship is close and intimate.

"Tom's Little Dog"[①] is a poem in the collection of poems written for children entitled *Bells and Grass* (1941) by Walter de la Mare (1873–1956). In this poem, the boy Tom gives his dog the name Tim, as if they were twin brothers. Tim is a very obedient dog and is at Tom's beck and call. When Tom asks Tim to do the action of begging, we can see that "up at once he sat, / His two clear amber eyes fixed fast, / His haunches on his mat" (lines 2-4). When Tom gives out the instruction "Trust" after putting a lump of sugar on Tim's nose, "Stiff as a guardsman sat his Tim; / Never a hair stirred he" (6-7). In front of temptation and allure of delicious and tasty food, if there is no permission from the boy, the dog is not supposed to have a taste of it. The word of instruction "Trust" is of great significance, since trustworthiness is one of the most remarkable virtues of dogs in general. From Tim's response, it is safe to say that Tom's dog can resist the temptation and can be trusted. Tom's next instruction is "Paid for", which means you are rewarded for your trustworthiness. Upon hearing this instruction, we can see that

>   ... in a trice

---

① https://www.poemhunter.com/poem/tom-s-little-dog/

Chapter Two Great Concern for Animals

> Up jerked that moist black nose;
>
> A snap of teeth, a crunch, a munch,
>
> And down the sugar goes! " (8-11)

From the quickness of the dog's swallowing the sugar, it is seen that he is extremely eager to eat it, but before he is allowed to do so, he manages to hold himself back. The boy and the dog cooperate very well to show the readers a vivid performance and demonstrate the harmony between man and animals.

Having discussed the pet poems, let's move on to the bird poems. The first to be analyzed is Clare's "The Skylark" (1835), in which we can see

> ... the skylark flies,
>
> And o'er her half-formed nest, with happy wings
>
> Winnows the air, till in the cloud she sings,
>
> Then hangs a dust-spot in the sunny skies,
>
> And drops, and drops, till in her nest she lies (lines 12-16)

As is shown in the above excerpt, the skylark flies freely and happily. "Happy wings" is the use of transferred epithet, since it is not that the wings are happy but the skylark herself is happy. She soars high into the sky and sings merrily, which reminds us of Shelley's skylark "singing still dost soar, and soaring ever singest". And finally she flies back into her nest. The poem ends:

> Oh, were they but a bird!
>
> So think they, while they listen to its song,
>
> And smile and fancy and so pass along;
>
> While its low nest, moist with the dews of morn,
>
> Lies safely, with the leveret, in the corn. (26-30)

While listening to the singing of the skylark, the school boys wish that they were birds, with freedom and carefreeness. If they were the birds, they would build their nest upon the cloud where they are "As free from danger as the heavens are free / From pain and toil" (23-24), instead of on the ground

/95/

"where any thing / May come at to destroy" (19-20). What comes next is very significant in showing the harmonious co-existence between the bird and human beings. Even though the bird's nest is low, the boys pass by his nest without infringement, to be specific, without endangering the eggs, baby birds or the skylark itself.

Dante Gabriel Rossetti (1828–1882) has written a poem entitled "Beauty And The Bird" (1855), which deals with the harmonious relationship between a bird and a beautiful lady. After the lady "fluted with her mouth as when one sips" (line 1), the bird "with little turns and dips, / Piped low to her of sweet companionships" (3-4), from which we can see that the lady's fluting and the bird's piping are in perfect harmony. The phrase "her fond bird" shows the love of the lady for the bird, and "sweet companionships" shows the bird's enjoyment of the cooperation in singing with the lady. Their happiness is mutual, natural and spontaneous, without any enforcement or affectedness.

What follows is a very touching scene. In order to reward the bird for his cooperation, the lady feeds him with some seeds. But the way she feeds the bird is very unique, that is, she puts the seeds on her tongue, from where the bird helps himself to the food. The lady is not afraid of being hurt by the bird's beak, and of course the bird is very careful so as not to hurt the lady. The two have tacit understanding and mutual trust. The poet's use of the simile "rosily / Peeped as a piercing bud between her lips" (7-8), in other words, the comparison of the lady's protruding tongue to a budding flower, shows the beauty of such a scene. Next, the bird-lover lady is deified as the Blessed Mary in Chaucer's story. Finally, the poet expresses his appreciation and commending of the lady's love of the bird by saying "I heard the throng / Of inner voices praise her golden head" (13-14).

Chapter Two Great Concern for Animals

"Bird Watcher"[①] by Robert William Service (1874–1958) deals with a kind-hearted bird watcher. The bird watcher was once a "potent power" (line 1), i.e. a powerful or authoritative person, and now he is a "multi-millionaire" (2), a very rich man. But he lives a frugal life because he wears clothes that even his servant are loath to wear. His hobby is to watch the birds with field glasses, a kind of telescope, from which he sees "Spies downy nestlings five days old" (9). A nestling is a bird that is too young to depart from the nest. The joy of watching the baby birds brings him so much joy that he deems the experience more precious than gold. Seeing the birds, he is as happy as a child.

But later on, he is filled with "hate and dread" and he "shakes a clawlike fist" (12, 13). The reason is that he sees a kestrel (small North American falcon) in the sky, which is a threat to the baby birds. Even though the kestrel threatens the life of the baby birds, the bird watcher "would never shoot it dead" (15), because he cannot kill this bird in order to protect other birds. He would let it be, that is, let the balance of nature and the rule of survival of the fittest decide everything. He can only do what he is able to do. For example, he is a vegetarian since he "lives on milk and porridge" (18).

> And now it is his last delight
> At eve if one lone linnet lingers
> To pick crushed almonds from his fingers. (19-21)

As an old man, his last pleasure is that he can be a bird feeder. He and the linnet form a good and intimate relationship, in which the man does not hurt the bird and the bird is not afraid of the man and dares to pick food from his fingers, creating a picture of harmony.

Finally, let's talk about poems about other animals. Blake's "The Shepherd" (1789) is a short poem of only eight lines, which I will quote in full length:

[①] https://www.poemhunter.com/poem/bird-watcher/

A Study of British Animal Poems

How sweet is the shepherd's sweet lot!

From the morn to the evening he strays;

He shall follow his sheep all the day,

And his tongue shall be filled with praise.

For he hears the lambs' innocent call,

And he hears the ewes' tender reply;

He is watchful while they are in peace,

For they know when their shepherd is nigh.

Blake thinks that the shepherd is lucky as far as fate is concerned, on the ground that he can follow his sheep all day long and wander here and there from the morning to the evening. The shepherd can hear that the young lambs are calling and the female sheep or the lambs' mothers are replying, which creates a peaceful picture. The sheep feel safe and sound because they know that the watchful and vigilant shepherd is on guard against danger or accidents, preventing the sheep from being hurt. As Nicholas Marsh argues, "The shepherd's presence gives them [the sheep] this 'peace', while their innocence affects him by giving him a 'sweet' life, and filling his tongue with 'praise'. The dependent and caring interrelationship of shepherd and sheep is idyllic" (14).

Hardy's "The Fallow Deer at the Lonely House" (1922) depicts an interesting scene. While people indoors "sit and think / By the fender-brink" (lines 5-6), the curious fallow deer outdoors looks in "Through the curtain-chink" (2). But due to the fact that the curtain-chink is very narrow and the rosy lamp light in the house is brighter than the darkness outside, the people inside cannot see clearly or recognize what kind of animal it is by judging merely from its eyes, though they are aglow. But the deer does not want to bother the people in the house since it wanders tiptoe in the snow. And the people inside do not want to disturb the deer either, since from the beginning to the end of the poem, the narrator does not mention the name of the animal outside. The fallow deer appears only once in the title, which means only Hardy the omniscient poet knows what kind of animal it is. The reason why the people in the poem do not bother to know what kind of animal it is reminds us of John Keats' poetic theory of "Negative Capability", "that is when man is capable of being in uncertainties, Mysteries, doubts without any irritable reaching after fact & reason"[①] (*Selected Letters* 60). As a result, peace and tranquility between man and the animals are preserved. As F.B. Pinion puts it, "the fascinating spectacle of curiosity in the deer suggests a natural affinity between man and the animal world" (*Commentary* 173).

III. Irony or Criticism of People's Lack of Concern for Animals

Even though most people tend to show love and concern to animals, and the relationship between man and animals is harmonious in general, there are still some people who are lacking in care and concern. This section is going to deal with poets' irony or criticism of this phenomenon. Since people who keep pets will love them and care about them, there are no poems of irony or criticism in this regard. Let's first look into the abundant bird poems.

At the beginning of "Fable XV. Philosopher and Pheasant" (1727) by John Gay (1685–1732), we see the animals' fear of man:

> But where he passed he terror threw,
> The song broke short, the warblers flew,
> The thrushes chatter'd with affright,
> And nightingales abhorr'd his sight;
> All animals before him ran

[①] Keats' letter to his brothers George and Tom Keats on December 21, 1817.

To shun the hateful sight of man. (lines 7-12)

It seems as if man were synonymous of "terror" in the eyes of the animals and so the animals hate seeing man. As a result, when the philosopher passes by, the birds stop singing and fly away. Even if some birds do not stop crying, there is fright in their voice. Not only the birds in the trees, but also the animals on the ground flee from him. The philosopher cannot help musing "Whence is this dread of ev'ry creature? / Fly they our figure or our nature?" (13-14). The reason is analyzed as follows:

> Sooner the hawk or vulture trust
> Than man; of animals the worst;
> In him ingratitude you find,
> A vice peculiar to the kind.
> The sheep, whose annual fleece is dy'd
> To guard his health and serve his pride,
> Forc'd from his fold and native plain,
> Is in the cruel shambles slain.
> The swarms, who, with industrious skill,
> His hives with wax and honey fill,
> In vain whole summer days employ'd,
> Their stores are sold, their race destroy'd.
> What tribute from the goose is paid!
> Does not her wing all science aid?
> Does it not lovers' hearts explain,
> And drudge to raise the merchant's gain?
> What now rewards this general use?
> He takes the quills and eats the Goose. (25-42)

The fear of animals towards man is due to the lack of trust of animals in man who is ungrateful and vicious. Man takes fleece from the sheep and

Chapter Two Great Concern for Animals

butchers them cruelly for their meat. Man takes the honey away by force from the hardworking bees. Man cuts the feathers of the geese to make quills and kills them for meat. Therefore, the seemingly simple-minded bird has taught the learned and erudite philosopher a lesson, as Frank Palmeri puts it, the pheasant's fundamental teaching is that humans are the least trustworthy of animals and a bird of no extraordinary intelligence teaches the philosopher why human nature falls below that of the worst predator (92).

"The Deserted Village" (1770) by Oliver Goldsmith (1728–1774) is a long pastoral elegy that condemns rural depopulation, the enclosure of common land, the creation of landscape gardens and the pursuit of excessive wealth (Bell 747-49). Apart from the major commentary, the influence of people's desertion of the village on the animals is also shown. The village Auburn used to be "sweet" and "loveliest village of the plain" (line 1). But now, with people's immigration to somewhere else, probably an urban area in the US, great changes have taken place, "Thy sports are fled, and all thy charms withdrawn" (36) and "Where wealth accumulates, and men decay" (54). The influence of the desertion on the birds is illustrated as follows:

> Along thy glades, a solitary guest,
>
> The hollow-sounding bittern guards its nest;
>
> Amidst thy desert walks the lapwing flies,
>
> And tires their echoes with unvaried cries. (45-48)

The bittern is a European bird of the heron family which has a loud call. Now with people leaving the land, the bittern becomes lonely and its cry becomes hollow. The lapwing is a small dark green bird which has a white breast and feathers sticking up on its head. It flies above the deserted place and gives out nothing but dull and monotonous cries.

Again in the past, we can see a pleasant scene:

> The swain responsive as the milkmaid sung,

> The sober herd that lowed to meet their young;
>
> The noisy geese that gabbled o'er the pool,
>
> The playful children just let loose from school;
>
> The watchdog's voice that bayed the whisp'ring wind,
>
> And the loud laugh that spoke the vacant mind;
>
> These all in sweet confusion sought the shade,
>
> And filled each pause the nightingale had made. (62-69)

The young man and girl's singing, the playful children's cry and people's laughter are combined with the lowing of the cattle, the hollering of the geese, the barking of the dog, and the cry of the nightingale, and they are "in sweet confusion" (68). The phrase "sweet confusion" employs the rhetorical device of oxymoron. Even though confusion generally means a situation in which everything is in disorder, this confusion of sounds in the village is sweet, so that they are actually in concordance with each other, instead of in confusion. But now, in sharp contrast, "the sounds of population fail, / No cheerful murmurs fluctuate in the gale, / No busy steps the grass-grown footway tread, / For all the bloomy flush of life is fled" (70-73), from which we can feel a strong sense of loss of the good old days.

Coming next is "The Brigs Of Ayr" (1787) by Robert Burns (1759–1796). "Brig" is Scottish word which means bridge and Ayr is a small harbour town situated on the south-west coast of Scotland. From the title of the poem, we can see nothing about animals. But the reading of it will lead us to the meeting with various birds at the very beginning of the poem.

> The chanting linnet, or the mellow thrush,
>
> Hailing the setting sun, sweet, in the green thorn bush;
>
> The soaring lark, the perching red-breast shrill,
>
> Or deep-ton'd plovers grey, wild-whistling o'er the hill; (lines 3-6)

We can see all kinds of birds like linnet, thrush, lark, red-breast and

Chapter Two Great Concern for Animals

plover, and all of them are singing heartily and sweetly in different ways, either chanting, or shrilling, or whistling.

However, the harmony and peace are broken by man, "that tyrant o'er the weak".

> The thundering guns are heard on ev'ry side,
>
> The wounded coveys, reeling, scatter wide;
>
> The feather'd field-mates, bound by Nature's tie,
>
> Sires, mothers, children, in one carnage lie: (35-38)

This is a hunting scene, in which a group of grouse or partridges are killed mercilessly. The word "carnage" refers to the violent killing of a large number of people or animals, which means many families of birds are killed, including fathers, mothers and baby birds. Therefore, Burns regards this slaughter of birds as "man's savage, ruthless deeds!" (40).

Cowper's "Strada's Nightingale" (1799–1800) deals with the competition in music between a shepherd and a philomel (nightingale), though the story may be fabricated. In the first stanza, we can see that whatever the shepherd plays by reed, the nightingale can catch the melody.

> The peevish youth, who ne'er had found before
>
> A rival of his skill, indignant heard,
>
> And soon (for various was his tuneful store)
>
> In loftier tones defied the simple bird. (lines 5-8)

So the bad-tempered shepherd becomes irritated, and maybe he is also jealous. He is aggressive and bellicose, and he wants to defeat the bird in musical performance. Thus he makes full use of the storage of his music to challenge the bird. In response, the bird does not admit defeat and sings "With all the force that passion gives inspired" (10). The result of the competition is very tragic, because the bird "Exhausted fell, and at his feet expired" (12). The "fatal strife" is lethal (13), and leads to the death of the bird. Is the shepherd satisfied with the triumph? The answer is definitely "No", because the poet comments that this is "sad victory" (15), which is the use of oxymoron, showing that the victory is not desirable and advisable. The last line of the poem is very meaningful, which goes "And he may wish that he had never won! " (16). Despite the tragedy in the story, this wish still gives us hope, because as the saying goes, it is never too late to mend. In the competition between man and nature, with the bird as its representative, there is no permanent winner, and only by respecting and loving each other, can we build up a relationship of harmonious co-existence.

Shelley's view on the suffering of creatures has been uttered through his mouthpiece Prometheus in his long poem *Prometheus Unbound*, that is, "I wish no living thing to suffer pain" (1.305). However, Shelley's poem "The Woodman and the Nightingale" (1818) tells a tragic story between a woodman and a nightingale. What the nightingale does is to "satiate the hungry dark with melody" (line 5). But it is a great pity that the woodman "hated to hear" the sweet music of the nightingale (3). No wonder Shelley says in the very first line of the poem that the woodman has a "rough heart" (1).

Shelley goes on illustrating the influence of the singing of the happy nightingale as follows:

> The folded roses and the violets pale
>
> Heard her within their slumbers, the abyss
> Of heaven with all its planets; the dull ear
> Of the night-cradled earth; the loneliness
>
> Of the circumfluous waters, — every sphere
> And every flower and beam and cloud and wave,
> And every wind of the mute atmosphere,

And every beast stretched in its rugged cave,

And every bird lulled on its mossy bough,

And every silver moth fresh from the grave (15-24)

So we can see that the influence of the nightingale's singing is not only limited to living things such as the roses, the violets, the flowers, the beasts, the birds and the moths, but also the inanimate things such as heaven, the earth, beams, clouds, waves, and wind. But pitifully, the positive influence does not extend to the woodman, who with axe and saw, kills the tree in which the nightingale is nesting and singing. In Ramananda Chatterjee's view, the poem portrays "the blatant insensitiveness of a rough-hearted woodman" (48).

At the end of the poem, Shelley moans regretfully:

The world is full of Woodmen who expel

Love's gentle Dryads from the haunts of life,

And vex the nightingales in every dell. (68-70)

Unfortunately, there is not only one rough-hearted woodman, but many of them, who break the nightingales' peaceful life, disturb them and even threaten their existence.

"Frog" (1896) by Hilaire Belloc (1870–1953) indirectly criticizes people's unfair treatment of the frog and calls on people to treat it kindly:

Be kind and tender to the Frog,

And do not call him names,

As 'Slimy skin,' or 'Polly-wog,'

Or likewise 'Ugly James,'

Or 'Gap-a-grin,' or 'Toad-gone-wrong,'

Or 'Bill Bandy-knees'. (lines 1-6)

However, Belloc is not talking about physical abuse or maltreatment towards the frog, but verbal disrespect, by giving it unpleasant or even humiliating nicknames. What Belloc is appealing here is not to hurt the frog emotionally, because he thinks "The Frog is justly sensitive / To epithets like these" (7-8). But as a matter of fact, no matter how sensitive the frog is, it cannot understand the human language, however vulgar it is. Nevertheless, what Belloc proposes here is not a groundless statement, because if we think it does not matter so much when we hurt the animals verbally, it is very likely for us to hurt them bodily in the future. Finally, Belloc emphasizes the significance of our kind and fair treatment of the frog:

>No animal will more repay
>
>A treatment kind and fair;
>
>At least so lonely people say
>
>Who keep a frog (and, by the way,
>
>They are extremely rare). (9-13)

In his opinion, the frog will give human beings the most payback in return of our kind-hearted treatment, as can be showcased by those lonely people who keep the frog as a pet. By a logical extension of this point, if we treat animals in general in a kind and tender way, we will be rewarded by our kind deed.

As a major contributor of animal poems, Hardy has written several poems concerning the topic under discussion. The first one is about birds' starvation in winter, which is entitled "Winter in Durnover Field" (1901). It is about the scene of three birds (a hook, a starling and a pigeon) talking about the lack of food in a frozen filed:

>Rook. — Throughout the field I find no grain;
>
>   The cruel frost encrusts the cornland!
>
>Starling. — Aye: patient pecking now is vain
>
>   Throughout the field, I find ...
>
>Rook. — No grain!
>
>Pigeon. — Nor will be, comrade, till it rain,
>
>   Or genial thawings loose the lorn land

Chapter Two Great Concern for Animals

> Throughout the field.
>
> Rook. — I find no grain:
>
> The cruel frost encrusts the cornland!

Indeed it is the cruel frost that encrusts the cornland and makes it hard for the birds to find any grain. However, if human beings give them some consideration, care and love, maybe they will not be on the verge of starvation. Hardy's "lifelong compassion for suffering birds suggests that he felt the scene as a tragedy" (Bailey, *Handbook and Commentary* 165). No wonder in his talk with Collins, he says "it was thoughtless [...] to say 'What a lovely frosty day!' when one remembered the suffering caused by wintry weather to birds and animals" (37).

Hardy's "The Bullfinches" (1902) has a kind of *carpe diem* beginning, or as Pinion puts it, a hedonistic philosophy of life is fancifully advocated (*Art and Thought* 147), so we can hear the bullfinch narrator says:

> BROTHER Bulleys, let us sing
>
> From the dawn till evening! —
>
> For we know not that we go not
>
> When to-day's pale pinions fold
>
> Where they be that sang of old. (lines 1-5)

What the bullfinch means is that since birds cannot predict their future, so to speak, whether they are still alive or not and whether they can still sing the old songs or not, they should enjoy the present moment, seize the day and sing all day long.

What makes their future so unpredictable? It is the lack of protection from Mother Nature, even though she is supposed to be the mother of birds and animals. The fact is that she

> never shows endeavour
>
> To protect from warrings wild

> Bird or beast she calls her child. (13-15)

As a result, "beneath her groping hands / Fiends make havoc in her bands" (19-20). The word "havoc" denotes a lot of damage or destruction and "fiends" refers to cruel, wicked and inhuman people. Actually nature is only a symbolic mother who cannot do anything to protect the birds or animals from being injured or killed by human beings. Only when human beings themselves realize their great mistake, change their image from evil and ruthless people into kind and compassionate people, show love and concern to the birds and animals, will the protection of the living creatures be secured.

Hardy's "The Reminder" (1909) shows us the miserable life of the birds in winter due to the lack of proper care and concern from human beings.

> There, to reach a rotting berry,
>
> Toils a thrush, — constrained to very
>
> Dregs of food by sharp distress,
>
> Taking such with thankfulness.
>
> Why, O starving bird, when I
>
> One day's joy would justify,
>
> And put misery out of view,
>
> Do you make me notice you! (lines 5-12)

The setting of this poem is Christmas, which is a time when people are all enjoying their happy time, without giving attention to a thrush who is toiling to reach for a rotting berry as food. Though he is constrained to very limited dregs of food in the cold winter and is in great distress, the bird is still grateful for what nature or human beings have given him. The narrator of the poem, possibly Hardy himself, would like to spend a happy Christmas day and does not want to see any scene of misery, but the appearance of the starving bird spoils his day, or as William W. Morgan puts it, it "interrupts the narrator's Christmas contentment and brings him back to awareness of suffering in the natural world" (235). Seemingly a complaint towards the bird, but actually it is uttered towards those people who fail to give enough concern and care to the starving birds in the cold winter while enjoying themselves in warm rooms. Hardy cannot help partaking of the suffering of the bird because "he could not help becoming involved in the misery of others" (Bailey, *Handbook and Commentary* 241).

Hardy's "The Faithful Swallow" (1923) deals with the regret of a faithful swallow who chooses to stay where he belongs and refuses to go to warmer places in the winter. The personified swallow tells us in the first person point of view that he does not want to follow the footsteps of those birds who migrate to other places and deems them "fickle" (line 8). However, he is not rewarded for his "Fidelity" (12), since the cold winter brings him nothing but "frost, hunger, snow" (14). Therefore, he regrets that he did not go with others and now it is "too late to go!" (16) His fidelity is shown not only to the familiar place but also to the people in the neighbourhood, but he is not rewarded by his fidelity. Indeed it is the mistake or even the foolishness of the swallow to choose to stay instead of migrating to warmer places, but if human beings provide him with shelter and food, in other words, show love and concern to him, maybe he will not have such a miserable life and regrets so much for his wrong choice.

Hardy's "A Bird-Scene at A Rural Dwelling" (1924) shows the relationship between man and birds through a series of actions of both. At the beginning of the poem, we see the birds are singing sweetly on the window-ledge or on the step of the door. "When the inmate stirs, the birds retire discreetly" (line 1). The word "discreetly" shows that the birds' action is very careful, for they do not want to offend the dweller of the house. When "the dweller is up", "they flee" (5). When "he comes fully forth", "they seek the garden" (7). We see the distance between the man and the birds is becoming larger and larger, and their relationship is becoming more and more strained. As Rosemarie Morgan argues,

"Unsettling discordancy is part of Hardy's purpose" (180). So the birds retreat

> And call from the lofty costard, as pleading pardon
> For shouting so near before
> In their joy at being alive: — (8-10)

We know from the previous illustration that the birds and the dweller are not on equal terms and they are rather afraid of the man. Actually, the birds who "whislted sweetly" should be rewarded with food and gratefulness, but they are now pleading pardon for shouting so close to the dweller, probably because the man does not show any friendliness or hospitality. The birds feel happy, not because human beings have shown love and respect to them, but simply because they are not killed by human beings. When survival is threatened, equality, concern and love become extravagant hopes.

After detailed discussion of some bird poems, let's move on to talk about poems concerning other animals. The first to be discussed is a poem by Burns, who wrote to his friend Mr. Cunningham on May 4th, 1789, about a neighbor farmer's son Thomson's shooting of a hare:

> One morning lately, as I was out pretty early in the fields, sowing some grass seeds, I heard the burst of a shot from a neighbouring plantation, and presently a poor little wounded hare came crippling by me. You will guess my indignation at the inhuman fellow who could shoot a hare at this season, when all of them have young ones. Indeed there is something in that business of destroying, for our sport, individuals in the animal creation that do not injure us materially, which I could never reconcile to my ideas of virtue. (*Letters*).

In this letter, "He expresses real anger at man's barbarity" (Simpson 106), and the experience mentioned in this letter leads to his poem "On Seeing a Wounded Hare Limp by Me Which A Fellow Had Just Shot at" (1789), the first four lines of which go as follows:

> Inhuman man! curse on thy barb'rous art,
>
> And blasted be thy murder-aiming eye;
>
> May never pity soothe thee with a sigh,
>
> Nor ever pleasure glad thy cruel heart; (1-4)

"Inhuman man" with "barb'rous art", "murder-aiming eye" and "cruel heart" is a further indictment of man as "tyrant" with "savage, ruthless deeds" in Burns' "The Brigs Of Ayr". We can see that many negative words are used to show the brutality and inhumanity of man, and at the same time Burns is cursing the wicked hunter and poor wanderer, wishing harm on him, such as something wrong with his aiming eye, and the deprivation of pleasure, home, food, or pastime. As for the wretched hare, finally he can do nothing but press his "bloody bosom" upon the "cold earth" (12), waiting for his death. At the end of the poem, Burns says that he will miss the hare "sporting o'er the dewy lawn" (15). The aim of the poem is twofold, one is to "mourn thy hapless fate", and the other is to "curse the ruffian's aim" (16). As Andrew Herbert Dakers proposes, "Whether he [Burns] could right the wrong mattered nothing; it was wrong, and he must condemn it" (196).

In some people's eyes, the animals are not living things but bags of meat, as can be seen in Hardy's poem "Bags of Meat" (1881–1883), the last stanza of which tells us:

> Each beast, when driven in,
>
> Looks round at the ring of bidders there
>
> With a much-amazed reproachful stare,
>
> As at unnatural kin,
>
> For bringing him to a sinister scene
>
> So strange, unhomelike, hungry, mean;
>
> His fate the while suspended between

> A butcher, to kill out of hand,
>
> And a farmer, to keep on the land;
>
> One can fancy a tear runs down his face
>
> When the butcher wins, and he's driven from the place. (lines 35-45)

We can see that the feeling of the beasts taken to the market or fair is a mixture of surprise and blame towards their owners for taking them away from home to a sinister place which is "So strange, unhomelike, hungry, mean". There are two kinds of fate for them, either to be slaughtered by the butchers or to toil in the field for the farmers. Even though the latter fate is also not so satisfactory, compared with the destiny of being killed, it is still the best choice, and this explains why one of the beasts sheds tears when he is unfortunately delivered to the butcher. As a matter of fact, the animals have no choice at all, and human beings fail to give adequate consideration to their feelings, let alone their rights.

As Florence recalls in *Life*, "The sight of animals being taken to market or driven to slaughter always aroused in Hardy feelings of intense pity, as he well knew, as must anyone living in or near a market-town, how much needless suffering is inflicted" (434). In 1919, Hardy joined the Wessex Pig Society, after supporting the use of a humane killer. In his will, he leaves 50 pounds (a large sum of money at that time) each to both the Society for the Prevention of Cruelty to Animals and the Council of Justice to Animals "to be applied so far as practicable to the investigation of the means by which animals are conveyed from their houses to the slaughter-houses with a view to the lessening of their sufferings in such transit and to condemnatory action against the caging of wild birds and the captivity of rabbits and other animals" (qtd. in F. Hardy 434), which shows that Hardy is a staunch supporter of animal welfare.

The same idea is also shown in another poem by Hardy "The Calf" (1911).

> Whether we are of Devon kind,
>
> Shorthorns, or Herefords,

Chapter Two Great Concern for Animals

> We are in general of one mind
>
> That in the human race we find
>
> Our masters and our lords. (lines 6-10)

The personified calves are telling the readers that they unanimously think that human beings are their masters and lords. But how can the calves have such awareness? Therefore, it is actually human beings' consciousness that they are superior to the calves and gain the upper hand in the human-animal relationship. The calves' jeremiad continues as follows:

> When grown up (if they let me live)
>
> And in a dairy-home,
>
> I may less wonder and misgive
>
> Than now, and get contemplative,
>
> and never wish to roam. (11-15)

The life of the calves is completely determined and controlled by human beings. If human beings want to raise them for meat, they will be slaughtered; if human beings want to raise them for milk, they will survive and work strenuously in a dairy, which may not necessarily be a better fate, because they might be overused and will not be able to roam freely as the time when they were calves. Hardy's criticism of the view on the inferiority of animals is in correspondence with the idea of the German philosopher Albert Schweitzer, that is, "To the man who is truly ethical all life is sacred, including that which from the human point of view seems lower in the scale" (qtd. in Joy 269).

The next poem is "Stupidity Street" (1917), written by Ralph Hodgson (1871–1962), which goes as follows:

> I SAW with open eyes
>
> Singing birds sweet
>
> Sold in the shops
>
> For people to eat,

> Sold in the shops of
> Stupidity Street.
>
> I saw in vision
> The worm in the wheat,
> And in the shops nothing
> For people to eat;
> Nothing for sale in
> Stupidity Street.

The poem is written in a cause-and-effect logic. Because people hunt birds, and kill birds for meat, the worms — the natural enemy of the birds — will prosper and they will destroy the crops. As a result, people will have no food to eat. As Victor Kutchin argues, "it is stupid to kill song birds for food, they are the real wardens of all growing things" (161). Of course, the poet is only foreshadowing the catastrophic consequence of human beings' breaking the balance of nature. But if people keep on behaving in such an unecological way, what the poet predicts may really come true in the future. According to Hilda Kean, larks, sold at Leadenhall market in the City of London, became sought after as roast delicacies (120). The attitude of the poet towards those who sell and buy bird's meat is shown in the ironic title of the poem, that is, people who do harm to the birds and endanger the ecological equilibrium are stupid. No wonder Kutchin says ironically that if he were a devout churchman, he would suggest an addition to the Prayer Book, that is, "from the besotted ignorance of 'Stupidity Street', Good Lord, deliver us" (161).

Stevie's "Nature and Free Animals" (1937) is about a conversation between God and man, in which God says to man:

> I will forgive you everything.
> But what you have done to my Dogs

Chapter Two   Great Concern for Animals

> I will not forgive.
>
> You have taught them the sicknesses of your mind
>
> And the sicknesses of your body
>
> You have taught them to be servile
>
> To hang servilely upon your countenance
>
> To be dependent touching and entertaining
>
> To have rights to be wronged
>
> And wrongs to be righted.
>
> You have taught them to be protected by a Society. (lines 1-11)

God is not satisfied with what man has done to the dogs. In God's opinion, man has negatively influenced the dogs both physically and mentally. In particular, man has made the dogs his subservient servants, wanting too much to please him and obey him. As Janice Thaddeus proposes, "Like Blake, she [Stevie] objects to their [animals'] enslavement by men" (91). What is hard to understand is that God is even not pleased with the protection of the dogs by a Society. We have no idea which society the God narrator is referring to, maybe the aforementioned RSPCA. The reason why God is not contented may be that human beings should be kind to animals is something natural and does not need to be enforced by any institution. Once such an institution is founded, it means that the situation of the ill-treatment of the dogs has already become very serious. Therefore, God says that he will not forgive human beings for what they have done to the dogs. To what God has said, man replies:

> Well, God, it's all very well to talk like this
>
> And I dare say it's all very fine
>
> And Nature and Free Animals
>
> Are all very fine,
>
> Well all I can say is
>
> If you wanted it like that

> You shouldn't have created me
> Not that I like it very much
> And now that I'm on the subject I'll say,
> What with Nature and Free Animals on the one side,
> And you on the other,
> I hardly know I'm alive. (14-25)

From what man has said, it seems as if he is very innocent. In his view, to give freedom to animals and to protect nature, it is easier said than done. On the one hand, man has to show love and respect to God, and on the other hand, man has to show care and concern to animals and nature. As far as man is concerned, he thinks he is double-burdened and it is too tough a task to be accomplished. However, what man has said does not hold water at all. By means of sophistry, he is only intending to shirk his responsibility in showing love and concern to animals, dogs in this case. As Malamud argues, "The poem's human speaker responds to God's admonishments with a wilting ambivalence that reflects Stevie's discomfort in a world where people diminish animals" (145).

Philip Larkin (1922–1985) also cares much about animal welfare, and in his will he leaves half of his estate to the RSPCA. He writes two animal poems in this regard as well. One is "Wires" (1955), which tells the story of young bulls and electric fences. The old cattle are experienced, sophisticated and weather-beaten, so they stay far away from the electric fences, which have hurt them in the past. But due to the fact that they cannot talk, they are not capable of warning the young ones against the potential danger, so the young can only experience and learn the hard truth by themselves. The reason for their attempt to break through the fences is that there is "purer water" beyond (line 3), which "leads them to blunder up against the wires" (5). As a result, they meet with "muscle-shredding violence" from the electric fences and are shocked. They get to know that they have to stay within their region of the wide prairie and cannot go beyond. Man's lack of concern and care to the cattle deprives the cattle of their freedom and puts "electric limits to their widest senses" (8).

The other is "Take One Home for the Kiddies" (1960), in which the name of the animal is not mentioned, but from the line "No dark, no dam, no earth, no grass" (line 3), we may guess that the animal is a beaver, who is an inborn dam-builder. However, it does not matter much as to what kind of animal it is, since the infringement of the animal's freedom and natural instinct is the same. The animal taken home for the kids are just "living toys" (5). Far away from their natural living environment, the animals are likely to wither and die. The last two lines of the poem "Fetch the shoebox, fetch the shovel — / *Mam, we're playing funerals now*" tell us the miserable dénouement of the beaver (7-8). J. R. Watson goes further to analyze the theme of the poem from a stylistic or linguistic perspective, as he argues, the thoughtless cruelty to animals, which so distressed Philip, is associated with a coarseness of speech, since there are no polite words like "please" or "thank you", no shape or grace to the expression as far as the kids are concerned (99).

"The Animal Refugees" (2010) by Sheena Blackhall (1947–) is one of the animal poems newly written in the twenty-first century, which deals with three cases of animal refugees in three different places in Southeast Asia. The poem is inspired by what she hears from the tour guide in her visit to Cambodia in 2010. It is written in the form of monologue by various animals:

> I'm the only elephant in Phnomh Penh
> No more of my kind you'll see
> My wife ran off from the killing fields
> She's an animal refugee
>
> I'm a Mekong crocodile from Vietnam
> When the napalm scorched each tree

> I swam to Laos at dead of night
> I'm an animal refugee
>
> I'm a slithery snake from Angkor Wat
> Where the mountains churned the sea
> Now tourists squat in my habitat
> I'm an animal refugee
>
> When people's homes are ripped apart
> There's appeals on world TV
> No one saves us. There's little fuss
> For an animal refugee.

  The narrator in the first stanza is a male elephant in Phnomh Penh, the capital city of Cambodia. He says that he is the only elephant of his kind left in this city and his wife has become a refugee, escaping to another place in order to avoid being killed. The narrator in the second stanza is a crocodile in Vietnam. In order to run away from the attack of napalm bombs, he escapes to the neighbouring country Laos. The narrator in the third stanza is a snake in Angkor Wat, a famous temple in Cambodia. Due to the fact that Angkor Wat is a well-known tourist attraction, visitors throng in great numbers and the tranquil life of the snake is affected. The word "squat" means to live in a building or on land without the owner's permission, which is kind of illegal act. In order to seek a quiet place, the snake also flees away from the boisterous temple and becomes a refugee. The last stanza is a complaint from the animal refugees, when human beings become homeless, there will be charitable appeals on TV worldwide. However, when the animals suffer from the same misfortune, there is no concern or attention given to them. The connotation here is that the world is still anthropocentric, lacking in love and concern for animals. As Anuradha

Chapter Two Great Concern for Animals

Murthi says, "No one even bothers about them because they are not able to put their feelings in words" (144). Sheena Blackhall is a Scottish poetess, but she is talking about the animal problems in Asia, which shows that this is a worldwide problem that needs cross-country and international concern and consideration.

IV. Remorse for Wrongdoings

In the above section, we have seen many examples of some people's lacking in care and love towards animals. Sometimes when people fail to show care and concern to animals, they will afterwards feel conscience-bitten, and even tend to show remorse for their wrongdoings towards animals. In my view, showing remorse for one's wrongdoing towards animals is hindsight, a redeeming and compensatory way to show concern to animals, since "it is never too late to mend". However, comparatively speaking, there are not so many poems of this kind. One reason might be that there are not so many such cases, and another reason might be that people are not bold enough to confess to the public that they have erred in the treatment of animals.

The first poem I'd like to talk about is "I Killed the Cat"① by Robert Roberts (1839–1898), in which the narrator kicks and kills a cat by accident. We do not know clearly what has happened that makes the narrator kick the cat, maybe because the cat does something wrong or offensive. Whatever the reason, he indeed kicks the cat, though not intending to hurt it, let alone kill it. But the fact is that the cat is dead now due to his kick, which is out of his expectation. The word "damn" at the very beginning of the poem shows the narrator's annoyance and disappointment. And his inner self is talking to him or blaming him "it's not your life to take / you killed a living thing" (lines 8-9). He is having

---

① https://www.poemhunter.com/poem/i-killed-the-cat/

self reflection and thinks that it is wrong to kill a living thing.

But later on another side of his inner self consoles himself that it does not matter so much since "it only a cat / there no where near extinction / so you have no problem" (10-12). So it's no big problem that he kills the cat since it is not a rare animal and his action will not result in the extinction of a kind of animal. But another problem pops up, how should he explain this to the kids who love the cat so much? To "bury it and say it ran away" (15)? This can be a white lie to cover his mistake, but no matter it is that he kills the cat by accident or the cat goes stray, the kids will be sad for the disappearance of the cat. Thinking of the sad face of the kids, he feels tortured, and thinking of the moaning of the cat when it passes away, he feels guilty. The ending of the poem goes "my god I killed the cat / I killed the cat" (21-22). The exclamation phrase "my god" again shows his regret and remorse. The use of repetition or epizeuxis of "I killed the cat" emphasizes his vexation and penitence for his involuntary wrongdoing. There is one more possible reason for the narrator's pang of conscience, that is, the cultural background of the nineteenth century, in which "the cat was at last securely established as a friend: humane feelings for animals and tender affection for pets became more widespread than the previous century" (Rogers 91).

Lawrence's well-known animal poem "Snake" (1920–1921) can also be interpreted from this perspective. The poem deals with the narrator's encounter with a snake. The conflict between the two arises when the narrator goes to the water-trough to fetch water with a pitcher on a hot day and a yellow-brown snake comes to the trough to drink water prior to him. As a result, he "must stand and wait" (line 6). And at that moment,

> The voice of my education said to me
>
> He must be killed,
>
> For in Sicily the black, black snakes are innocent, the gold are venomous.

Chapter Two Great Concern for Animals

>And voices in me said, If you were a man
>You would take a stick and break him now, and finish him off.
>
>But must I confess how I liked him,
>How glad I was he had come like a guest in quiet, to drink at my water-trough
>And depart peaceful, pacified, and thankless,
>Into the burning bowels of this earth? (22-30)

So there is a conflict in his mind, his previous education tells him that he is supposed to kill the snake who might be poisonous, but his conscience makes him tend to treat the snake simply like an uninvited guest. He is troubled and inflicted by his inner conflict, and he is not sure whether his act is one of "cowardice", "perversity", or "humility" (31, 32, 33). Finally, after some mental struggle, before the snake's "withdrawing into that horrid black hole" (52), he throws a log at the water trough, which makes a clatter sound. Even though the log does not hit the snake, "suddenly that part of him that was left behind convulsed in undignified haste, / Writhed like lightning, and was gone" (59-60). The snake is frightened or panicked and withdraws in a hasty and undignified way.

>And immediately I regretted it.
>I thought how paltry, how vulgar, what a mean act!
>I despised myself and the voices of my accursed human education.
>
>And I thought of the albatross,
>And I wished he would come back, my snake.
>[...]
>And so, I missed my chance with one of the lords
>Of life.

> And I have something to expiate;
>
> A pettiness. (63-67, 71-73)

The ending of the poem is filled with a sense of regret and remorse. As M.J. Lockwood puts it, "he [the narrator] listens to the human voices, and is left in the end feeling guilty and penitent" (125). The narrator uses four derogatory words to do self-blaming, namely, "paltry", "vulgar", "mean" and "pettiness". He even despises himself for his narrow-mindedness. Like the ancient mariner in S.T. Coleridge's "The Rime of the Ancient Mariner", the narrator in this poem also wants a chance to expiate or atone for his sin, so he wishes that the snake would come back, to whom he will show his hospitality instead of hostility.

In Larkin's "The Mower" (1979), he shares with us his feelings of killing a hedgehog by accident while he is mowing the grass. The hedgehog is not a stranger, since Larkin has ever seen it several times and fed it once, and even took photograph of it according to James Booth's biography (456). But now the harsh reality is that he has killed the hedgehog due to his carelessness. The "unobtrusive world" of the hedgehog shows its innocence, and Larkin's use of the word "maul" denoting unpleasantness and violence shows his self-accusation. "Unmendably. Burial was no help" shows the irrevocability of the accident and his feeling of regret and remorse (line 6). According to A. Banerjee, Larkin shows his deep remorse for the accidental killing of the hedgehog, and the poem serves as an indirect appeal for kindness toward animals and care for animal welfare (441). In real life, Larkin expresses similar feelings, he wrote to his close writer friend Judy Egerton about this incident, "This has been rather a depressing day: killed a hedgehog when mowing the lawn, by accident of course. It's upset me rather" (*SL* 601).

The ending of the poem goes as follows:

> Next morning I got up and it did not.
>
> The first day after a death, the new absence

Chapter Two Great Concern for Animals

Is always the same; we should be careful

Of each other, we should be kind
While there is still time. (7-11)

In the line "Next morning I got up and it did not", there is a tint, not so much, of survivor guilt, a theory from the German-American psychiatrist William G. Niederland (233). Survivor guilt is also referred to as "survivor syndrome", often experienced by those who escaped from a disaster that seriously injured and killed others. The lines "The first day after a death, the new absence / Is always the same" are of mourning and elegiac nature due to the fact that expressing the sense of loss or absence is a major feature of elegies.

The very ending of the poem is rather significant and meaningful. From a specific case, Larkin comes to a general proposal, that is, human beings and animals should be careful and kind to each other before it is too late, especially human beings who are apt to gain the upper hand in the human-animal relationship. As Malamud puts it, "This sentiment reflects an ecological consciousness (not much time remains before we have mown down all the nature and animals in the world), as well as an eschatological one (there's not much time before our mortal hourglasses run out of sand, as the hedgehog's has already done)" (159).

The last poem to be discussed in this section is Burns' "To A Mouse" (1785). The reason why it is not discussed first even though it is chronologically the first one written among the several poems under discussion is that it goes to an extreme in showing remorse for the injury brought to an animal because the mouse is universally considered as a pest, or an unwanted, harmful and repugnant animal that attacks food or crops. But if one can even show sympathetic feelings towards a pest, there is no doubt that he will show such feelings to beneficial or useful animals. Actually, in Perkins's view, "No poet writes of animals with more sympathy than Robert Burns" ("Human Mouseness" 3).

The background of the poem is that "Middle-class intellectuals in Robert Burns's time waged a campaign for kindness to animals" and "The opinion of Descartes [in the seventeenth century] that animals were organic machines and could not feel pain was entirely given up" (Perkins, "Human Mouseness" 1, 2), and so various kinds of practices that involve cruelties to animals were denounced by Burns and his contemporary middle-class intellectuals. The narrator in Burns' poem shares a similar experience with that of Larkin, since both are working, during which they endanger the life of the animal, and the difference is only in the degree as regards the damage to the animal. Larkin's hedgehog is unfortunately killed but Burns' mouse is only startled or brattled.

Even though Burns' narrator only startles the mouse while he is plowing, he still feels very remorseful for destroying the mouse's hole and disturbing its peaceful life, or "he laments his unwitting destruction of the mouse's nest" (McGuirk 65). He apologizes to the mouse:

> I'm truly sorry man's dominion,
>
> Has broken nature's social union,
>
> An' justifies that ill opinion (lines 7-9)

"The depth and universality of his sympathy is shown" in this poem (J. Hughes 128). He thinks that it is not only his fault but the fault of human beings on the whole who usually do something wrong to break the harmonious relationship between man and animals, and more often than not find excuses for their wrongdoings. In John Simons' view, "seeing the mouse's panic Burns meditates on the commonality between himself and the mouse and brings the non-human and the human into an idealised partnership that is challenged by Burns's own humanity" (88).

Thinking that his plough has demolished the mouse's cell, he feels very

Chapter Two Great Concern for Animals

sorrowful and the exclamation mark in the line "Thy wee bit housie, too, in ruin!" shows his strong sense of remorse (19). Especially when he thinks of the coming "bleak December's winds" and "weary winter" (23, 26), his regretful feelings grow even stronger.

In the penultimate stanza of the poem, the narrator says:

> The best-laid schemes o' mice an' men
>
> Gang aft agley,
>
> An' lea'e us nought but grief an' pain,
>
> For promis'd joy! (39-42)

The word "agley" is a Scottish word, which means wrong or awry, that is, away from the correct course. So Burns thinks the current man-and-mouse relationship is wrong, and in the long run it gives human beings nothing but grief and pain, since they base their happiness upon the mice's suffering. Burns' argument is also true without fail in terms of the relationship between human beings and animals on the whole.

To put an end to this section, I would like to talk about a very important animal poet Hughes, though it is a pity that up to now I have not found any poem written by him directly showing his remorseful view on hurting animals. However, from biographical writings on Hughes, I have discovered some relevant information. For example, according to Reddick, Ted Hughes and his brother Gerald Hughes look back on killing animals during their youth with nostalgia, sometimes mingled with traces of guilt (61). And in Jonathan Bate's *Ted Hughes: The Unauthorised Life*, he says that at the age of fifteen, Ted accused himself of disturbing the lives of animals. He began to look at them from their own point of view. That was when he started writing poems instead of killing creatures (53). Even though I fail to find Hughes' poems with regard to this topic, I have found that he ever wrote a short story entitled "The Head", in which the hero's over-enthusiastic killing of animals leads to his being hunted down himself. It is a story whose moral is that evil is rewarded with evil, which shows Hughes' ambivalence about his brother's obsession with hunting.

V. Elegies or Epitaphs to Dead Animals

Human beings' love to animals is not limited to the time when animals are alive, but extends to the time after their death. The way of expressing that "posthumous" love for an animal is through writing elegies or epitaphs, in which a poet shows grief over the death of the animal, recalls the good virtues of the dead animal or the memorable moments they spend together, and sometimes even expresses a kind of regret for not giving more concern and love to the animal when it is alive. Almost all the elegies or epitaphs to be discussed in this section are devoted to pet animals, which is understandable, because they have more intimate relationship with human beings than the wild animals.

Most of the animal elegies are dedicated to dogs, one of the most popular pets. Gay's "An Elegy on A Lap-Dog"[①] (1720) is devoted to mourn the death of a dog named "Shock". As an elegy usually does, it shows the poet's strong sense of loss by the use of repetition in lines like "poor Shock is now no more" (line 1), and

> Thy wretched fingers now no more shall deck,
> And tie the fav'rite ribbon round his neck;
> No more thy hand shall smooth his glossy hair,
> And comb the wavings of his pendent ear. (5-8)

The negative expression "no more" is repeated three times in order to emphasize the tragic fact of the death of the dog and the subsequent loss of the intimate interaction between the maids and the dog. The sense of loss is felt not

---

① https://www.poemhunter.com/poem/an-elegy-on-a-lap-dog/

Chapter Two Great Concern for Animals

only by the poet but by the maids as well. The phrase "wretched fingers" makes use of the rhetorical device of transferred epithet, which shows the sadness of the maids.

Apart from the sense of loss, sadness or grief is also a key element of an elegy. However, the poet does not directly express his own sadness, but shows the sadness of the maids who mourn, deplore, and are stricken with "flowing grief" (9), as well as his wife Celia's sadness who is "frantic with despair" (13), whose grief is shown through "streaming eyes, wrung hands, and flowing hair" (14), and who tears up her fan to express her "real signs of woe" (16). The reason why Celia is so grieved may be that the pampered dog, itself a kind of consumer of luxury goods, becomes an extension of its owner's subjectivity, reflecting her relationship to self in ways that inanimate commodities could not (Braunschneider 40).

Unlike what an elegy usually does, the poet himself is not overwhelmed with sadness; what's more, he persuades other people from being too depressed or melancholic. First of all, he tells his maids to "cease thy flowing grief" on the ground that "All mortal pleasures in a moment fade" (10). Then he tells his wife "Stream eyes no more, no more thy tresses rend" (20). It is not that he does not feel sad, but that he deems it is in vain to be so grieved, for he thinks that no lover is supposed to die of grief for the death of the dog.

Gay tells his wife and the maids that they must accept the undeniable fact that the dog is dead and what they should do next is to "lay him gently in the ground" (29). The line "may his tomb be by this verse renown'd" (30) reminds us of the ending of "Sonnet 18" by Shakespeare, that is, "So long as men can breathe or eyes can see, / So long lives this and this gives life to thee" (lines 13-14). Just as Shakespeare's verse endows literary immortality to his lover, so Gay's verse gives literary immortality to his dog.

In the last two lines, another key element of an elegy is involved, that is, singing high praise of the dead. The dog is "the pride of all his kind", and what's more important, he is a dog of faithfulness and loyalty because he "fawn'd like man, but ne'er like man betray'd" (32).

The next elegy on the dog is Wordsworth's "Tribute. To the Memory of the Same Dog" (1805). At the beginning of the poem, he explains to us why there is no tomb stone for the dog. It is not because of "unwillingness to praise" or "want of love" (line 3, 4), nor because the dog does not deserve a tomb stone, but because Wordsworth is taking things in nature as a memorial for the dog, as he says "This Oak points out thy grave; the silent tree / Will gladly stand a monument of thee" (9-10).

Wordsworth and his family members surely feel sad for the death of the dog since he says "We grieved for thee" (11) and "tears were shed; / Both man and woman wept" (22-23), but taking into consideration of the weakness and frailty of the dog in extreme old age, which is depicted as

Thy ears were deaf, and feeble were thy knees, —

I saw thee stagger in the summer breeze,

Too weak to stand against its sportive breath (17-19)

Wordsworth confesses that "we were glad" (21) since the dog will no longer have to drag out its feeble existence or linger on in a steadily worsening condition. Though death takes the dog out of the abyss of misery, Wordsworth and his family members still feel sorrowful for its departure as an old friend, and they could not help shedding tears, but their tears come not from sentimentality but "from passion and from reason" (35), since the dog is praised, as an elegy usually does, to be a dog of virtues (seen in "thy virtues made thee dear"), "a soul of love" and "an honoured name" (7, 34, 36).

Kipling's "The Power of the Dog" (1909) discusses the issue whether we should shed tears for our pet dog when it dies from "asthma, or tumour, or fits" (line 14). Kipling asks at the very beginning of the poem since in our life, there

Chapter Two Great Concern for Animals

has already been enough sorrow, "Why do we always arrange for more?" (4) Therefore, his suggestion to the readers is to "beware / Of giving your heart to a dog to tear" (5-6), which is similar to what Gay says to his wife and the maids in his "An Elegy on A Lap-Dog".

In the second stanza, Kipling says it is worthwhile to buy a pet dog who will give you "Love unflinching" and "Perfect passion and worship" (8, 9). But he says it is still not fair for us to wring our heart and shed tears for the death of a dog.

In the fourth stanza, Kipling makes a contrast between the past when the dog was alive and the present when it is dead, which is a typical way of writing an elegy.

> When the body that lived at your single will,
>
> With its whimper of welcome, is stilled (how still!);
>
> When the spirit that answered your every mood
>
> Is gone — wherever it goes — for good,
>
> You will discover how much you care,
>
> And will give your heart for the dog to tear. (19-24)

When the dog was alive, every day it welcomed its owner's homecoming with low crying sound, but now, the sound is stilled. The repetition of the word "still" and the exclamation mark after "how still" show a strong sense of loss. Robert Thurston Hopkins thinks that Kipling believes the dog is capable of determining fear, good-will, and anger with its highly developed olfactory organs (281). So when the dog was alive, its spirit could be adapted in accordance with its owner's mood, but now it is gone forever. At this moment, we will find how much we care for the dog and will naturally shed tears for the dog.

In the last stanza, Kipling argues

> That the longer we've kept 'em, the more do we grieve:
>
> For, when debts are payable, right or wrong,

A short-time loan is as bad as a long — (31-33)

What he means is that if a dog is mortal and is doomed to die sooner or later, we should not feel sadder and shed more tears only because we have kept it longer. Kipling ends the poem with a rhetorical question "So why in Heaven (before we are there) / Should we give our hearts to a dog to tear? " (33-34), which, if we know of the function of a rhetorical question, is to emphasize the unnecessity of being so grieved for the death of a dog if we have treated them well when they were alive. Nevertheless, few people can keep detached or apathetic when a beloved pet dies, as the title of the poem "The Power of the Dog" shows, no matter how the poet suggests or advises, the power of the deceased dog who can tear up our heart still exists and will influence the feelings and emotions of its owner to a great extent, due to the reciprocal love and affection between each other.

In an elegiac poem "Dead 'Wessex', the Dog to the Household" (1926–1928), Hardy shows his deep love for his faithful and unflinching pet dog "Wessex" who dies at the age of thirteen, the loss of whom makes him feel much bereaved. "There were those among Hardy's friends who thought that his life was definitely saddened by the loss of Wessex" (F. Hardy 435). The company of the dog for walking on that grassy path up the hill, the lovely jumping or trotting of the dog on the stair or path or plot, all have disappeared due to the death of the dog. Hardy inquires wailfully of the deceased dog:

> Do you look for me at times,
>
> When the hour for walking chimes,
>
> On that grassy path that climbs
>
> Up the hill? (lines 13-16)

Actually the dead dog can never look for Hardy any more, and it is him who is looking for the dog. By repeating each of the questions "Do you think of me at all", "Do you look for me at times" and "Should you call as when I knew

Chapter Two Great Concern for Animals

you" twice or even three times, Hardy emphasizes his deep sense of loss and his missing of Wessex.

Auden's "Talking to Dogs" (In memoriam Rolfi Strobl, run over, June 9th, 1970) first recalls what his neighbor's deceased dog liked and disliked when he was alive. He was fond of "gristly bones", "exciting odorscapes", "a rabbit to chase" and "a fellow arse-hole to snuzzle at" (line 1, 2, 3, 4). What made the dog unhappy or even furious is going to a salon with his owner, "to be scratched on the belly and talked to" by the members of the salon (8), because he could not understand what they were talking about. So we can see that Auden "handles the theme in his usual humorous style and the poem betrays his sense of sympathy for dogs" (Pandey 77).

Then the poet's dog changes into dogs in general, and Auden asks, unlike shepherds, killers, or polar explorers who keep dogs for practical use or particular use, what do householders expect from the pet dog in return? The answer is:

> ... The admiration of creatures
>
> to whom mirrors mean nothing, who never
>
> false your expression and so remind us
>
> that we as well are still social retards,
>
> who have never learned to command our feelings
>
> and don't want to, really... (18-23)

In terms of how to express our feelings, perhaps we are supposed to learn from the dogs who are candid and honest, never hide their true feelings, and show their emotions like pleasure, anger, sorrow and joy unreservedly and straightforwardly. Despite dogs' candidness and integrity, pitifully, some famous people, either literary men or fictional figures, such as Goethe and Lear, disliked dogs, which makes Auden think it is "eccentric" (25). Reassuringly, "good people, / if they keep one, have good dogs" (25-26). Auden has a very low opinion of those who debase dogs and makes a comment on them:

> ... It's those who crave
>
> a querulous permanent baby,
>
> or a little detachable penis,
>
> who can, and often do, debase you. (28-31)

After rebuking those grumblers of dogs, Auden goes back to the topic of dogs' candidness in expressing their feelings by stating "Humor and joy to your thinking are one, / so that you laugh with your whole body" (32-33). However, dogs do not only know when they should be happy, but also know when they should be sad and are supposed to keep silent.

> Being quicker to sense unhappiness
>
> without having to be told the dreary
>
> details or who is to blame, in dark hours
>
> your silence may be of more help than many
>
> two-legged comforters. (39-43)

As can be seen, in comforting their owners who are in a low mood, sometimes dogs can do better and are more helpful than human beings, because more often than not, what the grieved people need is just tranquility, as well as a space and time of their own. Just as Alexander McCall Smith proposes, this poem shows "canine qualities that will strike an immediate chord with the dog owner who has turned, as all such must on occasion do, to the dog for support or encouragement" (118). Then Auden talks about the dog's obedience:

> ... In citizens
>
> obedience is not always a virtue,
>
> but yours need not make us uneasy
>
> because, though child-like, you are complete (43-46)

Obedience is one of the good qualities of dogs even though it is not considered as a virtue among human beings. Dogs' obedience is innocent, having

Chapter Two Great Concern for Animals

no egoistic or ulterior purposes, and then will not make human beings feel worried or uncomfortable. After reviewing the good qualities of dogs, Auden concludes the poem:

> ... Let difference
>
> remain our bond, yes, and the one trait
>
> both have in common, a sense of theatre. (50-52)

The way to keep a harmonious man-and-dog relationship or human-animal relationship in general is to seek common ground while reserving differences. All in all, human beings should not inflict their values and ways of conduct upon the dogs and other animals.

Apart from elegies for dogs, I have also chosen two elegies for cats to discuss. When one of Hardy's favorite cats named Snowdove was killed on the railway line near his household, he wrote an elegy in dedication to him, entitled "Last Words to a Dumb Friend" (1904), in which a strong sense of loss and pain is shown. After recollecting the moments they stayed together and praising the cat of its docility, Hardy makes some introspection:

> Strange it is this speechless thing,
>
> Subject to our mastering,
>
> Subject for his life and food
>
> To our gift, and time, and mood;
>
> Timid pensioner of us Powers,
>
> His existence ruled by ours (lines 30-35)

To Hardy's mind, it is wrong to regard the relationship between a cat and its owner as that of subject and master, and animals' existence is not supposed to be ruled by human beings. Otherwise, animals might live in timidity and under stress, but they cannot express their feelings due to the lack of human language. To Rod Preece, the cat's dumbness is "the source of compassion" of the poet (*Animals and Nature* 34). Apart from showing nostalgic feelings towards the deceased cat, a sense of remorse for man's ruling position in the animal-human relationship is also expressed, not only felt toward his own cat, but presumably animals as a whole.

"I Miss My Cat"[①] (1997) by the contemporary poet Rosemary Monahan is a poem simple in diction, with nursery-rhyme-like language. Both the title and the ending lines of the poem "I'll remember everything about you / I will miss my Honeye forever" show directly Monahan's love for the cat and the nostalgic feelings towards it (lines 17-18). She recalls in detail the appearance, cry and movements of the cat, such as its "carefree ways", "lazy days", "balls of fur" and "outloud purrs" (1, 2, 3, 4). Special attention is given to the cat's particular movements, including its sitting, napping, jumping, meowing, hissing, licking, and waiting for the homecoming of its owner. As Monahan says in the poem, "You being so lovable" (7), and that is why she cannot forget the cat and misses it so much, who keeps lingering on her mind.

There is also an elegy for a pet hare. Cowper's "Epitaph on A Hare" (1783) mourns the death of a pet hare named Tiney who dies at the age of nine. At the very beginning of the poem, Cowper endorses the idea that death ends everything, both happiness and sadness, since the hare will no longer be bothered by the hunting dogs' pursuit and the hunter's shout. In this sense, it is not such a bad thing to die for an old hare and maybe he should not feel so sad for its death, which serves as a kind of self-consolation.

What follows is a detailed recollection of the hare's life in Cowper's household. Special attention is given to the eating habit and diet of the hare, which includes various things such as bread, milk, oats, straw, thistles, lettuces, twigs of hawthorn, pipping's peel, juicy salads and carrots. Cowper also recalls the movements of the hare, including his dozing, bounding, skipping, gamboling,

---

① https://www.poemhunter.com/poem/i-miss-my-cat/

swinging his rump and frisking. The simile "like a fawn" shows the liveliness and playfulness of the hare since fawn is a very young deer, usually less than one year old (line 23).

In the last but two stanza, Cowper tells us the importance of the hare in his life as follows:

> I kept him for his humour's sake,
>
> For he would oft beguile
>
> My heart of thoughts that made it ache,
>
> And force me to a smile. (33-36)

From the above lines, we can see that the reason why Cowper keeps the hare or what he values most in the hare is its humor, or its quality of being funny. And whenever he is in low spirits or in a bad mood, the hare used to cheer him up and make him smile. As John Timbs proposes, Cowper's account of his pet hares (altogether three) is full of pathos and fine feeling, and they must have been congenial companions in his melancholy musings (151).

In the last stanza, considering his own old age and the shock or blow the hare's death brings to him, he begins to envisage his own approaching death as he says "Must soon partake his [the hare's] grave" (44), from which we can see that the death of his beloved pet does have some negative influence upon his mood and frame of mind. Just as Perkins argues, Cowper "describes animals affectionately and realistically, taking a sympathetic interest in the creatures they naturally are" (*Romanticism and Animal Rights* 48).

Finally is an elegy to a sheep, or an ewe to be exact, that is, Burns' "Poor Mailie's Elegy" (1783). The death of the sheep Mailie leads the bereaved poet to "Lament in rhyme, lament in prose" (1.1). People can see the poet's grief shown by "tears tricklin down your nose" (1.2), and "dowie [Scottish word for sad, melancholy], wear / The mourning weed" (2.3-4). In the poet's mind, the sheep is "a friend an' neebor [Scottish word for neighbour] dear" (2.5).

After showing his sadness upon the death of the sheep, Burns begins to make some recollections, in which their intimate relationship is shown.

> Thro' a' the town she trotted by him;
>
> A lang half-mile she could descry him;
>
> Wi kindly bleat, when she did spy him,
>
> She ran wi' speed. (3.1-4)

As can be seen, the sheep is the poet's company in his journey to the town. The sheep has such good eyesight that she can see her owner in the distance, and the moment she sees him, she will run to him as quickly as possible with happy and welcoming bleat. "[S]he always wanted to be near her master, a sentiment that especially melts the pet-keeping heart" (Perkins, "Human Mouseness" 6). Burns does not only recall their good relationship, but also the sheep's good qualities as well.

> I wat she was a sheep o' sense,
>
> An' could behave hersel' wi' mense:
>
> I'll say't, she never brak a fence,
>
> Thro' thievish greed. (4.1-4)

One of the virtues of the sheep is that she is very well-behaved, as she is not such a greedy one, and never breaks the fence and go to the neighbor's domain to steal food. The sheep's death does not only have a strong influence on Burns himself, but also on others, as we can see "It maks guid fellows girn an' gape, / Wi' chokin dread" (7.3-4). So their feeling is a mixture of anger, shock, and sadness, for death is such a "vile, wanchancie [Scottish word for unlucky] thing — a raip [Scottish word for rape]!" (7.2), due to the fact that the sheep dies of falling into a ditch and getting drowned.

In the penultimate line of the poem we can see that the sheep's death is such a great blow on Burns that "His heart will never get aboon" (8.5). The word "aboon" is a Scottish word which means "in good cheer", or "in a better

Chapter Two Great Concern for Animals

condition". So this line aims to show us that Burns will not easily recover from the bereavement of his beloved sheep. So to speak, he might be in a state of what Jahan Ramazani terms as "melancholic mourning" (4), that is, chronic or unresolved mourning for the dead.

All the animals discussed above are pet animals. There is also an epitaph devoted to a bird, which is not a pet though he is kind of tamed. The poem is Cowper's "Epitaph on a Free but Tame Red-breast: A Favorite of Miss Sally Hurdis" (1792). The poem begins:

> These are not dewdrops, these are tears,
>
> And tears by Sally shed
>
> For absent Robin, who she fears,
>
> With too much cause, is dead. (lines 1-4)

The beginning is typical of an epitaph or elegy, in that it shows the great sadness of the mourner for the death of a beloved. After showing Miss Sally's grief, Cowper goes on to recollect the happy time she spent with the redbreast, or robin when he was alive. The redbreast used to "on her finger perch'd, to stand / Picking his breakfast-crumb" (7-8). We can see that Miss Sally and the redbreast have intimate relationship and mutual trust, in that she feeds the bird every day and the bird is not a bit afraid of her, which portrays a harmonious picture of man and nature. In order to commemorate the redbreast, she even "raised him here a tomb" (13). In order to tell us why Miss Sally loves the redbreast so much, at the end of his poem, Cowper further praises the bird's good qualities:

> But Bob was neither rudely bold
>
> Nor spiritlessly tame;
>
> Nor was, like theirs, his bosom cold,
>
> But always in a flame. (21-24)

The bird is a bird of principle or a bird of the "Golden Means", since he is neither too wild nor too mild, but keeps a balance between the two characters.

In addition, he is always passionate and fervent. No wonder he wins the love of Miss Sally and his death is a severe blow on her. As Ernest Bernhardt-Kabisch argues, epitaphs like this have "the tender pathos and innocent humor" (115).

Chapter Three   Animals' Functions in People's Mental Life

The relationship between man and animals is reciprocal in that not only human beings are praising animals for their good qualities or virtues, showing love and concern to them, but also animals can pay human beings back, rewarding them by being beneficial to them. First of all, animals can serve as stimulus to good mood when human beings feel depressed, in trouble or setback. Secondly, animals can be the poets' poetic Muse, bringing them epiphany or teaching them a lesson in life. Thirdly, animals can arouse empathy in the poets, since they sometimes are in the same boat, and so poets tend to use animals as the mouthpiece to express their own emotions.

I. Animals as Stimulus to Good Mood

When human beings feel sad, down or depressed, the animals can sometimes cheer them up or help to relieve them of their sadness or grief. Even if they are not in a bad mood, animals can make their spirits even higher. This is especially shown in bird poems.

"Sonnet to the Nightingale" (1645) by John Milton (1608–1674) is such a poem. It is written in the form of an Italian or Petrarchan sonnet:

> O Nightingale! that on yon bloomy spray
> Warblest at eve, when all the woods are still,
> Thou with fresh hope the lover's heart dost fill,

> While the jolly hours lead on propitious May.
> Thy liquid notes that close the eye of day,
> First heard before the shallow cuckoo's bill,
> Portend success in love; O, if Jove's will
> Have linked that amorous power to thy soft lay,
> Now timely sing, ere the rude bird of hate
> Foretell my hopeless doom in some grove nigh;
> As thou from year to year hast sung too late
> For my relief, yet hadst no reason why:
> Whether the Muse, or Love, call thee his mate,
> Both them I serve, and of their train am I.

As can be seen, in the evening, when the whole nature is hushed, the nightingale begins its singing, which makes the time become happy, cheerful and lucky. What's more, its singing can fill the lover's heart with fresh hope for the bright future. According to Milton's view in the poem, the nightingale's propitious singing forms a sharp contrast with the shallow cuckoo's singing in that the former brings about happiness and love while the latter brings on "hopeless doom" as "the rude bird of hate", and this label adhered to the cuckoo may derive itself from the "medieval debates between the nightingale as harbinger of love and the cuckoo as emblem of infidelity" (Lewalski 39). Maybe the nightingale is the partner of the Nine Muses, the inspirational goddesses of literature and arts, or Venus, the Goddess of Love, and so is Milton himself under the influence of the nightingale.

At the beginning of Cowper's "To the Nightingale, Which the Author Heard Sing on New Year's Day" (1792), he asks two questions. The first one is why can he hear the "melody of May" on the morning of the very first day of January, a wintry month signified by "wither'd spray" (line 2, 1)? The second one is why is he the only one chosen to witness such a favorable scene among so many people who would be proud of hearing the nightingale's singing at such a time? He then gives his surmise.

> Or sing'st thou, rather, under force
> Of some divine command,
> Commission'd to presage a course
> Of happier days at hand? (13-16)

Maybe the nightingale is sent here to accomplish some holy or sacred mission, so to speak, to forecast or predict the advent or approaching of days that are more pleasant than the gloomy and bleak winter days. Hence Cowper gives the nightingale "Thrice welcome" (17), that is, three times greeting. The reason is that he is somewhat like the nightingale, since he also sings cheerfully "Beneath a wintry sky" during "many a long / And joyless year" (20, 17-18). The "wintry sky" can be symbolic, which stands for unfavorable or frustrating situations.

> But thee no wintry skies can harm,
> Who only need'st to sing
> To make e'en January charm,
> And every season spring. (21-24)

In comparison with the poet, the nightingale is still more optimistic, cheerful and happy-go-lucky, who is not bothered by unfavorable situations and able to make even the coldest month charming, warm and pleasant. The nightingale's happiness and optimism are contagious, which bring about positive and profound influence upon the poet.

In front of Wordsworth's "To a Butterfly", there is an introduction to the background of the poem, which goes: "Written in the orchard, Town-end, Grasmere. My sister and I were parted immediately after the death of our mother, who died in 1778, both being very young" (*Poetical Works*, Vol.2, 238). At the time of separation, Wordsworth was only eight years old and his younger sister Dorothy seven. In the poem, Wordsworth recollects the scene that he and

Dorothy were catching a butterfly, and thus the butterfly serves as a reminder of his sister, from whom he was separated in his childhood since they were under the custody of different relatives. He says to the butterfly:

> Stay near me — do not take thy flight
> A little longer stay in sight
> Much converse do I find in thee,
> Historian of my infancy!
> Float near me; do not yet depart
> Dead times revive in thee
> Thou bring'st, gay creature as thou art!
> A solemn image to my heart,
> My father's family! (lines 1-9)

The reason why Wordsworth does not want the butterfly to fly away is that seeing the butterfly will remind him of his sister with whom he pleasantly chased and caught the butterfly. Wordsworth deems the butterfly as a historian, whose role is to study or write about things that happened in the past, as he himself puts it, "Dead times revive in thee" (6). The butterfly does not only remind Wordsworth of his sister, but also his father's household in Grasmere as a whole, including the orchard where they played and enjoyed themselves. So the butterfly serves as kind of spiritual pillar for Wordsworth in his emotional life, helping him to reminisce the happy childhood.

Another of Wordsworth's poem "The Green Linnet" (1802) first depicts a beautiful background, with "fruit-tree", "snow-white blossoms", "brightest sunshine", "unclouded weather", "sequestered nook" and "birds and flowers" (line 1, 2, 3, 4, 5, 7). No wonder Wordsworth exclaims "how sweet / To sit upon my orchard-seat!" (6-7).

Among all the birds, the happiest is the linnet who is "far above the rest / In joy of voice and pinion" (11-12), and is the "Presiding Spirit" who "Dost lead the revels of the May" (14, 15). In other words, the linnet is the leader in the boisterous celebrations of the woods.

> Scattering thy gladness without care,
>
> Too blest with anyone to pair;
>
> Thyself thy own enjoyment. (22-24)

That the linnet's happiness is matchless and unrivalled is reemphasized in the above excerpt. What the linnet does is not to keep happiness exclusive to himself, but to scatter his gladness among others and to make it contagious, affecting Wordsworth as well.

In the penultimate stanza, Wordsworth reiterates the happiness of the linnet who "perched in ecstasies" (27). And in the last stanza, he calls the bird "A Brother of the dancing leaves" (34), thus extending the spirit of fraternity among human beings to the animal world. The happiness of the bird is again shown when he "Pours forth his song in gushes" (36), producing "exulting strain" (37).

Much different from the aforementioned sinister cuckoo in Milton's nightingale-centered poem, Wordsworth's cuckoo in the poem "To the Cuckoo" (1827) is rather hailed and welcomed. Wordsworth calls the bird "BLITHE Newcomer" (line 1), which shows that the bird is happy, carefree and not anxious. The influence of the bird's happiness upon the poet is that "I hear thee and rejoice" and "Thou bringest unto me a tale / Of visionary hours." (2, 11-12). "The blithe bird of this poem is, after all, another manic recuperation" (Gannon 108). Wordsworth says to the bird:

> Thrice welcome, darling of the Spring!
>
> Even yet thou art to me
>
> No bird, but an invisible thing,
>
> A voice, a mystery; (13-16)

Anna Sue Parrill argues that "Like Shelley, both Keats and Wordsworth doubt that their inspired singers are real birds or inhabitants of this world" and "the cuckoo is an emissary from a spiritual realm" (49, 50). I would rather say that the bird itself is physical, but its influence is spiritual. Even though the bird is singing in a tree too far to be seen due to its elusive nature, the influence of its penetrating call still exists. The cuckoo is much loved by the spring season and is warmly welcomed by the poet. The unseen cuckoo signifies "a hope, a love" (23), an alleviator of people's grieved feelings.

Clare's "The Wren" (1835) is a sonnet about a bird less commonly seen than the above-mentioned nightingale and cuckoo. According to Johanne Clare, John Clare wrote a lot of poems with regard to "the plainest, most common, least praised objects of nature: wrens, blackbirds, weeds, common grass, mice, hedgehogs and badgers" (137-38). I'll quote the poem in full length as follows:

> Why is the cuckoo's melody preferred
> And nightingale's rich song so fondly praised
> In poets' rhymes? Is there no other bird
> Of nature's minstrelsy that oft hath raised
> One's heart to extacy and mirth as well?
> I judge not how another's taste is caught:
> With mine, there's other birds that bear the bell
> Whose song hath crowds of happy memories brought.
> Such the wood-robin singing in the dell
> And little wren that many a time hath sought
> Shelter from showers in huts where I did dwell
> In early spring the tenant of the plain
> Tenting my sheep and still they come to tell
> The happy stories of the past again.

Clare also says that the cuckoo and the nightingale are more frequently praised for their singing than other birds, including the wren, however, in his view, the wren, together with the robin, can also fill people's heart with ecstasy and happiness. The wren can bring back "happy memories" and "happy stories of the past" to people, and cheer them up. Therefore, we are not supposed to only favor the gaudy and gorgeous birds but discriminate against those less well-known and praise-worthy birds. This idea is identical to what is proposed in another of Clare's poem "The Progress of Ryhme", that is, "everything in nature and anything in human experience was worthy of a poet's interest" (Johanne Clare 138).

Stevenson's "My Heart, When First the Black-Bird Sings"[1] (1918) is a short poem of only twelve lines in three stanzas.

> MY heart, when first the blackbird sings,
> My heart drinks in the song:
> Cool pleasure fills my bosom through
> And spreads each nerve along.
>
> My bosom eddies quietly,
> My heart is stirred and cool
> As when a wind-moved briar sweeps
> A stone into a pool
>
> But unto thee, when thee I meet,
> My pulses thicken fast,
> As when the maddened lake grows black
> And ruffles in the blast.

The poem deals with the influence of the black-bird's singing on the poet. "My heart drinks in the song" makes use of the rhetorical device synaesthesia, since "drinks" is about the gustatory sense while "song" is related to auditory

---

[1] https://www.poemhunter.com/poem/my-heart-when-first-the-black-bird-sings-2/

sense. The pleasure of the bird is gulped down by the poet in the way of listening to its singing, and then the pleasure enters into his bosom and spreads to the nerves of his whole body. The maddened lake that grows black and the blast may symbolize the unpleasant mood of the poet, which is dispelled by the blackbird's singing.

Monro's "The Nightingale Near the House" (1920) is "one of the loveliest of his poems" (Untermeyer 145). It praises the nightingale's singing and its influence on Monro's sleeping. While the nightingale is singing in the tranquil night, things in nature are listening attentively, including the cypress tree, the taller trees, the moon and the stars. And the song of the nightingale flows "From lawn to lawn down terraces of sound" and it is penetrating and swift like "white arrows" (line 6, 7). Comparatively speaking, the nightingale's singing has more effect on the poet than on the things in nature.

> My dreams are flowers to which you are a bee
> As all night long I listen, and my brain
> Receives your song, then loses it again
> In moonlight on the lawn.
>
> Now is your voice a marble high and white,
> Then like a mist on fields of paradise,
> Now is a raging fire, then is like ice,
> Then breaks, and it is dawn. (8-16)

Monro uses a metaphor to show the influence of the nightingale's singing on his dream, that is, the nightingale makes his dream become sweet, just like a bee who gathers honey from the flowers. But the poet is half asleep and half awoken, and so he sometimes can hear the singing and sometimes cannot. When he is awoken, the nightingale's voice is like a "marble high and white", which is a kind of favorite decorative stone used in sculpture and architecture, and a cultural symbol of refined taste, and the association between the tenor and the vehicle can be easily formed. When he is asleep, the nightingale's voice is like a "mist on fields of paradise"; mist is something that make things less visible or unclear, which just shows the vagueness of the nightingale's singing to somebody who is sleeping. However, though it is vague, it is still sweet, as is shown in the word "paradise". In the above-mentioned two metaphors, the rhetorical device of synaesthesia is also employed, since "voice" is related to the sense of hearing, while "marble" and "mist" are related to the sense of sight. In the penultimate line, "raging fire" and "ice" form an antithesis; the former signifies passion and energy while the latter signifies coolness and calmness, which reemphasizes the influence of the nightingale's singing when the poet is in different states of wakefulness and sleep. Accordingly, we can see the entertaining and soothing role of the nightingale on the poet. As Preece proposes, "animals behave according to their God-given natures and are to be respected as such" (*Animals and Nature* 134).

II. Animals as Source of Wisdom

Animals can not only serve as stimulus to human beings' good mood, making them feel delighted, but can also be a source of wisdom, teaching them a lesson, leading them to epiphany, or helping them to have a better, deeper or more acute understanding of life. As Aristotle contends, "just as in man we find knowledge, wisdom and sagacity, so in certain animals there exists some other natural potentiality akin to these" (qtd. in Preece, *Animals and Nature* 65).

Let's first discuss some poems in which animals can be teachers of human beings to some extent, teaching them a lesson or something. In Shakespeare's *King Henry V* (near 1599), the archbishop of Canterbury says to King Henry V:

... for so work the honey-bees,

> Creatures that by a rule in nature teach
> The act of order to a peopled kingdom.
> They have a king and officers of sorts,
> Where some, like magistrates, correct at home,
> Others like merchants, venture trade abroad,
> Others, like soldiers, armed in their stings,
> Make boot upon the summer's velvet buds,
> Which pillage they with merry march bring home
> To the tent-royal of their emperor;
> Who, busied in his majesty, surveys
> The singing masons building roofs of gold,
> The civil citizens kneading up the honey,
> The poor mechanic porters crowding in
> Their heavy burdens at his narrow gate,
> The sad-eyed justice, with his surly hum,
> Delivering o'er to executors pale
> The lazy yawning drone. (1.2.190-207)

In Shakespeare's view, the honey-bees can teach human beings the act of order. There exist different strata and a clear division of labor among the bees. There is a king, together with various officers and common civil citizens. There are various occupations like magistrates, merchants, soldiers, masons, porters, justice (judge) and executors in the bee world. There are bees busy working, either building roofs or kneading up honey or carrying heavy burdens, however, there are also lazy drones who do not work at all, and therefore are punished according to law. Hence human beings can learn something from the bees in terms of the administration of the country and the management of the society.

At the beginning of the poem "The Snayl" (1659), Richard Lovelace (1617–1657) calls the snail "Wise Emblem of our Politick World" and "Sage

Chapter Three Animals' Functions in People's Mental Life

snail" (line 1, 2), both addresses signifying wisdom and sagacity. Why is the slow snail accredited with such a great recognition? The first reason is that by being "within thine own self curl'd" (2), it teaches people the way of survival in the circle of politics, that is, to withdraw from conflicts and keep oneself from incurring troubles. As Randolph L. Wadsworth puts it, "The lesson of the snail, then, is simply that disengagement is more comfortable than involvement" (753). The second reason is that the snail "Instruct me softly to make hast, / Whilst these my Feet go slowly fast" (3-4). What the snail teaches Lovelace is actually one famous proverb, that is, "haste makes waste", or in Wadsworth's view, its "proverbial tardiness is likewise connected with circumspection" (752), that is, being cautious and prudent in words and deeds. As "Large Euclid's strict epitome" (6), the snail's trail can be in varied geometrical forms, including point, ring, triangular, oval, square and serpentine, which means that he can adapt himself to the changes of the world, in other words, he can trim the sail of his ship to suit the wind. So to speak, he is good at "a roundabout course which masks intentions and avoids risks" (Wadsworth 754). So if politicians can learn something conducive from the snail, they can play safe in their political career.

In "The Spider"[①] by Jane Taylor (1783–1824), we see the response of a little girl Ann's encountering of a spider. She screams out of fear and brushes it away with her fan, calling it "great ugly spider" and "frightful black creature" (line 1, 3). Seeing what she has done, her mother begins to moralize her. First of all, the mother says "For after the fright, and the fall, and the pain, / It has much more occasion than you to complain" (7-8). In her view, the spider is more frightened and more justified to make a complaint than the girl since it is hurt by her brushing. It is more understandable for the spiders to fear human beings who are so powerful and can instantly "tread them to dust" (14). However, human

---

① https://www.poemhunter.com/poem/the-spider/

beings "have no cause for alarm" (15), because the spiders "could do us no harm" (16). The most important lesson for the girl to learn from the spider is:

> "Now look! it has got to its home; do you see
> What a delicate web it has spun in the tree?
> Why here, my dear Ann, is a lesson for you:
> Come learn from this spider what patience can do!
>
> And when at your business you're tempted to play,
> Recollect what you see in this insect to-day,
> Or else, to your shame, it may seem to be true,
> That a poor little spider is wiser than you." (17-24)

Patience is a good quality or life wisdom of the spider shown in his making of the delicate web, and it is what the girl is supposed to learn from the spider. Especially in the future when she is not persevering enough and is likely to be distracted in her study or work by something tempting, she can think of the spider and be patient. Otherwise, she will not be so wise and smart as a spider, which is shameful in her mother's opinion.

"What the Thrush Said. Lines From A Letter to John Hamilton Reynolds" (1818) by John Keats (1795–1821) is about "a singing bird as an embodiment of creativity and spontaneity who could give the poet advice on inspiration" (Doggett 555). The poem is written in the first person point of view with the thrush as its narrator, who is talking to human beings. The first man to be talked to is in a winter season and is confronted with "Winter's wind", "snow-clouds" and "freezing stars" (line 1, 2, 3), and the thrush says to him "To thee the spring will be a harvest-time" (4). The thrush is encouraging the man that the harsh winter will be followed by a warm spring, which is in accordance with Shelley's optimistic outlook in "Ode to the West Wind", i.e. "If spring comes, can spring be far behind?" (5.14) The second man is reading in the dark night "Of supreme

Chapter Three Animals' Functions in People's Mental Life

darkness" (6), and the thrush says to him "To thee the Spring shall be a triple morn" (8). The thrush is encouraging the man that the pitch-dark night will be followed by a bright dawn.

What's more important is that the thrush is telling human beings "fret not after knowledge" (9, 11). This reminds us of Keats' well-known poetic theory of "Negative Capability", which he explains in the letter to his two brothers George and Tom Keats on December 21, 1817, "that is when man is capable of being in uncertainties, Mysteries, doubts, without any irritable reaching after fact and reason" (*Selected Letters* 60). And this idea is reemphasized in the letter to John Hamilton Reynolds on February 19, 1818, in which Keats says:

> Let us not therefore go hurrying about and collecting honey-bee like, buzzing here and there impatiently from a knowledge of what is to be arrived at; but let us open our leaves like a flower and be passive and receptive, budding patiently under the eye of Apollo and taking hints from every noble insect that favors us with a visit. (*Selected Letters* 93)

So it is a capacity for accepting uncertainty and the unresolved. The thrush *per se* is following such a principle, yet its "song comes native with the warmth" and "the Evening listens" (9, 12). All in all, from the thrush's point of view, or the thrush serving as Keats' mouthpiece, "Negative Capability" is an advisable policy that human beings are supposed to adopt or pursue in their life.

"The Spider and the Fly" (1828) by Mary Howitt (1799–1888) is a fable-like poem which is about the process of a cunning spider's seduction of a fly into his web. The spider tells the fly that his parlor is "the prettiest little parlor that ever you did spy" (line 2), and what's more, his parlor has "many pretty things to show when you are there" (4), which is really very attractive. However, the fly is sober, knows the danger and resists the temptation. The spider then starts the second round of lure, by inviting the fly who night be weary and tired to sleep on his little bed, where "There are pretty curtains drawn around, the sheets are fine and thin" (9). Again the sober-minded fly rejects the proposal. The next bait the spider employs is the tasty and delicious food, his "pantry good store of all that's nice" (15). Once again the clear-headed fly refuses the offer. Finally, the spider plays his master card, flattery. He fawns on the fly: "You're witty and you're wise! / How handsome are your gauzy wings, how brilliant are your eyes!" (19-20). If the fly wants to see how handsome she is, she should go to the spider's house and use his looking-glass. Now the vainglorious fly becomes hesitant, and says she will come another day, but the spider is sure that "the silly fly would soon be back again" (26). So the next day, he starts his final round of temptation:

> Come hither, hither, pretty fly, with the pearl and silver wing:
>
> Your robes are green and purple; there's a crest upon your head;
>
> Your eyes are like the diamond bright, but mine are dull as lead. (30-32)

As a consequence, "this silly little fly" and "poor foolish thing" is enchanted and carried away by the spider's flattering words (33, 37). In other words, she is shot by the spider's sugar-coated bullet, falls victim to him and becomes his dish on the menu. The ending of the poem may serve as the moral of the fable:

> And now, dear little children, who may this story read,
>
> To idle, silly, flattering words, I pray you ne'er give heed;
>
> Unto an evil counselor close heart, and ear, and eye,
>
> And take a lesson from this tale of the Spider and the Fly. (41-44)

So what Howitt is trying to tell us through this animal poem is that we should stay sober-minded and cool-headed while facing various kinds of temptations, especially that of flattery, which sometimes is disastrous and devastating to us.

"The Meerkats of Africa" by Gavin Ewart (1916–1995) deals with a mongoose-like animal residing mainly in South Africa. One of the living habits of the meerkats is that they "go about in packs, / They don't hang loose" (lines 1-2), in other words, they do not separate from each other and they take actions

Chapter Three Animals' Functions in People's Mental Life

in a group, united as a whole. To be in detail,

> They rescue each other's children
>
> And have lookouts when they're feeding
>
> And a system of babysitters. (9-11)

They live on a mechanism of coordination and mutual aid, so as to protect themselves from stronger enemies. The meerkats' collaborative system of living and team spirit make Ewart think that there is something for human beings to learn from the meerkats, as he concludes the poem in the following way: "The kind of co-operation / That the human race is needing" (12-13).

Secondly, animals' natural behaviors can also lead human beings to a kind of sudden insight or understanding of something, that is, epiphany. "The Lark's Nest"[①] (1807) by Charlotte Smith (1749–1806) is based upon one of the Aesop's fables with the title of "The Lark and the Farmer" (sometimes entitled "The Crested Lark and the Farmer" or "The Lark and Her Young Ones"). The poem begins with a maxim "TRUST only to thyself" (line 1), the complete version of which is "Trust thyself only, and another shall not betray thee". At the end of the first stanza, Charlotte reemphasizes the idea by stating:

> ...that even kindred, cousin, uncle, brother,
>
> Has each perhaps to mind his own affair;
>
> Attend to thine then; lean not on another. (8-10)

Then in the following stanzas, Charlotte retells the story of the fable in a poetic way. Unlike most other birds who build their nests in a high place, either in a tree or under the eaves of a tall building, the larks build their nests on the ground, which makes it easy for them, especially their eggs or baby birds, to fall victim to bird catchers. In the poem, the lark couple first build their nest "in a spot by springing rye protected" (19). While the female lark is hatching the

---

① https://www.poemhunter.com/poem/the-lark-s-nest/

eggs, "little slept, and little ate" (26), the male lark only sings and flies happily in the sky without paying enough heed to his lover's labor and hunger. In order to get some food, the female lark has to leave the nest reluctantly, but when she comes back, to her grief and woe, she sees that a setter (a large hunting dog) "Had crush'd her half-existing young" (51).

  This part of the story seems to serve as the prelude to the second part of the story, that is, the moving of the homestead. However, another function of this part cannot be neglected, that is the male lark's insinuation of a type of men who fail to shoulder domestic responsibility, since the male lark in the poem turns out to be a husband "with a careless heart" (27), and the reason is "As is the custom of his sex" (28). This may hint at Charlotte's husband Benjamin Smith who is a drunkard and a gambler and is put into prison for debt, leaving his wife taking care of nine children all by herself. This surmise is not ungrounded, because according to Judith Phillips Stanton, the image of her husband reflected in her letters is a "self-centered and selfindulgent man" (*Collected Letters* XXI). As we can see, Charlotte is trying to show the similarity in character between human beings and animals, but as Jacqueline M. Labbe argues, "her method is not to bestialize men by presenting them as animals; rather, she humanizes the bird so that she may derive from this literal figuration the idea of types and the relationships between such types" (168).

  As the story goes, after the setback, the couple birds manage to build a new nest in a field of wheat, a relatively safer place, where another brood of their baby birds are born. This time, the lark parents "Watch'd and provided for the panting brood" with "tender care" (75, 73). And there is also a great change in the male lark who used to be "the vagrant of the air" (76). Now, in order to feed the baby birds, he "Explor'd each furrow, every sod for food" (79), while the mother lark labors to reinforce the nest with various kind of plants. Despite the reinforcement, "too much risk / The little household still were doom'd to run" (94-95), and the poetess cannot help worrying "who against all evils can provide?" (91). The evils or the possible risks may include

> The reaper's foot might crush, or reaper's dog might trace,
> Or village child, too young to reap or bind,
> Loitering around, her hidden treasure find; (106-08)

Therefore, what the parent larks have to do is to move their babies away (if they still cannot fly) before the farmer begins to reap the wheat. When the mother lark gets to know that the farmer's neighbors are coming to help reap the wheat, she is not worried at all. When she gets to know that the farmer's relatives are coming to offer help, she is still not worried. But when she hears the farmer says to his son "try what we can do with it ourselves" (139), she knows that she cannot delay to move the house any more, because she thinks "What a man undertakes himself is done" (141). Charlotte deems that the mother lark is "a bird of observation" (142) and she ends the poem by concluding "that none / [...] / Is very likely to succeed, / Who manages affairs by deputation" (143, 148-49), which is in accordance with the moral of the fable, that is, "self-help is the best help" (Aesop 175). Therefore, the story of the birds may help human beings to have an epiphany, since they resemble each other in various ways. As Charlotte's biographer Loraine Fletcher argues, "Her [Charlotte's] recognition of close resemblance across species is Darwinian" (336).

"Ode on the Death of a Favourite Cat Drowned in a Tub of Gold Fishes" (1747) by Thomas Gray (1716–1771) mourns for the tragic death of a pet cat named Selima owned by Horace Walpole, one of the poet's good friends. The accidental death of the cat who attempts to catch the fish in the tub reminds us of the English proverb "curiosity killed the cat". The cat's miserable struggling scene in the tub is portrayed as follows:

> Eight times emerging from the flood
> She mew'd to ev'ry wat'ry god,

> Some speedy aid to send.
>
> No Dolphin came, no Nereid stirr'd;
>
> Nor cruel Tom, nor Susan heard.
>
> A Fav'rite has no friend! (lines 31-36)

We can see that the cat tries many times in order to survive. She puts up a last-ditch struggle and screams hysterically for help, but pitifully no one comes to her rescue, not the Dolphin, who is "in Greek legend, one rescued Arion from the sea" (McGowan 389), not the Nereids, who are referred to as sea nymphs or spirits with supernatural abilities, not even the servant and maid of the household, who are just absent when the accident happens. Even though a cat is believed to have nine lives in folklore, Gray's cat fails to have a narrow escape from the disaster and ends her life in a pathetic way. In addition to showing great sympathy and sorrow to the cat, Gray also does some meditation on this event.

> From hence, ye Beauties, undeceiv'd,
>
> Know, one false step is ne'er retriev'd,
>
> And be with caution bold.
>
> Not all that tempts your wand'ring eyes
>
> And heedless hearts is lawful prize,
>
> Nor all, that glisters, gold. (37-42)

The cat's tragedy may serve as an alarm bell for people in general, that is, a wrong action may be fatal and the damage may be irreversible, so we must be very cautious, discreet and heedful while making decisions or doing things. When confronted with temptations, we are supposed to stay sober and composed, and resist the lures, instead of succumbing to them, because not all that glitters is gold. Since the cat is not Gray's own pet, we may find that it is more of a matter-of-fact description of the cat's death rather than one with much affection or compassion. No wonder the poem arouses an attack from Gray's contemporary poet Samuel Johnson (1709–1784), who is an affectionate cat

Chapter Three Animals' Functions in People's Mental Life

lover, for the "callousness it reveals to feline suffering" (Rogers 89). Given that this is a required composition, it is understandable for Gray to focus more on drawing a universal lesson from the tragic incident. "And its moral seeks to move beyond the specific instance of one real cat into the realm of human, as well as animal, experience" (Tague 289).

Cowper's "Epitaph on Fop, A Dog Belonging to Lady Throckmorton" (1792) is a ten-line short poem.

> Though once a puppy, and though Fop by name,
> Here moulders one whose bones some honour claim;
> No sycophant, although of spaniel race,
> And though no hound, a martyr to the chase.
> Ye squirrels, rabbits, leverets, rejoice!
> Your haunts no longer echo to his voice;
> This record of his fate exulting view,
> He died worn out with vain pursuit of you.
> 'Yes' — the indignant shade of Fop replies —
> 'And worn with vain pursuit man also dies.'

The poem is written in memory of a deceased dog named Fop. He belongs to the spaniel type of dog, one of the characteristics of whom is being good at pleasing its masters, but his pleasing does not go to the degree of sycophancy or flattery. Though the dog is not a professional hunting dog, he sacrifices himself to the vain pursuit of the hunted animals. So the poet thinks in the shoes of the hunted animals, deeming them taking delight in the misfortune of the dog, who will not threaten their lives any more. The ending of the poem is very meaningful, as the ghost of the dog said angrily, "worn with vain pursuit man also dies". It dawns upon Cowper that people should be on guard against vainglorious pursuits in their life, which is lethal to them, just like the dog who has died of the vain pursuit of small wild animals.

In Burns's "Address to the Woodlark" (1795), he requests the woodlark to stay instead of flying away, because he, as a lover, is fond of the bird's songs, its "soothing fond complaining" (line 4). "[S]oothing fond complaining" makes use of the rhetorical device of oxymoron, in which two words with complimentary or positive meaning modify a word with derogatory or negative meaning. So to speak, though to the bird its singing is like a kind of complaining, to the poet it has certain comforting or relieving function. He thinks that the bird's "melting art" will have some effect on his lover and "would touch her heart" (6, 7). Just as Simons puts it, "the poet listens to the song of the woodlark and tries to catch in it an 'art' which will enable him to win over his lover" (89).

Keats' "Ode" (1818) addresses the nightingale as "Bards of Passion and of Mirth" (line 1), who is considered as a poet of strong feelings and happiness and who has two souls, one is in heaven, the other is on earth. In heaven,

> Where the nightingale doth sing
>
> Not a senseless, tranced thing,
>
> But divine melodious truth;
>
> Philosophic numbers smooth;
>
> Tales and golden histories
>
> Of heaven and its mysteries. (17-22)

As we can see, the nightingale sings about truth, philosophy, stories, histories and mysteries of heaven, all of which are dignified, advanced and sophisticated things. As Helen Vendler puts it, "the heavenly nightingale wonderfully adds propositional or philosophical truth to its truth of tale or history" (103). While on earth,

> Here, your earth-born souls still speak
>
> To mortals, of their little week;
>
> Of their sorrows and delights;
>
> Of their passions and their spites;

Chapter Three Animals' Functions in People's Mental Life

Of their glory and their shame;

What doth strengthen and what maim.

Thus ye teach us, every day,

Wisdom, though fled far away. (29-36)

What the nightingale sings on earth are more down-to-earth and balanced, dealing with four pairs of quasi binary oppositions including sorrow and delight, passions and spites, glory and shame, as well as strength and damage. Like a teacher, the nightingale is instructing some wisdom to human beings. The wisdom might be that real life is composed of both positive elements and negative ones. While being engaged in some noble pursuits, we are supposed to make a balance between the pros and cons in life, and achieve a kind of equilibrium, just like the nightingale with two souls, symbolizing "the double immortality of Poets" (*Selected Letters* 233).

One of Keats' most anthologized poems, "Ode to a Nightingale" (1819), starts with a negative image of himself, someone with aching heart, numb sense, and forthcoming forgetfulness. However, these unfavorable states of mind, according to the poet, are not due to the envy of the happy situation of the nightingale, who is addressed as the "light-winged Dryad of the tree" (line 7), but because of "being too happy in thy happiness" (6), which is in agreement with the saying "extreme joy begets sorrow" or "too great pleasure will bring about sadness". But the nightingale's happiness is natural and "her art is one of happy spontaneity, coming as naturally as leaves to a tree" (Vendler 70), while Keats' happiness is affected. He would like to drink some wine and get drunk, so that he can "leave the world unseen" and "Fade far away, dissolve, and quite forget / [...] / The weariness, the fever, and the fret" (19, 21, 23), so to speak, to dispel melancholy by means of drinking. Having no wings, he wishes that he could fly to the happy nightingale "on the viewless wings of Poesy" (33). By joining the nightingale in spirit, Keats achieves temporary mental withdrawal from the earthly world, obtaining some ephemeral relief.

Keats confesses that he has been "half in love with easeful Death" (52), one of the ways of which is "To cease upon the midnight with no pain" (56), and at this moment, when the nightingale is singing "In such an ecstasy" (58), he thinks "more than ever seems it rich to die" (55). As Harold Bloom argues, "The *Ode to a Nightingale* is the first poem to know and declare, wholeheartedly, that death is the mother of beauty" (7). And this may remind us of the ending line of Keats' "Bright Star", "And so live ever — or else swoon to death" (line 14), which shows that it is happy and rich to die while lying upon the breast of one's lover. But finally in the nightingale poem, Keats experiences an epiphany and realizes what comes to his mind is not true since he is at the mercy of illusion or fantasy, so he says to the nightingale that he will come "back from thee to my sole self" (82), because he thinks that "the fancy cannot cheat so well" (83). At the end of the poem, he questions himself, or the readers, or the nightingale *per se*, "Was it a vision, or a waking dream? / Fled is that music: — do I wake or sleep?" (89-90). This is one more employment of Keats' poetic concept of "Negative Capability" mentioned above.

Finally, animals can also help human beings to have a better, deeper or more acute understanding of something in their life. Judging either from the title of Wordsworth's "O Nightingale! Thou Surely Art" (1807), or from the first half of the poem, it is very likely for the readers to draw a hasty conclusion that this poem is another Romantic nightingale-centered poem. At the beginning of the poem, Wordsworth calls the nightingale "A creature of a 'fiery heart'" (line 2), which is supposed to possess strong passions. The singing of the bird has a penetrating quality and the notes "pierce and pierce" (3), from which we can perceive "Tumultuous harmony and fierce!" (4). Though the nightingale is singing of love, it is "A song in mockery" (7), and it seems that the nightingale shows contempt to other lovers in the world.

Chapter Three Animals' Functions in People's Mental Life

Then the poem transfers to what Wordsworth really values, the stock-dove's singing.

Although the dove's singing is about a "homely tale" (12), not so impressive as the nightingale's song of Valentine with the help of "the God of wine" (5), and although the dove's voice is "buried among trees" (13), not so penetrating as the nightingale's shrill notes, he does not stop cooing and does not give up wooing, and his singing is a combination of "serious faith, and inward glee" (19). Wordsworth concludes the poem by giving his view candidly, "That was the song — the song for me! " (20). So it is not the nightingale's song but the dove's song that attracts him, impresses him more and wins his heart. As Pinion puts it, Wordsworth's "preference for the quieter and more steadfast virtues of the stockdove is characteristic" (*Wordsworth Companion* 171). Thus we can see that two kinds of birds in nature help the poet as well as the readers to know better what kind of virtue we are supposed to value in animals and men alike.

In Mrs. Browning's "Bianca among the Nightingales" (1862), the nightingales' singing tortures the female speaker Bianca by reminding her that her treacherous lover has deserted her and left for another woman, because when her lover made a vow by saying "Sweet, above / God's Ever guarantees this Now" (3.3-4), the nightingales' simultaneous penetrating singing seems to foreshadow the tragic ending,

> ... through his words the nightingales
> Drove straight and full their long clear call
> Like arrows through heroic mails,
> And love was awful in it all. (3.5-8)

The nightingales keep on singing despite the separation between the speaker and her lover, hence the speaker complains, "The nightingales sing through my head" and "These nightingales will sing me mad!" (5.8; 6.8). The poem concludes:

> Giulio, my Giulio! — sing they so,
> And you be silent? Do I speak,
> And you not hear? An arm you throw
> Round someone, and I feel so weak?
> — Oh, owl-like birds! They sing for spite,
> They sing for hate, they sing for doom,
> They'll sing through death who sing through night,
> They'll sing and stun me in the tomb —
> The nightingales, the nightingales! (16.1-9)

As far as the deserted and depressed Bianca is concerned, the nightingales sing for spite, hate and doom, all of which are negative things. "The chorus of nightingales functions like that of a Greek tragedy, voicing the constraints of accepted meanings as a counterpoint to the speaker's desperate utterance" (J. Williams 145). The nightingales' singing will always haunt Bianca, and it will even have posthumous influence on her after her death. Taking the nightingales as her mouthpiece, Bianca is trying to say that she will never forget her lover's unfaithfulness and betrayal.

"The Owl" (1915) is one of the most anthologized poems by Edward Thomas (1878–1917). Nearly half of the four-stanza poem serves as the setting, in which we see the hungry, cold and tired poet comes to an inn where he has "food, fire, and rest" (line 5). At night, he hears "An owl's cry, a most melancholy cry" (8), which is

> No merry note, nor cause of merriment,
> But one telling me plain what I escaped
> And others could not, that night, as in I went.
>
> And salted was my food, and my repose,

Chapter Three Animals' Functions in People's Mental Life

> Salted and sobered too, by the bird's voice
> Speaking for all who lay under the stars,
> Soldiers and poor, unable to rejoice. (10-16)

The melancholy cry of the owl reminds the poet of those who are not happy because they have to suffer from hunger, coldness and tiredness, such as the soldiers in the war and the poor people, who cannot enjoy their repose with a full stomach in a warm and cosy room like him. So it is the owl that functions as an enlightenment. Gerald Roberts thinks that "Thomas speaks on behalf not just of soldiers, but of all the suffering" and that is why he considers the poem as a "'prayer' for the dying and lonely inspired by Nature" (66), with the owl as her representative. The idea shown in this poem is identical to what Thomas argues in his essay "Studying Nature" (1909), that is, "Knowledge aids joy by discipline, by increasing the sphere of enjoyment, by showing us in animals, in plants, for example, what life is, how our own is related to theirs, showing us, in fact, our position, responsibilities and debts among the other inhabitants of the earth" (*Green Studies Reader* 67-68).

Lawrence's "A Doe At Evening" (1917) deals with the poet's encounter with a doe. Lawrence's travelling through the marshes startles a doe in the corn field who runs up the hill. She is so frightened that she even abandons her young deer. She stands at the hillside, watching Lawrence as he is looking at her. In her eyes, the poet "became a strange being" (line 11). So Lawrence cannot help raising several questions to himself:

> Ah yes, being male, is not my head hard-balanced, antlered?
> Are not my haunches light?
> Has she not fled on the same wind with me?
> Does not my fear cover her fear? (17-20)

This series of rhetorical questions are actually more emphatic than statements. What Lawrence means is that, in face of danger, human beings will be like the doe, and we will run away immediately and quickly, gripped by fear. Thus the doe exchanges some eye contact with Lawrence, hesitates a little bit and then finally decides to run away, which makes Lawrence sink into meditation on the mentality of living creatures confronted with danger. Just as Jessie Chambers writes in her *Memoir* that "a living vibration passed between" Lawrence and "wild things" (qtd. in Pinto 135).

III. Animals as Evoker of Empathy

There are times when the state or condition which the animals are in will evoke empathy or arouse the same feeling in human beings, who will look at things in the animals' shoes and are able to understand or share the animals' experiences, feelings and emotions. In some animal poems, we can see animals as evoker of man's empathy.

The nightingale in Charlotte's "Sonnet III: To A Nightingale"[①] (1784) is a "melancholy bird" that tells a "tale of tender woe" with "mournful melody" (line 1, 2, 4), which inevitably makes us think of the mythological figure Philomel. And all the three words with negative meaning — "melancholy", "woe", and "mournful" — denote sadness. No wonder Charlotte says the nightingale is a member of "Pale Sorrow's victims" (9). She then asks the bird about the reason why she is so sad. Is it because she has "felt from friends some cruel wrong" or she has become a "martyr of disastrous love"? (11, 12). Whatever the reason, one thing is for sure, that is, the nightingale is a "songstress sad" (13). The bird's fate reminds the poet of her own tragic fate, so she concludes the poem with the line "To sigh and sing at liberty — like thee!" (14). As Fletcher puts it, she "reverts solipsistically to her own suffering, looking back at the past with regret" (50). As

---

① https://www.poemhunter.com/poem/sonnet-iii-to-a-nightingale/

Chapter Three Animals' Functions in People's Mental Life

a wife whose husband is in prison for debt and as a mother who has to support nine kids all by herself, with the heavy burden upon her fragile shoulders, she is very likely to be melancholic, woeful and mournful as the gloomy nightingale with certain "sad cause" (3). In this case, Charlotte and the bird become fellow sufferers in life, who are supposed to commiserate with each other.

In another poem "Sonnet VII: On the Departure of the Nightingale" (1786), Charlotte says farewell to the migrant nightingale. At the end of the sonnet, she hails the nightingale as:

> The gentle bird, who sings of pity best:
>
> For still thy voice shall soft affections move,
>
> And still be dear to sorrow, and to love! (lines 12-14)

She reiterates the idea that the nightingale is a bird of pity and sorrow, conveying sadness as well as love to its listeners. Bidding adieu to the bird, she looks forward to its annual return to the old residence, continuing to be her intimate and empathetic partner or companion.

In the last poem of Charlotte's trilogy of nightingale sonnets, "Sonnet LV: The Return of the Nightingale" (1791), the selfsame idea is reemphasized as follows:

> And bade thee welcome to our shades again,
>
> To charm the wandering poet's pensive way
>
> And soothe the solitary lover's pain;
>
> But now! — such evils in my lot combine,
>
> As shut my languid sense — to Hope's dear voice and thine! (lines 10-14)

Charlotte depends on the nightingale for spiritual consolation or mental support. The nightingale's singing can diminish the poetess's sadness and alleviate her painful solitude, on the ground that there is mutual understanding and resonance between her and the nightingale.

In Blake's "The Fly" (1794), the narrator is talking to the fly:

> Little Fly,
>
> Thy summer's play
>
> My thoughtless hand
>
> Has brushed away.
>
> Am not I
>
> A fly like thee?
>
> Or art not thou
>
> A man like me?
>
> For I dance
>
> And drink, and sing,
>
> Till some blind hand
>
> Shall brush my wing. (lines 1-12)

In the first stanza, the narrator seems to be apologizing regretfully to the fly for his inconsiderate and careless driving away of the insect. In the phrase "thoughtless hand", there is a use of the rhetorical device of transferred epithet, which means that it is not the hand that is thoughtless, but the narrator he himself is thoughtless.

Then the narrator puts forward the question as regards the similarity between himself and the fly. The reason why the narrator makes such a comparison is that human beings sometimes are as fragile as the small fly, especially when they are at the mercy of "some blind hand". The "blind hand" is very symbolic, as it may stand for some misfortunes or disastrous accidents in life, the "Hap" in Hardy's concept, or even the God of Death, or any immortal god who has supernatural powers. This may remind us of words said by Gloster in Shakespeare's *King Lear* (1605–1606): "As flies to wanton boys, are we to the gods, — /

Chapter Three Animals' Functions in People's Mental Life

They kill us for their sport" (4.1.38-39). Therefore, the narrator suggests to us that before we are brushed away by some unexpected, uncontrollable and unfathomable force, we are supposed to "dance / And drink, and sing", in other words, we should enjoy ourselves, following the epicurean principle of *carpe diem*. Blake concludes the poem as follows:

>Then am I
>
>A happy fly,
>
>If I live,
>
>Or if I die. (17-20)

If we adopt the right life attitude, we can always be happy as the carefree fly is, no matter we are alive or we cease to be. In Charles Gardner's view, Blake is influenced by the Swedish philosopher Emanuel Swedenborg, "To see humanity in a fly is Swedenborgian" (70), the main concept of which is the salvation of human soul is reliant not only on God's grace but also on human endeavor.

In Wordsworth's *The Prelude* (1799–1805), he depicts to us a scene of a hunger-bitten girl with a heifer on a country lane in France.

>... mixed with pity too
>
>And love; for where hope is, there love will be
>
>For the abject multitude. And when we chanced
>
>One day to meet a hunger-bitten girl.
>
>Who crept along fitting her languid gait
>
>Unto a heifer's motion, by a cord
>
>Tied to her arm, and picking thus from the lane
>
>Its sustenance, while the girl with pallid hands
>
>Was busy knitting in a heartless mood
>
>Of solitude, and at the sight my friend
>
>In agitation said, "'T is against that
>
>That we are fighting," I with him believed

A Study of British Animal Poems

> That a benignant spirit was abroad
>
> Which might not be withstood, that poverty
>
> Abject as this would in a little time
>
> Be found no more, that we should see the earth
>
> Unthwarted in her wish to recompense
>
> The meek, the lowly, patient child of toil. (Book IX, lines 507-24)

In a state of abject poverty, both the girl and the young female cow suffer a lot. The girl is too hungry to walk normally; she walks very slowly, and her manner of walking is listless, dispirited and lackadaisical. The cow also walks slowly, looking for possible edibles by the roadside to relieve her hunger. The miserable living condition of the girl and the cow arouses the anxiety and sympathy of Wordsworth and his friend, who wish that such dire poverty would exist no more in the near future, so that human beings and animals would no longer undergo impoverishment and suffer so much in their life.

Clare's "Vixen"[①] (1835–1837) deals with the turbulent life of foxes in the woods. The vixen, the fox mother, is a very responsible mother. She plays with her kids, and what's more important is that she safeguards them and ensures their security, since their life is "from danger never free" (line 6). In order to bluff and bluster or warn her kids of the potential danger, "She snuffs and barks if any passes by" (3). If a horseman gallops by, she is so cautious that she "bolts to see" (5). The reason why she is so alert is that the man on the horseback might be the fox-hunter, since according to what Roy Porter states in *English Society in the Eighteenth Century*, "fox-hunting as we know it was a Georgian invention, with horses bred specially for speed and jumping, and packs of hounds for scent" (237). If anybody stops, she "barks and snaps and drive them in the holes" (8). The shepherd and the boy try to get them out of the hole with a

---

① https://www.poemhunter.com/poem/the-vixen/

Chapter Three Animals' Functions in People's Mental Life

stick and catch them, but in vain. When it is secure, they go out again, and try to catch the blackbirds and the butterfly. The affectionate and protective fox mother may remind us of our own mother who protects us from harm and danger when we are kids. Supposing we are empathetic enough, we will neither injure the fox mother nor the baby foxes, because if the mother is hurt, the babies will be lack of love and care, and if the babies are hurt, the mother will feel worried and brokenhearted.

Seeing the birds flying high happily in the sunny sky, the boys in Clare's "The Skylark" (1835) begin to imagine and meditate as follows:

...Had they the wing

Like such a bird, themselves would be too proud

And build on nothing but a passing cloud

As free from danger as the heavens are free

From pain and toil — there would they build and be

And sail about the world to scenes unheard

Of and unseen — O were they but a bird — (lines 20-26)

The boys' wish is that they could have wings and fly freely like the bird. As children, say the school boys portrayed by Jaques in Shakespeare's *As You Like It* (1599–1600), "Then the whining school-boy, with his satchel / And shining morning face, creeping like snail / Unwillingly to school" (2.7.148-50), what they long for is freedom, freedom from danger, pain and toil. As is proposed by Robert Lynd, "To Clare the skylark was most wonderful as a thing seen and noticed: it was the end, not the beginning, of wonders" (341). That's why the skylarks evoke empathy in the boys who dream to become them.

Janet Hamilton (1795–1873) first praises the skylark in her "The Skylark — Caged And Free"[①] (1868) as "Sweet minstrel of the summer dawn" and "Bard of

---

[①] https://www.poemhunter.com/poem/the-skylark-caged-and-free/

the sky" (line 1, 2), that is, a singer or a poet, whose singing is "rapturous", "clear and loud" (3), which shows extreme happiness, pleasure or enthusiasm. She goes on saying that the skylark is "Dame Nature's first and fairest born" (6). What we see in stanza one is a bird of freedom, who flies high "in morning glories of the sky" (14). In the second stanza, the bird is unfortunately caged, however, it still sings blithely and joyously, and its singing is "full and clear / As silver lute" (27-28). It is "void of sorrow" (29), just as when it is free. The bird's attitude towards imprisonment makes the poetess feel deeply moved, and she calls the bird "Sweet captive" (45), which is the use of oxymoron to show the special condition of the bird. The bird's optimistic stand influences the poetess so that she says if she is in the same fate as the bird, she "will not languish — will not pine" (46). She wishes that her song and the bird's song could be blended. They both can fly high in a symbolic way; the bird in its prison cage can fly to its "own blue sky" (67), while the poetess, in her hermitage life can fly to a "loftier sphere on high" (68). As Kirstie Blair argues, "Hamilton perceives herself as more in tune with the 'prison song' of the captured lark than the free bird in nature" (536).

Chapter Four   Criticism Against the Cruelty to Animals

Even though human beings generally love animals and are kind to them, there are also some people who are cruel, merciless and ruthless to animals, which have aroused poets' criticism of this phenomenon. In this chapter, criticism against the cruelty to animals in British poetry is discussed from five aspects. The first four sections are about the abuse of animals in different fields, including animals with bondage, performing or racing animals, hunted animals and ordinary animals, showing the pain, distress and suffering of these animals and criticizing human beings' unkindness and brutality in the treatment of animals. The last section deals with the theme of Nemesis, analyzing how supernaturally animals will revenge on human beings who have ill-treated animals.

I. Pain of Animals with Bondage

The caging of animals has a long history, which can be traced back to Ancient Greece. In the engraving of an Ancient Greek vase of 490 B.C., there is a small boy with a rabbit and a cage. For human beings' entertainment or private interests, some animals are held in bondage, such as in cages, in pens, or in some other narrow, confined spaces, and as a result, their freedom to move at liberty is snatched away from them, and they are deprived of their natural instincts to some extent. The suffering of the caged animals arouses poets' sympathy and indignation and many related poems are composed. The large majority of the animal poems discussed in this section will be about shackled or caged birds, with only one exception about a caged lion.

As early as the Renaissance period, in Shakespeare's famous tragedy *Romeo and Juliet* (1595), there is a conversation between Romeo and Juliet that goes as follows:

> Juliet:
>
> 'Tis almost morning. I would have thee gone:
>
> And yet no farther than a wanton's bird;
>
> That lets it hop a little from his hand,
>
> Like a poor prisoner in his twisted gyves,
>
> And with a silk thread plucks it back again,
>
> So loving jealous of his liberty.
>
> Romeo:
>
> I would I were thy bird.
>
> Juliet:
>
> Sweet, so would I.
>
> Yet I should kill thee with much cherishing. (2.2.177-85)

Juliet mentions a bird in gyves, i.e. in handcuffs or shackles, here made of silk thread, so the bird has lost his liberty. Even though Shakespeare uses the imprisoned bird as a simile to mean that Juliet would like to be possessive about her love toward Romeo and make him like a captive animal under her control, his revelation of the miserable state of caged birds' imprisonment is clear. Shakespeare uses Juliet as his mouthpiece to utter the view that too much cherishing and control will kill the bird, symbolizing that possessive love without freedom is suffocating to the loved one. Similarly, old Lear in Shakespeare's *King Lear* also compares his state to that of caged birds in his talk to Cordelia, "Come, let's away to prison; / We two alone will sing like birds i'

Chapter Four Criticism Against the Cruelty to Animals

the cage" (6.3.9-10).

Cowper's "On A Goldfinch, Starved to Death in His Cage" (1782) is written in a way of contrast, that is, the life of the goldfinch before and after being caged. Before the bird is caught and caged, he was "free as air" (line 1). He lived on things from nature, feeding on "thistle's downy seed" and drinking "the morning dew" (2, 3); he took a rest on any twig of his own free will. The phrase "my plumage gay" makes use of the rhetorical device of transferred epithet, since it is not the bird's plume is happy but the bird himself is happy. Owing to his freedom and happiness, the bird gave out "strains for ever new" (6).

However, after the bird is caged, things change drastically. The bird makes a complaint against his tragic fate: "starved to death, / In dying sighs my little breath / Soon pass'd the wiry grate" (10-12). Ironically, the bird does not hate death but shows his gratitude to death instead, because it is death that puts an end to all his woes and "cure of every ill" (15). With the coming of death, "More cruelty could none express" (16), and there will be no more suffering for the imprisoned bird.

Cowper's "On the Death of Mrs. (Now Lady) Throckmorton's Bullfinch" (1789) deals with the story of a caged bullfinch being killed and eaten by a rat. The bullfinch is named Bully, and is the favorite bird of Maria. Maria has thought of the safety of the bird, so that "No cat had leave to dwell" (21), since the cat is one of the bird's natural enemies. Despite that, she still makes a silly mistake in that she buys a cage whose grate is not made of rough steel or brass, but wood, which makes it possible for the rat with strong teeth to gnaw through the grate, enter into the cage and victimize the bird. At this point, the name of the bird "Bully" seems to be kind of ironic, because he is not the one to bully but instead is cruelly bullied by the rat. However, the rat is not to blame, since it is the natural instinct of a starving animal to prey on smaller animals for food. At the end of the poem, we see "Maria weeps, — the Muses mourn" (61), but it is futile and in vain. After all, Maria is also not so much to blame as the long-standing practice of caging birds, which is the root cause of the tragedy.

The Romantic poet Keats' "Song. I Had A Dove" (1818) is a short ten-line poem, which I'll quote in full length:

> I had a dove, and the sweet dove died;
>
> And I have thought it died of grieving:
>
> O, what could it grieve for? its feet were tied
>
> With a single thread of my own hand's weaving;
>
> Sweet little red feet, why should you die —
>
> Why should you leave me, sweet bird, why?
>
> You lived alone in the forest tree,
>
> Why, pretty thing! Would you not live with me?
>
> I kiss'd you oft and gave you white peas;
>
> Why not live sweetly, as in the green trees?

The whole poem is full of the bird owner's questioning of the bird one after another, "what could it grieve for?", "why should you die", "Why should you leave me, sweet bird, why?", "Would you not live with me? " and "Why not live sweetly, as in the green trees?". The bird owner experiences limited epiphany, which means he only comes to know that the bird dies not of starvation or other physical reasons, but of grieving, nevertheless, it is a pity that he fails to know what kind of grief leads to the death of the bird. Actually, the readers can easily sense that what the chained dove grieves for is its lost freedom, so that it can not live sweetly as in the green trees, even though its owner loves it and feeds it well. In other words, we human beings are doing harm to animals unawares and unconsciously.

"The Lark in London" by Gerald Massey (1828–1907) deals with a lark who is "Captured and blinded" and whose "nest-mate and his younglings all are dead" (line 2, 3). The reason for the death of his mate and babies is that their

Chapter Four Criticism Against the Cruelty to Animals

feathers are used to make hats "on some foolish head" (4). Here the rhetorical device of transferred epithet is used, since it is not the head that is foolish, but those people who make, sell, buy and wear such hats are foolish. Despite the lark's misery, he is still "singing in the dark" "Of some lost Paradise" (2, 5). His present imprisoned life forms a stark contrast with his past paradise-like life:

> Wide field of morning, woods and waterfall:
> A world of boundless freedom over all.
> He sings that great glory far away;
> He sings his fervid life out, day by day; (7-10)

The words "wide", "boundless", "great glory" and "fervid" contrast sharply with the small, cramped cage and his blinded dark life. Nevertheless, the lark still sings, "Trying to make a little heaven here / For others, he who has lost his own, poor dear!" (17-18). We can see that the lark is very unselfish or altruistic, since he tries to make his listeners entertained regardless of his own agony, which is rather ironic.

Criticism against the cruelty to animals did not reach its peak until the nineteenth and twentieth century, during which people witnessed an explosion of interest in animal protection in Britain.

First of all, some related organizations were founded, such as Victoria Street Society for the Protection of Animals from Vivisection (1875), The Humanitarian League (1891), and British Union for the Abolition of Vivisection (1898). What needs to be particularly mentioned is that in 1824, with the help of Richard Martin MP (1754–1834), William Wilberforce MP (1759–1833) and the Reverend Arthur Broome (1779–1837) and some other Members of Parliament, the pioneering Society for the Prevention of Cruelty to Animals was founded, which is the first of its kind in the world, and it later became the Royal Society for the Prevention of Cruelty to Animals (RSPCA) in 1840 after being granted a royal charter by Queen Victoria. It is now the oldest and largest animal welfare organization in the world.

Secondly, some related laws were enacted, including "Treatment of Cattle Act" (1822), "Bill to Prevent the Cruel and Improper Treatment of Dogs" (1824), "Warburton Anatomy Act" (1832), "Cruelty to Animals Act" (1835, 1849, 1950, 1854, 1876), and "Wild Birds Protection Act" (1880, 1881, 1894, 1896, 1902). What needs to be particularly mentioned is that in 1822, with the effort of Richard Martin, the world's first major animal protection legislation, "Ill Treatment of Horses and Cattle Bill" or "Martin's Act", was enacted and was later given royal assent as "An Act to Prevent the Cruel and Improper Treatment of Cattle". To push things forward, the first British "Cruelty to Animals Act" in 1835 aims to protect bulls, dogs, bears and sheep, and to prohibit bear-baiting and cockfighting.

Thirdly, many books concerning animal rights were published, among others *Moral Inquiries on the Situation of Man and of Brutes* (1824) by Lewis Gompertz (1783/4-1861) and *Animals' Rights: Considered in Relation to Social Progress* (1894) by Henry Salt (1851–1939). What needs to be particularly mentioned is *Rights of an Animal* (1879) by Edward Nicholson (1849–1912), who argued that animals have the same natural right to life and liberty as human beings do.

Finally, animal rights are advocated by some philosophers, biologists, and ethicists. The British philosopher John Stuart Mill (1806–1873) endorsed animal rights by arguing "Granted that any practice causes more pain to animals than it gives pleasure to man; is that practice moral or immoral? And if, exactly in proportion as human beings raise their heads out of the slough of selfishness, they do not with one voice answer 'immoral,' let the morality of the principle of utility be for ever condemned" (qtd. in Garner 12). Likewise, the British biologist Charles Darwin (1809–1882) showed himself to be an advocate of this issue in his *The Descent of Man, and Selection in Relation to Sex* (1871)

Chapter Four Criticism Against the Cruelty to Animals

by stating that "the lower animals, like man, manifestly feel pleasure and pain, happiness and misery" (39).

Apart from British advocacy, the concept of animal rights was supported by Schopenhauer as well, who wrote that Europeans were "awakening more and more to a sense that beasts have rights, in proportion as the strange notion is being gradually overcome and outgrown, that the animal kingdom came into existence solely for the benefit and pleasure of man" (qtd. in Phelps 153-54). Schopenhauer also paid tribute to the pioneering work in the legalization of the protection of animals by saying "To the honor, then, of the English, be it said that they are the first people who have, in downright earnest, extended the protecting arm of the law to animals" (qtd. in Phelps, 153-54).

In the twentieth century, more laws or regulations related to the protection of animals are enacted, including "Wild Animals in Captivity Protection Act" (1900), "Protection of Animals Act" (1911, 1912, 1921, 1934, 1954, replaced by Animal Welfare Act 2006), "Abandonment of Animals Act" (1960), "Agriculture Act" (1968), "Animal Health Act" (1981), "The Wildlife and Countryside Act" (1981) and "Welfare of Animals Regulations" (1995). Some institutions or departments are founded, such as "The State Veterinary Service" (SVS, 1938), 'The Meat and Livestock Commission" (MLC,1967), "The Farm Animal Welfare Council" (FAWC, 1979), and Animal Welfare Division of the Ministry of Agriculture, Forestry and Fisheries (MAFF).

With the above-mentioned background knowledge, let's look at several poems concerning the caging of birds in the nineteenth and twentieth century. "The Caged Skylark"[1] (1877) by the Victorian poet Gerard Manley Hopkins (1844–1889) is written in the form of an Italian sonnet, which I will quote in full length:

    As a dare-gale skylark scanted in a dull cage

---

[1] https://www.bartleby.com/122/15.html

Man's mounting spirit in his bone-house, mean house, dwells —

That bird beyond the remembering his free fells;

This in drudgery, day-labouring-out life's age.

Though aloft on turf or perch or poor low stage,

Both sing sometimes the sweetest, sweetest spells,

Yet both droop deadly sómetimes in their cells

Or wring their barriers in bursts of fear or rage.

Not that the sweet-fowl, song-fowl, needs no rest —

Why, hear him, hear him babble and drop down to his nest,

But his own nest, wild nest, no prison.

Man's spirit will be flesh-bound when found at best,

But uncumbered: meadow-down is not distressed

For a rainbow footing it nor he for his bónes rísen.

Like Shakespeare who uses the bird as a vehicle in the simile, Hopkins is also making a comparison between man's confined spirit in his physical body and the skylark in the cage, showing their similar state of imprisonment. "In such a condition both caged bird and man are less than they ought to be, the bird 'scanted' or deprived, having forgotten the freedom of flight over the 'fells' or uplands, and the man condemned to Adam's curse, the 'drudgery' of work" (Watt 49-50). The phrase "dull cage" makes use of the rhetorical device of transferred epithet, since it is not the cage that is dull but the bird in the cage that feels life is dull, boring and monotonous. The caged bird cherishes the memory of his previous life of freedom, becomes sad or depressed for his current confinement, and tries in vain to break through the cage, in spite of his fear and rage. So does the man. In both the caged bird and the captive man, we can find "the tension prevailing between the infinite reaches of the spirit with material limitations imposed on it" (Samanta 150).

"The Caged Thrush"[①] by another Victorian poet Robert Fuller Murray (1863-1894) is a ten-line short poem which I will quote in full length:

> Alas for the bird who was born to sing!
> They have made him a cage; they have clipped his wing;
> They have shut him up in a dingy street,
> And they praise his singing and call it sweet.
> But his heart and his song are saddened and filled
> With the woods, and the nest he never will build,
> And the wild young dawn coming into the tree,
> And the mate that never his mate will be.
> And day by day, when his notes are heard
> They freshen the street — but alas for the bird.

Cruel human beings do not only put the thrush in the cage, but also clip his wings, which is an ill and malicious deep-rooted practice. Even though they deem his singing as being sweet, the thrush himself knows that his song is permeated with sadness. When the thrush is singing, he cannot help but think of the woods he used to live in, the morning sunlight there, his nest, and his mate, which are far away from him now and seem to be illusions. It is human being's caging that strips the thrush of its due happiness. The interjection word "alas" in the last line shows the poet's sorrow and sympathy towards the bird.

Hardy's "The Caged Thrush Freed and Home Again (Villanelle)" (1899) shows his "revulsion at the act of caging" (Persoon 71). At the beginning of the poem, the thrush tells us the attitude of man towards birds, that is, "Who count us least of things terrene" (line 2). In other words, arrogant human beings

---

① https://www.poemhunter.com/poem/the-caged-thrush/

think birds are much inferior to them and thus they put the birds into a very low position. Seriously, a man cannot be deemed as being truly ethical if he does not consider animals as equal members on earth. In Schweitzer's words, "A man is ethical only when life as such is sacred to him — the life of plants and animals as well as that of his fellow men — and when he devotes himself to helping all life that is in need of help" (157-58).

The most typical rhetorical device used in this poem is repetition, and the ironic lines "Men know but little more than we" and "How happy days are made to be" are repeated several times. In the bird's point of view, human beings are quite ignorant of happiness, which does not mean that human beings do not know their own happiness but that they do not know the birds' happiness. The overtone here is that sometimes human beings' happiness is based upon depriving the happiness of the birds by caging them and listening to their singing. Actually the bird's request is very simple, that is, to go back to "yonder tree" (7), to glean on the ground and fly in the sky. It is fortunate for this bird to be freed and to go back home, but for many other caged birds, their status of being enjailed will not be terminated until "Man's sagacity" comes back to him and he begins to know the significance of the equality between man and animals (16). Hardy's indignation at the caging of birds is not only demonstrated in his literary works but also in real life, which shows that he is a man whose deeds are in accordance with his words. According to the reminiscence of Arthur Compton-Rickett, Hardy once said vehemently to him of the cruelty of caging song birds, with eyes blazed with anger, "I saw a horrible sight — a thrush in a cage… How can people do it? — The cruelty of it!" (qtd. in Purdy 114).

The bird in Hardy's "The Caged Goldfinch" (1917) is not so lucky as the above-mentioned thrush. Hardy uses the word "jailed" so directly that it is easy for the readers to empathize with the bird's miserable *status quo*. What makes things worse is that the place the caged bird is hung is a recent grave in a

Chapter Four Criticism Against the Cruelty to Animals

churchyard, which adds weirdness to the atmosphere. Due to the absolute silence of the surroundings, the bird can do nothing but "hops from stage to stage" (line 4). Later on, the bird tries to sing, with "inquiry in its wistful eye" (5). The word "wistful" signifies "someone who is rather sad because he wants something and knows that he cannot have it", which shows exactly the present state of the bird, that is, he aspires for freedom but cannot obtain it. In Christine Roth's view, the inquiry of the bird shows that "Whatever knowledge the birds have about spiritual matters, however, does not enable them to understand the reasons for human cruelty. Cruelty is incomprehensible to the animals in Hardy's poem" (88).

As to the content of the inquiry of the bird, the last two lines tell us that "Of him or her who placed it there, and why, / No one knew anything" (7-8). The poem ends in a suspense, because nobody knows who hangs the bird there and why. The possibility of the bird's accompanying the dead person cannot be excluded, so to speak, he becomes the sacrifice to the dead person, which makes his fate even more tragic and the treatment of him more inhumane since he is very likely to starve to death. What Hardy intends to strive for is that, to quote Peter Singer, "What we must do is bring nonhuman animals within our sphere of moral concern and cease to treat their lives as expendable for whatever trivial purposes we may have" (20). With a view to giving posthumous concern to caged birds, in his will, Hardy left one hundred pounds to be used for "condemnatory action against caging of wild birds" (qtd. in Cox 2).

Stevie has also written a couple of poems showing consideration to the suffering of caged animals. One example is "Parrot" (1938), in which Stevie castigates people's oppression of pets and our heedlessness of their needs and desires, their nature (Malamud 139):

>The old sick green parrot
>High in a dingy cage
>Sick with malevolent rage

Beadily glutted his furious eye

On the old dark

Chimneys of Noel Park

Far from his jungle green

Over the seas he came

To the yellow skies, to the dripping drain,

To the night of his despair

And the pavements of his street

Are shining beneath the lamp

With a beauty that's not for one

Born under a tropic sun.

He has croup. His feathered chest

Knows no minute of rest.

High on his perch he sits,

Waiting for death to come.

Pray heaven it won't be long.

  The living environment of the parrot is very dirty as is shown in the "dingy cage". The parrot is old, sick and moribund, and his major feeling is anger, reflected by his "malevolent rage" and "furious eye". He is indignant at his unfair treatment and his incompetence to put an end to such a miserable life. What's more, he is not a native or local bird, but is snatched away from the tropic area, so that it is very likely for him to find himself in an unaccustomed climate, which we can perceive from "the night of his despair". Although the modern city with man-made broad streets and neon lamps is beautiful, it does not suit the bird from the natural green jungle. What makes things worse is that he has got croup, a disease that makes the patient cough a lot and have difficulty in breathing. His disease is so severe that his chest "Knows no minute of rest". Being in such a wretched and pathetic condition, he is expecting death to come. The sooner, the better. When one shows world-weariness and death wishes, we can sense how agonized he or she is, and how he or she is overwhelmed by grief and sorrow.

Another of Stevie's poem "The Zoo" (1942) depicts the suffering animals' experience as a result of being displaced from their habitats for human convenience and amusement (Malamud 140):

> The lion sits within his cage,
> Weeping tears of ruby rage,
> He licks his snout, the tears fall down
> And water dusty London town.
>
> He does not like you, little boy
> It's no use making up to him,
> He does not like you any more
> Than he likes Nurse, or Baby Jim.
>
> Nor would you do if you were he,
> And he were you, for dont you see
> God gave him lovely teeth and claws
> So that he might eat little boys.
>
> [...]
> His claws are blunt, his teeth fall out,
> No victim's flesh consoles his snout,
> And that is why his eyes are red,
> Considering his talents are misused.

Like the parrot in the cage in the previous poem, the lion in the cage in this poem is also filled with rage. Apart from showing his anger, he also sheds tears. His grief is so deep that his tears "water dusty London town", in which we can see the use of exaggeration or hyperbole to emphasize and show the degree of his sorrow. The lion should be in nature, in the wilderness, using his sharp claws and strong teeth to prey on lambs, antelopes and buffaloes, instead of being imprisoned in a cage in the zoo. For the lack of use, "His claws are blunt, his teeth fall out", and his natural instincts are suppressed. Being a hero with no place to display his prowess is the root cause of the lion's anger and sadness. Stevie's castigation of human being's misuse of animals is significant and just as Malamud puts it, "Her reproofs, if heeded, might encourage her audience to reform and to appreciate more keenly our relationship with animals" (159).

II. Distress of Performing or Racing Animals

The existence of performing animals and racing animals has a long history, which can date back to Ancient Greece. In the ancient Olympic Games, there were performances like a man standing with one foot on horseback and horse racing with four horses driving a cart. Britain is the head stream of modern horse racing. Charles II (1630–1685) is the first British king in support of horse racing in the seventeenth century. He started the horse racing called "King's Plates" and is thus known as the "Father of English Turf". The first circus in the world was set up by the famous equestrian Philip Astley (1742–1814) in 1768 in London, who is thus referred to as the "Father of the Modern Circus". With the increasing popularity of horse racing and circus performance in the seventeenth and eighteenth century respectively, poets' concern about the animals involved in these activities also increased, and many poems were written in this regard.

Chapter Four Criticism Against the Cruelty to Animals

"The Glove and the Lions"[①] (1836) by Leigh Hunt (1784–1859) deals with a royal sport played by the royal beasts, which King Francis and the noble men and proud ladies are fond of watching. The sport is about some lions fighting against one another:

> Ramped and roared the lions, with horrid laughing jaws;
> They bit, they glared, gave blows like beams, a wind went with their paws;
> With wallowing might and stifled roar they rolled on one another;
> Till all the pit with sand and mane was in a thunderous smother;
> The bloody foam above the bars came whisking through the air; (lines 7-11)

Actually the whole story is about how Count de Lorge's lover would like to test the bravery of her lover and prove the degree of his love to her by dropping one of her gloves into the pit and letting him get it back. Though he accomplished the task successfully, he did not hand the glove to the lady but threw it into her face, saying that "No love", "but vanity, sets love a task like that" (24). Despite the major theme of love and vanity, the minor theme of the cruelty of royal sport cannot be neglected. As we can see from Lawrence's vivid description, the fighting between the lions is very violent and fierce, which is shown through their actions like "roared", "bit", "glared", "gave blows" and "rolled on one another", and also through the descriptive words like "horrid jaws", "wallowing might", "thunderous smother" and "bloody foam". The royal people base their entertainment and happiness upon the misery and suffering of the performing animals, which is one of the corrupt customs in the past that deserves debunking and denouncing.

Hardy also criticizes man's cruelty to performing or competing birds.

---

① https://www.poemhunter.com/poem/the-glove-and-the-lions/

A Study of British Animal Poems

According to Pinion, Hardy "was averse to cruelty for pleasure" (*Hardy Companion* 182). A case in point is "The Blinded Bird" (1916), in which Hardy shows his protest against Vinkensport, a Dutch word meaning "finch sport", which is a sort of singing competition between male finches that started from the end of the sixteenth century in Belgium. His criticism is more targeted at a cruel practice of the early proponents of the sport, that is, to blind the birds with hot needles so as to reduce distractions, as is shown in the poem by "red-hot needle" and "stab of fire" (line 5, 12). Hardy regards this practice as kind of "indignity" on the bird (2), and what is more ironic is that the indignity is inflicted on the bird "With God's consent" (3), the claimed omnipotent and benevolent God. Hardy wonders how "So zestfully thou canst sing" regardless of the indignity (7). As a matter of fact, there is no other way for the bird to survive. Despite human beings' ill-treatment, the bird's response is quite generous:

> Resenting not such wrong,
> Thy grievous pain forgot,
> Eternal dark thy lot,
> Groping thy whole life long;
> After that stab of fire;
> Enjailed in pitiless wire;
> Resenting not such wrong! (8-14)

We can see that the bird harbors no hatred for the unfair treatment he receives, and he even forgets the agony he suffers while he is being blinded. Even though his whole life will be spent in darkness and groping, even though his whole life will be in a state of imprisonment, he bears no resentment for such unfairness and maltreatment. The rhetorical device of transferred epithet is employed in "pitiless wire", which means that it is not the wire that is pitiless but human beings who cage the birds are. In accordance with Bailey's analysis of this poem, "Hardy's irony indicts a

Chapter Four Criticism Against the Cruelty to Animals

society that calls itself Christian but practices cruelty" (*Handbook and Commentary* 357-58). Hence, in the last stanza, Hardy asks several questions and gives the answers by himself:

> Who hath charity? This bird.
> Who suffereth long and is kind,
> Is not provoked, though blind
> And alive ensepulchred?
> Who hopeth, endureth all things?
> Who thinketh no evil, but sings?
> Who is divine? This bird. (15-21)

The bird's state of life is pretty vividly shown in "alive ensepulchred", so to speak, "life in death", which means that the cage is the bird's tomb and he is kind of buried there alive in respect that he has no freedom and lives in woe. Even so, the bird "suffereth", "hopeth", "endureth" and "thinketh no evil", and "is kind" but "is not provoked". The conclusion drawn from this poem is that it is not God and human beings who have charity and divinity, but the bird has. So the poem shows Hardy's "reproof to a supposedly loving God who has not provided an economy merciful to forms of life" (Kerridge 136). Hardy is showing in an oblique way his protest against this cruel practice with a long history of over three hundred years and what he does is what a thinking man is supposed to do. Just as Schweitzer puts it, "the thinking man must therefore oppose all cruel customs no matter how deeply rooted in tradition and surrounded by a halo" (qtd. in Joy 305).

Lawrence contributes most to the poems about performing animals. He writes several circus elephant poems in his poetry collection *Pansies* (1929), and one of them is "When I Went to the Circus" (1928), which is separately published in the magazine *Dial* in May 1929. In this poem, the animals who first come onto the stage for performance include the monkeys, ponies, dogs and geese, and their performances are as follows:

> Monkeys rode rather grey and wizened
>
> on curly plump piebald ponies
>
> [...]
>
> and dogs jumped through hoops and turned somersaults
>
> and then the geese scuttled in in a little flock
>
> and round the ring they went to the sound of the whip
>
> then doubled, and back, with a funny up-flutter of wing (lines 6-7, 9-12)

What come next successively are the performances of the tight-rope lady and the trapeze man, and then animals take the stage again, including elephants and horses.

> The elephants, huge and grey, loomed their curved bulk through the dusk
>
> and sat up, taking strange postures, showing the pink soles of their feet
>
> and curling their precious live trunks like ammonites
>
> and moving always with soft slow precision
>
> as when a great ship moves to anchor.
>
> ...
>
> Horses, gay horses, swirling round and plaiting
>
> in a long line, their heads laid over each other's necks (25-29, 31-32)

While the audience are enjoying the spectacular performance, we may ask a question, that is, what are the feelings of the circus animals? And the poem tells us:

> They were happy, they enjoyed it;
>
> all the creatures seemed to enjoy the game
>
> in the circus, with their circus people (33-35)

So our following-up question is "are they genuinely happy?" or "do they

Chapter Four   Criticism Against the Cruelty to Animals

really enjoy the game?" The answer is dubious since uncertainty is shown in the word "seemed". As a matter of fact, the opposite is more true. The animals are far from being happy, and they suffer a lot and are therefore painful. Even the audience themselves, according to the poem, "were not really happy" (39), because they were "compelled to admire the bright rhythms of moving bodies" (36). And the children in the audience "vaguely know how cheated they are of their birthright / in the bright wild circus flesh" (55). The ending of the poem becomes more ironic when we turn to Lawrence's argument on animal consciousness in his essay "Hymns in a Man's Life" (1928), "Plant consciousness, insect consciousness, fish consciousness, animal consciousness, all are related by one permanent element, which we may call the religious element inherent in all life, even in a flea" (132).

The second circus elephant poem by Lawrence is "Elephants in the Circus" (1928), a very short poem with only four lines:

Elephants in the circus

have aeons of weariness round their eyes.

Yet they sit up

and show vast bellies to the children.

The elephants are not able to speak, so their feelings are merely shown in their eyes. According to Thomas Bewick, "In proportion to the size of the Elephant his eyes are very small; but they are lively, brilliant, and capable of great expression" (187-88), but ironically, the great expression here is "weariness", being tired of the repetitive and monotonous performance every day. Their weariness is not temporary or ephemeral, but long-lasting since the word "aeon" means thousands of years, or an extremely long period of time. However, as animals in the circus, and "inferior to none in sagacity and obedience" (Bewick 186), they have no choice but to obey the orders of the animal tamer, bringing happiness and entertainment to the audience despite their own misery and suffering. According to Mark Van Doren, it is Lawrence's "wit as well as his anger, his sense of absurdity as well as his conviction of the truth" that leads Lawrence to such significant observations (313), rather than "apparently simple, objective observation" as Lockwood proposes (150).

The third circus elephant poem by Lawrence is "On the Drum" (1928), which also consists of merely four lines:

> The huge old female on the drum
>
> shuffles gingerly round and smiles;
>
> the vastness of her elephant antiquity
>
> is amused.

The performing elephant is an aged one. Though we are not informed how old she is, we do know that elephants can live as long as sixty to eighty years in general, even longer than some human beings. It is hard to imagine that an acrobat over sixty is still performing on the stage in a circus, however, the old elephant in this poem is still performing. But from the word "shuffle", which means to move without lifting one's feet properly off the ground, and the word "gingerly", which means to do something in a careful way for fear of being hurt, we get to know that the elephant cannot move so agilely and dexterously as she used to do when she was young. Despite her slowness in movement, she still smiles as usual in order to amuse her audience, which is the requirement for a circus animal. Unfortunately, the audience fail to perceive the agony of the elephant behind its affected smile.

Lawrence's last circus elephant poem in *Pansies* is "Two Performing Elephants" (1928). The two performing elephants include one young male elephant and one elderly female elephant, the relationship between whom is unknown. One of the tricks they play is that the old female elephant creeps beneath the bridge archway formed by the young male elephant standing with his forefeet on a drum, in which we can see the female elephant

Chapter Four Criticism Against the Cruelty to Animals

> On her knees, in utmost caution
>
> all agog, and curling up her trunk
>
> she edges through without upsetting him. (lines 1-3)

In order to accomplish the task triumphantly, the female elephant is extremely cautious. There exists a paradox in her movement. On the one hand, she is "agog", in other words, she is eager to put the performance to an end since moving on her knees is uncomfortable and even painful, but on the other hand, she has to edge through, that is, she has to move very slowly so as not to knock the male elephant down.

Another trick is that the male elephant lies on the ground and the female elephant climbs over him, in which we can see

> with what shadow-like slow carefulness
>
> she skims him, sensitive
>
> as shadows from the ages gone and perished
>
> in touching him, and planting her round feet. (5-8)

As can be seen, in doing this trick, the female elephant's movement is also very slow and careful. But the reason is different, that is, due to her bulky body, she is afraid of pressing too hard and thus hurting the male elephant.

At the end of the poem, the audience's response is shown, the children's response, to be exact.

> While the wispy, modern children, half-afraid
>
> watch silent. The looming of the hoary, far-gone ages
>
> is too much for them. (9-11)

The children are watching the performance, not with pleasure and hilarity, but with half-fear and silence. The reason is that the age-old circus tricks are too much for them to understand and appreciate. If even the naive children who are easy to please cannot enjoy the circus performance, we may think about the necessity of the existence of this age-old way of amusement. Anyway, given the importance of the elephant poems in understanding Lawrence's criticism of the abuse of performing animals, I find it difficult to agree with N. Poovalingam's argument that "there is no obvious significance attached to this beast symbolically or otherwise" (251).

Stevie's "This is Disgraceful and Abominable" (1957) castigates the misuse of performing animals straightforwardly, calling it a completely disgraceful and abominable thing:

> Of all the disgraceful and abominable things
>
> Making animals perform for the amusement of human beings is
>
> Utterly disgraceful and abominable. (lines 1-3)

She then cites a specific example of a performing dog in a French circus.

> A disgraceful and abominable thing I saw in a French circus
>
> A performing dog
>
> Raised his back leg when he did not need to
>
> He did not wish to relieve himself, he was made to raise his leg.
>
> The people sniggered. Oh how disgraceful and abominable.
>
> Weep for the disgrace, forbid the abomination. (6-11)

The trainer in the circus forces the dog to do something against its nature or instinct. Usually only when a dog is urinating, will it raise one of its hind legs. But the circus trainer forces the dog to raise its hind leg as if it were urinating so as to make the audience laugh. Stevie deems this treatment of dogs disgraceful and completely unacceptable. Not only dogs, but also many other animals are trained brutally.

> The animals are cruelly trained,
>
> How could patience do it, it would take too long, they are cruelly trained.
>
> Lions leap through fire, it is offensive,
>
> Elephants dance, it is offensive

Chapter Four Criticism Against the Cruelty to Animals

> That the dignified elephant should dance for fear of hot plates,
> The lion leap or be punished.
> And how can the animals be quartered or carted except cheaply?
> Profit lays on the whip of punishment, money heats the prodding iron,
> Cramps cages. Oh away with it, away with it, it is so disgraceful and abominable. (12-20)

Animals including lions, elephants, and so on are offensively trained, and if they do not obey the training instructions or orders, they will be severely punished by the circus trainers. According to Romana Huk, Stevie's "interest is rather in the ways humans invade and colonise such otherness [of animals], and in how animals both resist and succumb to their captors' constructions of them" (23). What lies behind this merciless training is profit, and circus performance is benefit-driven. Finally, Stevie calls on the abolition of caging animals and the emancipation of the performing animals.

In addition, the words "disgraceful and abominable" are repeated five times in the poem in order to emphasize the firm negative attitude of Stevie towards human beings' abuse of performing animals. Just as Malamud argues, "Two elements characterize Smith's poetry about animals: a strident, righteous tenor, resounding with unabashed, sometimes impolite, and always fiercely polemical advocacy for animals; and a broad diversity of sub-topics concerning animals' existence in human culture" (139).

Apart from those poems about performing animals, there is also a poem about racing animals, i.e. horses. Larkin's "At Grass" (1950) deals with the life of two retired racing horses. The beginning stanza seems to show to the readers the uncomfortable life of the two horses by depicting "the cold shade they shelter in" (line 2). But the concluding stanzas reveal the truth to us. In comparison with the past glorious racing life filled with "The starting-gates, the crowds and cries" (22), the two horses prefer the current tranquil life with "the unmolesting meadows" (23), which indicates that the racing life is molesting, or harassing and annoying. Their racing achievements make their names well-known far and wide, but they do not care a pin about it, since "their names never had any meaning for the horses themselves" (Booth 157), and so they "Have slipped their names" (25). What they value now is that they can " stand at ease" (25), and they do not have to race intensely and ferociously any more. Even though they still gallop, that is "for what must be joy" (26), rather than for fierce competition. What's more, they are no longer slaves to the stop-watch. Unrestrained and unchained by racing, they return to their true selves. Just as Sisir Kumar Chatterjee argues, "They are their own masters. Their time is now their own, and so is their will" (159).

III. Suffering of Hunted Animals

Like the caging of animals, animal performance and horse racing, hunting also has a long history, and an even longer history, because hunting originally was for survival in the primitive society. Hunting as amusement in Britain started from the Middle Ages, or the beginning of the eleventh century to be specific, brought in from France with the Norman Conquest, but as a privilege of the royal family or the aristocratic class. Not until the eighteenth century, did organized hunting become popular among the whole upper class. Later on, many more hunting lovers joined in the game. Hunting as entertainment was not prohibited by law until the year 2004 in Britain.

In British history, there are many men of letters who are against hunting. One pioneer who is deprecatory of hunting is Thomas More (1478–1535), in whose *Utopia* (1516), the Utopians condemn hunting as follows:

>But if the hope of slaughter and the expectation of tearing the victim in pieces pleases you, you should rather be moved with pity to see

Chapter Four Criticism Against the Cruelty to Animals

an innocent hare murdered by a dog — the weak by the strong, the fearful by the fierce, the innocent by the cruel and pitiless. Therefore this exercise of hunting, as a thing unworthy to be used of free men, the Utopians have rejected to their butchers, to the which craft (as we said before) they appoint their bondsmen. For they count hunting the lowest, the vilest, and most abject part of butchery; and the other parts of it more profitable and more honest as bringing much more commodity, in that they (the butchers) kill their victims from necessity, whereas the hunter seeks nothing but pleasure of the seely and woeful animal's slaughter and murder (qtd. in H. Williams 92).

One of the earliest attack on hunting in British poetry appears in the Renaissance period. According to Edward Berry, throughout the reigns of Tudors (1485–1603) and Stuarts (1603–1714), hunting was an important part of the life of the court, and of the aristocratic households connected with it (4). In Shakespeare's long poem *Venus and Adonis* (1593), a scene of the hunting of rabbits is portrayed, in which we can see the misery of the hunted rabbit. Venus says:

By this, poor Wat, far off upon a hill,

Stands on his hinder legs with listening ear,

To harken if his foes pursue him still:

Anon their loud alarums he doth hear;

And now his grief may be compared well

To one sore sick that hears the passing-bell.

Then shalt thou see the dew-bedabbled wretch

Turn, and return, indenting with the way;

Each envious brier his weary legs doth scratch,

Each shadow makes him stop, each murmur stay:

For misery is trodden on by many,

And being low never relieved by any. (lines 720-36)

We can see that the hunted rabbit is very alert and vigilant, listening to the hunters' movement attentively. When he hears their alarm, it seems as if he hears the bell tolled to announce a death or a funeral. In order to run for life, he has to turn and return wearily regardless of the damp dew and the scratching brier in the field. As Berry argues, Venus is unexpectedly moved to pity the very animal she has been recommending as a prey, and she is psychologically and morally unable to sustain even the thought of killing such a beast (54). Venus' sympathetic view on the hunted animal shows Shakespeare as an anti-hunting poet. Incidentally, the hare is named Wat, which is a very ironic name, because etymologically the meaning of the name is "military ruler". However, being hunted, the miserable fleeing hare is more like an army deserter rather than a military ruler.

In Shakespeare's play *As You Like It*, Act II, Scene I, there is a conversation between Duke Senior and the First Lord about hunting deer.

The Duke says:

> Come, shall we go and kill us venison?
>
> And yet it irks me, the poor dappled fools,
>
> Being native burghers of this desert city,
>
> Should, in their own confines, with forked heads
>
> Have their round haunches gor'd. (lines 22-26)

Even though the Duke suggests hunting deer for meat, he feels annoyed about the deer being wounded with hunting weapons, say a javelin or spear.

The suffering of the hunted deer is depicted vividly by the First Lord as follows:

> To the which place a poor sequester'd stag,
>
> That from the hunter's aim had ta'en a hurt,
>
> Did come to languish; and, indeed, my lord,
>
> The wretched animal heav'd forth such groans,

Chapter Four Criticism Against the Cruelty to Animals

> That their discharge did stretch his leathern coat
>
> Almost to bursting; and the big round tears
>
> Cours'd one another down his innocent nose
>
> In piteous chase... (35-42)

The melancholy Jaques feels grieved at that and he does not only feel sad but also bursts into tears upon seeing the suffering of the deer, as he is seen standing "on the extremest verge of the swift brook, / Augmenting it with tears" (44-45). What's more, he moralizes that human beings

> Are mere usurpers, tyrants, and what's worse,
>
> To fright the animals, and to kill them up
>
> In their assign'd and native dwelling-place. (64-66)

Thus we can see that Shakespeare, with Jaques as his mouthpiece, utters one of the earliest literary attack on the hunting of animals.

In the seventeenth century, there is a female poet named Margaret Cavendish (1623–1673) who has written two heroic couplets opposing hunting. "Hunting was and is a debated topic. Margaret Cavendish took the side of the hunted" (McColley 192). One of her poems is "The Hunting of the Hare"[①] (1653). In the poem, before the hunters come, the hare named Wat, with the same name as the one in Shakespeare's *Venus and Adonis*, lives a leisurely and happy life:

> Thus rests he all the day till th' sun doth set;
>
> Then up he riseth, his relief to get,
>
> Walking about until the sun doth rise,
>
> Then coming back in's former posture lies. (lines 9-12)

Unfortunately, wretched Wat was found by the huntsmen and their dogs, and the game of fleeing and chasing begins.

---

① http://library2.utm.utoronto.ca/poemsandfancies/2019/04/29/the-hunting-of-the-hare/

> Whom seeing, he got up, and fast did run,
> Hoping some ways the cruel dogs to shun.
> But they by nature have so quick a scent,
> That by their nose they traced what way he went,
> And with their deep, wide mouths set forth a cry,
> Which answered was by echoes in the sky.
> Then Wat was struck with terror and with fear,
> Seeing each shadow, thought the dogs were there,
> And running out some distance from their cry,
> To hide himself his thoughts he did employ. (15-24)

In the process of escaping, the overwhelming feeling of the hare is terror and fear. He is so terrified that he mistakens all the shadows as the hunting dogs. Even though he can find a temporary hiding place, he will soon be found by the dogs who have very good olfactory sense. After the exhausting seesaw battle, "Poor Wat, being weary, his swift pace did slack" (38). But despite his tiredness, when he sees the dogs again, he has to run away for life once more.

> Fear gave him wings, and made his body light:
> Though weary was before, by running long,
> Yet now his breath he never felt more strong,
> Like those that dying are, think health returns,
> When 'tis but a faint blast, which life out burns (46-50)

In desperateness, he runs very fast as if he had wings, but ironically, it is like the last radiance of the setting sun, or like a dying man lingering on with one's last breath of life. Eventually, the hare is caught and killed cruelly by the dogs.

> At last the dogs so near his heels did get,
> That they their sharp teeth in his breech did set.
> Then tumbling down he fell, with weeping eyes

Chapter Four Criticism Against the Cruelty to Animals

Gave up his ghost, and thus, poor Wat, he dies. (79-82)

Seeing the hare being killed, the response of the hunters is "hooping loud, such acclamations made" (83), that is, they make loud and enthusiastic approval for it. So actually human beings are the real murderer of the hare, and the dogs are just the accomplice.

At the end of the poem, Cavendish makes a long stinging rebuke for human beings' hunting activity, "criticizing hunting as an enactment of human tyranny over the animal world" (Landry 470).

> As if God did make creatures for man's meat,
>
> To give them life and sense, for man to eat,
>
> Or else for sport or recreation's sake,
>
> Destroy those lives that God saw good to make,
>
> Making their stomachs graves, which full they fill
>
> With murthered bodies, which in sport they kill.
>
> Yet man doth think himself so gentle, mild,
>
> When of all creatures he's most cruel, wild,
>
> And is so proud, thinks only he shall live,
>
> That God a godlike nature did him give,
>
> And that all creatures for his sake alone
>
> Were made, for him to tyrannize upon. (95-106)

According to Cavendish, human beings usually hunt for two main reasons: one is for food, the other is for sport or recreation. She makes use of a shocking metaphor, that is, human beings stomachs are the graves of the killed animals. Accordingly, she thinks that human beings are the cruelest creatures in the world. Her line "When of all creatures he's most cruel" anticipates Friedrich Nietzsche's remark "For man is the cruelest animal" (169). The reason behind the unfair treatment of animals is that human beings have a sense of pride or a sense of superiority, deeming that God created all creatures for the sake of human beings.

A Study of British Animal Poems

In Cavendish's view, human beings are tyrants in the human-animal relationship, who treat animals in a cruel and unfair way. As Margaret E. Owens proposes, "In *Poems and Fancies*, Margaret Cavendish repeatedly challenges this orthodoxy, most memorably in 'The Hunting of the Hare', a poem that imagines, in poignant detail, the experience of a hunt from the viewpoint of the prey" (159).

The other anti-hunting poem by Cavendish is "The Hunting of the Stag"[①] (1653). Similar to the previous poem, this poem also starts with a description of the pleasant life of the stag:

> In summer's heat he in cool brakes him lay,
> Which, being high, did keep the sun away;
> In evenings cool and dewy mornings new
> Would he rise up, and all the forest view.
> Then walking to some clear and crystal brook,
> Not for to drink, but on his horns to look,
> Taking such pleasure in his stately crown,
> His pride forgot that dogs might pull him down. (lines 7-14)

In the forest, the stag enjoys the peaceful and agreeable life and is his own king. He is so indulged in this stately life that he even neglects the potential danger from the hunting dogs. In order to feed himself, he comes to a field. No sooner has he fed himself full and lied down, than he is espied by the owner of the field. As a result, we see a similar fleeing and chasing scene as we have previously seen in "The Hunting of the Hare".

> Straight called his dogs to hunt him from that place;
> At last it came to be a forest chase.
> The chase grew hot; the stag apace did run;
> Dogs followed close, and men for sport did come.

---

① http://library2.utm.utoronto.ca/poemsandfancies/2019/04/29/the-hunting-of-the-stag/

Chapter Four Criticism Against the Cruelty to Animals

> At last a troop of men, horse, dogs did meet,
> Which made the hart to try his nimble feet.
> Full swift he was; his horns he bore up high;
> The men did shout; the dogs ran yelping by.
> And bugle horns with several notes did blow;
> Huntsmen to cross the stag did sideways go. (57-66)

Because the stag is stronger and runs faster than the small hare, it is much more difficult to capture him. Therefore, more and more hunters come to join the hunting, with the assistance of dogs and horses, forming a troop, as if they were a group of soldiers intending to fight against a strong enemy. They obstruct and intercept, pursue and encircle, sparing no efforts to catch the stag. In order to run for life, much like the aforementioned hare to whom "Fear gave him wings, and made his body light" (46), the stag's feet "did like a feathered arrow fly, / Or like a wingèd bird, that mounts the sky" and "fear the stag made run, his life to save" (101-102, 115). As Landry puts it, "we never lose sight of the struggling animal in the field" (473).

Consequently there comes his stubborn last-ditch fight and eventual tragic death.

> Then men and dogs did circle him about.
> Some bit; some barked; all plied him at the bay,
> Where with his horns he tossèd some away.
> But Fate his thread had spun; he down did fall,
> Shedding some tears at his own funeral. (136-40)

Because the stag is much outnumbered by his enemy, fighting against heavy odds, he is doomed to failure. Apart from the stag's unyielding and courageous counter attack, what is most poignant is the terminating line of the poem, which tragically portrays the stag's mournful weeping for his own funeral. However, his bitter tears are futile, because no matter how moving this scene is, it can never touch the stony and callous heart of the hunters.

To conclude the discussion of the two hunting poems by Cavendish, I'd like to quote Alan Hager, who proposes that in each of these two poems, Cavendish breaks the hunting-poem tradition by giving the animals' perspectives, evoking pity or disgust in the reader (293).

Let's move on to the hunting poems in the eighteenth century. In the long poem "Windsor-Forest" (1713) by Pope, he describes a scene of the hunting of a pheasant:

> See! from the brake the whirring Pheasant springs,
> And mounts exulting on triumphant wings:
> Short is his joy; he feels the fiery wound,
> Flutters in blood, and panting beats the ground.
> Ah, what avail his glossy, varying dyes,
> His purple crest and scarlet-circled eyes —
> The vivid green his shining plumes unfold,
> His painted wings, and breast that flames with gold? (lines 111-18)

By instinct, the pheasant who is shot tries to fly away at once. The fact that he can still fly makes him take it for granted that he is still able to run away successfully. He is so naive and so his joy does not last long. No sooner has he begun to fly, than he suddenly feels the sharp pain from the wound. Blood gushes out from his body and he drops hard on the ground, breathing quickly and heavily. Pope wonders, to the shot and dying pheasant, what is the use of his fabulous beauty. His various shining colours, his purple crest, his scarlet-circled eyes, his vivid green plumes, his painted wings and his golden breast, all come to nothing due to human beings' hunting activity.

> With slaughtering guns the unwearied fowler roves,
> When frosts have whitened all the naked groves,
> Where Doves, in flocks, the leafless trees o'ershade,

Chapter Four Criticism Against the Cruelty to Animals

>And lonely Woodcocks haunt the watery glade —
>He lifts the tube, and level with his eye,
>Straight a short thunder breaks the frozen sky.
>Oft, as in airy rings they skim the heath,
>The clamorous Lapwings feel the leaden death:
>Oft, as the mounting Larks their notes prepare,
>They fall and leave their little lives in air. (125-34)

In the phrase "slaughtering guns", the rhetorical device of transferred epithet is used, since it is not the guns that are to blame, but the hunters or fowlers who make use of the guns to kill the birds. The word "slaughter" signifies the killing of a large number of animals in a way that is cruel or unnecessary. The hunted birds include not only the above-mentioned pheasants, but also doves, woodcocks, lapwings and larks. The hunters disturb the peaceful life of the birds, frighten them to the utmost, and deprive them of their lives. From this poem, we can see Pope's direct criticism of hunting, just as H. Williams argues, "Whenever occasion arises, Pope fails not to stigmatise the barbarity of slaughtering for food" (131).

In the "Autumn" section[①] (1730) of the long poem *The Seasons* by James Thomson (1700–1748), a hunting scene is vividly portrayed:

>The pack full-opening, various; the shrill horn
>Resounded from the hills; the neighing steed,
>Wild for the chase; and the loud hunter's shout;
>O'er a weak, harmless, flying creature, all
>Mix'd in mad tumult, and discordant joy. (lines 421-25)

The above description tells us that the hunting of animals is a tumultuous and joyful event for the hunters. From the diction of the poem, such as "mad"

---

① https://www.poemhunter.com/poem/the-four-seasons-autumn/

and "discordant", we know that the poet holds a rather negative attitude toward people's hunting mania, which is in tune with his view in the "Summer" section of the same poem, in which he calls it "the madness of mankind" (732). And the description of the "weak, harmless, flying creature" shows his sympathy over the hunted animals.

The following description is about the escaping movement of the hunted stag:

> At first, in speed
> He, sprightly, puts his faith; and, roused by fear,
> Gives all his swift aërial soul to flight;
> Against the breeze he darts, that way the more
> To leave the lessening murderous cry behind:
> Deception short! though fleeter than the winds
> Blown o'er the keen-air'd mountain by the north,
> He bursts the thickets, glances through the glades,
> And plunges deep into the wildest wood;
> If slow, yet sure, adhesive to the track
> Hot-steaming, up behind him come again
> The inhuman rout, and from the shady depth
> Expel him, circling through his every shift. (428-40)

We can see that the stag is so overwhelmed by fear that he runs as swiftly as he can to flee from the hunters, even "fleeter than the winds". Phrases like "murderous cry" and "inhuman rout" directly show the poet's antagonistic and indignant view on hunting.

Regardless of the stag's fast and desperate running for life, he fails to avoid the tragedy and as a result,

> The big round tears run down his dappled face;
> He groans in anguish: while the growling pack,

Chapter Four Criticism Against the Cruelty to Animals

> Blood-happy, hang at his fair jutting chest,
>
> And mark his beauteous chequer'd sides with gore. (454-57)

The tear-shedding of the stag cannot move the hunters, and his painful groan cannot arouse their sympathy, because they are stony-hearted and "Blood-happy". The stag's beauteous chequered sides and the thick blood from its wound form a sharp contrast, so as to show how the animal's natural beauty is mercilessly destroyed by human beings' ill practice of hunting. According to H. Williams, "As far as ordinary life was concerned, the last age [of the eighteenth century] is only too obnoxious to the charge of selfishness and heartlessness. Callousness to suffering, as regards the non-human species in particular, is sufficiently apparent in the common amusements and 'pastimes' of the various grades of the community" (134).

The Scottish poet James Beattie (1735–1803) also deals with the hunting issue in his long 244-line poem "The Hares. A Fable" (1760). At the beginning of the poem, the hunters and their hounds are getting ready for the hunting, while the hares are having a meeting, in which we can hear "Long lists of grievances" and "general discontent" about human beings hunting of hares, and one of them says:

> "Our harmless race shall every savage
>
> Both quadruped and biped ravage?
>
> Shall horses, hounds, and hunters still
>
> Unite their wits to work us ill?
>
> [...]
>
> In every field we meet the foe,
>
> Each gale comes fraught with sounds of woe;
>
> The morning but awakes our fears,
>
> The evening sees us bath'd in tears.
>
> But must we ever idly grieve,

A Study of British Animal Poems

> Nor strive our fortunes to relieve?
> Small is each individual's force:
> To stratagem be our recourse;
> And then, from all our tribes combin'd,
> The murderer to his cost may find
> No foes are weak, whom Justice arms,
> Whom Concord leads, and Hatred warms.
> Be rous'd; or liberty acquire,
> Or in the great attempt expire." (lines 37-40, 49-62)

We can see that first of all the hare is complaining about the damage the "savage" hunters have brought to their peaceful life; their daily life is filled with fears and tears, and they cannot bear it any more. Therefore, he thinks that they cannot only grieve in vain for their misery and have to think about some countermeasures against the hunters. To begin with, they have to be united and make use of collective force and concerted efforts. In addition, they have to employ elaborate or deceitful schemes. They are going to make the hunters — their murderers — know that they are not weak defenders. The last two lines in the above selection are coincidentally identical to what the American revolutionist Patrick Henry said on March 23, 1775: "Give me liberty or give me death". Despite the leader hare's appeal and encouragement, when the hunters come, unfortunately the hares "distracted scour the grove, / As terror and amazement drove; / But danger, wheresoe'er they fled" (103-05), and "All hope extinct, they wait their doom" (108). At this moment a young hare with "bloody eye, and furious look" arises and encourages his fellow hares by saying "Must we, with fruitless labour, strive / In misery worse than death to live" (111, 125-26). He says if they keep striving, the final result will be "All hail, eternal peace!" (130). And a sedate hare also encourages the hares by remarking:

Chapter Four Criticism Against the Cruelty to Animals

> At least be firm, and undismay'd
>
> Maintain your ground; the fleeting shade
>
> Ere long spontaneous glides away,
>
> And gives you back th' enlivening ray. (219-22)

Incidentally, according to the study of William George Black, the hare is often credited with supernatural powers (86). Hence, supernaturally or magically, while the sedate hare is speaking calmly, something miraculous and marvelous happens:

> ... our danger past!
>
> No more the shrill horn's angry blast
>
> Howls in our ear; the savage roar
>
> Of war and murder is no more. (223-26)

So as luck would have it, the hunters mysteriously retreat and the hares win the battle without a single fight. And at the end of the poem, we see a very happy ending or a very harmonious picture of nature: "Discord and care were put to flight, / And all was peace, and calm delight" (243-44). Thus Beattie expresses his disapproval of hunting and his best wishes for the compatible human-animal relationship in a fictional way.

In Book VI "The Winter Walk at Noon" of *The Task* by Cowper, he puts forward his view on hunting.

> Not so when, held within their proper bounds
>
> And guiltless of offence, they range the air,
>
> Or take their pastime in the spacious field.
>
> There they are privileged; and he that hunts
>
> Or harms them there is guilty of a wrong,
>
> Disturbs the economy of Nature's realm,
>
> Who, when she formed, designed them an abode. (lines 574-80)

As Cowper sees it, hunting is guilty and wrong, for the reason that it invades the proper bounds of animals, disturbs their peaceful life and joyful pastime, offends them and takes away their privilege endowed by mother nature.

The next poem is Cowper's "On A Spaniel, Called Beau, Killing A Young Bird" (1793), which is not absolutely a hunting poem, but a quasi one. "Beau" is Cowper's favorite dog, but when he kills a bird, Cowper still blames him for that. First of all, the dog does not kill the bird for food since he is "Well fed" (2), but for fun, for sport, or as a way of amusement. Secondly, the bird is a very tiny young bird, or a fledgling, which "flew not till to-day" (6). Thirdly, the dog kills the bird "Against my [Cowper's] orders" because Cowper shouts at him "Forbidding you the prey" (7, 8). Fourthly, the bird is not a pest, nor "of the thievish sort" (13), nor one "whom blood allures" (14), so it is not right to kill such a good bird. Cowper concludes his blame by saying "But innocent was all his sport, / Whom you have torn for yours" (15-16), meaning the dog should not have killed such an innocent bird for his own amusement. The concluding lines are very thought-provoking: "I see you, after all my pains, / So much resemble man!" (19-20). Therefore, by rebuking the dog's behavior, Cowper is indirectly criticizing human beings' corrupt practice of hunting animals for fun or sport.

Coming to the nineteenth century, several well-known Romantic poets' poems on hunting cannot be overlooked. According to Perkins, in Wordsworth's time, animals had been endowed by nature with rights and middle-class intellectuals often felt acute guilt at the suffering inflicted by humans on animals ("Polemic Against Hunting" 421). Wordsworth's "Hart-Leap Well" (1800) is about the hunting of a hart. The 7th stanza describes the hunting pack:

> Where is the throng, the tumult of the race?
> The bugles that so joyfully were blown?
> This chase it looks not like an earthly chase;
> Sir Walter and the hart are left alone. (1.25-28)

Much similarity can be found between Wordsworth's description and that of

Chapter Four Criticism Against the Cruelty to Animals

Thomson's in the previously discussed "Autumn" section of the long poem *The Seasons*. Thomson describes the hunting pack as "in mad tumult, and discordant joy", and Wordsworth deals with the "tumult of the race" and joyful bugles.

Wordsworth goes on telling us the running away and being killed of the hart just as Thomson portrays the fleeing of the stag.

> The poor hart toils along the mountain-side;
>
> I will not stop to tell how far he fled,
>
> Nor will I mention by what death he died;
>
> But now the knight beholds him lying dead. (29-32)
>
> At last, the hunter Sir Walter says:
>
> I'll build a pleasure-house upon this spot,
>
> And a small arbor, made for rural joy;
>
> 'T will be the traveller's shed, the pilgrim's cot,
>
> A place of love for damsels that are coy. (57-60)

What Sir Walter says is very ironic on the ground that a place where animals are hunted cannot be regarded as pleasure-house, cannot bring true rural joy to visitors, and is even far from being a place of love. Even the title of the poem is ironic, since in a place called "Hart-Leap Well", the hart is killed and cannot leap any more, and as a result, "Such sight was never seen by human eyes" (54).

The ending of the poem is very thought-provoking, "Never to blend our pleasure or our pride / With sorrow of the meanest thing that feels" (2.83-84). "More broadly, the poem pleads for sympathy with animals" (Perkins, *Romanticism and Animal Rights* 80). Wordsworth is arguing that we should not base our happiness upon the sadness or suffering of other living things, no matter how mean, lowly or humble we think they are. Perkins thinks that Wordsworth expresses misanthropy in this poem, believing it is very difficult for a lover of nature also to be a lover of man, most especially when man is a hunter ("Polemic

A Study of British Animal Poems

Against Hunting" 445).

If we consider hunting in a broad sense, fishing or angling can also be taken into account. In Byron's long satiric epic *Don Juan* (1819–1824), we can find his criticism against angling:

> And angling, too, that solitary vice,
>
> Whatever Izaak Walton sings or says:
>
> The quaint, old, cruel coxcomb, in his gullet
>
> Should have a hook, and a small trout to pull it. (13.106)

Byron regards angling as something vice, in other words, an evil or immoral behaviour. The British writer Isaac Walton (1593–1683) has ever written a book entitled *The Compleat Angler* (1653), which is dedicated to the art and spirit of fishing. Byron holds a different opinion and describes Walton as a quaint and cruel guy. He even curses Walton by remarking that he wishes the fish and the angler could change their roles, and so the fish could hook the throat of the angler.

Clare's "The Marten" (1835–1837) praises the animal in the very first line of the poem as "The marten cat long shagged of courage good" (1). He then goes on to describe the character of the marten, including his shape, hair, eyes, size and head. Before the hunters come, the marten lives an undisturbed peaceful life, in that "He keeps one track and hides in lonely shade / Where print of human foot is never made" (7-8). But the hunters and their dogs break the tranquility, and the marten has to run for life, hence we can see "The marten hurries through the woodland gaps / And poachers shoot and make his skin for caps" (15-16). So this poem is one of Clare's poems that "describe animals as victims of humans who harass, torture, hunt, and kill them" (Chun 50).

The story ends with a surprise ending, that is, the marten is finally saved by a grey owl.

> When the grey owl her young ones cloaked in down

Chapter Four Criticism Against the Cruelty to Animals

> Seizes the boldest boy and drives him down
>
> They try agen and pelt to start the fray
>
> The grey owl comes and drives them all away
>
> And leaves the marten twisting round his den
>
> Left free from boys and dogs and noisy men. (23-28)

As a matter of fact, the grey owl is trying hard to drive away the birdnesting boys in order to protect her own baby birds. Fortunately, the owl's battle of defence also brings benefit to the marten, who successfully escapes from the hunters and their dogs. Or maybe the owl is also trying to help the marten as the mutual aid between animals, since the owl has already seen that the marten is in danger, as we see "The great brown hornèd owl looks down below / And sees the shaggy marten come and go" (13-14). The group of animal poems to which this poem belongs all show Clare's sympathy with hunted creatures, and his obsession with the struggle of existence in the wild (M. & R. Williams 241).

The last poem to be discussed in the nineteenth century is "The Dying Swan" (1899) by Thomas Sturge Moore (1870–1944):

> O SILVER-THROATED Swan
>
> Struck, struck! A golden dart
>
> Clean through thy breast has gone
>
> Home to thy heart.
>
> Thrill, thrill, O silver throat!
>
> O silver trumpet, pour
>
> Love for defiance back
>
> On him who smote!
>
> And brim, brim o'er
>
> With love; and ruby-dye thy track
>
> Down thy last living reach
>
> Of river, sail the golden light —

> Enter the sun's heart — even teach
>
> O wondrous-gifted Pain, teach Thou
>
> The God of love, let him learn how

As can be seen, the swan is severely wounded by the hunter's dart. Ironically, the poet is suggesting the silver-throated swan to pour out the last swan song, requiting the cruel hunter who hurts it with a song of love, instead of a tooth-for-tooth retaliation. The phrase "wondrous-gifted Pain" makes use of the rhetorical device of oxymoron, showing the lenient attitude of the swan toward the perpetrator. More ironically, one may wonder where the "God of love" is when this misconduct happens, who is negligent in the performance of duties. But it is advisable to say that the root cause of this tragedy is more of human beings' moral degeneration than God's negligence.

Talking about views on the hunting of animals, we cannot avoid discussing the cross-century poet Hardy. In the light of Bailey's view, "Hardy's revulsion at the suffering of birds extended to active and scornful hostility toward the breeding the shooting of game-birds for sport" (*Handbook and Commentary* 164). And according to Michael Millgate, "Hardy himself was particularly oppressed by the mass slaughter of game birds on local estates: Lord Wimborne's guests, a few weeks before the ball which the Hardys attended in December 1881, had killed in one day 1,418 pheasants, 35 hares, 48 rabbits, and 2 partridges" (218). And the poem "The Puzzled Game-Birds (Triolet)" (1899) might be a reflection of this or related experience.

> They are not those who used to feed us
>
> When we were young — they cannot be —
>
> These shapes that now bereave and bleed us?
>
> They are not those who used to feed us, —
>
> For would they not fair terms concede us?
>
> — If hearts can house such treachery

Chapter Four   Criticism Against the Cruelty to Animals

>They are not those who used to feed us
>
>When we were young — they cannot be!

The game birds find it hard to believe that the people who are now bereaving them, bleeding them, and killing them are just those people who used to feed them. The birds persuade themselves into believing that these people brutalizing them are not those who fed them in the past so as not to feel so depressed at the "treachery" of human beings. The bubble of "fair terms" they dreamed to have at the beginning now gets burst. Using the game birds as a mouthpiece, Hardy expresses his criticism of those treacherous human beings who are not touched by the ethic of reverence for life, just as Schweitzer puts it, "If he [man] has been touched by the ethic of reverence for life, he injures and destroys life only under a necessity which he cannot avoid, and never from thoughtlessness. So far as he is a free man he uses every opportunity of tasting the blessedness of being able to assist life and avert from it suffering and destruction" (qtd. in Joy 276). To put it more seriously, if people kill animals for fun or entertainment, they may even be at the risk of being labeled as speciesists, since in Singer's opinion, "Just as most human beings are speciesists in their readiness to cause pain to animals when they would not cause a similar pain to humans for the same reason, so most human beings are speciesists in their readiness to kill other animals when they would not kill human beings" (17). Hardy is so concerned with the game birds that even in one of his love poems "She, to Him. I" (1866), he also makes a vivid comparison between the man who loved and deserted his lover to "That Sportsman Time but rears his brood to kill" (line 10).

In Alma Evers' view, the form of cruelty which roused Hardy's deepest indignation was hunting and he found the concept of it as a sport incomprehensible[①]. In the poem "Winter Night in Woodland" (1923), we can see a vivid description of a hunting scene:

> With clap-nets and lanterns off start the bird-baiters,
> In trim to make raids on the roosts in the copse,
> Where they beat the boughs artfully, while their awaiters
> Grow heavy at home over divers warm drops.
> The poachers, with swingels, and matches of brimstone, outcreep
> To steal upon pheasants and drowse them a-perch and asleep. (lines 7-12)

We can see that the hunters are fully prepared, with their outfit, with artful skills, and with clear labor division for night hunting. They invade the home of the pheasants while they are sound asleep. At the end of the poem, though they are "tired and thirsty", the hunters are "cheerful", because they can make profit by selling those pheasants. The cheerfulness of the hunters and the sadness of the birds form a sharp contrast. What is ironic is that "they home to their beds". After hunting, the hunters can go home and have a sound sleep but the home of the pheasants has been destroyed and their life deprived. In Bailey's mind's eye, this poem shows "Hardy's compassion for animals and birds and his scorn for men who cruelly trick, trap, and kill them for sport" (*Handbook and Commentary* 521). Even though the hunting in this poem is more profit-oriented than amusement-oriented, Bailey's argument about Hardy's scorn for the hunters does hold water.

Hardy's critical view towards hunting and other sports using animals can be seen in his reply to the Rev. S. Whittel Key, who has inquired of him concerning "sport", in which Hardy writes:

> I am not sufficiently acquainted with the many varieties of sport to pronounce which is, quantitatively, the most cruel. I can only say

---

[①] Alma Evers, "Thomas Hardy: A Man Who Used to Notice Such Things." http://www.all-creatures.org/ca/ark-200-thom.html

Chapter Four Criticism Against the Cruelty to Animals

> generally that the prevalence of those sports which consist in the pleasure of watching a fellow-creature, weaker or less favoured than ourselves, in its struggles, by Nature's poor resources only, to escape the death-agony we mean to inflict by the treacherous contrivances of science, seems one of the many convincing proofs that we have not yet emerged from barbarism. (qtd. in F. Hardy 321)

Generally speaking, if we refer to someone's behaviour as "barbarism", we strongly disapprove of it because we think that it is extremely cruel or uncivilized. This is exactly Hardy's state of mind when he is criticizing the hunting of birds.

Hardy is so concerned with the welfare of the animals that even when he is asked by Millicent Garrett Fawcett, the leading figure in the women's suffrage movement, to write something for a related pamphlet, he still takes advantage of this opportunity to express his own view on animal protection. I'd like to quote what he says as follows for a better understanding of his standpoint:

> I am in favour of it [women's suffrage] because I think the tendency of the women's vote will be to break up the present pernicious conventions in respect of manner, customs, religion, illegitimacy, the stereotyped household (that it must be the unit of society), the father of a woman's child (that it is anybody's business but the woman's own, except in cases of disease or insanity), sport (that so-called educated men should be encouraged to harass & kill for pleasure feeble creatures by mean stratagems), slaughter-houses (that they should be dark dens of cruelty), & other matters which I got into hot water for touching on many years ago. (qtd. in Millgate 413-14)

Finally, let's talk about other hunting poems in the twentieth century. "To a Squirrel at Kyle-na-no" (1912) by W. B. Yeats (1865–1939) is a very short poem dealing with the scare of a squirrel at Kyle-na-no, one of the seven woods at

Coole in Ireland:

> Come play with me;
>
> Why should you run
>
> Through the shaking tree
>
> As though I'd a gun
>
> To strike you dead?
>
> When all I would do
>
> Is to scratch your head
>
> And let you go.

Yeats is puzzled why the squirrel runs away from him as what he wants to do is simply to touch it gently and let it go without hurting it. The reason is very clear, that is, the vigilant squirrel is afraid of being hunted by man with a gun. It is their natural instinct to flee from potential danger. So to speak, "once bitten, twice shy". Yeats' pretended ignorance is a subtle criticism of what hunting has brought to the relationship between man and animals. In his autobiography, Yeats confirms his abstinence of the killing of live animals when he was young: "I fished for pike at Castle Dargan and shot at birds with a muzzle-loading pistol until somebody shot a rabbit and I heard it squeal. From that on I would kill nothing but the dumb fish" (qtd. in Jeffares 189).

Hodgson's "The Birdcatcher" (1917) is a short eight-line poem which goes:

> WHEN flighting time is on I go
>
> With clap-net and decoy,
>
> A-fowling after goldfinches
>
> And other birds of joy;
>
> I lurk among the thickets of
>
> The Heart where they are bred,

Chapter Four Criticism Against the Cruelty to Animals

And catch the twittering beauties as

They fly into my Head.

Judged from the equipment, including the clap-net and decoy, the speaker in the poem is a professional bird-catcher. He knows exactly when to go, what to take and where to lurk for successful bird-catching or bird-hunting. His hunting targets are goldfinches and other birds of joy. It is ironic that even though the bird-catcher knows what he catches are birds of joy, he does not feel regretful or conscience-bitten for bringing misery to those joyful birds, changing them into birds of sorrow.

The beginning of Lawrence's "Mountain Lion" (1923) is very blunt to show the fearfulness of men in the eyes of animals.

Men!

Two men!

Men! The only animal in the world to fear! (lines 1-3)

When human beings are discussing who are stronger, more threatening, and are thus the king of the animal kingdom, the lions or the tigers? The lions themselves may think that human beings are the most fearful animals in the world, on the ground that "They have a gun" (6), which is a lethal weapon for the animals.

The "we" in the poem describe their encounter with the two hunters, especially the one who carries the killed dead lion, as follows:

He smiles, foolishly, as if he were caught doing wrong.

And we smile, foolishly, as if we didn't know.

He is quite gentle and dark-faced. (16-18)

The foolish smile between the hunter and the "we" is tacit, in that the hunter knows he is doing something wrong while the "we" choose to stand aloof, in lieu of admonishing him or even reporting him. By this mutual foolish smile, an unvoiced pact has been made, or even some kind of "conspiracy". The word "gentle" is ironic, since a gentle man has done such a brutal thing.

The dead body of the mountain lion, or puma, is not portrayed in a horrible way, but in a beautiful way instead:

> Lift up her face,
> Her round, bright face, bright as frost.
> Her round, fine-fashioned head, with two dead ears;
> And stripes in the brilliant frost of her face, sharp, fine dark rays,
> Dark, keen, fine rays in the brilliant frost of her face.
> Beautiful dead eyes. (23-28)

The "we" go on walking and see the lion's lair, and begin to meditate:

> So, she will never leap up that way again, with the yellow
> flash of a mountain lion's long shoot!
> And her bright striped frost face will never watch any more,
> out of the shadow of the cave in the blood-orange rock,
> Above the trees of the Lobo dark valley-mouth. (35-37)

Though dead, her beauty still remains, however, her valiant, valorous and vigorous movement will no loner exist. Despite her strength and power, she has to admit defeat pathetically to the more powerful gun. As Pinion puts it, "More moving is the lament for the mountain lion Lawrence saw being carried down the Lobo canyon" (*Lawrence Companion* 113).

At the end of the poem, the narrator regrets for "what a gap in the world" (45). It may mean the huge gap existing between human beings and animals. By continuous hunting and killing of animals, the gap is becoming larger and larger, and the disbelief of animals towards human beings is becoming stronger and stronger. Harmonious co-existence between man and animals turns out to be a mirage, too unrealistic to be tangible. To Lawrence, perchance it is more than regret or complaint, since according to Inniss, this poem even shows one of Lawrence's recurring moments of misanthropy (85).

Chapter Four Criticism Against the Cruelty to Animals

Auden's "Our Hunting Fathers" (1934) is a poem with ambiguous ideas and has already been interpreted in varied ways. For example, Hecht believes that the theme of the poem is love, and argues that love is conceived in the first stanza as divine, rational, beneficent, and in the second stanza as warped, private and guilt-ridden (59). Craig Raine thinks that the poem deals with reason and love and proposes that the first stanza argues that our primitive ancestors imagined that, granted reason, animals would be raised to godlike status — that love and reason would supply a deficiency; while the second stanza examines the idea of love itself, challenges our unquestioned assumptions about love, and finds that love isn't the liberal nostrum we like to imagine, or that our ancestors imagined[1]. As far as I am concerned, the poem is also about Auden's view on hunting, as the title of the poem suggests. For better discussion, I will quote the two stanzas in full length.

> Our hunting fathers told the story
> Of the sadness of the creatures.
> Pitied the limits and the lack
> Set in their finished features;
> Saw in the lion's intolerant look.
> Behind the quarry's dying glare.
> Love raging for the personal glory
> That reason's gift would add.
> The liberal appetite and power.
> The rightness of a god.
>
> Who, nurtured in that fine tradition.
> Predicted the result.

---

[1] http://wwword.com/6/think/school-room/how-to-read-a-poem/

A Study of British Animal Poems

> Guessed Love by nature suited to
>
> The intricate ways of guilt.
>
> That human ligaments could so
>
> His southern gestures modify
>
> And make it his mature ambition
>
> To think no thought but ours.
>
> To hunger, work illegally,
>
> And be anonymous?

Here the hunting fathers do not necessarily refer to Auden's previous generations, but rather the distant ancestors of human beings or even those early predators who ate animal flesh raw and drank animal blood. While they were killing the animals, they could feel the sadness of these animals, they could see the intolerant look of the lion as well as the frightening and desperate glare of the hunted animals, and they felt sympathetic towards the preyed animals. Regardless of the conscience and sympathy towards the animals, they still hunt them so as to survive, because survival is their top priority. Later on, what the hunters do was endorsed by the privilege or superiority over animals that God bestowed on human beings in the Bible. Henceforth, hunting is done in a justified way, since hunters are hunting with the support of the "rightness of a god". Yet whether our 'rightness' is justified remains questionable, for the poem's construction of nature as inferior is evidently a projection of the human appetite for power (Emig 215).

Nevertheless, for the hunting fathers, hunting is not done without any qualm of conscience, even though it has become a "fine tradition". The feeling of love is intertwined with that of guilt, but both were submerged by the necessity of livelihood. To hunger or to work illegally (or immorally), that is the question confronting and bothering the hunting fathers who hunted for survival. But what about those who hunt just for fun? A plausible explanation is definitely needed, or else, a public denunciation.

The last poet I'd like to talk about is Hughes, whose attitude towards hunting changes in different periods of his life, at times even contradictory. In Hughes' "The Seven Sorrows"[①] (1976), the second and sixth sorrows are about the hunting of animals, pheasants and foxes respectively.

> The second sorrow
> Is the empty feet
> Of a pheasant who hangs from a hook with his brothers.
> The woodland of gold
> Is folded in feathers
> With its head in a bag.
> [...]
> And the sixth sorrow
> Is the fox's sorrow
> The joy of the huntsman, the joy of the hounds,
> The hooves that pound
> Till earth closes her ear
> To the fox's prayer. (lines 7-12, 31-36)

Both stanzas are written in a way of contrast. In the second stanza, the previous beautiful and lively pheasant, the "woodland of gold", is contrasted with the dead bird, hung "from a hook", "folded in feathers" and "head in a bag". In the sixth stanza, the joy of the hunters and the hunting dogs is contrasted with the sorrow of the fox, whose prayer turns out to be futile. Ironically, even mother earth turns a deaf ear to the fox's suffering, conniving in the hunting. "Hughes himself was torn between his sympathy for the individual animal and his desire for its species to be preserved — for hunting" (Reddick 202). By the early

---

① http://www.poetseers.org/poets/ted-hughes-poetry/seven-sorrows/

1970s, Hughes holds "an ambivalent attitude towards hunting" (Reddick 205).

Hughes' "The Black Rhino" was written for the Duke of Edinburgh as President of the World Wildlife Fund, being a contribution to the Rhino Rescue Appeal of 1987. Hughes depicts the portending extinction of the Black Rhino as follows:

> For this is the Black Rhino, who vanishes as he approaches
> Every second there is less and less of him
> By the time he reaches you nothing will remain, maybe, but the horn
>   — an ornament for a lady's lap
> [...]
> Quickly, quick, or even as you stare
> He will have dissolved
> Into a gagging stench, in the shimmer.
> Bones will come out on the negative.
> [...]
> The Black Rhino
> Is vanishing
> Into a soft
> Human laugh (lines 10-12, 22-25, 133-36)

People kill black rhinos especially for their horns, which can be used in medicine, sculptures, or ornaments as is mentioned in the poem, which leads to the gradual reduction in the number of black rhinos. Consequently, the body of the dehorned black rhino will dissolve into "a gagging stench", sending out very disgusting unpleasant smell, as a way to show their posthumous protest against hunting. The poem "conveys the horror of poaching an endangered species" (Reddick 278). However, pitifully, towards the approaching distinction of the rhinos, human beings' attitude is not worry and regret, but laugh and indifference.

However, in the late 1980s, Hughes began to express surprisingly favourable opinions of the hunt, siding with the elite (Reddick 206). And from the mid-1990s, Hughes was attempting to develop a conservationist defence of hunting and fishing (Reddick 286), since some conservationists hold the view that hunting activity helps to manage the growing numbers of predators, protect the weaker animals and thus make the balance of nature. Hence Hughes ambivalent attitude towards hunting is not ungrounded.

IV. Abuse of Other Animals

Apart from the abuse of those animals which can be categorized generally, there are also some other animals who suffer from ill-treatment as well, such as wild birds in nature, laboring animals, animals in the butcher house, animals in transportation, post horses, war horses and so on.

As early as the Renaissance period, Shakespeare in his long poem *Venus and Adonis* describes the horse slavery as follows:

> How like a jade he stood, tied to the tree,
>
> Servilely master'd with a leathern rein!
>
> But when he saw his love, his youth's fair fee,
>
> He held such petty bondage in disdain;
>
> Throwing the base thong from his bending crest,
>
> Enfranchising his mouth, his back, his breast. (lines 415-19)

The palfrey, which is a light saddle horse, is so exhausted that he looks like an old or over-worked horse, bound and controlled by a rein. "Servilely master'd" shows his state of slavery. However, he is so brave that he shows contempt to his enthrallment, to the degree that he throws off the whip, the symbol of bullying and control. Unfortunately, he is far from being completely freed from his servitude.

Among the seventeenth-century animal poems, Cavendish's "A Dialogue of Birds"[①] (1653) is worth detailed discussion. In this poem, various birds are complaining the unfair or ill-treatment from human beings, including the lark, the nightingale, the owl, the robin, the sparrow, the magpie, the partridge, the woodcock, the peewit, the quail, the swallow, the pigeon, the parrot and so on. For example, the sparrow denounces men as follows:

> But men do with their nets us take by force.
>
> With guns and bows they shoot us from the trees,
>
> And by small shot, we oft our lives do leese
>
> Because we pick a cherry here and there,
>
> When God knows we do eat them in great fear. (lines 34-38)

Men try to catch the sparrows with various instruments, including nets, guns, and bows. Despite their danger, the sparrows have to take a risk in order to feed themselves, so that they have to eat the cherries in great fear.

Sometimes a sparrow is caught just as a toy for kids. As is shown in the following part:

> And if a child do chance to cry and bawl,
>
> They do us catch to please that child withal.
>
> With threads they tie our legs almost to crack,
>
> And when we hop away, they pull us back,
>
> And when they cry, "fip, fip!" straight we must come.
>
> And for our pains they'll give us one small crumb. (43-48)

When the kids are in low spirits or not well-behaved, in order to coax them or cheer them up, their parents will catch a sparrow for them. And so as to prevent the sparrow from running away, they will tie a thread to its leg. Though painful, the sparrow has to obey the instructions given by the kids.

---

① http://library2.utm.utoronto.ca/poemsandfancies/2019/04/28/a-dialogue-of-birds/

Chapter Four Criticism Against the Cruelty to Animals

Hearing the sparrow's bitter experience, the magpie says that his own fate is more tragic, because "For they our tongues do slit, their words to learn, / And with this pain, our food we dearly earn" (51-52). For the convenience of learning human language, the magpie's tongue is cruelly made a long narrow cut.

Many other birds join in the denunciation of gluttonous human beings:

> When we poor birds are by the dozens killed.
>
> Luxurious men us eat till they be filled,
>
> And of our flesh they make such cruel waste,
>
> That but some of our limbs will please their taste.
>
> In woodcocks' thighs they only take delight,
>
> And Partridge wings, which swift were in their flight.
>
> The smaller Lark they eat all at one bite,
>
> But every part is good of Quail and Snite. (71-78)

Edacious human beings are very good at eating various kinds of birds, knowing clearly the knack. For some of the birds, human beings will eat every part of their body, among others the quail, the snipe (snite in O.E.) and the lark, especially the smaller lark, which they will greedily swallow in one gulp. For some other birds, human beings do not like eating their flesh very much, but their limbs instead, such as the woodcocks' thighs and the partridges' wings. In order to glut themselves with delicacies, human beings have killed many innocent birds.

The helpless birds can do nothing but make a revenge-like curse in one voice at human beings who kill, cook and eat birds:

> But when they eat us, may they surfeits take;
>
> May they be poor when they a feast us make.
>
> The more they eat, the leaner may they grow,
>
> Or else so fat they cannot stir nor go. (87-90)

They wish vengefully that harm or hurt would be inflicted upon human beings by certain supernatural power, say the gluttons either grow too thin to be healthy or so fat that they cannot walk or move conveniently or normally.

What follows is an even more cruel treatment of birds, which is inflicted upon the swallows:

> Yet men will take us when alive we be
> (I shake to tell, O horrid cruelty!),
> Beat us alive till we an oil become.
> Can there to birds be a worse martyrdom?" (95-98)

It is hard to understand what people have done to the swallows without necessary background information. According to the study of Michelle DiMeo and Rebecca Laroche, in the ancient recipe books between the late sixteenth century and the early eighteenth century, there are many medicinal recipes concerning "Oil of Swallow" ("Oyle", "Oyl", "Oile" in O.E.), a kind of ointment or remedy for physical ailments or illness, such as sore eyes. The similarity between some of these recipes is that they "are filled with graphic descriptions of swallows being beaten to death 'feathers and all'" (88), or specific references about "placing birds into the mortar 'alive' or 'quick,' 'beating' them as their 'guts' are spread out 'raw' before us" (96). No wonder the swallow in this poem call this treatment of birds "horrid cruelty". The word "martyrdom" in line 97 shows that the swallows are made to suffer greatly before they breathe their last, and what's more, the swallows think their martyrdom is the worst one among all birds, which is without exaggeration.

After the above-mentioned revelation of human beings' maltreatment of birds, the ending of the poem turns out to be very ironic.

> But all their songs were hymns to God on high,
> Praising his name, blessing his majesty.
> And when they asked for gifts, to God did pray
> He would be pleased to give them a fair day. (197-200)

Chapter Four Criticism Against the Cruelty to Animals

Having complained to one another about human beings' ill-treatment of birds, and put human beings under a curse, which are all presumably in vain, the birds turn to God for help, the last straw to clutch at. But unfortunately, God would only be pleased to give them a fair day, in lieu of giving them what they really want, that is, fair treatment and peaceful living lifelong. Though there seems to be no way out for the birds, by revealing in detail some people's harsh treatment of birds, Cavendish is trying to arouse the public's awareness of the necessity and urgency of protecting birds. "Poetry is one way in which songbirds speak to us about their plight, and it is to poetry that we must turn to save them" (Ortiz-Robles 88).

In the eighteenth century, in Pope's famous long poem *An Essay on Man* (1733–1734), he writes about the innocent lamb which is going to be butchered:

> The lamb thy riot dooms to bleed to-day,
> Had he thy reason would he skip and play?
> Pleas'd to the last he crops the flowery food,
> And licks the hand just rais'd to shed his blood. (Epistle I, lines 81-84)

The lamb is so innocent and is totally unaware of his portending death. He skips and plays as usual, he feeds on the food with pleasure, and he licks the hand of his owner intimately, having no knowledge that it is just this hand that is going to shed his blood and put an end to his life. There is more irony than criticism of the treachery of man in the human-animal relationship.

In fact, long before the composition of *An Essay on Man*, Pope has already published an article entitled "Against Barbarity to Animals" in *The Guardian* newspaper in 1713, expressing his view on the ill-treatment of animals:

> I cannot think it extravagant to imagine that mankind are no less, in proportion, accountable for the ill use of their dominion over the lower ranks of beings, than for the exercise of tyranny over their own species.

> The more entirely the inferior creation is submitted to our power, the more answerable we must be for our mismanagement of them; and the rather, as the very condition of Nature renders them incapable of receiving any recompense in another life for ill-treatment in this.

This fact shows that Pope's view on the abuse of animals is identical, no matter it is in poetry or in prose, no matter it is when he is in his younger twenties or in his more mature forties.

The "Spring" section (1728) of Thomson's *The Seasons* takes up the cudgels against the injustice done to those peaceful animals.

> ... but you, ye Flocks,
> What have you done? Ye peaceful people, what
> To merit death? You who have given us milk
> In luscious streams, and lent us your own coat
> Against the winter's cold? And the plain Ox,
> That harmless, honest, guileless animal,
> In what has he offended? He, whose toil,
> Patient and ever ready, clothes the land
> With all the pomp of harvest — shall he bleed,
> And struggling groan beneath the cruel hands
> E'en of the clowns he feeds, and that, perhaps,
> To swell the riot of the autumnal feast
> Won by his labour? ... (lines 357-69)

In Thomson's view, unlike the beasts of prey, who are themselves bloodstained, the relatively mild animals like the sheep and the ox do not deserve death. In terms of disposition, the sheep are meek and peaceful, and the oxen are harmless, honest, and guileless. In terms of provision, the sheep have provided people with milk and wool, and the oxen have toiled patiently on the farmland. Thomson is well-grounded to ask why these gentle and useful animals should

Chapter Four Criticism Against the Cruelty to Animals

struggle and groan beneath the cruel hands of the butchers. "To the author of *The Seasons* belongs the everlasting honour of being the first amongst modern poets earnestly to denounce the manifold wrongs inflicted upon the subject species, and, in particular, the savagery inseparable from the Slaughter-House" (H. Williams 134).

In S.T. Coleridge's "To a Young Ass, Its Mother Being Tethered Near It" (1794), at the very beginning of the poem, he does not beat about the bush, but instead comes straight to the point and utters his view very directly, that is "Poor little Foal of an oppressèd Race!" (line 1), exploited by human beings. Though oppressed, the ass shows "languid Patience" (2). Coleridge is sympathetic towards the ass, so he gives it bread, claps his coat, and pats his head to show his love and care to him. Coleridge wonders why the young ass is not like most other young animals who are fond of sporting on the glade. So he asks the ass: "Do thy prophetic Fears anticipate, / Meek Child of Misery! thy future fate?" (9-10). In other words, is it the foreseeing of the doomed future fate that prevents him from enjoying the present life or forsaking the life style of *carpe diem*? No wonder Coleridge addresses the young ass as "Child of Misery", who endures "The starving meal, and all the thousand aches" (11). But compared with him, his mother's fate is more grim and pitiable, because she is "Chained to a Log within a narrow spot" (16), deprived of freedom, bemoaning her inadequacy in the face of the tempting green grassland in the distance.

After showing sympathy to the ass and his mother, Coleridge turns to rebuke their owner, who "should have learnt to show / Pity — best taught by fellowship of Woe!" (19-20). Finally, Coleridge shows his firm attitude towards the ass:

> Innocent Foal! thou poor despised Forlorn!
> I hail thee Brother — spite of the fool's scorn!
> And fain would take thee with me, in the Dell

Of Peace and mild Equality to dwell. (25-28)

Though others despise and scorn the ass, without showing care to him, Coleridge by contrast regards him as a brother, and would like to live together with him in an Arcadia or a Utopia where there is peace and equality between man and animals, and where the ass "wouldst toss thy heels in gamesome play, / And frisk about, as lamb or kitten gay!" (31-32). Just as Ortiz-Robles puts it, the poem ends with "an extended Utopian fantasy" and "this Utopia is named 'Pantisocracy' and constitutes a realm of equality in which antagonisms are reversed and where rats and terriers, mice and cats, poets and asses can coexist in 'Mirth'" (45).

"The Farmer's Boy" (1798) by Robert Bloomfield (1766–1823) is a long rural poem, which is composed of four individual poems, namely, "Spring", "Summer", "Autumn" and "Winter". In the "Winter"[①] poem, there is an episode about the ill-treatment of a post horse.

> Could the poor post-horse tell thee all his woes;
> Shew thee his bleeding shoulders, and unfold
> The dreadful anguish he endures for gold:
> Hir'd at each call of business, lust, or rage,
> That prompt the trav'eller on from stage to stage.
> Still on his strength depends their boasted speed;
> For them his limbs grow weak, his bare ribs bleed;
> And though he groaning quickens at command,
> Their extra shilling in the rider's hand
> Becomes his bitter scourge:... 'tis he must feel
> The double efforts of the lash and steel;
> Till when, up hill, the destin'd inn he gains,

---

① https://www.poemhunter.com/poem/the-farmer-s-boy-winter/

Chapter Four Criticism Against the Cruelty to Animals

>   And trembling under complicated pains,
>
>   Prone from his nostrils, darting on the ground,
>
>   His breath emitted floats in clouds around: (lines 162-76)

The post-horse cannot speak, therefore he is not able to tell people his misery. He is not capable of showing his bleeding shoulders or revealing the severe pain he suffers from. He can only endure silently and patiently. Even though "his limbs grow weak, his bare ribs bleed", yet when the rider is given extra money for higher speed and faster delivery, unfortunately the horse will fall victim to "bitter scourge", that is, he will be whipped brutally for speeding up. Not only is the horse tormented by the whip, but also by the sharp-pointed spur on the heels of the rider's boots. The suffering of the horse does not come to an end until he reaches the next destination exhaustedly, where he can have some rest.

>   Ah, well for him if here his suff'rings ceas'd,
>
>   And ample hours of rest his pains appea'd!
>
>   But rous'd again, and sternly bade to rise,
>
>   And shake refreshing slumber from his eyes,
>
>   Ere his exhausted spirits can return,
>
>   Or through his frame reviving ardour burn,
>
>   Come forth he must, tho' limping, maim'd, and sore;
>
>   He hears the whip; the chaise is at the door:...
>
>   The collar tightens, and again he feels
>
>   His half-heal'd wounds inflam'd; again the wheels
>
>   With tiresome sameness in his ears resound,
>
>   O'er blinding dust, or miles of flinty ground.
>
>   Thus nightly robb'd, and injur'd day by day,
>
>   His piece-meal murd'rers wear his life away. (185-98)

But the horse's rest is only temporary. When the day breaks, he has to embark again on the long journey, even though he has not recovered from yesterday's exhaustion yet, neither physically, nor spiritually. Despite his weariness, when the chaise is ready and when the whip is cracked, he has no choice but to go "limping, maim'd, and sore". As a result, his half-healed wounds are ruthlessly torn open again and recovery is virtually out of the question, which is like the miserable Prometheus in Greek mythology, whose liver is torn out by the eagle every day, unable to completely recover from his wound. Ironically, even the inanimate and lifeless wheels also feel tired, let alone the post horse with flesh and blood. No wonder the poet considers the horse-riders as robbers and calls them "piece-meal murd'rers", who injure the horse day by day and take away the horse's life in a gradual and painful way. As A. H. R. Fairchild argues, in Bloomfield's poetry, there is "a marked sympathy for animals, a sentiment by no means familiar then as now" (91).

Let's move on to the animal poems in the nineteenth century. "The Donkey and His Panniers"[①] (1826) by Thomas Moore (1779–1852) starts with the breaking down of a donkey named Neddy:

> A donkey whose talent for burdens was wondrous,
>
> So much that you'd swear he rejoiced in a load,
>
> One day had to jog under panniers so ponderous,
>
> That — down the poor Donkey fell smack on the road! (lines 1-4)

It is very ironic that because the donkey is not able to complain about the heavy load, his owner thinks he is pleased with such strenuous work. As a result, the burden is aggravated, which leads to the eventual collapse of the donkey. His owner boasts about his donkey's fame "For vigor, for spirit, for one thing or other" (11), however, it is tragic that "'mid his praises, the Donkey came down!" (12) While passers-by give advice to the owner, such as, leaving

---

① http://fullonlinebook.com/poems/the-donkey-and-his-panniers-a-fable/wymb.html

Chapter Four Criticism Against the Cruelty to Animals

the donkey alone and letting him recover by himself, or providing the donkey with metal shoes, "the poor Neddy in torture and fear / Lay under his panniers, scarce able to groan" (25-26). Luckily, a wise adviser comes at last to his rescue by suggesting "Quick — off with the panniers, all dolts as ye are, / Or your prosperous Neddy will soon kick his last!" (31-32). Before the donkey eventually dies, the best solution is to relieve him of the ponderous load. There is no difference between man and animals in feeling exhaustion and pain. Never take it for granted that because they are the so-called "lower animals", they can endure much more than human beings can. As for the relief of the burden of laboring animals, the principle is "better late than never".

Clare contributes the most among the nineteenth-century poets to the criticism of human beings' abuse of animals. First of all, his "Summer Evening" (1820) strongly denounces the wanton destruction of sparrows and their nests (McKusick 84).

> Prone to mischief boys are met
> Gen the eaves the ladder's set
> Sly they climb and softly tread
> To catch the sparrow on his bed
> And kill 'em O in cruel pride (lines 91-95)

If the boys only catch the sparrows to play with them, perhaps we can say they are just ignorant, naughty and mischievous, but if they later kill the sparrows "in cruel pride", mischief can no more be an acceptable and sound excuse. The narrator of the poem is so angry at such savage treatment of the birds that he calls these boys "Cursd barbarians" (97). He shouts at them:

> Come not, turks, my cottage nigh
> Sure my sparrows are my own
> Let ye then my birds alone (98-100)

The word "turks" means Turkish people, signifying invaders, which shows the attitude of detestation of the narrator towards these boys. After warning the boys not to come to his domain to snatch the sparrows under the eave of his house, the narrator then encourages the sparrows to come to his house for shelter:

> Sparrows, come from foes severe,
> Fearless come, ye're welcome here
> My heart yearns for fates like thine
> A sparrow's life's as sweet as mine
> To my cottage then resort
> Much I love your chirping note
> Wi' my own hands to form a nest
> I'll gi' ye shelter peace and rest
> Trifling are the deeds ye do
> Great the pains ye undergo (101-10)

He asks the sparrows to run away from their enemies, i.e. those cruel human beings. He promises to the sparrows that he will make a nest for them, and provide them with a "shelter peace and rest". He is sympathetic towards the sparrows for their sufferings inflicted upon by the cruel people, who he thinks

> ... woud Justice serve
> Their crueltys as they deserve
> And justest punishment pursue
> And do as they to others do (111-14)

In his opinion, those who do cruel things to others will be retaliated or punished. In addition, he also alludes to the Bible to further elaborate his view, that is "So in everything, do unto others what you would have them do to you, for this sums up the Law and the Prophets" (Matthew 7:12). He then goes on to criticize human beings who fail to see the advantage of sparrows and regard them as absolutely injurious birds:

Chapter Four Criticism Against the Cruelty to Animals

> Your blinded eyes, worst foes to you,
>
> Ne'er see the good which sparrows do
>
> Did not the sparrows watching round
>
> Pick up the insect from your grounds
>
> Did not they tend your rising grain
>
> You vain might sow — to reap in vain
>
> Thus providence when understood
>
> Her end and aim is doing good (119-26)

Actually, although the sparrows steal grains for food from the peasants, they also feed on the harmful insects, and thus protect the peasants' crops from injury and give them prospects of harvest. Clare concludes the stanza as follows:

> O God let me the best pursue
>
> As I'd have other do to me
>
> Let me the same to others do
>
> And learn at least Humanity (131-34)

The narrator prays to God to let him always be in pursuit of philanthropic things, and not only does he himself seek goodness, but he also hopes other people will follow suit. All in all, let human beings learn to be caring and humane towards the animals.

Clare's "The Badger" (1830) deals with the corrupt local custom of baiting badgers. The poem consists of five stanzas, four of which are sonnets, one stanza being a 12-line stanza. That is the reason why this poem is also referred to as "badger sonnets".

Here is a description of badger baiting in Bewick's *A General History of Quadrupeds* (1790):

> Few creatures defend themselves better, or bite with greater keenness, than the Badger. On that account it is frequently baited with Dogs trained for the purpose. This inhuman diversion is chiefly confined

to the idle and the vicious, who take a cruel pleasure in seeing this harmless animal surrounded by its enemies, and defending itself from their attacks, which it does with astonishing agility and success. Its motions are so quick, that a Dog is frequently desperately wounded in the first moment of assault, and obliged to fly. (281-82)

In the second and fourth badger sonnets written by Clare, we can discover something similar to Bewick's objective description, that is, the nimbleness and bravery of the badger. In the second sonnet, we see the badger

... beats and scarcely wounded goes away

Lapt up as if asleep he scorns to fly

And siezes any dog that ventures nigh (lines 4-6)

Clare's depiction pictures for us a brave badger who seldom gets injured in the fierce fight against dogs and who fights to the last ditch, disdaining to run away during the fight. In the fourth sonnet, Clare shows to us that

When badgers fight and every one's a foe

The dogs are clapt and urged to join the fray

The badger turns and drives them all away

Though scarcely half as big, dimute and small

He fights with dogs for hours and beats them (4-8)

In spite of the disadvantage in size compared with the huge dogs, the badgers are never timid and cowardly. Apart from courage and nerve, they have endurance and stamina in the fighting, which enable them to defeat the dogs.

In the third sonnet, we can find something more similar to Bewick's description, that is, the cruel pleasure people take in the baiting of the badger.

And bait him all the day with many dogs

And laugh and shout and fright the scampering hogs

He runs along and bites at all he meets

They shout and hollo down the noisey street (11-14)

Chapter Four Criticism Against the Cruelty to Animals

This is a bustling, cacophonous and chaotic scene. Very much outnumbered, fighting for the whole day with men and dogs, the badger is very exhausted. But the baiting lovers take great pleasure in chasing the badger, frightening him and seeing him scamper here and there. They just base their wicked happiness upon the extreme suffering and infliction of the badger. So Clare does not merely pontificate on abstract moral issues, but lends his voice to the powerless victims of human violence (McKusick 85).

The idea of cruel pleasure is reemphasized in the last 12-line stanza, "The blackguard laughs and hurrys on the fray" (2). Taking into consideration the meaning of the word "blackguard", which refers to someone who is dishonest and who has no sense of right and wrong, the attitude of Clare towards those who participate in badger baiting is pretty clear.

Brave though the badger is, he is not able to fight against so many people and so many dogs, and so he is doomed to fail and die, since this is the ultimate fun of the baiting game. In the last stanza, we are grieved to see the tragic ending of the badger.

> But sticks and cudgels quickly stop the chace
> He turns agen and drives the noisey crowd
> And beats the many dogs in noises loud
> He drives away and beats them every one
> And then they loose them all and set them on
> He falls as dead and kicked by boys and men
> Then starts and grins and drives the crowd agen
> Till kicked and torn and beaten out he lies
> And leaves his hold and cackles groans and dies (4-12)

The attack of the baiting lovers and dogs goes on round after round. When the badger finally lies on the ground, as if he were dead, he is ruthlessly "kicked by boys and men". He had no choice but to fight back again until he is "kicked and torn and beaten out" and breathes his last miserably and tragically, which is a very brutal scene. According to John Goodridge, "it seems the poet must cast around for a familiar image of violence and brutality in order to convey the strength of his feelings of anger, betrayal and loss" (132). As one of the poems of the Middle Period of his creation, Clare's condemnation of the local custom of badger baiting in this poem is severe, different from his attitude in his early writing career, when he "accepted fox-hunting and badger-baiting as part of rural life, neither totally condemning nor approving of these pursuits" (Chun 57). Hence we can see his progress as an ecological poet.

Clare's "The Puddock's Nest" (1832–1837) is a sonnet. The puddock bird refers to the kite or fork-tailed buzzard.

> And lay three eggs and spotted o'er the red
>
> The schoolboy often hears the old ones cry
>
> And climbs the tree and gets them ere they fly
>
> And take them home and often cuts their wing
>
> And ties them in the garden with a string. (lines 10-14)

The naughty schoolboy not only snatches the bird eggs, but also catches the puddocks, mercilessly cuts their wings, and puts them in bondage. No wonder Merryn Williams and Raymond Williams think this is one of Clare's darkest poems (241). But we may wonder who is more to blame for this tragic incident, the ignorant schoolboy, or his parents and teachers? As far as I am concerned, apart from subjective factor on the kids' side, dereliction of duty in moral and ethical education and laissez-faire attitude on the guardians' side are to some extent responsible for the ill-treatment of birds among kids.

Clare's "The Fox" (1835–1837) deals with the narrow escape of a wounded fox. The ploughman wounds a weary fox while he is plowing, and what he does is not to save the fox or show some regret as Burns does in his poem "To A Mouse", but to cruelly "beat him till his ribs would crack" (line 9). A shepherd who passes by with his dog wants the skin of the fox, so after the ploughman beats the fox out, the shepherd "slung him at his back" (10). So we can see the cruelty of the ploughman and the shepherd in their treatment of the fox. As Sarah Houghton-Walker puts it, "the taking of pleasure in inflicting gratuitous pain (laughing, posthumous beating), rather than the attempt to kill (itself understandable in the rural economy), is grotesque" (180). While they stop to have a rest, to their astonishment, the fox who pretends to be dead suddenly starts to run for life. The fox runs away so abruptly and swiftly that it is impossible for the two men and the dog to respond at once and to catch up with him. Even though the shepherd throws his hook towards the fox and a woodman who witnesses the incident helps to stop the fox by throwing his hatchet towards him, the fox still escapes successfully into a badger hole, and "lived to chase the hounds another day" (28). The result of the pursuit is that the shepherd breaks his hook and loses the skin. The hunting which ends in failure proves that "These hunters are clumsy, vacant, malcoordinated, late: all the things the fox isn't" (Houghton-Walker 181). And just as M. & R. Williams put it, Clare admired animals' qualities like the fox's resourcefulness (241).

Christina's "Hear What the Mournful Linnets Say" (1870) is also taken from her *Sing-Song*. The poem is written with the linnets as the speaker of the poem, or in other words, the complainer, as we hear they say mournfully:

> We built our nest compact and warm,
> But cruel boys came round our way
> And took our summerhouse by storm.
>
> They crushed the eggs so neatly laid;
> So now we sit with drooping wing,
> And watch the ruin they have made,
> Too late to build, too sad to sing. (lines 2-8)

The small boys are so cruel that they not only destroy the linnets' nest but also break their eggs into small pieces. The linnets can only watch the boy's savage act sorrowfully and helplessly, as the word "droop" signifies the lack of strength or firmness. The heavy blow on the linnets makes it hard for them to sing any more. As Virginia Sickbert argues, this is one of Christina's poems that promote empathic understanding of animals (397).

The last series of animal poems to be discussed in the nineteenth century is from Kipling's monograph *Beast and Man in India — A Popular Sketch of Indian Animals in Their Relations with the People* (1891). At the beginning of some chapters, there are animal poems written by Kipling himself, for example, Chapter V, Of Goats and Sheep; Chapter VII, Of Buffaloes and Pigs; Chapter IX, Of Elephants; and Chapter XIII, Of Animal Calls. The goat is actually the scapegoat, who "bled in that Babe's stead / Because of innocence" (lines 3-4). For their own sake, human beings take advantage of the innocence of the lamb. The innocent goat thus complains, "I bear the sins of sinful men / That have no sin of my own" (5-6), and "I am the meat of sacrifice, / The ransom of man's guilt" (9-10). For the pigs and buffaloes, they belong to the "folk of low degree" (line 4). For the elephants, they are "our slave" and "servant of the Queen" (line 7, 8), which shows their inferior position. Due to the low position of the beasts, human beings ill-treat them, so we can see

> But man with goad and whip,
>
> Breaks up their fellowship,
>
> Shouts in their silky ears
>
> Filling their soul with fears. (lines 7-10)

When the beasts are disobedient of their orders due to extreme tiredness or the toughness of the task, human beings will use a pointed stick or a whip to beat them severely or violently to make them do something against their will. Apart from beating the beasts, they will also shout at the beasts or curse them,

Chapter Four Criticism Against the Cruelty to Animals

which frighten them a lot. Human beings think that the beasts are supposed to understand their job, but in the beasts' view, "'twas the whip that spoke" (16).

The twentieth century saw Hardy's concern with war horses, which appears in his verse-play *The Dynasts* (1903–1908). After describing the soldiers with "crazed cries" in the war, Hardy turns to show the response of the war horses:

> Are horses, maimed in myriads, tearing round
>
> In maddening pangs, the harnessings they wear
>
> Clanking discordant jingles as they tear! (3.1.5.343-45)

In the war, there are an extremely large number of horses that are injured seriously. They feel so painful that the pain seems to make them become mad. As a result, they run on the battlefield wildly and violently, with the jingles on their body making an inharmonious and unpleasant sound.

Hardy's representative war poem "Horses Aboard" (1922–1925) shows again his sympathy towards and criticism of the ill-treatment of the war horses, probably those in the Second Boer War (1899–1902).

> Horses in horse cloths stand in a row
>
> On board the huge ship that as last lets go:
>
> Whither are they sailing? They do not know,
>
> Nor what for, nor how.
>
> They are horses of war,
>
> And are going to where there is fighting afar;
>
> But they gaze through their eye-holes unwitting they are,
>
> And that in some wilderness, gaunt and ghast,
>
> Their bones will bleach ere a year has passed,
>
> And the item be as "war-waste" classed.
>
> And when the band booms, and the fold say
>
> "Good bye!"
>
> And the shore slides astern, they appear wrenched awry.

> From the scheme Nature planned for them —
>
> wondering why.

The wretched war horses have no idea where they are heading for and what they are going to do, so to speak, unaware of their fate. Tragically, the predestined result for them is that when they become exhausted, "gaunt and ghast", and die on the battle field, they will be classed as "war-waste" and thus their miserable life comes to an end. According to Millgate, Hardy expressed his distress at the involuntary and uncomprehending sufferings of horses and mules on the battlefields of the Boer War (380). In the summer of 1901, Hardy said that it was in any circumstances "immoral and unmanly to cultivate a pleasure in compassing the death of our weaker and simpler fellow-creatures by cunning, instead of learning to regard their destruction, if a necessity, as an odious task, akin to that, say, of the common hangman" (*Collected Letters*, Vol. 2, 283). Only when the war is over, can the horses be freed from harsh treatment. As is illustrated in the poem "And There Was A Great Calm" (On the Signing of the Armistice, Nov. 11, 1918): "Worn horses mused: 'We are not whipped to-day'" (8.4).

However, much earlier than the composition of his verse-play and war poem, Hardy has already shown his view on the abuse of war horses in the nineteenth century. In Hardy's journal on July 13, 1888, he writes:

> What was it on the faces of those horses? — Resignation. Their eyes looked at me, haunted me. The absoluteness of their resignation was terrible. When afterwards I heard their tramp as I lay in bed, the ghosts of their eyes came in to me, saying, 'Where is your justice, O man and ruler?'. (qtd. in F. Hardy 211)

In Hardy's reply to the letter from Mr. W. T. Stead, who has asked him to voice his opinion on "A Crusade of Peace" in 1899, Hardy remarks:

> As a preliminary, all civilized nations might at least show their

Chapter Four Criticism Against the Cruelty to Animals

humanity by covenanting that no horses should be employed in battle except for transport. Soldiers, at worst, know what they are doing, but these animals are denied even the poor possibilities of glory and reward as a compensation for their sufferings. (qtd. in F. Hardy 303)

Other than showing consideration to war horses, Hardy's criticism of cruelty to animals also goes to other common animals. Based on Florence Hardy's recollection, "The sight of animals being taken to market or driven to slaughter always aroused in Hardy feelings of intense pity, as he well knew, as must anyone living in or near a market-town, how much needless suffering is inflicted" (*Life* 434). As can be seen in the poem "A Sheep Fair" (1922–1925):

The day arrives of the autumn fair,

And torrents fall,

Though sheep in throngs are gathered there,

Ten thousand all,

Sodden, with hurdles round them reared:

And, lot by lot, the pens are cleared,

And the auctioneer wrings out his beard,

And wipes his book, bedrenched and smeared,

And takes the rain from his face with the edge of his hand,

As torrents fall.

The wool of the ewes is like a sponge

With the daylong rain:

Jammed tight, to turn, or lie, or lunge,

They strive in vain.

Their horns are soft as finger-nails,

Their shepherds reek against the rails,

The tied dogs soak with tucked-in tails,

The buyers' hat-brims fill like pails,

> Which spill small cascades when they shift their stand
>
> In the daylong rain.

We can imagine the situation with which the sheep are confronted at the fair. It is a rainy day, and the sheep become "sodden" because they have stayed in the rain for a whole day. There are so many of them within a limited and constrained space, and they "jammed tight"; it is impossible for them "to turn, or lie, or lunge", and even though they struggle, it is in vain. They can do nothing but suffer the tiredness, humidity and suffocation. Descriptions like "woolly wear", "meek, mewed band" in the Postscript imply some sympathy for the hapless sheep (T. Johnson 125). By showing the poor condition of the sheep, Hardy insinuated his criticism.

Hardy's "The Mongrel" (1924–1928) tells the story of how the owner of a dog murders him. The reason why the owner has to kill the dog is stated clearly at the beginning of the poem, that is "taxpaying day was coming along, / So the mongrel had to be drowned" (lines 3-4). The practice of collecting taxes from dog owners in Britain actually started in the nineteenth century, and there was even "The Dog Tax War" in 1898 in opposition to the enforcement of dog tax. Accordingly, in order not to pay the dog tax, the owner in this poem chooses to kill his dog. Pinion's comment on this poem is very brief but ironic: "Which is the mongrel, man or dog?" (*Commentary* 246). Considering the figurative meaning of the word "mongrel" as "a derogatory term for a variation that is not genuine", it is easy to get what Pinion means by such a question.

The way the owner kills the dog is to take advantage of his inborn faithfulness and pride in pleasing his owner. The owner throws a stick into the ebbing tide of the sea, and the dog jumps into the water without any hesitation with the aim of taking back the stick for his owner. But it is a pity that he underestimates the power of the "treacherous trend" (12). Here the rhetorical device of transferred epithet is used, because it not the trend that is treacherous, but the dog's owner who has coaxed him into doing such a risky thing. While the dog is struggling in the water, its owner just indifferently and apathetically "standing to wait the end" (16), even though "The loving eyes of the dog inclined / To the man he held as a god enshrined" (17-18), which is a very ironic apotheosis. The dog has never suspected that this tragic incident is out of his owner's premeditated plot or scheme. However, before he breathes his last, he has got a painful epiphany.

> Just ere his sinking what does one see
>
> Break on the face of that devotee?
>
> A wakening to the treachery
>
> He had loved with love so blind?
>
> The faith that had shone in that mongrel's eye
>
> That his owner would save him by and by
>
> Turned to much like a curse as he sank to die,
>
> And a loathing of mankind. (25-32)

When his faith in his owner's coming to his rescue is shattered, he suddenly comes to know mankind's treachery. And his previous love of human beings turns into a curse and hatred towards them. To William H. Pritchard, the poem is "a quite unbearable piece" (395).

Hardy writes the commemorative poem "Compassion: An Ode: in Celebration of the Centenary of the Royal Society for the Prevention of Cruelty to Animals" (1924) at the request of the RSPCA when its 100-year anniversary is around the corner.

In the beginning stanza of the poem, Hardy first recalls the history of the foundation of the organization. The "dusky years" in the first line means the time when animals suffered from harsh use and maltreatment, such as in driving the carriages, scientific experiments and fields of entertainment. "A lonesome lamp" in the second line refers to the RSPCA whose function is to give light to the "dusky years". The "few fain pioneers" in the third line represent the aforementioned founding fathers of the organization, headed by Richard Martin MP, William Wilberforce MP and the Reverend Arthur Broome. And "incredulous eyes" in the fourth line stand for those people who cannot believe in such a progressive and audacious act, and who even tend to impede its setting up. The purpose of this organization is to "plead / Their often hunger, thirst, pangs, prisonment" (lines 7-8).

Seen from the second stanza, thanks to what the RSPCA has done in the past 100 years since its foundation, much progress has been made in the protection of animals, as "A larger louder conscience saith / More sturdily to-day" (13-14). Despite the achievements made, some indifferent people are still not influenced, especially in the foreign countries, as we can see

> But still those innocents are thralls
> To throbless hearts, near, far, that hear no calls
> Of honour towards their too-dependent frail,
> And from Columbia Cape to Ind we see
> How helplessness breeds tyranny
> In power above assail. (15-20)

And those who advocate the rights for animals are forced to keep silent, and sometimes are even punished or persecuted secretly. As Hardy describes in the third stanza:

> Cries still are heard in secret nooks,
> Till hushed with gag or slit or thud;
> And hideous dens whereon none looks
> Are sprayed with needless blood. (21-24)

Nevertheless, Hardy is still very proud of what has been accomplished, confident and hopeful of the future development of animal protection, as he says:

> But here, in battlings, patient, slow,

Chapter Four Criticism Against the Cruelty to Animals

> Much has been won — more, maybe, than we know —
> And on we labour hopeful. "Ailinon!"
> A mighty voice calls: "But may the good prevail!"
> And "Blessed are the merciful!"
> Calls a yet mightier one. (25-30)

Apart from Hardy the major contributor, there are a couple of other poets who also contributed to the criticism of animal abuse. Hodgson's "The Bells of Heaven"[①] (1917) is short ten-line poem, which I'll quote in full length:

> 'TWOULD ring the bells of Heaven
> The wildest peal for years,
> If Parson lost his senses
> And people came to theirs,
> And he and they together
> Knelt down with angry prayers
> For tamed and shabby tigers
> And dancing dogs and bears,
> And wretched, blind pit ponies,
> And little hunted hares.

The poem shows sympathy to animals facing four different kinds of unfair treatment, namely, tigers in the zoo, dogs and bears in the circus, small horses moving coal in a mine, and hares that are hunted in the field. To be specific, the poem indicts human beings' misuse of animals from four perspectives: lifelong imprisonment, torturous training, laborious toil, and merciless hunting. It is understandable that people who kneel down to say prayers for the animals feel angry about this, and actually it is the poet's anger towards the maltreatment of animals. No wonder Mike Read argues that Hodgson "was one of the earliest

---

① https://www.poemhunter.com/poem/the-bells-of-heaven/

writers to be concerned with ecology, speaking out against the fur trade and man's destruction of the natural world" (105).

Lawrence's "Elephants Plodding" (1928) is a mini poem with only three lines:

> Plod! Plod!
>
> And what ages of time
>
> the worn arches of their spines support!

This is a poem about toiling elephants. We do not know what kind of work the elephants in this poem are doing, maybe carrying logs, or pulling carts. Whatever the work, it is burdensome, which is shown in the way of their walking, because the word "plod" means to walk slowly and heavily, a sign of hard work or tiredness. In the first line, the rhetorical device of epizeuxis is used to give emphasis to the repetitive, boring and onerous task the elephants undertake. The strenuous work the elephants have done over a long period of time is also shown in "the worn arches of their spines", because the word "worn" signifies damage caused by long-term use.

The last poem to be discussed in this section is Larkin's "Myxomatosis" (1954), in which the narrator is talking to a personified rabbit who poses a question to him as regards the unfair treatment the rabbits have received:

> Caught in the centre of a soundless field
>
> While hot inexplicable hours go by
>
> What trap is this? Where were its teeth concealed?
>
> You seem to ask.
>
> I make a sharp reply,
>
> Then clean my stick. I'm glad I can't explain
>
> Just in what jaws you were to suppurate:
>
> You may have thought things would come right again
>
> If you could only keep quite still and wait.

Chapter Four Criticism Against the Cruelty to Animals

Myxomatosis is a fatal viral disease of rabbits characterized by erupting skin tumors, and was intentionally introduced into Great Britain to reduce the rabbit population (Malamud 153), which is actually a maltreatment to the rabbits. The reason why the field is soundless is that a lot of rabbits have been killed by the malicious myxomatosis. When the innocent rabbit asks the narrator what trap this is, he is not able to give a satisfactory explanation, or actually he knows how to explain, but he does not want to tell the truth because truth hurts. And he thinks if he does not reveal the truth, the rabbit or rabbits in general can still cherish hope for the future if they are patient enough to wait. Despite the failure to give an appropriate answer to the rabbit's question, in Malamud's view, Larkin establishes an evenhanded relationship between himself and the rabbit with the second-person pronoun ("you") indicating dialogue between the poem's two characters, man and rabbit (154), so to speak, he is trying to provide a tentative remedy for the damaged relationship between human beings and the rabbits.

V. Theme of Nemesis

Nemesis is the Goddess of retribution for evil deeds in Greek mythology, and is used to mean deserved and inevitable punishment for one's wicked wrongdoings. The theme is frequently used in literature, and in some animal poems as well, so as to show the evil consequence or disastrous effect resulting from the maltreatment of animals, and at the same time serve as a warning or alarm to those potential or would-be animal abusers.

The first poem I would like to quote in this part is the eighteenth-century poet Gay's "Fable V. Wild Boar and Ram" (1727), which is mainly a dialogue between a boar and a ram, and the first half of which goes:

  Against an elm a sheep was tied,

> The butcher's knife in blood was dyed:
> The patient flock, in silent fright,
> From far beheld the horrid sight.
> A savage Boar, who near them stood,
> Thus mocked to scorn the fleecy brood.
> "All cowards should be served like you.
> See, see, your murderer is in view:
> With purple hands and reeking knife,
> He strips the skin yet warm with life;
>
> Your quartered sires, your bleeding dams,
> The dying bleat of harmless lambs
> Call for revenge. O stupid race!
> The heart that wants revenge is base." (lines 1-14)

Seeing one of their kindred is being killed by the butcher, the tamed and frightened flock of sheep just stand far away, watching patiently and silently, or even detachedly. Hence a savage boar nearby makes a remark in which he points out the cowardice of the sheep. In the boar's view, the sheep should rebel and fight back by themselves, instead of only calling for revenge, which is reliant upon others or supernatural powers, and which he thinks is base. As a reply to his criticism, an old ram says:

> We bear no terror in our eyes;
> Yet think us not of soul so tame,
> Which no repeated wrongs inflame;
> Insensible of every ill,
> Because we want thy tusks to kill.
>
> Know, those who violence pursue,

Chapter Four Criticism Against the Cruelty to Animals

>Give to themselves the vengeance due;
>
>For in these massacres they find
>
>The two chief plagues that waste mankind:
>
>Our skin supplies the wrangling bar,
>
>It wakes their slumbering sons to war,
>
>And well revenge may rest contented,
>
>Since drums and parchment were invented. (16-28)

The old male sheep thinks that the boar has misunderstood the sheep, since they are not so tame that no repeated ill-treatment can exasperate them, nor are they so numb that they are not sensible or aware of human beings' wrongdoings. But because the sheep are not strong enough to rebel, they hope that the boar who has sharp tusks can retaliate against human beings on their behalf. What the sheep can do is to turn to the Goddess of Nemesis for help and it really has worked, because human beings' massacre of animals has brought about plagues that hurt or torture them. One of the retributions is that when the skin of the sheep is used to make drums, the drums will drive the young men to fight and sacrifice themselves in the brutal war. And thus the sheep's vengeance is wreaked.

In the prophetic poet Blake's "Auguries of Innocence" (1803), he first describes the suffering of various animals in the hands of human beings, such as the robin imprisoned in the cage, the doves and pigeons shut in the dove house, the starving dog at the gate, the misused horse on the road, the hunted hare in the field, the wounded skylark in the woods, the game cock clipped for fight, as well as the misused lamb in the butcher's house.

And then he predicts how is human beings' cruelty to animals going to be revenged by Heaven:

>He who shall hurt the little Wren
>
>Shall never be belov'd by Men

A Study of British Animal Poems

> He who the Ox to wrath has mov'd
>
> Shall never be by Woman lov'd
>
> The wanton Boy that kills the Fly
>
> Shall feel the Spiders enmity
>
> He who torments the Chafers Sprite
>
> Weaves a Bower in endless Night
>
> The Catterpiller on the Leaf
>
> Repeats to thee thy Mothers grief
>
> Kill not the Moth nor Butterfly
>
> For the Last Judgment draweth nigh
>
> He who shall train the Horse to War
>
> Shall never pass the Polar Bar. (lines 29-42)

Even though Blake's sympathy towards animals has gone so far as to the harmful insects including chafers, flies and caterpillars, which is somewhat overdone, the concern about the welfare of other animals (such as wren, ox, and horse) are advisable. Blake suggests that if we human beings do not treat mammals, birds, insects well, we will be revenged on and bad consequences will be inflicted upon us naturally or supernaturally, for instance, we will not be loved by our fellow mankind; upon our death we will be reincarnated into the creature that we have killed and will be killed subsequently by its natural enemy; our unkind deeds will incur the Last Judgement by the stern Jesus Christ and what ensues is the end of the world; and we cannot enter into the posthumous spiritual world through a gate in the north. What's worse, the revenge is not only on individuals, but on the nation as a whole, since Blake states that the ill-treatment of animals "Puts all Heaven in a Rage" and "Predicts the ruin of the State" (6, 10). As Derek Wall proposes, "That we are all interconnected and what befalls one part of nature will influence the rest is lyrically captured by the poet" (63).

Chapter Four Criticism Against the Cruelty to Animals

S.T. Coleridge's most well-known and representative poem "Rime of the Ancient Mariner" (1798) is sometimes interpreted from an Eco-critical perspective. As the story goes, the old mariner kills an innocent and harmless albatross, a deed which in his own words is "a hellish thing" (2.9). His reckless act irritates the Goddess of Nemesis, and as a result, severe punishment is inflicted upon him and his fellow sailors. They is no wind over the sea at all and they are stuck in a stagnant situation, "nor breath nor motion" (2.34). They are deprived of drinkable water and their throats are parched. Finally, "With heavy thump, a lifeless lump, / They dropped down one by one" (3.76-77). Consequently, the old mariner's wrongdoing costs the lives of two hundred of his fellowmen as scapegoats, which is really a harsh and cruel punishment. What's more, he himself also has to suffer from loneliness and fear, with his "soul in agony" and his "heart as dry as dust" (4.12, 4.24). The mariner is mentally tormented and begins to repent for his wrongdoing. Then he sees the water snakes, and begins to bless them.

> O happy living things! no tongue
> Their beauty might declare:
> A spring of love gushed from my heart,
> And I blessed them unaware:
> Sure my kind saint took pity on me,
> And I blessed them unaware. (4.59-64)

As a result of his blessing the snakes, the albatross falls off his neck and his sin is repented. He gets redemption and salvation. However, the mariner's repentance is not finished yet, since one supernatural voice says, "The man hath penance done, / And penance more will do" (5.117-18). That is why the mariner has to intercept the wedding guest, and tell him the story. And he will tell the story to many more people in the future as a way of penance. The mariner's attitude or change of attitude towards animals in nature plays a crucial role in our understanding of the poem as an animal poem, and his remorse for his wrongdoing in the treatment of the albatross serves as the turning point of the story. As Neil Roberts and Terry Gifford propose, "In 'The Rime of the Ancient Mariner', Coleridge wrote perhaps our language's greatest ecological fable" (169). Even though the mariner eventually gets redemption and salvation by blessing the water snakes unawares and the story seems to end in a rather consummate way, the inserted theme of nemesis is also crucially important, which has a warning and alarming function for those animal abusers and murderers, including the potential ones, since according to John Blades, "Scapegoat and pariah, he [the old mariner] suffers terrible psychological torment as the punishment for his 'crime'" (191).

Another of Coleridge's nemesis poem is "The Raven. A Christmas Tale, Told by A School-Boy to His Little Brothers and Sisters" (1798). In the tale, the raven couple build their nest in a tall oak tree, with the young birds in it. But a woodman comes and cuts down the tree, which kills the young birds who still cannot fly and the raven mother dies of grief. The woodman then makes a boat using the wood of the oak tree. When the woodman and his friends put out to sea in this hand-made boat, an accident takes place:

> Such a storm there did rise as no ship would withstand.
> It bulged on a rock, and the waves rush'd in fast;
> Round and round flew the Raven, and cawed to the blast.
> He heard the last shriek of the perishing souls —
> See! see! O'er the topmast the mad water rolls! (lines 36-40)

So, revengefully, the woodman and his fellowmen are all killed by a ferocious and devastating storm. The raven father who witnesses the miserable death of those men cannot help feeling relieved and happy. And the poem ends:

> Right glad was the Raven, and off he went fleet,
> And Death riding home on a cloud he did meet,

And he thank'd him again and again for this treat:

They had taken his all; and Revenge it was sweet! (41-44)

So we can see that the God of Death comes to the raven's aid and punishes those wrongdoers severely and duly. The last sentence of the poem "Revenge it was sweet" makes use of the rhetorical device of oxymoron, since such a cruel revenge cannot be deemed as being sweet in human beings' eyes, and it is only true from the raven's perspective. If the woodman and his friends had treated the raven and his family in a humanitarian way, perhaps there would not have been any revenge at all on the raven's side, and both of them could live happily.

Unlike the three previous poems, Hardy's "The Bird-Catcher's Boy" (1912) uses an indirect way to show his protest against the cruelty to birds. This poem also contains some supernatural element and describes a child named Freddy who runs away from home because he is forced by his father to make his living through catching birds. Tragically, he only returns to his home as a ghost when the sea gives up his body.

At the beginning of the poem, the boy says to his father:

FATHER, I fear your trade:

Surely it's wrong!

Little birds limed and made

Captive life-long.

Larks bruise and bleed in jail,

Trying to rise;

Every caged nightingale

Soon pines and dies. (lines 1-8)

The little boy has realized that what his father does as a profession is not morally right, and he is afraid of such a bird-catching profession, because the birds are confined in a prison-like cage, and thus they become very depressed and even die of grief.

Hearing the little boy's worry and concern, his father replies in an authoritative manner:

> Don't be a dolt, my boy!
> Birds must be caught;
> My lot is such employ,
> Yours to be taught.
>
> Soft shallow stuff as that
> Out from your head!
> Just learn your lessons pat,
> Then off to bed. (9-16)

The father is persuading his son that they have no choice but to catch birds because it is their way of making a living, and what's more, the boy is supposed to inherit his father's trade when he grows up. In the father's eyes, what the boy has just said seems to be stupid words and "shallow stuff". However, in the eyes of the animal protectionists, the boy's remark is far from being shallow, instead, it is significant and enlightening.

As a way to rebel against his father, the little boy leaves home secretly and nobody knows where he has gone. Weeks and months have passed, and the heart-sick parents can only wait anxiously and painfully for their son's returning home. Nevertheless, the birds are still kept imprisoned in the cages:

> Hopping there long anon
> Still the birds hung:
> Like those in Babylon
> Captive, they sung. (37-40)

The story turns out to be a tragedy since the concluding stanza of the poem tells us that the boy becomes a sailor and is drowned in the sea. As the English proverb goes, "wickedness does not go altogether unrequited". On the ground that the boy's father has caught and caged many birds, nemesis falls upon the household, with the boy as the victim or scapegoat. This poem serves more as a premonition of danger rather than a wisdom of hindsight. If we do not treat animals in a more humane way, regard them as equal members of the earth, and take animal ethics into serious consideration, we are doomed to be punished in the long run. As Singer has argued, "Pain and suffering are in themselves bad and should be prevented or minimized, irrespective of the race, sex, or species of the being that suffers" (49).

The last poem in this section I would like to bring into discussion but feel reluctant to do so is "The Hare" (1910–1911) by the twentieth-century poet Wilfrid Wilson Gibson (1878–1962). It is a long poem of 415 lines about the legendary tale of a man, a hare and a girl. The reason why I hesitate to talk about this poem is because it is actually the opposite of the aforementioned poems, since it does not deal with retribution, but repaying the favor. At the very beginning of the poem, the man tells us his experience of catching a hare in a snare:

>My hands were hot upon a hare,
>
>Half-strangled, struggling in a snare —
>
>My knuckles at her warm wind-pipe —
>
>When suddenly, her eyes shot back,
>
>Big, fearful, staggering and black;
>
>And ere I knew, my grip was slack;
>
>And I was clutching empty air,
>
>Half-mad, half-glad at my lost luck... (lines 1-8)

The "Big, fearful, staggering and black" eyes of the hare staring back at the man startles him and makes him loosen his clutch of her, and so she runs away for life successfully. The man has ambivalent feelings toward such a loss, both anger and happiness. What he narrates seems to have happened in a dream, since soon after telling the story, he says "I awoke beside the stack" (9). But even he himself is not sure whether this is a dream or reality, as he later says "Last night I loosed you from the snare — / Asleep, or waking, who's for knowing!" (63-64).

However, when he wakes up and looks around, he indeed sees a hare. When he stands up, the hare quickly runs away. He then starts to follow her, but soon loses sight of her. But when he later sits down beside a river to have lunch, he again sees the hare, runs after her, and fails again to catch up with her. He goes on travelling, and at twilight, he tells us "dropped my hands in time to feel / The hare just bolting 'twixt my feet" (135-36), but again "She slipped my clutch" (137). The hare seems to be teasing him or playing a game with him. So he "cursed that devil-littered hare" (138), because she leaves him "stranded in the dark" (139). As luck would have it, he finds a caravan on his way, and the hostess warmly welcomes him to be a guest. In this household, he catches sight of a girl from whose eyes he detects the fearful look of the hare, and once again he recalls the scene in his dream. Up to this point, there is some supernatural or mythological element in the story, since the girl seems to be the embodiment of the hare, or kind of fairy-like figure, turning up to pay a debt of gratitude, which actually resembles the stories in *Strange Stories from a Chinese Studio*, a collection of bizarre stories written by Pu Songling in the Qing Dynasty.

Later on, the girl tells him that a leering and ignoble widower wants to marry her, and his shameful coveting makes her frightened. Supposing the girl is the embodiment of the hare, the widower may symbolize the hunter. Then the man falls in love with the girl and they decide to run away together. Even though six happy months has passed after their elopement, the man still fears that one day when the girl wakes up in the morning, he would see the fearful look of the

Chapter Four Criticism Against the Cruelty to Animals

hare in her eyes. One night, he dreams again the previous hare-catching scene, and startles from the nightmare, and finds the girl is absent from the bed. He looks for her and sees her standing in the darkness, with a "leveret cuddled to her breast" (398). She explains to him:

> ... she could not rest;
>
> And, rising in the night, she'd found
>
> This baby-hare crouched on the ground;
>
> And she had nursed it quite a while;
>
> But, now, she'd better let it go...
>
> Its mother would be fretting so...
>
> A mother's heart... (402-08)

So it turns out to be a false alarm. Even if the girl is not the embodiment of the hare, she is definitely a lover and protector of hares, or animals in general. The man's epiphany is conducive to their harmonious and consummate relationship.

> I saw her smile,
>
> And look at me with tender eyes;
>
> And as I looked into their light,
>
> My foolish, fearful heart grew wise...
>
> And now, I knew that never there
>
> I'd see again the startled hare,
>
> Or need to dread the dreams of night. (409-15)

If in his previous dream, he is still uncertain about whether or not it is the right choice to let the hare go, now he is assured that he has done the justified thing. In the future, he will be a wise man, and he will love and protect animals, just like what the girl is doing now. Moreover, he will never be conscience-bitten, never see the frightening look in the girl's eyes, and never have nightmares about hare-catching again. As the saying goes, one good turn deserves another. This long tale can also be regarded as an ecological fable, or a poem with the theme of anti-nemesis, since nemesis is really a cruel alternative in the animal rights movement when there are genial and peaceful solutions.

Chapter Five　Advocacy of Animal Freedom and Rights

In order to achieve the equality between man and animals and build up a more harmonious relationship between the two, it is not enough to only praise the animals, show love and concern to them, or reveal some people's ill-treatment of them. Poets are supposed to advocate animal freedom, animal rights and animal welfare in a more direct and unwavering way. The pioneering ideas of some of the poets in terms of animal rights movement even anticipate those of the well-known moral philosophers or animal ethicists, such as Albert Schweitzer, Peter Singer and Tom Regan, whose major views on reverence for life, animal liberation and animal rights came out in 1949, 1975 and 1983 respectively. The last chapter of this book is targeted at giving an analysis of the poems devoted to the advocacy of animal freedom and animal rights.

I. Proposal for the Protection and Welfare of Animals

The German philosopher Immanuel Kant thinks that all animals are equally free and from freedom there arises the desire for equality (28). Direct proposal for animal freedom, animals' equality with man, and the protection and welfare of animals in British poetry flourishes in the nineteenth and twentieth century. One of the representative poems of its kind is Service's "Bird Sanctuary"[1]. A

---

[1] https://www.poemhunter.com/poem/bird-sanctuary/

sanctuary is usually an area where birds or wild animals are protected. In the first stanza, Service portrays the beauty of the sanctuary as follows:

> With fig and olive, almond, peach,
>
> cherry and plum-tree overgrown;
>
> Glad-watered by a crystal spring
>
> That carols through the silver night,
>
> And populous with birds who sing
>
> Gay madrigals for my delight. (lines 3-8)

In the sanctuary, there are various kinds of fruit trees, which can serve as the food source for the birds. There is also a clear spring which is the water source for them. No wonder the speaker calls this sanctuary "A slip of emerald" to show its preciousness (2). As a result, there are many birds that come to inhabit this wood, living a happy life here.

This beautiful place also attracts the attention of some merchants who would like to purchase this place and construct a pleasure dome. Confronted with such a profitable and tempting offer, the response of the speaker is not happiness, but instead, he remarks justifiably:

> Poor fools! they cannot understand
>
> how pricelessly it is my home!
>
> So luminous with living wings,
>
> So musical with feathered joy ...
>
> Not for all pleasure fortune brings,
>
> Would I such ecstasy destroy. (12-16)

According to the speaker, this sanctuary is priceless and invaluable. He would not exchange such a beautiful place with money, nor destroy the ecstasy brought by the birds' singing with the pleasure brought by material wealth.

In the last stanza, the speaker stresses that "Their [the birds'] happiness is my delight" (20). The reason why the birds would like to stay here instead of moving to somewhere else is that "They know their lover and their friend" (22). Finally, the speaker makes a solemn promise, that is, "So I will shield in peace and praise / My innocents unto the end" (23-24). In other words, he will continue to sing praise of the innocent birds and protect them from harm and danger until the very end of his life, which means the protection of birds is a life-long career for him.

Hardy's proposal for the protection of animals is shown in "The Lady in the Furs" (1925). In the first stanza, we can see that the noble lady in furs is very self-conceited and arrogant, which is shown in the glance she casts on the poorer ladies around her and in her remarks about addressing herself as "a lofty lovely woman" (line 1). The reason for her self-importance is that she is wearing a robe "that cost three figures" (5). As for the raw material of this robe, the lady explains that

> And they, they only got it
> From things feeble and afraid
> By murdering them in ambush
> With a cunning engine's aid. (9-12)

In order to make such an expensive and luxurious dress, some fur animals have to be butchered. People kill the animals with guns mercilessly regardless of their fragility and fear.

The last stanza shows the attitude of those who are against the killing of animals for furs.

> Though sneerers say I shine
> By robbing Nature's children
> Of apparel not mine,
> And that I am but a broom-stick,
> Like a scarecrow's wooden spine. (20-24)

Those with disapproval show contempt for the lady, and they use the word "rob" to indicate the illegal nature of the lady's behavior. The original title of the poem is "The Lady in the Christmas Furs", which is very ironic, on the ground that Christmas is a holiday of peace, while the soul of the animals who have been killed for furs are not at peace at all. As Pinion argues, "Hardy's altruism extended to all life, and the irony for him was that goods derived from slaughter were fashionable gifts at the season which proclaims peace on earth" (*Hardy Dictionary* 158).

"Animal Rights"[①] by Frederick (Or Freddie) Nellist (1928–) shows his advocacy of animal rights directly in the title of the poem, as well as in the very first line of the poem "Animal rights should be respected by all" (line 1). He then appeals for the rights of various animals. The first one is the dog.

> Keeping a dog chained all day is wrong
>
> He can't plead with you or sing a song
>
> A canine creature is a potential friend
>
> Do we no longer have compassion to lend? (3-6)

He thinks that the dog should have freedom and should not be chained all day long. Dogs are human beings' friends and we are supposed to show sympathy to them. The next stanza deals with various animals including ponies, foxes, hares, and birds.

> Pony's in fields half starved and confused
>
> Their needs ignored and are daily abused
>
> Is there pleasure hunting foxes and hares?
>
> Stand and be counted, show someone cares
>
> Birds of a feather held prisoner in cages
>
> I for one think this is utterly outrages. (7-12)

The horses toiling in the field are abused every day, but what makes

---

① https://www.poemhunter.com/poem/animal-rights-7/

Chapter Five Advocacy of Animal Freedom and Rights

things worse is that they are not provided with enough food and they suffer from hunger. The entertaining sport of hunting foxes and hares is to base our happiness upon the suffering of animals, which shows human beings' lack of care for animals. The birds are imprisoned in cages and thus lose their freedom. Nellist thinks that this is an act that is violent, cruel and wrong, which makes him feel shocked and angry. He then goes on serving as the spokesman for other animals.

> Lions and tigers and some elephants too
> Being prodded with whips in circus or zoo
> They are forced to perform and entertain
> Now it's time for their rights to campaign (13-17)

The last group of animals are those performing animals in the circus or zoo, who are compelled to give performance to entertain the audience. If they are unwilling or afraid of doing some dangerous and difficult acts, they will be urged by whips, especially during the harsh training. After showing us what kind of animals are in need of rights, Nellist calls on people to carry out this campaign.

> I am saying animals do not have a voice
> Humans are different we can make a choice
> Give it some thought, who takes the blame?
> Let us be honest, hang our heads in shame. (17-20)

Because animals cannot speak, they are not able to ask for rights by themselves. Therefore, human beings should be responsible to give help to animals in need. More and more people should be the mouthpiece of animals, asking for rights on their behalf. If animals are not given the rights they deserve, human beings are to blame and are supposed to feel shameful. We cannot shirk our responsibility or pass the buck.

Another poem entitled "Animal Rights"[①] is written by terence nabbs (born in 1940s). The poem is about a lawsuit between the owners of battery hens and the advocates of animal rights movement. Battery hens means the egg-laying hens which are raised in cages connected together in a unit, as in an artillery battery in the battle, and this way of raising hens will lead to the restriction of movement and prevention of many natural behaviors.

The poem starts from a piece of good news, that is, "two / Animal rights movement members, were elected to Holland's Parliament" (lines 1-2). And the first thing they are going to do is to "prosecute, / On behalf of Battery Hens for, / Cruelty" (3-5). Before the court hearing begins, the judge warns the two sides that "There will be no long winded speeches or Rabbiting on / Trying to Worm your way into my good Bucks" (8-9), in other words, the two sides are not supposed to waste time on this case because time is money in such a commercialized society, which shows that he deems the lawsuit insignificant and he does not care so much about the case. The defendants find a man and an old lady as witnesses, especially the latter one, whose "crocodile tears were soon flowing like a river" (22). With the heedless attitude of the judge and the "touching" evidence from the defendants' witnesses, it is not difficult to give an estimation of the verdict of the case. The defendants win the case, in spite of the protest of the prosecutors' lawyers that the owners of the battery hens should be charged. And the poet could not help saying "We've been Badgered by the Judge and Out Foxed by the Defence / It's a Cat-Astrophy" (30-31). The poet capitalizes the word "catastrophe" on purpose so as to show that injustice in the court is a big disaster for the hens, which will cause them great suffering and damage. Despite the failure in the lawsuit, we can see that the advocates for animals rights are indeed fighting bravely.

---

① https://www.poemhunter.com/poem/animal-rights-2/

Chapter Five Advocacy of Animal Freedom and Rights

The last poem in this section is "Animal Rights, Human Wrongs"[①], which is written by the contemporary poet Vincent Jolliffe. The title is a possible allusion to Regan's monograph *Animal Rights, Human Wrongs: An Introduction to Moral Philosophy* (2003). The whole poem goes as follows:

> this must be wrong what humans do
>
> to breed animals to use as food
>
> chefs disguise the flesh in such a way
>
> that as children we do not realise
>
> an animal has died for our dish of the day
>
> vegetarians will not be deceived
>
> they will get by eating their greens
>
> there are enough vegetables to go around
>
> one day an empty stomach will not be found
>
> in years to come people will not conceive
>
> the suffering we created just so we could feed
>
> and to fill the pockets of weakness with greed
>
> religious people hold the key
>
> to the animals right to be free
>
> before you say your prayers tonight
>
> you religious people who think you are so right
>
> please spare a thought for animal rights

Like what Nellist does in the above-mentioned "Animal Rights", Jolliffe also thinks depriving animals of their rights is wrong. What's more, he puts his view straightforwardly both in the title and the first line of the poem. But unlike Nellist who asks for rights of various animals, Jolliffe is merely stressing the right of the animals who are raised only to be killed and used as meat, and whose

---

① https://www.poemhunter.com/poem/animal-rights-human-wrongs/

bitter suffering is ignored. In Jolliffe's view, vegetarians are praiseworthy in this perspective since they feed on vegetables and fruits. It is ironic that many of the people who do harm to animals are religious people, who pray to God every day for mercy. At the end of the poem, Jolliffe is requesting those people to take animal rights into consideration in their future prayers. In other words, in term of protecting animals and gaining rights for them, human beings should be identical with themselves and cannot be hypocrites who say one thing, but do another.

II. Protest Against Experiment on Animals and Vivisection

Looking back into the British history, we may find experiments on animals of various kinds started early in ancient times, but vivisection was not introduced from the European Continent into British laboratories and medical schools until the mid-nineteenth century. And anti-vivisection movement in Britain started from the nineteenth century as well. Surprisingly, anti-vivisection started from the doctors who carried out vivisection experiments, as "medical practitioners complained it was contrary to the compassionate ethos of their profession" (Bates xxi). And later on, some Christian anti-cruelty organizations and individuals joined in the movement and became the dominant force, worrying that "callousness among the professional classes would have a demoralizing effect on the rest of society" (Bates xxi). Nevertheless, neither side thinks about the issue from the animals' perspective. Not until the RSPCA's involvement into this movement in the 1850s did it become more animal-protection-oriented. There was once heated debate on the issue of vivisection, especially when people began to see the benefit it brought to human beings in terms of medicare. Since the abolition of vivisection is impossible under current scientific conditions, what animal rights advocates were and are supposed to do is to request experimenters to reduce the number of vivisection experiments and the degree of suffering of the animals in the experiments, say by the use of anaesthesia. Under such circumstances, what the poets as part of the cultural force can do is to reveal the cruelty of the experiment on animals and vivisection, and their disapproval of or protest against it.

One of the earliest disapproval of experiment on animals occurs in the early seventeenth century in Shakespeare's play *Cymbeline* (1611), which is shown in a conversation between Cymbeline's wife the Queen and Cornelius the physician:

> **Queen:** ... Hast thou not learned me how
> To make perfumes? distil? preserve? yea, so
> That our great king himself doth woo me oft
> For my confections? Having thus far proceeded —
> Unless thou think'st me devilish — is 't not meet
> That I did amplify my judgement in
> Other conclusions? I will try the forces
> Of these thy compounds on such creatures as
> We count not worth the hanging — but none human —
> To try the vigour of them and apply
> Allayments to their act, and by them gather
> Their several virtues and effects.
> **Cornelius:** Your highness
> Shall from this practice but make hard your heart;
> Besides, the seeing these effects will be
> Both noisome and infectious. (1.5.12-27)

In order to win the love and favor of the King, the Queen has to try her best to keep herself young, beautiful and attractive by means of using drugs or compounds, some of which might be poisonous or having side effects. So as to ensure the safety and effectiveness of using these compounds, the Queen would like to apply them first on the animals and thus try the vigor of them.

Upon hearing the Queen's proposal, the physician's response is that such practice will harden her heart, in other words, doing experiments on animals will make her into a stony-hearted or cold-hearted lady. What's more, the side effects of these compounds on the animals will be obnoxious and can be spread to others. The physician's dissuasion of the Queen from carrying out her devilish plan proves him to be a pioneering protester against experiment on animals.

By the 1690s an active anti-vivisection movement had already taken root in France, and the early years of the eighteenth century this sentiment had spread to England (Guerrini 407), but of course at its rudimentary stage, instead of a large-scaled social activity as what is stated at the beginning of this section. Poets in the eighteenth century, like Pope and Johnson, are also concerned with these issues. For example, Pope ever made a comment on the English botanist and physiologist Stephen Hales (1677–1761), "he is a good man, only I'm sorry he has his hands so much imbued in blood [...] he commits most of these barbarities with the thought of being of use to man. But how do we know that we have a right to kill creatures that we are so little above dogs, for our curiosity?" (qtd. in French 16). As for Johnson, according to Richard D. French's view, "The quotation from Johnson captures the flavor of mid-eighteenth century indignation and skepticism toward animal experiment" (17).

Since the publication of Henry Crowe's *Zoophilos, Or, Considerations on the Moral Treatment of Inferior Animals* (1819), "Experiments upon animals joined bull-baiting, cock-fighting, abuses in animal husbandry, and casual cruelty to beasts of burden as evils to be stamped out" (French 24). However, it was not until 1857 that the RSPCA got actively involved in the practical problems of controlling vivisection. Among the nineteenth-century poets, Christina Rossetti paid close attention to the issue of vivisection. As J. Marsh notes in her

Chapter Five Advocacy of Animal Freedom and Rights

biography of Christina, Christina had long been sympathetic, as her concern over French veterinary dissection of live horses in 1863 indicated, and like others she was shocked to learn that British regulations established in 1870 to provide for anaesthesia in animal experimentation were not being implemented (599). And according to Palazzo, "Her anger against vivisection is well known and she actively petitioned against it" (79), and "There follows an angry outburst against animal cruelty and the exploitation of animals for research or for fashion" (80).

In a letter to her brother Dante Gabriel in December 1875, Christina writes:

> I used to believe with you that chloroform was so largely used as to do away with the horror of vivisection ... but a friend has so urged the subject upon me, and has sent me so many printed documents alleging and apparently establishing the contrary, that I have felt compelled to do what little I could to gain help against what (I now fear) is cruelty of revolting magnitude. (qtd. in Palazzo 79)

Hence we can see, both biographically and epistolarily speaking, as a female poet, Christina is bold and courageous enough to show her negative view on vivisection. Nevertheless, it is a pity that I fail to find any of Christina's poems directly devoted to this topic, though she has written several animal poems, which have been discussed previously. To be added, in one of her devotional prose entitled "Whales and All That Move in the Waters", she also utters her view distinctly: "One thing however is absolutely clear: they [creatures] are entrusted to man's sovereignty for use, not for abuse" (324) and " the groans of a harmless race sacrificed to our vanity or our curiosity should rise up in the judgment with us and condemn us" (325).

The nineteenth century is a critical epoch in terms of anti-vivisection. According to J. Marsh, in 1874, anti-vivisectors began pressing for legislation, collecting signatures from influential people, including Tennyson, Browning, Carlyle and Ruskin, for a parliamentary petition (599). In Chris Snodgrass' view, poetry in the 1890s made assaults on social injustice of all sorts, including urban poverty, child labour, prostitution, animal vivisection and treatment of the insane (336), among which the assault on animal vivisection must be under the influence of the previous anti-vivisection movement.

In the twentieth century, Hardy also shows his view on vivisection in the aforementioned letter written to an anonymous lady of New York:

> Therefore the practice of vivisection, which might have been defended while the belief ruled that men and animals are essentially different, has been left by that discovery [the law of evolution] without any logical argument in its favour. (qtd. in F. Hardy 346-47)

According to Pinion, Hardy "knew that his craving to write denied him the 'manysidedness possessed by some men', and for that reason refused to consider his adoption as a vice president at the International Anti-Vivisection and Animal Protection Congress in July [1909]" (*Life and Friends* 299). Despite the fact that Hardy fails to become the vice president of the Congress, it is undeniable that he is an important figure in the anti-vivisection circle as a man of letters. But pitifully, just like my study of Christina, I only find Hardy's view on vivisection, rather than his related poems.

Another twentieth-century poet I would like to bring into discussion is Larkin. In the letter to his lover Monica Jones on September 14, 1952, Larkin shows his support to Monica's devotion to the animal welfare by saying "I'm glad, by the way, that you are fighting the cause of animals in your circle of life". Accordingly, Anthony Thwaite remarks that "The two of them [Larkin and Monica] shared a sympathy with animals, in the sense that both of them deplored bullfights, vivisection, myxomatosis and pet-shops" (*Letters to Monica*, Introduction).

In a letter to Monica on December 30, 1953, Larkin tells us one of his potential ambitions in writing:

Chapter Five Advocacy of Animal Freedom and Rights

>If I were a titled eccentric I should devote my life to writing a study of *Men and Animals*: a history of the animal in society. As Food; As Property; As Game; As friends; As Gods (that should come earlier); As Philosophical concepts (pre-&post-Darwin). There's six fat volumes! And I'd pack into 2 & 3 every monstrous outrage I could find authenticated, whale hunting, seal slaughtering, bullfighting, bear baiting & all the Bertram Mills [a British circus owner] stuff, lineal descendant of the 'mad bull covered with fireworks & released in the market, 3 p.m. However, as I'm not a titled eccentric I suppose I shan't.

Although Larkin denies himself of the possibility of writing about the relationship between man and animals, he indeed shows his meditation on this issue and his outrage at the ill-treatment of animals. And even though he fails to come up with a monograph elaborating on the human-animal relationship, yet in his animal poems, "Something lurking in his treatment of these animals suggests a perspective that contributes importantly to the enterprise of envisioning and expressing human-animal relationships" (Malamud 159).

Larkin's "Ape Experiment Room" (originally named "Laboratory Monkeys", 1965) deals with the practice of using monkeys in doing experiments in laboratories.

>Buried among white rooms
>Whose lights in clusters beam
>Like suddenly-caused pain,
>And where behind rows of mesh
>Uneasy shifting resumes
>As sterilisers steam
>And the routine begins again
>Of putting questions to flesh

> That no one would think to ask
> But a Ph.D. with a beard
> And nympho wife who —
> But
> There, I was saying, are found
> The bushy T-shaped mask,
> And below, the smaller, eared
> Head like a grave nut,
> And the arms folded round.

As for the background of the poem, according to Larkin's letter to Monica on February 24, 1965, "it was inspired by the photo on *The Listener* cover a week or so ago of a rhesus monkey & her baby monkey [...] It carried that complete & utter condemnation of the human race monkeys seem to be able to convey. It was accompanied by accounts of fatuous American experiments of taking baby monkeys away from their mothers & noting that they are unhappy" (qtd. in *Complete Poems* 577).

The first stanza of the poem introduces to us the typical features of the laboratory, which include the white rooms, the light beam, rows of mesh and sterilisers. The word "buried" insinuates that the laboratory is like a tomb which encompasses the dead body of the animal used as a subject of experiment. And "suddenly-caused pain" may indicate that anaesthesia is not used in this process, which is very cruel to the animal.

If the value of the experiment is really very significant and may bring about a scientific breakthrough, it might as well be worthwhile. However, the purpose of this experiment is to find the answer to a question no one would ask or be interested except the experimenter, a Ph.D., and his wife who is a nympho. Larkin does not finish the line, but ends it with a dash instead, leaving space to give the readers some food for thought. Based upon the meaning of the word "nympho", that is, a woman with abnormal sexual desires, we are likely to surmise that the experiment is presumably related to this personal abnormality. All in all, the poem shows Larkin's disapproval of using animals in experiments. As Booth argues, the poem is "a poem of anti-vivisectionist propaganda" (327). And as far as Malamud is concerned, "Larkin certainly aligns himself here, even if in an understated fashion, with the spirit of animal rights protest and exposé by detailing the tableau of torture" (156).

The last poet to be discussed in this section is John Amsden. According to the information at PoemHunter.com, Amsden is a contemporary British poet in Cranmore, Yarmouth, Isle of Wight, whose date of birth is unknown. He has written a poem which is directly entitled "Vivisection"[1]. The poem goes:

> The darkest of arts
>
> In magic vile, obscene
>
> The cruelest of acts
>
> In torture: we must lean
>
> A tottering, sickening,
>
> Diseased, dying world,
>
> Poisoned, near mindless
>
> Or bared to herald
>
> Scientific misnomer
>
> Few flee obeisance
>
> What e'er their beliefs fruitless
>
> Invalid now conscience.

---

[1] https://www.poemhunter.com/poem/vivisection/

> And the animals
> Suffer as never before
> In vile persecution:
> For more ... and yet more.

As can be seen, Amsden has a very low opinion of vivisection, calling it "The darkest of arts" and "The cruelest of acts" due to the torture it incurs upon the animals, using derogatory words like "vile" and "obscene" to modify it. In his view, the world relying on the discovery from vivisection is a "tottering, sickening, / Diseased, dying world". Human beings do experiments on live animals in the name of medical or scientific research, without showing due respect to the vivisected animals, not feeling conscience-smitten. As is known, experiment after experiment has to be done before the final result is gained, so more and more animals will be used in vivisection, and thus "the animals / Suffer as never before".

Poignantly, bitterly and earnestly, Amsden has revealed to us the vileness of vivisection, even though he does not portray the bloody scene of the experiment and he does not directly call a halt to vivisection, his negative attitude towards this practice is clearly shown in this poem. In my mind's eye, it is not that all vivisection experiments have to be abandoned, but to reduce the number of them, especially those relatively unnecessary ones. For those necessary ones, the suffering and affliction of the experimented animals should be reduced to its minimum amount.

III. Promotion of Vegetarianism

People adopt the vegetarian way of life for different reasons, such as for nutritional, ascetic, ethical, or environmental reasons. In my study, I only focus on the vegetarianism for ethical reasons, since that is directly related to the

Chapter Five Advocacy of Animal Freedom and Rights

protection of animals. As early as the seventeenth century, two female writers, Katherine Philips (1631/2 -1664) and Margaret Cavendish, discussed the issue of meat eating in their poetry as well as positing the Golden Age as vegetarian.

Another female writer concerning about vegetarianism in the seventeenth century is Aphra Behn (1640–1689). She has ever written a poem in praise of the writings of Thomas Tryon (1634–1703), whose seventeenth-century books on behalf of vegetarianism has influenced her to stop meat eating. Behn's commendatory poem was first published with Tryon's *The Way to Make All People Rich: or, Wisdom's Call to Temperance and Frugality in a Dialogue between Sophronio and Guloso* (1685) and later was republished as "On the Author of that Excellent Book Intituled *The Way to Health, Long Life, and Happiness*" (1697). In this poem, Behn first criticizes man's moral degradation in food and drink, which has a bad influence on the country:

>Till wild Debauchery did Mens minds invade,
>
>And Vice, and Luxury became a Trade;
>
>Surer than War it laid whole Countrys wast,
>
>Not Plague nor Famine ruins half so fast;
>
>By swift degrees we took that Poison in,
>
>Regarding not the danger, nor the sin;
>
>Delightful, Gay, and Charming was the Bait,
>
>While Death did on th' inviting Pleasure wait,
>
>And ev'ry Age produc'd a feebler Race,
>
>Sickly their days, and those declin'd apace,
>
>Scarce Blossoms Blow, and Wither in less space.
>
>Till Nature thus declining by degrees,
>
>We have recourse to rich restoratives,
>
>By dull advice from some of Learned Note,
>
>We take the Poison for the Antidote;

> Till sinking Nature cloy'd with full supplys,
>
> O'er-charg'd grows fainter, Languishes and dies.
>
> These are the Plagues that o'er this Island reign,
>
> And have so many threescore thousands slain; (lines 20-38)

Behn has a very low opinion of man's debauchery, that is, being indulged in excessive eating and drinking, which in her view is unhealthy. She deems that way of life as "Poison" and thinks it is even worse than war, plague or famine in wrecking people and ruining the country. People who are allured by the delicious and attractive food ignore the danger brought to their health by a life of indulgence and forget that gluttony is one of the seven deadly sins. As a result, their heath declines severely and rapidly, and many people die consequently. In order to satisfy their overwhelming needs, people are taking too much from nature in a predatory manner, which does great harm on nature and threatens its normal development, and thus nature becomes fainter and weaker, like a moribund patient. At this crucial moment, Tryon comes up with his book to call on a life of temperance and frugality and appeal to vegetarianism, with the overriding aim of "Man's eternal health, eternal good" (52).

> Till you the saving Angel, whose blest hand
>
> Have sheath'd that Sword, that threatned half the Land;
>
> More than a Parent, Sir, we you must own,
>
> They give but life, but you prolong it on;
>
> You even an equal power with Heav'n do shew,
>
> Give us long life, and lasting Vertue too: (39-44)

Behn calls Tryon "the saving Angel", so to speak, the savior saving people from an unhealthy lifestyle. In Behn's eyes, Tryon is even more important than parents in people's life, on the ground that parents only give birth to us but Tryon makes us live longer. Apart from that, by following vegetarianism advocated by Tryon, people become more virtuous in terms of the protection of animals.

Chapter Five Advocacy of Animal Freedom and Rights

Finally, Behn endorses Tryon by saying:

> Let Fools and Mad-men thy great work condemn,
>
> I've tri'd thy Method, and adore thy Theme;
>
> Adore the Soul that you'd such truths discern,
>
> And scorn the fools that want the sense to learn. (63-66)

As we can see that Behn is a pious disciple of Tryon and follows his proposal earnestly and strictly. In her opinion, those who express very strong disapproval of Tryon's idea are either foolish or mad, towards whom she holds a contemptuous attitude. Even though both Tryon and Behn kind of exaggerated the advantage of vegetarianism, the propaganda for it is definitely beneficial to the protection of animals.

In the eighteenth century, Gay wrote two poems in this regard. One is "Fable XVII. Shepherd's Dog and Wolf" (1727), in which the wolf gives an explanation of the necessity of wolves' eating the sheep:

> Friend, says the Wolf, the matter weigh.
>
> Nature design'd us beasts of prey,
>
> As such, when hunger finds a treat,
>
> 'Tis necessary wolves should eat. (lines 23-26)

The wolves are inherently "beasts of prey" or carnivorous animals, so they have no choice but to eat other weaker animals when suffering from hunger. Biologically, the sheep are on the food chain of the wolves and it is part of the balance of nature. In other words, omnivorous human beings have choices between meat and vegetables, but the carnivorous wolves have no alternatives. The wolf goes on with his remark:

> A wolf eats sheep but now and then,
>
> Ten thousands are devour'd by men.
>
> An open foe may prove a curse,
>
> But a pretended friend is worse. (31-34)

In terms of the frequency and the amount of sheep eating, the wolves only eat the sheep occasionally and so the number is relatively small, but in contrast, human beings have eaten an extremely large number of sheep to meet the needs of their appetite. Ironically, human beings pretend to be the friends of the sheep in the process of raising them, but when it comes to kill the sheep for meat, they become a treacherous and merciless foe. The wolf concludes his remark by saying something like the moral of the fable, that is, false friends are worse than bitter enemies, because we are apt to slacken our vigilance towards pretended friends. As the old Chinese saying goes, overt shots are easy to dodge, but hidden arrows are difficult to guard against.

The other is "Fable XXXVI. Pythagoras and Countryman" (1727), which compares again gluttonous human beings with carnivorous animals. This time the ancient Greek mathematician and philosopher Pythagoras, who is known for his temperance and abstinence, says:

> But if these tyrants of the air
> Demand a sentence so severe,
> Think how the glutton man devours;
> What bloody feasts regale his hours!
> O impudence of power and might!
> Thus to condemn a hawk or kite,
> When thou perhaps, carniv'rous sinner,
> Hadst pullets yesterday for dinner! (lines 23-30)

When the countryman tells Pythagoras about the kite's rapine of his hens and turkeys, and being killed and nailed to the wall as a terror or warning to other kites, the sage replies that the kite does not deserve such a severe punishment compared with human beings whose lavish banquets are filled with various animals. To Pythagoras, this is an abuse of man's power and authority. Human beings are hypocritical for the reason that they rebuke the hawk or kite for grabbing the chickens while they themselves eat young chickens heartily at the dinner table. Even though there is a fallacy here, that is, human beings are eating their own chickens while the hawk or kite is kind of snatching away chickens raised by others, the fact that the people mentioned in this poem are carnivorous and glutinous rather than vegetarian is beyond doubt.

Pope was a literary influence on the practice of vegetarianism in the Enlightenment period. In the aforementioned article "Against Barbarity to Animals", he writes, "I know nothing more shocking or horrid than the prospect of one of their [human beings'] kitchens covered with blood, and filled with the cries of creatures expiring in tortures". Pope regarded the slaughter of animals for meat as a practice of tyranny and believed that animal consumption was the product of man's longing for control over the inferior animals. So he was in favor of vegetarianism as a way of rebellion against such tyranny. But it is a pity there are no related poetic works by Pope.

Among the nineteenth-century Romantic poets, both Byron and Shelley are renowned vegetarians. Byron's view on vegetarian diet is shown in a couple of his letters. In the letter to his mother on June 25, 1811, Byron writes, "I must only inform you that for a long time I have been restricted to an entire vegetable diet neither fish or flesh coming within my regimen" (*Letters and Journals* 78). In his letter to Thomas Moore on January 28, 1817, Byron writes, "The remedy for your plethora is simple — abstinence. I was obliged to have recourse to the like some years ago, I mean in point of *diet*" (*Letters and Journals* 262). Byron's vegetarian diet is also shown in biography about him, according to John Galt's biography *The Life of Lord Byron*, Byron was in delicate health, and upon an abstemious regimen. He rarely tasted wine, nor more than half a glass, mingled with water, when he did. He ate little; no animal food, but only bread and vegetables (76). From the above information, it seems as if Byron's vegetarianism is not ethics-oriented, but health-oriented. This view is endorsed by Janet Barkas, who thinks Byron practiced a meatless diet sporadically throughout his life (not for philosophical or ethical reasons but for vanity), and might have influenced Shelley's vegetarianism (84). But if we turn to Moore's biography *Life of Lord Byron*, we find him saying:

> We frequently, during the first months of our acquaintance, dined together alone... Though at times he would drink freely enough of claret, he still adhered to his system of abstinence in food. He appeared, indeed, to have conceived a notion that animal food has some peculiar influence on the character; and I remember one day, as I sat opposite to him, employed, I suppose, rather earnestly over a 'beef-steak,' after watching me for a few seconds, he said in a grave tone of inquiry, — "Moore, don't you find eating beef-steak makes you ferocious?". (64)

Byron's view that eating meat makes people become ferocious is not simply health-oriented or vanity-oriented, but also related to ethics, that is, eating the meat of animals is a practice which is fierce, violent and aggressive, and thus should be seriously considered for the sake of animals.

Though a vegetarian in life, Byron does not write any poem directly attacking meat eating, but only slightly touches upon the subject in *Don Juan*:

> For we all know that English people are
>
> Fed upon beef — I won't say much of beer,
>
> Because 't is liquor only, and being far
>
> From this my subject, has no business here;
>
> We know, too, they very fond of war,
>
> A pleasure — like all pleasures — rather dear. (2.156)

Byron only mentions English people's carnivorous eating habit of feeding on beef, but he does not show his view on it. However, after referring briefly to this subject, he turns to talk about ironically English people's fondness of war,

Chapter Five Advocacy of Animal Freedom and Rights

which he thinks is one of their pleasures, including eating beef, which are all rather dear and done at a high cost in the long run.

Unlike Byron whose view is not clearly shown in his poetry, Shelley bluntly expresses his view on vegetarianism in his long poem *Queen Mab: A Philosophical Poem* (1812–1813):

> ... no longer now
>
> He slays the lamb that looks him in the face,
>
> And horribly devours his mangled flesh. (8.211-13)

Shelley provides the readers with a long note of approximately eight pages to the above lines, which shows the special attention he pays to this issue. In this note, Shelley clearly expresses his view on the abstention of animal food:

> How can the advantages of intellect and civilization be reconciled with the liberty and pure pleasures of natural life? How can we take the benefits, and reject the evils, of the system which is now interwoven with all the fibres of our being? I believe that abstinence from animal food and spirituous liquors would, in a great measure, capacitate us for the solution of this important question. (*Complete Poetical Works* 242)

As far as Shelley is concerned, abstinence from animal food is so important that it can even solve some social problems. Shelley hatefully describes the butchers of animals as "man of violent passions, blood-shot eyes, and swollen veins" (244). Shelley's advocacy of returning to vegetable diet is shown by his remark: "In no cases has a return to vegetable diet produced the slightest injury; in most it has been attended with changes undeniably beneficial" shows him to be one of the pioneers of vegetarianism among the men of letters (244). For further proof, in real life, Shelley and his first wife Harriet were confirmed vegetarians on May 21, 1813 (Morton 68, Ruston 83).

In addition to poetry, Shelley also writes a couple of essays concerning vegetarianism, including "A Vindication of Natural Diet" (1813), "Essay on the Vegetable System of Diet" (1814–15), as well as a section of "A Refutation of Deism" (1814), from which we can see that he is definitely the most ardent supporter of vegetarianism among Romantic poets.

The poem "We Are the Living Graves of Murdered Beasts" (or "Song of Peace", 1951) is usually attributed to Shelley's pious follower Bernard Shaw, though it can not be found in any of his published works. The poem goes:

> We are the living graves of murdered beasts,
> Slaughtered to satisfy our appetites,
> We never pause to wonder at our feasts,
> If animals, like men, can possibly have rights.
> We pray on Sundays that we may have light,
> To guide our footsteps on the paths we tread,
> We're sick of war, we do not want to fight,
> The thought of it now fills our heart with dread,
> And yet we gorge ourselves upon the dead.
> Like carrion crows, we live and feed on meat,
> Regardless of the suffering and pain
> We cause by doing so. If thus we treat
> Defenseless animals, for sport or gain,
> How can we hope in this world to attain
> The PEACE we say we are so anxious for?
> We pray for it, o'er hecatombs of slain,
> To God, while outraging the moral law,
> Thus cruelty begets its offspring — War.

Shaw is also a well-known vegetarian among writers, who started his vegetarian diet when he was only 25 years old, and this diet lasted almost sixty years, so the attribution of the poem to him is not ungrounded. Dating back to 1886, as a thirty-year-old young man, at the first general meeting of the Shelley

Chapter Five Advocacy of Animal Freedom and Rights

Society, Shaw endorsed Shelley by remarking: "Like Shelley, I am a Socialist, an Atheist, and a Vegetarian" (qtd. in Duerksen 115). Hence Shaw expressed his stand as a vegetarian clearly and outright. And he reiterated this idea by saying in his *Sixteen Self Sketches* (1949) as an old man, "I was a cannibal for twenty-five years. For the rest I have been a vegetarian. It was Shelley who first opened my eyes to the savagery of my diet" (53).

The title of Shaw's poem "We Are the Living Graves of Murdered Beasts", which is also the very first line, makes use of a shocking metaphor, human beings are the tombs of murdered beasts. So to speak, the dead bodies of the animals are buried in our stomach, which make the readers feel disgusting. After that Shaw uses a simile, that is, we are like carrion crows who feed on the decaying flesh of dead animals, which again creates a disgusting scene. In Archibald Henderson's view, "a vegetarian, he [Shaw] abhorred the slaughter of animals, in sport or in the butcher's yard" (411). While we are killing the animals, we ignore the suffering and pain inflicted upon them.

So Shaw poses a rhetorical question, that is, if we treat the barehanded and unarmed animals in such a way, how can we achieve real peace in the world? As Richard H. Schwartz's puts it, Shaw wants to show that the killing of animals today logically leads to the killing of men on the battlefield tomorrow (99). This idea is in line with John Locke's view "custom of tormenting and killing of beasts will, by degrees, harden their minds even towards men" (112), and Kant's view "for a person who already displays such cruelty to animals is also no less hardened towards men" (212). Then Shaw prays to God that this kind of mass slaughter or massacre could be over, for if this immoral and cruel act continues, there will be a bad consequence, and the cruelty to animals may result in the cruelty to man, and peace will be spoilt. Therefore, "His persistent vegetarianism is not based upon a scientific inquiry into the amount of hydrocarbons, uric acid, or what not deleterious stuff there may be in meat, but in his perfectly natural and humane distaste for the shedding of blood" (Henderson 478), since the shedding of the blood of animals is likely to have a slippery-slope effect.

Shaw's vegetarian idea is not only shown in the poem discussed above, but also in some of his remarks, including "animals are my friends and I don't eat my friends" (qtd. in Gold 154), "while we ourselves are the living graves of murdered beasts, how can we expect any ideal conditions on this earth?" (qtd. in Goodale 155), and "I choose not to make a graveyard of my body for the rotting corpses of dead animals" (qtd. in Freston and Cohn 86).

What's more, according to Shaw's biographer Pearson, in his late years, Shaw fell off from his bicycle and sprained his ankle, and the doctors who could do nothing for him blamed his diet. And to the blame Shaw replied, "But death is better than cannibalism. My will contains directions for my funeral which will be followed not by mourning coaches but by herds of oxen, sheep, swine, flocks of poultry, and a small travelling aquarium of live fish, all wearing scarves in honour of the man who perished rather than eat his fellow-creatures" (185). So we can see that Shaw would rather die than eat the meat of animals.

Apart from Shaw's poem, another poem in the twentieth century is Chesterton's "The Logical Vegetarian"[①] (1915), in which he is advocating a special kind of vegetarian diet, that is, to have vegetarian drink.

> You will find me drinking rum,
>
> Like a sailor in a slum,
>
> You will find me drinking beer like a Bavarian
>
> You will find me drinking gin
>
> In the lowest kind of inn
>
> Because I am a rigid Vegetarian. (lines 1-6)

Rum is a kind of alcoholic drink made from the juice of sugar cane, beer is

---

① https://www.poetry.net/poem/16005/the-logical-vegetarian

made from grain, and gin is made from grain and flavoured with juniper berries. None of the raw materials of the drinks is related to meat or fish, hence as far as Chesterton is concerned, alcoholic drinks are supposed to be on the vegetarian diet, even though they are not vegetables, fruits or grain in appearance. And this is the reason why Chesterton entitles the poem as "The Logical Vegetarian". As the poem shows, because Chesterton is a vegetarian, he gives all his pork to a doctor named Gluck, and eats vegetables only, "Shoving peas in with a knife" (23). What's more,

>No more the milk of cows
>Shall pollute my private house
>Than the milk of the wild mares of the Barbarian
>I will stick to port and sherry,
>For they are so very, very,
>So very, very, very, Vegetarian. (25-30)

For a rigid or an ascetic vegetarian, referred to as a vegan, not only meat and fish are forbidden, but also eggs, milk, butter and cheese, because these food is directly related to animals. And Chesterton is one member of them, especially in the control of milk. In order to find a substitute drink, he turns to alcoholic drinks like port and sherry. The ending of the poem works in concert with the beginning, proposing vegetarian drinking. Especially in the last two lines, the word "very" is repeated five times to emphasize his firm standpoint, that is, drinking alcoholic drinks is absolutely vegetarian.

The "Prayer for Animals" is a prayer attributed to Schweitzer in some books, such as Lisa Kemmerer's *Speaking Up for Animals: An Anthology of Women's Voices*, Nathaniel Altman's *The Little Giant Encyclopedia of Meditations & Blessings*, and *A Prayer Treasury: A Collection of Best-loved Prayers* published by Lion Publishing, with a little variation from each other, but similar to Shaw's case, it is not found in any of Schweitzer's published writings.

And the prayer is sometimes considered as a poem and is patterned in the form of a poem. The prayer goes:

> Hear our humble prayer oh God, for our friends the animals. Especially for animals who are suffering. For all those who are overworked and underfed and cruelly treated. For all who are hunted and frightened and lost. For those who beat their wings against bars. For all who must be put to death. We entreat for them all Thy mercy and pity and for those who deal with them, we ask a heart of compassion, kind words and gentle hands. May we, ourselves, be friends to Animals, and so share the blessings of the Merciful. (qtd. in Kemmerer)

The attribution is well-grounded due to what Schweitzer has done in the field of animal welfare, especially his notable idea of "Reverence for Life". In recognition of his contribution to animal ethics, "The Albert Schweitzer Animal Welfare Fund" was established in 1981. In this prayer or poem, Schweitzer appeals to God, requesting mercy and sympathy from God towards animals who are overworked, underfed, starved, hunted, deserted, frightened, encaged, cruelly treated, and meant to be killed for meat. He is not only asking for compassion from God, but also from those who ill-treat animals. He prays to God to make human beings and animals become real and genuine friends, instead of hypocritical or treacherous ones.

The twentieth century witnessed the increase of consciousness of vegetarianism among people and poets alike, so we can see that many more poets have written about this issue. The next poem is Stevie's "Death Bereaves our Common Mother, Nature Grieves for my Dead Brother" (1937), in which she grieves for the death of a lamb:

> Lamb dead, dead lamb,
> He was, I am,
> Separation by a tense

Chapter Five Advocacy of Animal Freedom and Rights

> Baulks my eyes' indifference.
> Can I see the lately dead
> And not bend a sympathetic head?
> Can I see lamb dead as mutton
> And not care a solitary button?

By using the immediate repetition of "lamb dead" and "dead lamb", the state of death of the lamb is emphasized. Stevie reemphasizes the lamb's death by contrasting its pastness or past existence with his own presentness or present existence. She then uses two rhetorical questions to stress the necessity of her sympathy towards and care for the dead lamb. Not only is the poetess deeply grieved for the lamb's death, but also mother nature, as is shown in the title of the poem, which is the use of the literary device of pathetic fallacy, in which inanimate or nonhuman objects or nature laments or mourns for the death of someone. According to Malamud, the title of the poem and the poem itself form a nice "poetic conceit", on the ground that "One doesn't eat one's relatives — so, if we do eat these lambs, we must be giving the lie to the relationship that the title posits. Animals can't really be our brothers, and we don't have a common mother" (143).

An important event in the development of vegetarianism is the foundation of the Vegan Society, which was founded by Donald Watson, Elsie B. Shrigley (also known as Sally Shrigley), and some other leading vegans in the UK in 1944, and is the first of its kind in the world. And the term "vegan" was also coined simultaneously by Watson.

The next poem to be discussed is Hughes' "View of a Pig" (1957). The speaker of this poem looks at a dead pig and tells us how completely dead it is. In Oliver Tearle's view, the poem contrasts the pig's now deadened and lifeless state with the warm, active creature that is the living pig[①]. The pig is so insignificant as an animal that the speaker treats its dead body in a casual way:

> I thumped it without feeling remorse.
> One feels guilty insulting the dead,
> Walking on graves. But this pig
> Did not seem able to accuse. (lines 9-12)

The speaker does not give due respect to the dead body of the pig as he does to the dead body of human beings, and the reason is quite simple, because the pig is not capable of accusing, no matter it is dead or alive. When the pig breathes its last, "Its last dignity had entirely gone" and "Too dead now to pity" (15, 17). Since the pig is a very large pig, having the weight of three men, a long deep cut is necessary when killing it. In the speaker's view, "The gash in its throat was shocking, but not pathetic" (24). The reason why the speaker does not feel sympathetic towards the pig's shocking gash is that it is nothing to be fussy about the death of a meat-supplying animal. After all, the meaning of their existence lies in their role as meat-suppliers, so the way how they are killed does not matter much, let alone the way they are treated after their death, as we can see "They were going to scald it, / Scald it and scour it like a doorstep" (35-36). In the eyes of the butchers, the dead pigs are no more animals, they are objectified, as lifeless as a doorstep, and thus can be treated in whatever way the butchers like. Given the tragic ending of the pig, its previous "earthly pleasure" "Seemed a false effort, and off the point" (19, 20).

"A Registered Vegetarian"[②] is written by Pete Crowther, who was once a cataloguer at the the University of Hull where he served under the poet and librarian Larkin. In this poem, he tells us the process of his daughter's

---

① https://interestingliterature.com/2017/11/22/10-of-the-best-poems-about-animals/
② https://www.poemhunter.com/poem/a-registered-vegetarian/

Chapter Five Advocacy of Animal Freedom and Rights

registration as a vegetarian.

> At the tender age of twelve
> my daughter, bless her,
> was registered as a vegetarian.
> She was duly accredited
> with the appropriate documents
> and vaccinated with chlorophyll.
> Now she is authorized
> to eat zucchinis, papayas
> and winter cabbages
> not to mention
> French beans, celeriac
> and best of all —
> mouth-watering mangold wurzel.

We are not sure to what organization is his daughter registered, perhaps the above-mentioned Vegan Society. However, it does not matter so much. What is more important is the fact that she has become a vegetarian. Crowther thinks that this is something good and right because he says "bless her" to express his best wishes. From this poem, we also get to know that the procedure of registration consists of two parts, that is, accreditation through documents and vaccination with chlorophyll, the green substance in plants. After registration, the girl can eat vegetables and fruits solely in a justifiable way, which include zucchinis, papayas, winter cabbages, French beans, celeriac, and mangold wurzel. From Crowther's description, we can see that he feels proud of his daughter's becoming a registered vegetarian and he is proved to be an advocate of vegetarianism.

The last poem to be discussed in this section is the contemporary poet

Amsden's "Vegan Assist"[①].

> The lands lost
>
> To brutal killing
>
> The seas lost
>
> Their light to life bleeding.
>
> Most to vivisection toss'd
>
>
> The skies
>
> 'times silent to the wings of yore
>
> The air poisoned
>
> Vapid vapour for the swift breeze.
>
> These our sighs, terrible our cries.

  Amsden talks about human beings' killing of animals for meat from three dimensions or perspectives, that is, animals on the land, animals in the sea and animals in the sky, or animals, fish and birds to be specific. The word "vivisection" does not refer to that in the laboratory, but the act of butchering animals for meat, in which people kill the animals, fish or birds alive, skin them, scale them or pluck off their feathers, and disembowel them. Amsden's diction "brutal", "bleeding" and "poison" shows his deep loathing of meat-oriented animal killing. Being much outnumbered by meatarians, vegetarians or vegans cannot help but to heave sighs and utter cries to arouse people's awareness or draw their attention to cut down on the killing of animals.

IV. Proposition of Anti-Anthropocentrism

  The idea of anthropocentrism probably originates from the Bible, in which

---

①   https://www.poemhunter.com/poem/vegan-assist/

Chapter Five Advocacy of Animal Freedom and Rights

we see "God said, Let us make man in our image, after our likeness: and let them have dominion over the fish of the sea, and over the fowl of the air, and over the cattle, and over all the earth, and over every creeping thing that creepeth upon the earth" (Genesis 1:26-27). Anthropocentrism is one of the root causes of human beings' lack of concern to animals and abuse of animals. Those advocates of animal liberation and animal rights are actually opposed to anthropocentrism, because human-centered standpoint will put animals in an inferior or subordinate position. Many poets have expressed their view on anthropocentrism or anti-anthropocentrism in their animal poems either directly or indirectly.

First, I intend to deal with three poems in the seventeenth century that are anthropocentric. "To Penshurst" (1616) by Ben Jonson (1572–1637) belongs to the genre of country house poem popular in the first half of the seventeenth century in Britain. It describes the leisurely, comfortable and luxurious life at Penshurst, a land or homestead in Kent, England, which was inhabited by the nobles, represented by "Thy Lord, and Lady" (line 50). This is a self-sufficient and self-contained place, where

> Thy Copp's too, nam'd of Gamage, thou hast there,
>
> That never fails to serve thee season'd Deer,
>
> When thou would'st Feast, or exercise thy Friends. (19-21)

There are deer which can either serve as food for a banquet or as a quarry in the hunting game for the proprietor of Penshurst as well as his friends. Apart from deer, there are many other animals that are taken as food at the dinner table, including the pheasant, the partridge, and various kinds of fish such as carps, pikes and eels. Hence as the guest of this house, Jonson can eat to his heart's content, since

> ...nor, standing by
>
> A Waiter, doth my Gluttony envy:
>
> But gives me what I call for, and lets me eat,

He knows, below, he shall find plenty of Meat. (67-70)

Queerly and ironically, the animals sacrifice themselves to human beings on their own initiative, for example, the partridge "is willing to be kill'd" (30); the carps "run into thy Net" (33); the pikes "themselves betray" (36); and the eels "leap on Land, / Before the Fisher, or into his Hand" (37-38). The undertone here is that all animals serve human beings voluntarily and wholeheartedly because human beings are the masters and they are the subordinates, thus insinuating anthropocentrism. As Erica Fudge puts it, "In running into nets, willingly offering themselves for sacrifice, asking for human aid, the animals are fulfilling human ideals, but are fulfilling them in anthropomorphic ways" (4).

"To Saxham"[①] (written in early 1620s, published in 1640) by Thomas Carew (1595–1640) also belongs to the genre of country house poem. It gives a high praise of the estate named Saxham to please the landlord, which is modeled right after Jonson's "To Penshurst".

Similarly, there are various kinds of birds in this homestead. "The pheasant, partridge, and the lark / Flew to thy house, as to the Ark" (lines 21-22). Carew compares this place to Noah's Ark, the animal sanctuary in time of the world-engulfing flood. However, this house is far from being a place of shelter or protection, but a slaughtering house instead. Much alike to the animals in "To Penshurst", the animals in this poem also sacrifice themselves voluntarily:

> The willing ox of himself came
> Home to the slaughter with the lamb,
> And every beast did thither bring
> Himself, to be an offering.
> The scaly herd more pleasure took,
> Bathed in thy dish than in the brook. (23-28)

---

① http://www.luminarium.org/sevenlit/carew/saxham.htm

Chapter Five Advocacy of Animal Freedom and Rights

The ox and the lamb would fain be the offerings either at the feasts or in the ceremonies of religious worship. Ridiculously and ironically, the fish are even more pleased to bathe in the cooking pot than swimming at liberty in the river. As Fudge argues, "Animals represent human power: their self-sacrifice is an image of man's control" (4). Hence we can see that Carew goes even further than Jonson in portraying the willing servitude of the animals towards their human master.

"Providence" (1633) by George Herbert (1593–1633) continues to emphasize the central position of human beings among living things on earth as follows:

> Of all the creatures both in sea and land
> Only to Man thou hast made known thy ways,
> And put the pen alone into his hand,
> And made him Secretary of thy praise.
>
> Beasts fain would sing; birds ditty to their notes;
> Trees would be tuning on their native lute
> To thy renown: but all their hands and throats
> Are brought to Man, while they are lame and mute.
>
> Man is the world's high Priest: he doth present
> The sacrifice for all; while they below
> Unto the service mutter an assent,
> Such as springs use that fall, and winds that blow. (lines 5-16)

Herbert proposes that man is endowed with the central position by God, because only man knows the divine order and God's ways of behavior. Accordingly, only man is entitled with literacy, who is able to read and write, and sing praise of God. Herbert's statement "Man is the world's high Priest" earns man full recognition of their human-centred position on earth, and the diction "they below" shows directly the inferior or subordinate status of animals in the human-animal relationship. As Fudge proposes, "To underline this anthropocentrism even further, while Herbert's animals cannot speak to the divine they can speak to the god on earth, man: 'The beasts say, Eat me.' Their servitude underlines human centrality" (4).

Having discussed three poems showing anthropocentrism, I will turn to one of the earliest poems expressing the idea of anti-anthropocentrism, which appeared in the early seventeenth century. "Holy Sonnet VIII: Why Are Wee by All Creatures Waited On?" (1609–1610) by the metaphysical poet John Donne (1572–1631) begins with a series of questions for human beings and animals:

> Why are wee by all Creatures waited on?
>
> Why doe the prodigall Elements supplye
>
> Life, and foode to mee, being more pure then I,
>
> Simpler, and further from corruption?
>
> Why brook'st thou ignorant horse, subjection?
>
> Why dost thou, Bull and Bore soe sillilye,
>
> Dissemble weaknes, and by one mans stroke dye,
>
> Whose whole kinde you might swallowe, and feed vpon? (lines 1-8)

The questions for human beings include why the animals should serve us and why natural elements should provide food to us. And the questions for the animals include why the ignorant horse accepts submission to be enthralled by human beings, and why the silly bull or boar feigns weakness, and is thus butchered by the slaughter-man. These questions are all rhetorical questions which need no answers at all, and the real purpose of using these questions is to emphasize, stressing that human beings should not be anthropocentric and be the masters of animals. To quote James Reeves, "It is a wonder that nature should be subject to man, who is more sinful and corrupt" (101).

Chapter Five Advocacy of Animal Freedom and Rights

The sonnet ends with a preaching to the animals:

Weaker I am, woe is mee, and worse then you,

You haue not sinn'd, nor neede bee timorous;

But wonder at a greater wonder, for to vs

Created Nature doth these things subdue.

But their Creatour, whom sinne, nor nature tied,

For vs his Creatures, and his foes hath died. (9-14)

The reason why the animals are submissive and timorous (i.e. nervous and easily frightened) may be that they think they are sinful, but according to Donne, they have not sinned at all, and hence do not have to be compliant or servile.

There are more animal poems with anti-anthropocentrism in the eighteenth century. In section three of Chapter Four, I have already discussed Thomson's criticism of hunting in the "Autumn" section of his long poem *The Seasons*. To say the least, if hunting is for survival or making a living, it is very likely to be forgiven, but in many occasions hunting is just for entertainment.

... Not so [he reproaches] the steady tyrant Man,

Who with the thoughtless insolence of Power,

Inflamed beyond the most infuriate wrath

Of the worst monster that e'er roamed the waste,

For Sport alone pursues the cruel chase,

Amid the beamings of the gentle days.

Upbraid, ye ravening tribes, our wanton rage,

For hunger kindles you, and lawless want;

But lavish fed, in Nature's bounty rolled —

To joy at anguish, and delight in blood —

Is what your horrid bosoms never knew. (lines 390-400)

As H. Williams argues, this poem denounces the amateur slaughtering (euphemised by the mocking term of *Sport*) unblushingly perpetrated in the broad light of day (137). The "tyrant Man" with "thoughtless insolence of Power" shows that the world is a human-centered world, where human beings have absolute controlling power over animals and use it in an indiscriminate and unfair way. They just hunt for sport, and base their happiness upon the misery and suffering of the animals, being filled with "joy at anguish, and delight in blood", without giving consideration to the feelings of animals. As for the general feature of Thomson's poetry and his position in the development of British poetry, H. Williams remarks that

> Natural enthusiasm, sympathy, and love for all that is really beautiful on Earth forms his chief characteristic. But, above all, his sympathy with suffering in all its forms, not limited by the narrow bounds of nationality or of species but extended to all innocent life — his indignation against oppression and injustice, are what most honourably distinguish him from almost all of his predecessors and, indeed, from most of his successors. (135)

In Epistle III entitled "Of the Nature and State of Man with Respect to Society" of Pope's *An Essay on Man*, he discusses the relationship between man and animals. He thinks that the ideal human-animal relationship should be "beast in aid of man, and man of beast: / All served, all serving — nothing stands alone" (lines 24-25). However, "Man exclaims, 'See all things for my use!'" (45), which Pope deems is not the right and advisable standpoint. For those "Who thinks all made for one, not one for all" (48), Pope thinks they are unreasonable or irrational, and are doomed to fall.

> Ah, how unlike the man of times to come —
> Of half that live the butcher and the tomb!
> Who, foe to Nature, hears the general groan,
> Murders their species, and betrays his own.
> But just disease to luxury succeeds,

And every death its own avenger breeds:

The fury-passions from that blood began,

And turned on man a fiercer savage, man. (161-68)

For the sake of our own interests and benefits, human beings have butchered many animals, ignoring their painful groan while being killed. However, the gluttony of meat may lead to diseases, which may be the so-called "affluenza", or disease of the wealthy people. This can also be regarded as the posthumous revenge of the butchered animals upon man, "a fiercer savage" in the eyes of the animals. This deteriorated relationship between man and animals forms a sharp contrast to that in the good old days long in the past, when "Man walk'd with beast, joint tenant of the shade" and "No murder clothed him [man], and no murder fed" (152, 154). According to H. Williams, Pope "expresses his detestation of the selfishness of our species" (131), who "Destroy all creatures for their sport or gust" (Epistle I, line 117).

Goldsmith's "An Elegy on the Death of A Mad Dog"[①] (1766) is a narrative poem that tells the ironic story of the death of a dog.

This dog and man at first were friends;

But when a pique began,

The dog, to gain some private ends,

Went mad, and bit the man.

Around from all the neighbouring streets

The wond'ring neighbours ran,

And swore the dog had lost its wits

To bite so good a man.

---

① http://www.poetry-archive.com/g/an_elegy_on_the_death_of_a_mad_dog.html

> The wound it seemed both sore and sad
>
> To every Christian eye;
>
> And while they swore the dog was mad,
>
> They swore the man would die.
>
> But soon a wonder came to light
>
> That showed the rogues they lied, —
>
> The man recovered of the bite,
>
> The dog it was that died!

The story seems to tell us that whenever there is a conflict between a man and an animal, people tend to stand on the side of the man and would take it for granted that the animal is responsible and is to blame, as the saying goes, preconceived ideas keep a strong hold.

In the story, the man and the dog used to be good friends, but later on bitter feelings develop between the two. However, we have no idea who is responsible for the grudge and the breakup, but we know the result is that the dog goes mad and bites the man. Again we have no idea why the dog goes mad and whether the man is accountable or not. The fact is that people in the neighborhood all think that the dog should take full responsibility for this accident because the man is a good man in people's eyes, taking it for granted that a good man will always do good deeds. They sympathize with the man and assert that he will die from the dog's bite. But the end of the story is different from people's expectation, that is, the man recovers from the bite but the dog dies instead. The speaker thinks people in the neighborhood are rogues who tell lies. But actually, they are not telling lies on purpose, because their anthropocentric thinking or mentality is deep-rooted, and they've just made a hasty conclusion subconsciously.

Goldsmith becomes known as an essayist after the publication of a collection of letters or essays entitled *The Citizen of the World: or, Letters*

Chapter Five Advocacy of Animal Freedom and Rights

from a Chinese Philosopher, Residing in London, to His Friends in the East (1762), where we can find his disapproval of and protest against brutality to animals, especially letter XV entitled "Against cruelty to animals. A story from the Zendevest of Zoroaster", in which we see animals like the boar, the sheep, and the hen make a complaint against man's cruel treatment and in which Goldsmith remarks, "he [man] was born to share the bounties of heaven, but he has monopolized them; he was born to govern the brute creation, but he is become their tyrant" (52). In Goldsmith's biographer E. S. Lang Buckland's view, "These appeals then were rare indeed, and even now are only revealed in any earnestness through a slowly dawning purer spirit" (47), which shows that Goldsmith is one of the pioneering figures in the animal rights movement.

The last poem to be discussed in the eighteenth century is Burns' "On Scaring Some Waterfowl in Loch Turit: A Wild Scene Among the Hills of Oughtertyre" (1787), in which he asks the waterfowls at the beginning of the poem:

> Why, ye tenants of the lake,
>
> For me your wat'ry haunt forsake?
>
> Tell me, fellow-creatures, why
>
> At my presence thus you fly? (lines 1-4)

At first Burns cannot understand why the birds fly away from their habitat upon seeing his presence. But on second thought, he comes to realize that it is for the fear of human beings that the birds flee away. Unlike the squirrel in Cowper's "The Winter Walk At Noon" who runs away due to the "prettiness of feign'd alarm", the waterfowls in Burns' poem run away because of real fear.

> Conscious, blushing for our race,
>
> Soon, too soon, your fears I trace,
>
> Man, your proud, usurping foe,
>
> Would be lord of all below:
>
> Plumes himself in freedom's pride,

Tyrant stern to all beside. (13-18)

The root cause of this disbelief of the birds in human beings is that human beings are arrogant and anthropocentric, regarding themselves as the master of all lower animals, taking away by force whatever they want from the animals. Therefore, in the eyes of the animals, human beings are usurpers and tyrants. And this can fairly explain why the birds are afraid of human beings and run away from them. Accordingly, the epiphany makes Burns feel ashamed of what his fellow men have done to the animals in nature, imperiling the harmonious relationship between man and animals.

Burns goes on criticizing human beings' barbarous behaviors towards animals as below:

> But Man, to whom alone is giv'n
>
> A ray direct from pitying Heav'n,
>
> Glories in his heart humane —
>
> And creatures for his pleasure slain! (23-26)

If starving human beings kill animals for food, maybe it is forgivable. But more often than not, human beings kill animals just for fun, for entertainment. In other words, they base their pleasure upon the misery and suffering of the animals, which is immoral and improper.

Finally, Burns gives practical advice to the waterfowls as follows:

> Or, if man's superior might
>
> Dare invade your native right,
>
> On the lofty ether borne,
>
> Man with all his pow'rs you scorn;
>
> Swiftly seek, on clanging wings,
>
> Other lakes and other springs;
>
> And the foe you cannot brave,
>
> Scorn at least to be his slave. (33-40)

Chapter Five Advocacy of Animal Freedom and Rights

Due to the birds' fragility and inability to protest or defend against powerful human beings' attack, Burns suggests to the waterfowls that if human beings do invade the birds' holy residence, what they can do is to show contempt to human beings' behavior and flee away to seek a new habitat, instead of being captured or killed by them. Burns' consciousness of animal ethics is noted by his biographer John Campbell Shairp, who remarks:

> And then his humanity was not confined to man, it overflowed to his lower fellow-creatures. His lines about the pet ewe, the worn-out mare, the field-mouse, the wounded hare, have long been household words. In this tenderness towards animals we see another point of likeness between him and Cowper. (199)

At the beginning of the nineteenth century, Shelley, in his *Queen Mab*, depicts to us prophetically a Utopian world where man and animals have equality and live harmoniously together.

> No longer now the winged habitants,
> That in the woods their sweet lives sing away,
> Flee from the form of man; but gather round,
>
> And prune their sunny feathers on the hands
> Which little children stretch in friendly sport
> Towards these dreadless partners of their play.
> All things are void of terror: man has lost
> His terrible prerogative, and stands
> An equal amidst equals. (Section VIII, lines 219-27)

In such an envisioned pantisocracy, the birds will not be afraid of human beings any more and will not fly away from them as they do in Burns' poem discussed above. Instead, they stand on the stretched-out hands of young children and prune their feathers there leisurely. The birds will become the "dreadless partners" of human beings and the world will be in universal harmony. The most important of all is that man will not have prerogative or privilege over animals. Anthropocentrism will no longer exist, and man and animals will become equal members of the society.

Another nineteenth-century poem, Clare's "Summer Evening" (1830), does not portray a beautiful, peaceful and auspicious evening. As can be seen, the frog jumps in a "half-fearful" way (line 1), the little mouse "Nimbles with timid dread" (3), the hare jumps "Cheat of its chosen bed" (9), and the yellowhammer "flutters in short fear" (10), from which we can see that dread or fear is the dominant feeling of the animals in the evening, and human beings are the initiators of evil who disturb the animals' tranquil life, frightening and intimidating them. So Clare ends the poem with the following lines: "Thus nature's human link and endless thrall: / Proud man still seems the enemy of all" (13-14). This is corresponding to the view in the poem "British Georgics. August"① by the Scottish poet James Grahame (1765–1811), in which he says "To man, bird, beast, man is the deadliest foe / 'Tis he who wages universal war" (lines 13-14). Therefore, in the eyes of the animals, the arrogant and anthropocentric human beings are still their enemies, the sight of whom will make them run for life. Though Clare is against killing wild animals, his disapproval is not so determined and strong-minded, since according to Chun, Clare only shows a lackadaisical (i.e. not so enthusiastic) opposition, the reason is that those cruelties to animals are culturally accepted by rural folks and the urban poor as a part of ordinary life or a means of redirecting their social anger to blood sports (57).

Let's finally turn to the twentieth-century animal poems. The first one to be discussed is Lawrence's "Elephant" (1923), which deals with Perahera, or

---

① https://www.poemhunter.com/poem/british-georgics-august/

Chapter Five Advocacy of Animal Freedom and Rights

the Festival of the Tooth, a religious festival in August in Sri Lanka, featured by a parade of dancers, musicians, singers and other performers accompanied by elephants. Lawrence and his wife Frieda visited Kanty, Ceylon (old name for Sri Lanka) in 1922. The vivid description of the parade in the poem "Elephant" is based upon this actual visit. The most part of the poem is devoted to the procession of men and elephants.

Before going into the portrayal of the Perahera festival, Lawrence first describes the laborious work that the elephants do: "you meet a huge and mud-grey elephant advancing his frontal bone, his trunk curled round a log of wood" and "the slim naked man slips down, and the beast deposits the lump of wood, carefully" (line 8, 12). As Achsah Brewster records in her recollection "In Ceylon", Lawrence "had a wholesome respect for the size and disposition of the elephants hauling timber on the road" (165). What's more, the owner of the elephant will force the elephants to lift up their knee as a way of salute to visitors or passers-by in order to get a bonus, as is seen in the following depiction:

> The keeper hooks the vast knee, the creature salaams.
>
> White man, you are saluted.
>
> Pay a few cents. (13-15)

In the religious festival Perahera, people are enthusiastic and even fanatical, but the elephants are not. At the tail of the procession, people can catch sight of the younger elephants, who are described as "smaller, more frightened elephants" (51), from which we can see that they are not enjoying the ceremony, but feeling terrified instead, maybe by the tumult and the fire-flare. For the larger adult elephants, they have to make "clumsy, knee-lifting salaam" to the royalty (32). From the word "clumsy", we can sense the difficulty for the "hugest, oldest of beasts" to make such a salute (33).

When the parade is finished and the elephants are dismantled, Lawrence expresses his feelings towards them as follows:

A Study of British Animal Poems

> Then I knew they were dejected, having come to hear the repeated
> Royal summons: *Dien! Ihr!*
> Serve!
> Serve, vast mountainous blood, in submission and splendour, serve royalty. (86-89)

Being summoned or ordered repeatedly to serve the royalty makes the elephants feel dejected or depressed. But since human beings are the masters, and the elephants are subordinates, and thus they have no choice but to obey human beings in submission. Once the ceremony is over, the elephants brook no delay in going back home, as is said in the poem, "in haste to get away" (97). They are so bored with such events that even "Their bells sounding frustrate and sinister" (98).

At the end of the poem, one more summoning or command for the elephants is given:

> *First great beasts of the earth*
> *A prince has come back to you,*
> *Blood-mountains.*
> *Crook the knee and be glad.* (123-26)

The elephants are asked to kneel down and salute to the royalty because they are inferior animals. The command is not only a physical one, but also a mental one. In other words, the elephants are not only requested to do clumsy salutes but also have to pretend to be happy, even though they feel grieved inside. However, as Poovalingam argues, "The poet holds that the prince being diffident, does not deserve to be aloft the elephant; he lacks the pride of power...The poem reveals how man is increasingly becoming superannuated for animals" (252), so this poem is actually anti-anthropocentric, standing by the side of the elephants. Some critics say that Lawrence sometimes has opposing attitudes towards animals, but I agree with Jamie Johnson's argument that

Lawrence's so-called contradictions may reflect his progressive struggle against anthropocentrism (145).

Stevie's "Friends of the River Trent" (1966) deals with the influence of water pollution on the fish, or "the environmental danger people pose to animals" (Malamud 146). The title *per se* is ironic, because what people are doing to the environment is far from being eco-friendly to their animal friends.

> Because of water pollution, my boys,
>
> And a lack of concerted action,
>
> These fish of what they used to be
>
> Is only a measly fraction
>
> A-swimming about most roomily (lines 5-9)

The spacious living space prior to the water pollution and the small space after the pollution form a stark contrast. But when pollution happens, providing people can take some concerted actions to solve the problem, the negative influence on the fish can be dwindled. Unfortunately, no positive measures are taken to relieve the serious situation. As a result, the fish are dying. What the speaker calls on the boys to do is very ironic.

> Then three cheers for the ageing fish, my boys,
>
> Content in polluted depths
>
> To grub up enough food, my boys,
>
> To carry 'em to a natural death.
>
> And may we do the same, my boys,
>
> And carry us to a natural death. (13-18)

The speaker asks the boys to cheer for the fish as if the fish had triumphed in a significant match or competition. As a matter of fact, the reason for their cheer is that the fish are satisfied to live in the polluted water. However, actually the fish are not satisfied at all. They are just trying to be forbearing and tolerant since they have no choice but to endure and suffer. They are already aging fish and they are awaiting their death. What the speaker says finally to the boys are a kind of warning or prophesy, that is, if anthropocentric human beings still do not take actions to tackle pollution, they will die from it like the fish, since their destinies are interrelated. As Malamud puts it, "This reiterates the deluge of contemporary ecological warnings that Western industrial society is inclined to ignore: the survival of animals and people is mutually codependent" (146).

The last poem to be analyzed in this section is "Hedgehog" (1973) by Paul Muldoon (1951–), which again deals with the distrust of animals in human beings.

>The snail moves like a
>Hovercraft, held up by a
>Rubber cushion of itself,
>Sharing its secret
>
>With the hedgehog. The hedgehog
>Shares its secret with no one.
>We say, Hedgehog, come out
>Of yourself and we will love you.
>
>We mean no harm. We want
>Only to listen to what
>You have to say. We want
>Your answers to our questions.
>
>The hedgehog gives nothing
>Away, keeping itself to itself.
>We wonder what a hedgehog
>Has to hide, why it so distrusts. (lines 1-16)

Chapter Five Advocacy of Animal Freedom and Rights

The snail would like to share its secret with the hedgehog, which shows the mutual trust between animals. However, the hedgehog does not want to share the secret with human beings, which signifies the lack of trust of animals in human beings. Even though human beings say "we will love you" and "we mean no harm", the hedgehog still hides itself and does not want to come out of its hole, let alone reveal the secret. The speaker wonders why this happens and the ending of the poem seems to provide an answer:

> We forget the god
> under this crown of thorns.
> We forget that never again
> will a god trust in the world. (17-20)

The god here is not necessarily a religious one, but someone who is admired very much by people, and is referred to as a god. The respect in hedgehog may date back to the seventh century B.C., when the Greek poet Archilochus says, "The fox knows many things, but the hedgehog just one big thing" (qtd. in Harris 96), which shows the depth and profundity of the hedgehog in thinking. Here Muldoon means that anthropocentric human beings fail to show due respect to animals, and even hurt or kill them for their own sake, therefore, they have lost the trust of animals and severely jeopardized the human-animal relationship.

To conclude, anthropocentrism leads to man's lack of concern towards animals and ill-treatment of them, as well as animals' distrust in man and regarding man as enemies or potential enemies. The animal poems studied in this section criticize anthropocentrism, appeal for equality between man and animals, try to arouse people's consciousness of animal rights, and thus help to remedy the endangered and corrupted human-animal relationship. We human beings are supposed to show due sympathy and concern to animals around us, as Schopenhauer argues, "boundless compassion for all living beings is the surest and most certain guarantee of pure moral conduct, and needs no casuistry" (213).

Conclusion

Through the analysis of over two hundred animal poems by more than eighty British poets from the sixteenth century to the twenty-first century, bridging a history of British literature for over four hundred years, the study has made a thorough, comprehensive and systematic research into the British animal poetry.

The study helps us to find that there are always British poets who have been making strenuous efforts to push the animal rights movement forward, striving for the fair treatment of animals, the freedom of animals and the equal rights between animals and man. With the help of literary critics and scholars of cultural studies, my study has tried to provide a close reading of animal poems giving high praise of animals' good qualities or virtues, poems showing human beings' concern, love or sympathy to animals, poems portraying the harmonious relationship between man and animals, poems criticizing some people's lack of care and concern for animals, poems showing some people's remorse for their wrongdoings towards animals, poems illustrating animals' functions in human beings' mental life, poems revealing some people's abuse or ill treatment of animals, and especially poems fighting for animal freedom and animal rights.

No matter to which literary school does a poet belong to, either Renaissance or Metaphysical, either Neoclassical or Romantic, either Victorian or Modern, there is no difference between their concern with the welfare of animals. They all have contributed to the development of British animal poetry, and they are supposed to win our respect, and deserve our careful study and research. There is still relatively a long way to go in terms of the protest against the abuse of animals and the fight for animal rights. Animal rights activists, writers, literary critics, and the society as a whole, have to work concertedly for a better future of animal welfare.

In addition to what has been achieved, there are also some limitations as regards this study. The first one is that the animal poems related to my focal points are not exhausted, there are still other poems that I may have failed to discover and bring into discussion, even though I have already analyzed over two hundred and twenty poems in total. Secondly, for poets who are my previous research focus, like the Romantic poets and some modern poets such as Thomas Hardy, I find myself able to handle at ease, and can bring in more critical engagements in my argument, for some other poets, critics' support of my standpoints seem to be less adequate, especially for some contemporary new poets or the less well-known poems by noted poets, there is even no other criticism found despite my strenuous efforts. Thirdly, for some arguments, I only find the poets' approval of such an idea or concept in his letters, journals, or essays, in stead of his poems, which is a deficiency. Fourthly, the attribution of a couple of poems to certain poets have not been confirmed yet in the literary or critical circle, so they are only the assumed or alleged writers of the poems. These above-mentioned limitations leave some space for me and other scholars to fill in concerning the future and further study of the British animal poetry.

Upon the completion of the book at the beginning of 2020, the COVID-19 (Corona Virus Disease 2019) pandemic broke out earlier in China and later in many other countries in the world. Some people surmised that it might be related to the consumption of wild animals. Though this surmise has never been confirmed by experts or authorities, it does once again arouse people's consciousness of the protection of wild animals for the sake of both animals themselves and human beings alike. As a conscientious researcher in animal poems and an ardent lover of animals, I would rather believe that the surmise is incorrect, and I sincerely wish that people would stop consuming wild animals and a more harmonious relationship between man and animals could be established.

References

Abrams, M. H., ed. *The Norton Anthology of English Literature*. 4th ed. Vol.1. New York; London: W.W. Norton & Company, 1979.

Aesop. *Aesop's Fables*. Intro. and Notes. D. L. Ashliman. Trans. V.S. Vermon Jones. New York: Barnes & Noble Books, 2003.

Altman, Nathaniel. *The Little Giant Encyclopedia of Meditations & Blessings*. New York: Sterling Publishing Co., Inc., 2000.

Auden, W. H. *W. H. Auden: Collected Poems*. Ed. Edward Mendelson. New York: Random House, 1976.

Bailey, J. O. "Evolutionary Meliorism in the Poetry of Thomas Hardy." *Studies in Philology* 60.3 (1963): 569-87.

---. *The Poetry of Thomas Hardy: A Handbook and Commentary*. Chapel Hill: University of North Carolina Press, 1970.

Baker, James V. "The Lark in English Poetry." *Prairie Schooner* 24.1 (Spring 1950): 70-79.

Banerjee, A. "Larkin Reconsidered." *Sewanee Review* 116.3 (2008): 428-41.

Barkas, Janet. *The Vegetable Passion: A History of the Vegetarian State of Mind*. London: Routledge & Kegan Paul; New York: Charles Scribners Sons, 1975.

Barker, Juliet. *Wordsworth: A Life*. New York: HarperCollins Publishers Inc., 2000.

Bate, Jonathan. *Ted Hughes: The Unauthorised Life*. Glasgow: William Collins Sons & Company, Ltd., 2015.

Bates, A. W. H. *Anti-Vivisection and the Profession of Medicine in Britain: A Social History*. London: Palgrave Macmillan, 2017.

Beattie, James. *The Poetical Works of James Beattie*. Memoir. Alexander Dyce. Boston: Little, Brown and Company; New York: Evans and Dickerson, 1854.

Beauchamp, Tom L. "Introduction." In *The Oxford Handbook of Animal Ethics*, eds. Tom L. Beauchamp and R. G. Frey. Oxford; New York: Oxford University Press, 2011.

Behn, Aphra. *The Complete Works of Aphra Behn*. Eds. Delphi Classics editors. Hastings: Delphi Publishing Ltd., 2016.

Bell, Howard J. "The Deserted Village and Goldsmith's Social Doctrines." *PMLA* 59.3 (1994): 747–72.

Belloc, Hilaire. *Bad Child's Book of Beasts*. London; Southampton: The Camelot Press Limited, 1896.

Bernhardt-Kabisch, Ernest. "The Epitaph and the Romantic Poets: A Survey." *Huntington Library Quarterly* 30.2 (1967):113-46.

Berry, Edward. *Shakespeare and the Hunt: A Cultural and Social Study*. Cambridge: Cambridge University Press, 2001.

Bewick, Thomas. *A General History of Quadrupeds: With Figures Engraved on Wood* 1885. Chicago; London: The University of Chicago Press, 2009.

Black, William George. "The Hare in Folk-Lore." *The Folk-Lore Journal* 1.3 (1883): 84-90.

Blades, John. *Wordsworth and Coleridge: Lyrical Ballads*. Houndmills, Basingstoke,Hampshire: Palgrave Macmillan, 2004.

Blair, Kirstie. "'He Sings Alone': Hybrid Forms and the Victorian Working-Class Poet." *Victorian Literature and Culture* 37. 2 (2009): 523-41.

Blake, William. *William Blake: Collected Poems*. 1905. Ed. W.B.Yeats. London; New York: Routledge Classics, 2002.

Bloom, Harold. "Introduction." In *Bloom's Modern Critical Views: John Keats*, ed. Harold Bloom. New York: Chelsea House Publishers, 2007. 1-12.

---. *Bloom's Classic Critical Views: Percy Shelley*. New York: Infobase Publishing, 2009.

Booth, James. "Larkin as an Animal Poet." *About Larkin* 2006 (22): 5-9.

---. *Philip Larkin — Life, Art and Love*. New York; London; New Delhi; Sydney: Bloomsbury, 2014.

Braunschneider, Theresa. "The Lady and the Lapdog: Mixed Ethnicity in Constantinople, Fashionable Pets in Britain." In *Humans and Other Animals in Eighteenth-century British Culture: Representation, Hybridity, Ethics*, ed. Frank Palmeri. Aldershot: Ashgate Publishing Limited; Burlington: Ashgate Publishing Company, 2006. 31-48.

Brewster, Achsah. "In Ceylon." In *D. H. Lawrence Interviews and Recollections* (Vol. 2), ed. Norman Page. London; Basingstoke: The Macmillan Press Ltd., 1981. 159-65.

Browning, Elizabeth. *Poetical Works of Elizabeth Barrett Browning*. Eds. F. T. Merrill, Mary B. Smith, F. H. Hayden, and F. E. Wright (illustrator). New York: Thomas Y. Crowell & Co., 1886.

Browning, Robert. *The Complete Poetical Works of Robert Browning*. Ed. Augustine Birrell. 1907. New York: The Macmillan Company, 1916.

Buckland, E. S. Lang. *Oliver Goldsmith*. London: George Bell & Sons, 1909.

Burns, Robert. *The Complete Poetical Works of Robert Burns*. Ed. Horace E. Scudder. Boston; New York: Houghton Mifflin Company, 1897.

---. *The Letters of Robert Burns*. Ed. J. Logie Robertson. Ebook, The Project Gutenberg, 2006.

Byron, George Gordon. *Complete Works of Lord Byron*. Eds. Delphi Classics editors. Hastings: Delphi Publishing Ltd., 2012.

---. *Byron's Letters and Journals: A New Selection*. Ed. Richard Lansdown. Oxford: Oxford University Press, 2015.

Chambers, E.K. "Review of Marvell in the Muses' Library Series." In *Andrew Marvell: The Critical Heritage*, ed. Elizabeth Story Donno. London; New York: Routledge, 1978. 267-70.

Chatterjee, Ramananda, ed. *The Modern Review*. Vol. 89-90. Calcutta: Prabasi Press Private, Limited, 1951.

Chatterjee, Sisir Kumar. *Philip Larkin: Poetry That Builds Bridges*. New Delhi: Atlantic Publishers & Distributors, 2006.

Chen, Hong. "To Set the Wild Free: Changing Images of Animals in English Poetry of the Pre-Romantic and Romantic Periods." *Interdisciplinary Studies in Literature and Environment* 13.2 (2006):129-49.

Chesterton, Gilbert Keith. *A Chesterton Calendar*. London: Kegan Paul, Trench, Trübner & Co. Ltd., 1911.

---. *Wine, Water, and Song*. London: Methuen & Co. Ltd., 1915.

Chun, Sehjae. "'An Undiscovered Song': John Clare's 'Birds Poems'." *Interdisciplinary Literary Studies* 6.2 (Spring 2005): 47-65.

Clare, Johanne. *John Clare and the Bounds of Circumstance*. Kingston; Montreal: McGill-Queen's University Press, 1987.

Clare, John. *John Clare: Selected Poems*. Ed. Geoffrey Summerfield. London: Penguin Books Ltd, 1990.

---. *John Clare: By Himself*. 1996. Ed. Eric Robinson and David Powell. Manchester: Carcanet Press, 2002.

Cohn, Elisha. "'No insignificant creature': Thomas Hardy's Ethical Turn." *Nineteenth-Century Literature* 64. 4 (2010): 494-520.

Coleridge, Samuel Taylor. Samuel Taylor Coleridge: *The Complete Poems*. ed. William Keach. London; New York; Victoria; Toronto; Auckland; Harmondsworth: Penguin Books, 1997.

Collins, Vere H. *Talks with Thomas Hardy at Max Gate 1920 to 1922*. New York: Doubleday, Doran and Co., 1928.

Cotner, June. *Animal Blessings: Prayers and Poems Celebrating Our Pets*. San Francisco: HarperOne, 2010.

Coupe, Laurence, ed. *The Green Studies Reader: From Romanticism to Ecocriticism*. 2000. London; New York: Routledge, 2004.

Cowper, William. *The Works of William Cowper: His Life, Letters and Poems*. Ed. Rev. T. S. Grimshawe. London: William Tegg and Co., 1849.

Craik, Roger. "Animals and Birds in Philip Larkin's Poetry." *Papers on Language & Literature* 38.4 (2002): 395-412.

Craze, Michael. *The Life and Lyrics of Andrew Marvell*. London; Basingstoke: The Macmillan Press Ltd., 1979.

Dakers, Andrew Herbert. *Robert Burns, His Life and Genius*. London: Chapman & Hall, Ltd., 1923.

Darwin, Charles. *The Descent of Man, and Selection in Relation to Sex*. 1871. Chichester: Princeton University Press, 1981.

David, Deirdre. *Intellectual Women and Victorian Patriarchy: Harriet Martineau, Elizabeth Barrett Browning, George Eliot*. Houndmills, Basingstoke, Hampshire; London: The Macmillan Press Ltd., 1987.

DiMeo, Michelle and Rebecca Laroche. "On Elizabeth Isham's 'Oil of Swallows': Animal Slaughter and Early Modern Women's Medical Recipes." in *Ecofeminist Approaches to Early Modernity*, ed. Jennifer Munroe and Rebecca Laroche. New York: Palgrave Macmillan, 2011.

Dodd, Henry Philip. *The Epigrammatists: A Selection from the Epigrammatic Literature of Ancient, Mediæval, and Modern Times*. London: Bell and Daldy, 1870.

Doggett, Frank. "Romanticism's Singing Bird." *Studies in English Literature, 1500–1900* 14.4 (1974): 547-61.

Donne, John. *The Variorum Edition of the Poetry of John Donne, Volume 7, Part 1. The Holy Sonnets*. Eds. Gary A. Stringer and Paul A. Parrish.

Bloomington; Indianapolis: Indiana University Press, 2005.

Donovan, Josephine. "Aestheticizing Animal Cruelty." *College Literature* 38.4 (2011): 202-17.

Doren, Mark Van. "Mark Van Doren in *New York Herald Tribune Books*, 15 December 1929, 15." In *The Critical Heritage: D. H. Lawrence*. 1970. Ed. R. P. Draper. Abingdon: Taylor & Francis e-Library, 2002. 312-13.

Drew, Samuel. *The Imperial Magazine; Or, Compendium of Religious, Moral, & Philosophical Knowledge*. Vol.12. London: H. Fisher, Son, and Co., 1830.

Duerksen, Roland A. "Shelley and Shaw." *PMLA* 78. 1 (1963): 114-27.

Emig, Rainer. "Auden and ecology." In *The Cambridge Companion to W. H. Auden*, ed. Stan Smith. Cambridge: Cambridge University Press. 2005. 212-25.

Fairchild, A. H. R. "Robert Bloomfield." *Studies in Philology* 16.1 (1919): 78-101.

Ferguson, Margaret, Mary Jo Salter and Jon Stallworthy. *The Norton Anthology of Poetry*. 5th ed. New York; London: W.W. Norton & Company, 2005.

Feuerstein, Anna. *The Political Lives of Victorian Animals: Liberal Creatures in Literature and Culture*. Cambridge: Cambridge University Press, 2019.

Fletcher, Loraine. *Charlotte Smith: A Critical Biography*. 1998. Houndmills, Basingstoke, Hampshire; New York: Palgrave, 2001.

Flint, and F. Cudworth. "Auden's Our Hunting Fathers Told the Story." *The Explicator* 2.1 (1943): 3-4.

French, Richard D. *Antivivisection and Medical Science in Victorian Society*. Princeton; London: Princeton University Press, 1975.

French, Roberts W. "Lawrence and American Poetry." In *The Legacy of D. H. Lawrence: News Essays*, ed. Jeffrey Meyers. New York: St. Martin's Press, Inc., 1987.

Freston, Kathy, and Rachel Cohn. *The Book of Veganish: The Ultimate Guide to*

Easing into a Plant-Based, Cruelty-Free, Awesomely Delicious Way to Eat, with 70 Easy Recipes Anyone Can Make. New York: Pam Krauss Books, 2016.

Fudge, Erica. *Perceiving Animals: Humans and Beasts in Early Modern English Culture*. Houndmills, Basingstoke, Hampshire; London: Macmillan Press Ltd., 2000.

Galt, John. *The Life of Lord Byron*. Paris: Baudry, Bookseller in Foreign Languages, 1835.

Gannon, Thomas C. *Skylark Meets Meadowlark: Reimagining the Bird in British Romantic and Contemporary Native American Literature*. Lincoln; London: University of Nebraska Press, 2009.

Gardner, Charles. *William Blake: The Man*. London: J. M. Dent & Sons Limited; New York: E. P. Dutton & Co., 1919.

Garner, Robert. *Political Animals: Animal Protection Politics in Britain and the United States*. Houndmills, Basingstoke, Hampshire; London: Macmillan Press Ltd., 1998.

---. *The Political Theory of Animals Rights*. Manchester: Manchester University Press, 2005.

Garrett, Martin. *The Palgrave Literary Dictionary of Byron*. Houndmills, Basingstoke, Hampshire; New York: Palgrave Macmillan, 2010.

Gay, John. *Fables of John Gay*. Ed. John Benson Rose. London: William Clowes & Sons, 1871.

Gibson, Wilfrid Wilson. *Fires — Book III: The Hare, and Other Tales*. London: Elkin Mathews, 1912.

Gold, Scott. *The Shameless Carnivore: A Manifesto for Meat Lovers*. New York: Broadway Books, 2008.

Goldsmith, Oliver. *The Citizen of the World, Or, Letters from a Chinese Philosopher*. Vol.1. London: Taylor & Hessey, 1809.

Gonel, Tuba, and John Dayton. "Animal Images as Metaphors in Ted Hughes' Poetry." In 2nd International Conference on Foreign Language Teaching and Applied Linguistics (FLTAL '12). 4-6 May 2012, Sarajevo.

Goodale, Greg. *The Rhetorical Invention of Man: A History of Distinguishing Humans from Other Animals*. Lanham: Lexington Books, 2015.

Goodridge, John. *John Clare and Community*. New York: Cambridge University Press, 2013.

Graves, Robert. *On English Poetry*. New York: Haskell House Publishers Ltd., 1972.

Greenblatt, Stephen, and M. H. Abrams, eds. *The Norton Anthology of English Literature*. 8th ed. Vol.2. New York; London: W.W. Norton & Company, 2006.

Guerrini, Anita. "The Ethics of Animal Experimentation in Seventeenth-Century England." *Journal of the History of Ideas* 50.3 (1989): 391-407.

Guiccioli, Teresa. *My Recollections of Lord Byron*. New York: Harper & Brothers Publishers, 1869.

Hager, Alan, ed. *Encyclopedia of British Writers: 16th, 17th, and 18th Centuries*. New York: Facts On File, Inc., 2005.

Hands, Timothy. *A Hardy Chronology*. Houndmills, Basingstoke, Hampshire, and London: Macmillan, 1992.

Hardy, F. E. *The Life of Thomas Hardy, 1840–1928*. London: Macmillan Press Ltd., 1962.

Hardy, Thomas. *The Complete Poems of Thomas Hardy*. Eds. James Gibson and Trevor Johnson. Houndmills, Basingstoke, Hampshire; New York: Palgrave, 2001.

---. *The Collected Letters of Thomas Hardy*. Eds. Richard Little Purdy and Michael Millgate. Oxford: The Clarendon Press, 1978.

Harris, William. *Archilochus: First Poet after Homer*. Unpublished MS, Middlebury College.

Harrison, Michael and Christopher Stuart-Clark, ed. *The Oxford Book of Animal Poems*. Oxford: Oxford University Press, 1992.

Hartley, Lodwick Charles. *William Cowper: Humanitarian*. Chapel Hill: The University of North Carolina Press, 1938.

Hasan, Sheikh Mehedi. "Ted Hughes' Animal Poems: An Embodiment of Violence or Vitality?" *The Dawn Journal* (2012): 174.

Hawlin, Stefan. *The Complete Critical Guide to Robert Browning*. London: Routledge, 2002.

Heaney, Seamus. *Seamus Heaney: New Selected Poems: 1966–1987*. London: Faber and Faber, 1990.

Hecht, Anthony. *The Hidden Law: Poetry of W.H. Auden*. Cambridge: Harvard University Press, 1993.

Henderson, Archibald. *George Bernard Shaw: His Life and Works*. Cincinnati: Steward & Kidd Company, 1911.

Herbert, George. *George Herbert: The Complete English Poems*. 1991. Ed. John Tobin. London: Penguin Books Ltd., 2004.

Hibberd, Dominic. *Harold Monro: Poet of the New Age*. New York: Palgrave, 2001.

Hodgson, Ralph. *Poems*. New York: Macmillan Company, 1917.

Hollander, John, ed. *Animal Poems*. London; New York; Toronto: Everyman's Library, 1994.

---. "On *A Child's Garden of Verses*." In *Bloom's Modern Critical Views: Robert Louis Stevenson*, ed. Harold Bloom. Philadelphia: Chelsea House Publishers, 2005. 245-60.

Hopkins, Gerard Manley. *Selected Poems of Gerard Manley Hopkins*. Ed. R.J.C.Watt. Houndmills, Basingstoke, Hampshire; London: Macmillan Education Ltd., 1987.

Hopkins, Robert Thurston. *Rudyard Kipling: A Literary Appreciation*. London:

Simpkin, Marshall, Hamilton, Kent & Co. Ltd., 1915.

Houghton-Walker, Sarah. *John Clare's Religion*. Farnham: Ashgate Publishing Limited, 2009.

Hughes, Glenn. "The Passionate Psychologist." In *D. H. Lawrence's Poetry: Demon Liberated: A Collection of Primary and Secondary Material*, ed. A. Banerjee. Houndmills, Basingstoke, Hampshire; London: The Macmillan Press Ltd., 1990. 110-24.

Hughes, J. L. *The Real Robert Burns*. London; Edinburgh: W. & R. Chambers, Ltd., 2011.

Hughes, Ted. *New Selected Poems 1957–1994*. London: Faber & Faber, 1995.

---. *Letters of Ted Hughes*. Ed. Christopher Reid. London: Faber & Faber, 2007.

Huk, Romana. *Stevie Smith: Between the Lines*. Houndmills, Basingstoke, Hampshire; New York: Palgrave Macmillan, 2005.

Inniss, Kenneth. *D. H. Lawrence's Bestiary: A Study of his Use of Animal Trope and Symbol*. The Hague: Mouton & Co. N. V., Publishers, 1972.

Istiak, Ashik. "Human Animals in Ted Hughes' Poetry: A Thorough Study of the Animal Poems of Ted Hughes." In International Conference on Language, Literature, Culture and Education (4th ICLLCE). 30th-31st, January, 2016. Kuala Lumpur, Malaysia.

Janik, Del Ivan . "D. H. Lawrence and Environmental Consciousness." *Environmental History Review* 7.4 (1983): 359-72.

Jeffares, A. Norman. *A Commentary on the Collected Poems of W. B. Yeats*. London: Macmillan and Co. Ltd., 1968.

Johnson, Jamie. "The Animal in D. H. Lawrence: A Struggle Against Anthropocentrism." In *D. H. Lawrence: New Critical Perspectives and Cultural Translation*, ed. Simonetta de Filippis. Newcastle: Cambridge Scholars Publishing, 2016. 145-64.

Johnson, Trevor. *A Critical Introduction to the Poems of Thomas Hardy*.

Houndmills, Basingstoke, Hampshire; London: Macmillan Education Ltd., 1991.

Johnston, Kenneth R. "'Home at Grasmere': Reclusive Song." *Studies in Romanticism* 14.1 (Winter, 1975): 1-28.

Jonson, Ben. *The Complete Works of Ben Jonson*. Eds. Delphi Classics editors. Hastings: Delphi Publishing Ltd., 2013.

Joy, Charles, R. *Albert Schweitzer: An Anthology*. Boston: The Beacon Press, 1947.

Kant, Immanuel. *Lectures on Ethics*. Trans. Peter Heath. Cambridge: Cambridge University Press, 1997.

Karremann, Isabel. "Human/Animal Relations in Romantic Poetry — The Creaturely Poetics of Christopher Smart and John Clare." *European Journal of English Studies* 19.1 (2015): 94-110.

Kean, Hilda. *Animal Rights: Political and Social Change in Britain Since 1800*. London: Reaktion Books Ltd., 1998.

Keats, John. *Poetical Works of John Keats*. Ed. William T. Arnold. London: Kegan Paul, Trench, & Co., 1884.

---. *Selected Letters of John Keats*. Ed. Grant F. Scott. Cambridge: Harvard University Press, 2005.

Keenleyside, Heather. *Animals and Other People: Literary Forms and Living Beings in the Long Eighteenth Century*. Philadelphia: University of Pennsylvania Press, 2016.

Kemmerer, Lisa. *Speaking Up for Animals: An Anthology of Women's Voices*. 2012. New York: Routledge, 2016.

Kennedy, David, ed. *The Waldorf Book of Animal Poetry*. Viroqua, Wisconsin: Living Arts Books, 2013.

Kennedy, Richard S., and Donald S. Hair. *The Dramatic Imagination of Robert Browning: A Literary Life*. Columbia: University of Missouri Press, 2007.

Kenyon-Jones, Christine. *Kindred Brutes: Animals in Romantic-period Writing*. Aldershot: Ashgate Publishing, 2001.

Kerridge, Richard. "Ecological Hardy." In *Beyond Nature Writing: Expanding the Boundaries of Ecocriticism*, ed. Karla Armbruster and Kathleen R. Wallace. Virginia: The University Press of Virginia, 2001. 126-43.

Kipling, Rudyard. *Complete Works of Rudyard Kipling*. Eds. Delphi Classics editors. Hastings: Delphi Publishing Ltd., 2011.

Kutchin, Victor. *What Birds Have Done with Me*. Boston: The Gorham Press, 1922.

Labbe, Jacqueline M. *Writing Romanticism: Charlotte Smith and William Wordsworth, 1784–1807*. Houndmills, Basingstoke, Hampshire; New York: Palgrave Macmillan, 2011.

Landry, Donna. "Green Languages? Women Poets as Naturalists in 1653 and 1807." *Huntington Library Quarterly* 63.4 (2000): 467-489.

Larkin, Philip. *Philip Larkin: Selected Letters*. Ed. Anthony Thwaite. London: Faber & Faber, 1992.

---. *Letters to Monica*. Ed. Anthony Thwaite. London: Faber & Faber Ltd., 2010.

---. *The Complete Poems of Philip Larkin*. Ed. Archie Burnett. London: Faber & Faber Ltd., 2012.

Lawrence, D. H. *Complete Works of D. H. Lawrence*. Eds. Delphi Classics editors. Hastings: Delphi Publishing Ltd., 2012.

---. "Hymns in a Man's Life." In *Late Essays and Articles: D. H. Lawrence*, ed. James T. Boulton. New York: Cambridge University Press, 2004. 128-34.

Li, Yudi. "The Relationship between Man and Animal in Ted Hughes' Poems." *Canadian Social Science* 3.1 (2007): 95-98.

Locke, John. *The Works of John Locke*. Vol. 9. London: Rivington, 1812.

Lockwood, M. J. *A Study of the Poems of D. H. Lawrence: Thinking in Poetry*. Houndmills, Basingstoke, Hampshire; New York: Palgrave, 1987.

Lomas, Herbert. "The Poetry of Ted Hughes." *Hudson Review* 40.3 (Autumn 1987): 409.

Lynd, Robert. "Robert Lynd on Clare and Mr Hudson." 1921. In *John Clare: The Critical Heritage*, ed. Mark Storey. London; New York: Routledge, 1973.

Malamud, Randy. *Poetic Animals and Animal Souls*. New York: Palgrave Macmillan, 2003.

Malay, Michael. *The Figure of the Animal in Modern and Contemporary Poetry*. New York: Springer International Publishing, Macmillan, 2018.

Marsh, Jan. *Christina Rossetti: A Literary Biography*. London: Faber and Faber Ltd., 1994.

Marsh, Nicholas. *William Blake: The Poems*. 2001. Houndmills, Basingstoke, Hampshire; New York: Palgrave Macmillan, 2012.

Marson, Janyce, ed. *Bloom's Classic Critical Views: William Wordsworth*. New York: Infobase Publishing, 2009.

Mazzeno, Laurence W., and Ronald D. Morrison, eds. *Animals in Victorian Literature and Culture: Contexts for Criticism*. London: Palgrave Macmillan, 2017.

McColley, Diane Kelsey. *Poetry and Ecology in the Age of Milton and Marvell*. Aldershot: Ashgate Publishing Limited; Burlington: Ashgate Publishing Company, 2007.

McGowan, Ian, ed. *Macmillan Anthologies of English Literature. Vol. 3: The Restoration and Eighteenth Century*. Houndmills, Basingstoke, Hampshire; London: Macmillan Education Ltd., 1989.

McGuirk, Carol. *Reading Robert Burns: Texts, Contexts, Transformations*. 2014. Abingdon; New York: Routledge, 2016.

McHugh, Susan. "Literary Animal Agents." *PMLA* 124.2 (2009): 487-95.

McKusick, James C. *Green Writing: Romanticism and Ecology*. New York: St. Martin's Press, 2000.

Meredith, George. *Complete Works of George Meredith*. Eds. Delphi Classics editors. Hastings: Delphi Publishing Ltd., 2013.

Millgate, Michael. *Thomas Hardy: A Biography Revisited*. Oxford; Melbourne: Oxford University Press, 2004.

Milne, Anne. "The Power of Testimony: The Speaking Animal's Plea for Understanding in a Selection of Eighteenth-Century British Poetry." In *Speaking for Animals: Animal Autobiographical Writing*, ed. Margo DeMello. New York; London: Routledge, 2013. 163-77.

Milton, John. *The Complete Poems of John Milton*. Vol. 4. ed. Charles W. Eliot. New York: P.F. Collier & Son Company, 1909.

Moffatt, James. "Meredith in perspective." In *George Meredith: The Critical Heritage*, ed. Ioan Willams. London; New York: Routledge, 1971. 497-502.

Moine, Fabienne. *Women Poets in the Victorian Era: Cultural Practices and Nature Poetry*. London; New York: Routledge, 2016.

Moore, Thomas. *Life of Lord Byron: With his Letters and Journals*. Vol. 2. London: John Murray, 1854.

Morgan, Rosemarie. *Student Companion to Thomas Hardy*. Westport; London: Greenwood Press, 2007.

Morgan, William W. "Aesthetics and Thematics in Hardy's Volumes of Verse: The Example of *Time's Laughingstocks*." In Thomas Hardy Reappraised: Essays in Honour of Michael Millgate, ed. Keith Wilson. Toronto; Buffalo; London: University of Toronto Press Incorporated, 2006.

Morton, Timothy. *Shelley and the Revolution in Taste: The Body and the Natural World*. Cambridge: Cambridge University Press, 1994.

Muldoon, Paul. *Paul Muldoon: Poems 1968–1998*. London: Faber and Faber Ltd., 2001.

Murthi, Anuradha. *Mosaic Reader*. Vol. 6. 2013. New Delhi: Madhubun Education Books, 2015.

Newey, Vincent. "Cowper Prospects: Self, Nature, Society." In *Romanticism and Religion from William Cowper to Wallace Stevens,* eds. Gavin Hopps and Jane Stabler. Hampshire; New York: Ashgate Publishing Limited, 2006. 41-56.

Niederland, William G. "The problem of the survivor." *The Journal of Hillside Hospital* 10 (1961): 233-47.

Nietzsche, Friedrich. *Thus Spake Zarathustra.* Trans. Thomas Wayne. New York: Algora Publishing, 2003.

O'Halloran, Meiko. *James Hogg and British Romanticism: A Kaleidoscopic Art.* Houndmills, Basingstoke, Hampshire; New York: Palgrave Macmillan, 2016.

Ortiz-Robles, Mario. *Literature and Animal Studies.* Abingdon, Oxon; New York: Routledge, 2016.

Owens. Margaret E. "'A hodge-podge of diseases tasteth well': Arcimboldesque portraits in Margaret Cavendish's *Poems and Fancies* (1653)." *Word & Image: A Journal of Verbal/Visual Enquiry* 25.2 (2009): 154-65.

Packer, Lona Mosk. *Christina Rossetti.* Berkeley; Los Angeles: University of California Press, 1963.

Palazzo, Lynda. *Christina Rossetti's Feminist Theology.* Houndmills, Basingstoke, Hampshire; New York: Palgrave, 2002.

Palmeri, Frank. "The Autocritique of Fables." In *Humans and Other Animals in Eighteenth-century British Culture: Representation, Hybridity, Ethics,* ed. Frank Palmeri. Aldershot: Ashgate Publishing Limited; Burlington: Ashgate Publishing Company, 2006. 83-100.

Pandey, Maya Shankar. "Animal Imagery in the Poetry of A.K. Ramanujan." *The Aligarh Journal of English Studies* 19. 1 (1997): 73-83.

Parrill, Anna Sue. "Romantic Songbirds." *Innisfree* (1978): 44–58.

Pearson, Hesketh. *Bernard Shaw: His Life And Personality.* Looe: House of Stratus, 1942.

Perkins, David. "Wordsworth and the Polemic Against Hunting: 'Hart-Leap Well'." *Nineteenth-Century Literature* 52. 4 (1998): 421-45.

---. "Sweet Helpston! John Clare on Badger Baiting." *Studies in Romanticism* 38.3 (1999): 387–407.

---. "Human Mouseness: Burns and Compassion for Animals." *Texas Studies in Literature and Language* 42.1 (Spring 2000): 1-15.

---. *Romanticism and Animal Rights: 1790–1830*. Cambridge: Cambridge University Press, 2003.

Persoon, James. *Hardy's Early Poetry: Romanticism Through a "dark Bilberry Eye"*. Lanham; Oxford: Lexington Books, 2000.

Phelps, Norm. *The Longest Struggle: Animal Advocacy from Pythagoras to PETA*. Brooklyn: Lantern Books, 2007.

Pielak, Chase. *Memorializing Animals during the Romantic Period*. New York: Routledge, 2016.

Pinion, F. B. *A Hardy Companion: A Guide to the works of Thomas Hardy and their background*. New York: Palgrave Macmillan; St. Martin's Press, 1968.

---. *A Commentary on the Poems of Thomas Hardy*. Houndmills, Basingstoke, Hampshire; London: The Macmillan Pressed Ltd., 1976.

---. *Thomas Hardy: Art and Thought*. Houndmills, Basingstoke, Hampshire; London: The Macmillan Pressed Ltd., 1977.

---. *A D. H. Lawrence Companion: Life, Thought, and Works*. Houndmills, Basingstoke, Hampshire; London: The Macmillan Pressed Ltd., 1978.

---. *A Wordsworth Companion: Survey and Assessment*. Houndmills, Basingstoke, Hampshire; London: The Macmillan Pressed Ltd., 1984.

---. *A Thomas Hardy Dictionary: with maps and a chronology*. Houndmills, Basingstoke, Hampshire; London: The Macmillan Pressed Ltd., 1989.

---. *Thomas Hardy: His Life and Friends*. Houndmills, Basingstoke, Hampshire; London: The Macmillan Pressed Ltd., 1992.

Pinto, V. de S. "Poet Without a Mask." In *D. H. Lawrence: A Collection of Critical Essays*, ed. Mark Spilka. Englewood Cliffs: Prentice-Hall, Inc., 1963.

Poovalingam, N. *Animal Imagery in D. H. Lawrence: Gospels of Horizontal Life*. Ph.D. Diss. Pondicherry University, 1992.

Pope, Alexander. "Against Barbarity to Animals." *The Guardian* No. 61 Thursday, May 21, 1713.

---. *The Complete Poetical Works of Alexander Pope*. Ed. Henry W. Boynton. Boston; New York; Chicago; Dallas; San Francisco: Houghton Mifflin Company, 1903.

Porter, Roy. *English Society in the Eighteenth Century*. 1982. London: Penguin Books Ltd., 1991.

Preece, Rod. *Animals and Nature: Cultural Myths, Cultural Realities*. Vancouver: UBC Press, 1999.

---. *Awe for the Tiger, Love for the Lamb: A Chronicle of Sensibility to Animals*. New York: Routledge, 2002.

Prelutsky, Jack, ed. *The Beauty of the Beast: Poems from the Animal Kingdom*. New York: Knopf Books for Young Readers, 2006.

Pritchard, William H. "Hardy's Winter Words." *The Hudson Review* 32.3 (Autumn, 1979): 369-97.

Quijano, Johansen. "Morality, Ethics, and Animal Rights in Romantic Poetry and Victorian Thought." In *Issues in Ethics and Animal Rights*, ed. Manish Vyas. New Delhi: Regency Publications, 2013.

Raine, Craig. "How to Read a Poem." <http://wwword.com/6/think/school-room/how-to-read-a-poem/>

Ramazani, Jahan. *Poetry of Mourning: The Modern Elegy from Hardy to Heaney*. Chicago: University of Chicago Press, 1994.

Read, Mike, ed. *Classic FM One Hundred Favourite Poems*. London: Hodder &

Stoughton, 1997.

Reddick, Yvonne. *Ted Hughes — Environmentalist and Ecopoet*. Houndmills, Basingstoke, Hampshire; New York: Palgrave Macmillan, 2017.

Reeves, James, ed. *Selected Poems of John Donne*. London: Heinemann, 1952.

Regan, Tom. *The Case for Animal Rights*. Oakland: University of California Press, 1983.

---. *Animal Rights, Human Wrongs: An Introduction to Moral Philosophy*. Lanham: Rowman & Littlefield Publishers, Inc., 2003.

Ridley, Florence H. "The Treatment of Animals in the Poetry of Henryson and Dunbar." *The Chaucer Review* 24. 4 (Spring, 1990): 356-66.

Roberts, Gerald. *Selected Poems of Edward Thomas*. Houndmills, Basingstoke, Hampshire; London: Macmillan Education Ltd., 1988.

Roberts, Neil, and Terry Gifford. "The Idea of Nature in English Poetry." In *Literature of Nature: An International Sourcebook*, ed. Patrick D. Murphy. Chicago: Fitzroy Dearborn Publishers, 1998.

Robinson, Vanessa. "Poetry's Language of Animals: Towards a New Understanding of the Animal Other." *The Modern Language Review* 110. 1 (2015): 28-46.

Rogers, Katharine M. *The Cat and the Human Imagination: Feline Images from Bast to Garfield*. Ann Arbor: The University of Michigan Press, 1998.

Rossetti, Christina. *Complete Poetical Works of Christina Rossetti*. Eds. Delphi Classics editors. Hastings: Delphi Publishing Ltd., 2012.

Rossetti, Dante Gabriel. *Complete Poetical Works of Dante Gabriel Rossetti*. Ed. William M. Rossetti. Boston: Little Brown and Company, 1910.

Roth, Christine. "The Zoocentric Ecology of Hardy's Poetic Consciousness." In *Victorian Writers and the Environment: Ecocritical Perspectives*, eds. Laurence W. Mazzeno, and Ronald D. Morrison. Abingdon; New York: Routledge, 2017. 79-96.

Ruston, Sharon. *Shelley and Vitality*. Houndmills, Basingstoke, Hampshire; New York: Palgrave Macmillan, 2005.

Salt, Henry S. *Animals' Rights: Considered in Relation to Social Progress*. London: G. Bell and Sons, Ltd., 1922.

Schnakenberg, Robert. *Secret Lives of Great Authors: What Your Teachers Never Told You About Famous Novelists, Poets and Playwrights*. Philadelphia: Quirk Productions, Inc., 2008.

Schopenhauer, Arthur. *The Basis of Morality*. Trans. Arthur Brodrick Bullock. London: George Allen & Unwin Ltd. 1915.

Schwartz, Richard H. *Judaism and Vegetarianism*. New York: Lantern Books, 2001.

Schweitzer, Albert. *Out of My Life and Thought : An Autobiography*. 1933. Trans. Antje Bultmann Lemke. Baltimore: The Johns Hopkins University Press, 1998.

Scodel, Joshua. *The English Poetic Epitaph: Commemoration and Conflict from Jonson to Wordsworth*. Ithaca; London: Cornell University Press, 1991.

Searl, Edward, ed. *In Praise of Animals: A Treasury of Poems, Quotations and Readings*. Boston: Skinner House Books, 2007.

Sells, A. Lytton. *Animal Poetry in French and English Literature and the Greek Tradition*. London: Thames and Hudson, 1957.

Shairp, John Campbell. *Robert Burns*. London: Macmillan and Co., Limited; New York: The Macmillan Company, 1909.

Shakespeare, William. *The Complete Sonnets and Poems*. Ed. Colin Burrow. Oxford: Oxford University Press, 2002.

---. *Romeo and Juliet*. Ed. Burton Raffel. Chicago: R.R.Donnelley & Sons, 2004.

---. *King Lear*. Ed. Philip M. Parker. San Diego: ICON Group International, Inc., 2005.

---. *As You Like It*. Ed. Philip M. Parker. San Diego: ICON Group International,

Inc., 2005.

---. *King Henry V.* Ed. Philip M. Parker. San Diego: ICON Group International, Inc., 2005.

---. *Cymbeline.* Ed. John Dover Wilson. New York: Cambridge University Press, 2009.

Shaw, George Bernard. *Sixteen Self Sketches*. London: Constable and Company, 1949.

Shea, Victor, William Whitla, eds. *Victorian Literature: An Anthology*. Chichester: John Wiley & Sons, Ltd., 2015.

Shelley, Percy Bysshe. *The Complete Poetical Works of Percy Bysshe Shelley*. 3 Vols. Ed. William Michael Rossetti. London: Gibbings and Company Ltd., 1894.

Sherman, George W. "Thomas Hardy and the Lower Animals." *Prairie Schooner* 20.4 (1946): 304-09.

Sickbert, Virginia. "Christina Rossetti and Victorian Children's Poetry: A Maternal Challenge to the Patriarchal Family." *Victorian Poetry* 31.4 (Winter 1993): 385-410.

Simons, John. *Animal Rights and the Politics of Literary Representation*. Houndmills, Basingstoke, Hampshire; New York: Palgrave, 2002.

Simpson, K. G. *Love and Liberty: Robert Burns: A Bicentenary Celebration*. East Lothian: Tuckwell Press, 1997.

Singer, Peter. *Animal Liberation*. New York: HarperCollins Publishers Inc., 1975.

Singla, Om Prakash. *W.H. Auden's Quest for Values*. Rohtak: Manthan Publications, 1989.

Smith, Alexander McCall. *What W. H. Auden Can Do for You*. Princeton; Woodstock: Princeton University Press, 2013.

Smith, Charlotte. *The Collected Letters of Charlotte Smith*. ed. Judith Phillips

Stanton. Bloomington: Indiana University Press, 2003.

Smith, Stevie. *All the Poems of Stevie Smith*. Ed. Will May. London: Faber and Faber, 2015.

Snodgrass, Chris. "The Poetry of the 1890s." In *A Companion to Victorian Poetry*, eds. Richard Cronin, Alison Chapman, and Antony H. Harrison. Oxford: Blackwell Publishers Ltd., 2002.

Squire, J.C. "The 'precious residuum'." In *D. H. Lawrence: The Critical Heritage*, ed. R.P. Draper. London; New York: Routledge, 1970. 330-34.

Stevenson, Robert Louis. *Complete Works of Robert Louis Stevenson*. Eds. Delphi Classics editors. Hastings: Delphi Publishing Ltd., 2011.

Stone, Marjorie, and Beverly Taylor, eds. *Elizabeth Barrett Browning: Selected Poems*. Peterborough; Plymouth; Sydney: Broadview Press, 2009.

Sultzbach, Kelly. *Ecocriticism in the Modernist Imagination: Forster, Woolf, and Auden*. Cambridge: Cambridge University Press, 2016.

Swingle, L. J. "Stalking the Essential John Clare: Clare in Relation to His Romantic Contemporaries." *Studies in Romanticism* 14.3 (Summer 1975): 273-84.

Tague, Ingrid H. "Dead Pets: Satire and Sentiment in British Elegies and Epitaphs for Animals." *Eighteenth-Century Studies* 41. 3 (Spring 2008): 289-306.

Taylor, Dennis. "The Chronology of Hardy's Poetry." *Victorian Poetry* 37.1 (Spring, 1999): 1-58.

Tearle, Oliver. "10 of the Best Poems about Animals." <https://interestingliterature.com/2017/11/22/10-of-the-best-poems-about-animals/>

Thaddeus, Janice. "Stevie Smith and the Gleeful Macabre." In *In Search of Stevie Smith*, ed. Sanford Sternlicht. Syracuse: Syracuse University Press, 1991. 84-96.

Thomas, Edward. "Studying Nature." In *The Green Studies Reader: From*

Romanticism to Ecocriticism, ed. Laurence Coupe. London, New York: Routledge, 2000. 66-69.

Timbs, John. *Knowledge for the People: Or, The Plain Why and Because*. London: Hurst, Chance, & Co., 1831.

Untermeyer, Louis, ed. *Modern British Poetry*. New York: Harcourt, Brace & Company, 1920.

Vendler, Helen. *The Odes of John Keats*. 1983. Cambridge; London: The Belkbap Press of Harvard University Press, 2003.

Wadsworth, Randolph L. "On 'The Snayl' by Richard Lovelace." *The Modern Language Review* 65.4 (1970): 750-60.

Wall, Derek. *Green History: A Reader in Environmental Literature, Philosophy and Politics*. London; New York: Routledge, 1994.

Wang, Qiusheng. "Animal Ethics in Thomas Hardy's Bird Poems." In *Proceedings of the 2015 Northeast Asia International Symposium on Linguistics, Literature and Teaching*, eds. Jacob A. Haskell and Hao Bo. Las Vegas: New Vision Press, 2015. 105-11.

---. "Thomas Hardy's Animal Poems Seen in the Light of Animal Ethics." In *Proceeding of The Fifth Northeast Asia International Symposium on Language, Literature and Translation*, eds. Lisa Hale, Jin Zhang, Linda Sun and Qi Fang, et al. Marietta: American Scholars Press, 2016. 302-09.

---. "Theme of Nemesis in British Animal Poems." *Journal of Literature and Art Studies* 9.11 (2019): 1153-59.

---. "A Study of Anti-anthropocentrism in British Animal Poems." In *Proceedings of The 2019 Northeast Asia International Symposium on Linguistics, Literature and Teaching* (Volume A), eds. Jacob A. Haskell and Hao Bo. Las Vegas: New Vision Press, 2019. 41-48.

Warren, Michael J. *Birds in Medieval English Poetry: Metaphors, Realities, Transformations*. Cambridge: D.S.Brewer, 2018.

Watson, J. R. "Philip Larkin: Voices and Values." In *Philip Larkin: The Man and his Work*, ed. Dale Salwak. Houndmills, Basingstoke, Hampshire; London: The Macmillan Pressed Ltd., 1989. 90-111.

Webb, Laura. "Mythology, Mortality and Memorialization: Animal and Human Endurance in Hughes' Poetry." In *Ted Hughes: From Cambridge to Collected*, eds. Mark Wormald, Neil Roberts, and Terry Gifford. London: Palgrave Macmillan, 2013. 33-47.

Weiner, Stephanie Kuduk. "Listening with John Clare." *Studies in Romanticism* 48.3 (Fall 2009): 371-90.

West, Anna. *Thomas Hardy and Animals*. Cambridge and New York: Cambridge University Press, 2017.

Wikipedia Editors. "Animal Ethics." En.wikipedia.org. Wikipedia Foundation, Inc., 2001. Web. 24 Dec. 2018.

Wild, Min. *Christopher Smart and Satire*. Hampshire: Ashgate Publishing Limited, 2008.

Williams, Howard. *The Ethics of Diet: A Catena of Authorities Deprecatory of the Practice of Flesh Eating*. London: F. Pitman, 1883.

Williams, Ioan, ed. *George Meredith: The Critical Heritage*. London; New York: Routledge, 1971.

Williams, Jeni. *Interpreting Nightingales: Gender, Class and Histories*. Sheffield: Sheffield Academic Press, 1997.

Williams, Merryn, and Raymond Williams, eds. *John Clare: Selected Poetry and Prose*. London: Methuen, 1986.

Wordsworth, William. *The Poetical Works of William Wordsworth*. 8 vols. Ed. William Knight. New York: Macmillan & Co., 1896.

Yang, Jeffrey, ed. *Birds, Beasts, and Seas: Nature Poems from New Directions*. New York: New Directions Publishing, 2011.

Yeats, W. B. *The Collected Poems of W. B. Yeats*. 1983. Ed. Richard J. Finneran.

New York: Macmillan Publishing Company, 1989.

陈柏羽，"泰德·休斯对人与自然关系的建构 ——《乌鸦》诗集的生态解读"，《文学艺术》，2012 (6): 57-58

陈贵才，原一川，"英国浪漫派诗歌动物书写的互文性和现代性 —— 以休斯的'鹰'和劳伦斯的'鹰'为例"，《西南科技大学学报（哲学社会科学版）》，2018 (6): 32-38

陈红，Bestiality, Animality, and Humanity. 武汉：华中师范大学出版社，2005。

陈红，"戴·赫·劳伦斯的动物诗及其浪漫主义道德观"，《外国文学研究》，2006 (3): 47-55

陈红，"人与兽，孰为暴力？—— 再议泰德·休斯的动物诗"，《当代外国文学》，2006 (4): 33-40

陈晞，《城市漫游者的伦理衍变：论菲利普·拉金的诗歌》。博士论文。华中师范大学，2011。

陈晞，"生物、生态、环境 —— 菲利普·拉金诗歌的生态伦理"，《2008 文学与环境武汉国际学术研讨会论文集》，442-48

丁礼明，"论劳伦斯诗歌《蛇》的动物美学与伦理主题"，《青海师范大学学报》（哲学社会科学版），2018 (4): 118-22

方英，方玲，"哈代作品中的生态伦理思想"，《宁波大学学报》（人文社科版），2011 (2): 21-25

何宁，"论当代英国动物诗歌"，《当代外国文学》，2017 (2): 79-86

胡家峦，"'和平的王国' —— 文艺复兴时期英国园林诗歌与动物象征"，《外语与外语教学》，2006 (1): 32-35

胡洁雯，王丽明，"特德·休斯的现代动物寓言"，《中国矿业大学学报》，（社会科学版），2008 (1): 124-27

胡澎，"生态文明中的多维情结观 —— 对泰德·休斯动物诗的再认识"，《上饶师范学院学报》，2014 (4): 69-71, 86

姜慧玲，"托马斯·哈代动物书写诗歌中的生态伦理观解析"，《文化学刊》，

2015 (2)：109-10

姜慧玲，"同写催难的动物：哈代与拉金动物书写诗歌生态伦理观之比较"，《名作欣赏》，2016 (3)：136-37

姜慧玲，"D.H. 劳伦斯动物书写诗歌中的'众生平等观'"，《大众文艺》，2016 (21)：38

姜慧玲，苏晓丽，"善待动物，追求和谐美 —— 拉金与休斯动物诗歌中的生态理想"，《大众文艺》，2017 (11)：34-35

姜慧玲，崔希芸，"从'非英雄'到'英雄'—— 从拉金与休斯的动物诗歌看战后英国人社会心理的变化"，《名作欣赏》，2017 (18)：22-24

李成坚，"后现代视域下浪漫主义精神的复归—— 塔特·休斯诗歌意义的再诠释"，《外国文学研究》，2002 (9)：39-42, 169

林玉鹏，"野性与力亦有情评泰德·休斯的诗"，《当代外国文学》，1999 (1)：139-43

刘国清，《从断裂到弥合：泰德·休斯诗歌的生态思想研究》。博士论文。东北师范大学，2008。

刘昊多，"孤独的勇者 —— 动物寓言诗人泰德·休斯述评"，《吉林师范大学学报》（人文社会科学版），2007 (5)：54-56

刘影倩，刘须明，"在自然中探询人类的未来 —— 读劳伦斯诗歌《鸟·兽·花》"，《东南大学学报》（哲学社会科学版），2007 (9)：201-02

吕爱晶，"失落的伊甸园 —— 看拉金式的风景"，《2008 文学与环境武汉国际学术研讨会论文集》，449-55

吕爱晶，"小之美 —— 从拉金诗歌中的动物意象看其'非英雄'思想"，《湘潭大学学报》（哲学社会科学版），2009 (6)：107-10

吕爱晶，"寻找英国的花园 —— 菲利浦·拉金诗歌中的生态意识"，《外国语文》，2010 (4)：16-20

苗福光，《生态批评视角下的劳伦斯》。博士论文。山东大学，2006。

潘灵剑，"劳伦斯《鸟·兽·花》：人的复归与宇宙和谐秩序的祈唤"，《上

海师范大学学报》（哲学社会科学版），2002 (1)：96-102

邵夏沁，"解读菲利普·拉金诗歌中的伦理思想"，《湖北第二师范学院学报》，2016 (6)：15-18

王育烽，陈智淦，"菲利普·拉金诗歌中的生态思想初探"，《安徽理工大学学报》（社会科学版），2011 (2)：72-76

肖谊，"世纪末的沉思——论哈代《黑暗中的鸫鸟》"，《怀化师专学报》，2000 (3)：53-54

谢超，"英国浪漫主义诗歌中人与动物的关系"，《江苏大学学报》（社会科学版），2018 (3)：35-41

姚志勇，吾文泉，"泰德·休斯及其'动物世界'"，《江苏教育学院学报》，1997 (1)：60-62

余娟，"论D.H.劳伦斯诗歌中的动物书写"，《湖南科技学院学报》，2016 (4)：47-48

张静，"D.H.劳伦斯的动物哲学"，《云南师范大学学报》（哲学社会科学版），2012 (1)：152-56

张丽萍，"从《鸟·兽·花》看劳伦斯诗歌中的生态意识"，《盐城师范学院学报》（人文社会科学版），2010 (2)：94-99

张林，郑晓清，"鹰，人，自然——从《鹰之栖息》看泰德休斯的动物诗歌创作"，《徐州师范大学学报》（哲学社会科学版），2006 (6)：42-46

张中载，"塔特·休斯——英国桂冠诗人"，《外国文学》，1985 (10)：26-29

赵越，"泰德·休斯《牧神》中的动物隐喻解析"，《哈尔滨学院学报》，2016 (10)：97-99

郑思明，"人对自然的暴力——泰德·休斯诗中的生态意识"，《现代语文》，2016 (12)：58-59

周维贵，"天真世界与经验世界：论劳伦斯动物诗的存在主题"，《重庆科技学院学报》（社会科学版），2011 (8)：93-97

Index

Amsden, John
"Vegan Assist", 292
"Vivisection", 275

Auden, W. H.
"Address to the Beasts", 65
"Bird-Language", 50
"Cats and Dog", 93
"Our Hunting Fathers", 219
"Short Ode to the Cuckoo", 34
"Talking to Dogs", 131

Beattie, James
"The Hares. A Fable", 205

Behn, Aphra
"On the Author of that Excellent Book Entitled *The Way to Health, Long Life, and Happiness*", 277

Belloc, Hilaire
"Frog", 105

Blackhall, Sheena
"The Animal Refugees", 117

Blake, William
"Auguries of Innocence", 251
"The Fly", 166
"The Lamb", 33
"The Shepherd", 97

Bloomfield, Robert
"The Farmer's Boy: Winter", 230

Browning, Elizabeth Barrett
"To Flush, My Dog", 29, 59

Browning, Robert
"How They Brought the Good News from Ghent to Aix", 62

Burns, Robert
"Address to the Woodlark", 158
"The Brigs Of Ayr", 102, 111
"On Scaring Some Waterfowl in Loch Turit: A Wild Scene Among the Hills of Oughtertyre", 301
"On Seeing a Wounded Hare Limp by Me Which A Fellow Had Just Shot at", 110

"Poor Mailie's Elegy", 135

"To A Mouse", 3, 123, 238

Byron, George Gordon

Don Juan, 210, 282

"Epitaph to a Dog", 58

"Inscription On The Monument Of A Newfoundland Dog", 58

Carew, Thomas

"To Saxham", 294

Cavendish, Margaret

"A Dialogue of Birds", 224

"The Hunting of the Hare", 197, 200

"The Hunting of the Stag", 200

Chesterton, Gilbert Keith

"The Donkey", 53

"The Logical Vegetarian", 286, 287

Clare, John

"The Badger", 235

"The Fox", 238

"The Marten", 210

"The Nightingale's Nest", 41, 77

"The Progress of Ryhme", 145

"The Puddock's Nest", 238

"The Skylark", 95, 169

"A Spring Morning", 52

"Summer Evening" (1820), 233

"Summer Evening" (1830), 304

"Vixen", 168

"The Wren", 144

Coleridge, David Hartley

"On the Death of Echo, A Favourite Beagle", 51

Coleridge, Samuel Taylor

"The Nightingale: A Conversation Poem", 40

"The Raven. A Christmas Tale, Told by A School-Boy to His Little Brothers and Sisters", 254

"The Rime of the Ancient Mariner", 22, 254

"To a Young Ass, Its Mother Being Tethered Near It", 229

Cowper, William

"The Dog and the Water Lily. No Fable", 29, 55

"Epitaph on a Free but Tame Red-breast: A Favorite of Miss Sally Hurdis", 137

"Epitaph on A Hare", 134

"Epitaph on Fop, A Dog Belonging

to Lady Throckmorton", 157

"On A Goldfinch, Starved To Death in His Cage", 173

"On A Spaniel, Called Beau, Killing A Young Bird", 208

"On the Death of Mrs. Throckmorton's Bullfinch", 173

"Strada's Nightingale", 103

The Task: A Poem, in Six Books, 38, 70, 86, 207

"To the Nightingale, Which the Author Heard Sing on New Year's Day", 140

de la Mare, Walter

"Tom's Little Dog", 94

Donne, John

"Holy Sonnet VIII: Why Are Wee by All Creatures Waited On?", 296

Erskine, Thomas

"The Liberated Robins", 77

Ewart, Gavin

"The Meerkats of Africa", 152

Gay, John

"An Elegy on A Lap-Dog", 126, 129

"Fable V. Wild Boar and Ram", 249

"Fable XV. Philosopher and Pheasant", 99

"Fable XVII. Shepherd's Dog and Wolf", 279

"Fable XXXVI. Pythagoras and Countryman", 280

Gibson, Wilfrid Wilson

"The Hare", 257

Goldsmith, Oliver

"The Deserted Village", 101

"An Elegy On The Death Of A Mad Dog", 299

Grahame, James

"British Georgics. August", 304

Graves, Robert

"Epitaph on a Favorite Dog", 60

Gray, Thomas

"Ode on the Death of a Favourite Cat Drowned in a Tub of Gold Fishes", 155

Hamilton, Janet

"The Skylark — Caged And Free", 169

Hardy, Thomas

"Ah, Are You Digging on My Grave?", 60

"And There Was A Great Calm", 242

"Bags of Meat", 111

"The Bird-Catcher's Boy", 255

"A Bird-Scene at A Rural Dwelling", 109

"Birds at Winter Nightfall", 79

"The Blinded Bird", 1, 7, 186

"The Bullfinches", 107

"The Caged Goldfinch", 180

"The Caged Thrush Freed and Home Again", 7, 179

"The Calf", 112

"Compassion: An Ode", 245

"Dead 'Wessex', the Dog to the Household", 130

The Dynasts, 7, 241

"The Faithful Swallow", 109

"The Fallow Deer at the Lonely House", 98

"Horses Aboard", 241

"The Lady in the Furs", 263

"Last Words to a Dumb Friend", 133

"The Mongrel", 244

"A Popular Personage at Home", 91

"The Puzzled Game-Birds (Triolet)", 7, 212

"The Reminder", 108

"A Sheep Fair", 243

"Snow in the Suburbs", 14, 75

"Winter in Durnover Field", 106

"Winter Night in Woodland", 214

Heaney, Seamus

"The Badgers", 84

"Nesting-Ground", 80, 81

Herbert, George

"Providence", 295

Hodgson, Ralph

"The Bells of Heaven", 247

"The Birdcatcher", 216

"Stupidity Street", 113

Hogg, James

"The Skylark", 43

Hopkins, Gerard Manley

"The Caged Skylark", 177

Howitt, Mary

"The Spider and the Fly", 151

Hughes, Ted
"The Black Rhino", 222
"Little Whale Song", 36
"The Seven Sorrows", 221
"View of a Pig", 289

Hunt, Leigh
"The Glove and the Lions", 185

Jolliffe, Vincent
"Animal Rights, Human Wrongs", 267

Jonson, Ben
"To Penshurst", 293, 294

Keats, John
"Bright Star", 160
"Ode", 158
"Ode to a Nightingale", 3, 159, 160
"Song. I Had A Dove", 174
"What the Thrush Said. Lines From A Letter to John Hamilton Reynolds", 155

Kipling, Rudyard
Beast and Man in India, 240
"The Power of the Dog", 128, 130
"Seal Lullaby", 85

Larkin, Philip
"Ape Experiment Room", 19, 273
"At Grass", 18, 19, 193
"The Mower", 10, 122
"Myxomatosis", 19, 248
"Take One Home for the Kiddies", 18, 117
"Wires", 9, 19, 116

Lawrence, D. H.
"A Doe At Evening", 163
"Elephant", 304, 305
"Elephants in the Circus", 189
"Elephants Plodding", 248
"Hymns in a Man's Life", 189
"Mountain Lion", 16, 217
"Snake", 8, 9, 16, 17, 120
"Two Performing Elephants", 190
"When I Went to the Circus", 187

Lovelace, Richard
"The Snayl", 148

Marlowe, Christopher
"The Passionate Shepherd to His Love", 72

Marvell, Andrew
"The Mower to the Glowworms", 64

Massey, Gerald
"The Lark in London", 174

Meredith, George
"The Lark Ascending", 49, 50
"To A Nightingale", 42

Milton, John
"Il Penseroso", 40
"Sonnet to the Nightingale", 139

Monahan, Rosemary
"I Miss My Cat", 134

Monro, Harold
"Dog", 90
"Goldfish", 35
"The Nightingale Near the House", 146

Moore, Thomas
"The Donkey and His Panniers", 232

Moore, Thomas Sturge
"The Dying Swan", 211

Mrs. Holland
"The Robins' Reply to Their Benefactor (Lord Erskine) at Hampstead", 77

Muldoon, Paul
"Hedgehog", 308

Murray, Robert Fuller
"The Caged Thrush", 179

nabbs, terence
"Animal Rights", 266

Nashe, Thomas
"Spring", 85

Nellist, Frederick
"Animal Rights", 264, 267

Pope, Alexander
"Argus", 54
An Essay on Man, 227, 298
"Windsor-Forest", 202

Roberts, Robert
"I Killed the Cat", 119

Rossetti, Christina
"Bread and Milk for Breakfast", 47-48
"The Dog Lies in His Kennel", 89
"A Green Cornfield" ("The Skylark"), 47, 48

"Hear What the Mournful Linnets Say", 239

"Hurt No Living Thing", 82

Rossetti, Dante Gabriel

"Beauty And The Bird", 96

Service, Robert William

"Bird Sanctuary", 261

"Bird Watcher", 97

Seward, Anna

"An Old Cat's Dying Soliloquy", 88

Shakespeare, William

As You Like It, 169, 196

King Henry V, 147

King Lear, 166, 172

Romeo and Juliet, 172

"Sonnet 18", 127

Venus and Adonis, 195, 197, 223

Shaw, Bernard

"Puppy Dog", 92

Shelley, Percy Bysshe

"Ode to the West Wind", 46, 150

Queen Mab, 283, 303

Revolt of Islam, 87

"To a Skylark", 3, 34, 44, 48, 50

"Verses On A Cat", 73

"The Woodman and the Nightingale", 104

Smart, Christopher

"For I Will Consider My Cat Jeoffry", 30

Smith, Charlotte

"The Lark's Nest", 153

"Sonnet III: To A Nightingale", 164

Smith, Stevie

"Death Bereaves our Common Mother, Nature Grieves for my Dead Brother", 288

"Friends of the River Trent", 307

"My Cat Major", 75

"Nature and Free Animals", 114

"Parrot", 181

"This is Disgraceful and Abominable", 192

"The Zoo", 183

Spencer, William Robert

"Beth Gêlert, or The Grave of A Greyhound", 56

Stevenson, Robert Louis

"The Cow", 63

"My Heart, When First the

Black-Bird Sings", 145

Taylor, Jane

"The Spider", 149

Tennyson, Frederick

"The Skylark", 48

Thomas, Edward

"The Owl", 162

Thomson, James

The Seasons, 203, 209, 228, 297

Todd, Ruthven

"The Sea Horse", 83

Wordsworth, William

"Fidelity", 56

"The Green Linnet", 142

"Hart-Leap Well", 208

"The Kitten and the Falling Leaves", 32

"O Nightingale! Thou Surely Art", 160

"The Pet-Lamb. A Pastoral", 72

"Peter Bell. A Tale", 61

The Prelude, 167

"To a Butterfly", 81, 141

"To a Skylark" (1805), 46

"To a Skylark" (1825), 47

"To the Cuckoo", 3, 143

"Tribute. To the Memory of the Same Dog", 128

"Water-Fowl Observed Frequently over the Lakes of Rydal and Grasmere", 33

Yeats, W. B.

"To a Squirrel at Kyle-na-no", 215